BEN'S WORLD

WILLIAM G. COOK

Copyright © 2015 by William G. Cook.

All rights reserved. This book or any portion thereof may not be reproduced or used in any manner whatsoever without the express written permission of the publisher except for the use of brief quotations in a book review.

Printed in the United States of America

First Printing, 2015

ISBN 978-1-62217-241-2

Nuns fret not at their convent's narrow room,
And hermits are contented with their cells.

— William Wordsworth

Chapter 1

He never tired of smelling the damp earth. The dark, damp earth that was beneath the layer of leaves that covered the floor of these woods. His woods, as he liked to think of them. Ben's woods. The reason he liked to smell the earth was, he spent a great deal of time on his stomach, burrowed down like a rabbit. Hiding. Becoming part of the leaves, the dark earth, the soft wind that blew across the ridge behind him.

The sudden movement of the wind caused the large buck to lift his head. It was feeding on the acorns that had fallen from the huge oak tree just down the slope from where Ben lay. The buck sniffed the air. The strange man smell came to him stronger this morning. He had been living with it for the past few years, so it was becoming a natural smell to him. At first it had been a danger smell. He had tossed his tail over his back and fled. Now there was no danger attached to the smell. Just an awareness that it was there, along with the strange creature that carried it.

The man could still remember his first name. His mind said it frequently. Maybe something inside him was trying to make sure he didn't forget it.

So he referred to the large deer with the huge rack as his. Ben's deer. The deer owed Ben his life, maybe three times over. That's how many times Ben had spooked him when the hunters got too close. There were no hunters on this particular piece of property. If Ben could only make the deer stay here. Now he was eating, and his belly was starting to swell from the acorns. But that was all right, for Ben knew that when the rutting season began, he might not eat for two weeks. That's how dominant that phase of his life was.

The only sounds that didn't belong in these woods were the harsh, motorized noises that came up from the interstate highway that ran about three hundred yards from where Ben lay. The big buck never lifted his head at these sounds. He was like Ben. He had learned to filter all other sounds through the traffic noise. It was amazing how the smallest sound could come through this large barrier and find its way straight to the tuned ear. Which was what Ben's and the buck's were.

The interstate was I-65. The state was Tennessee. The county was McCord. The nearest town was Lewiston. That much Ben had remembered from the legal papers. The rest of it was starting to go. After all, he had tried to forget most of it. That's why he was here. The memories and his life ran into a roadblock. He had known on that fateful day that the two couldn't continue. He had to choose either memories or life. He had slithered under the roadblock in an attempt to outrun the memories. But they kept finding him, especially when he was at peace with himself. The times spent watching the buck were such.

When the memories jarred into his being, the buck seemed to sense it. He would throw his head up and look Ben's way. He didn't know what it was, but he knew something was in the air. That's how powerful the memories were. They were so electrifying they charged the atmosphere.

Suddenly the buck was off and running through the trees. Whatever it was, he had heard if before Ben had. Ben hated to move but something told him he had to. He rolled over behind a shaggy bark hickory tree and looked back up the slope. That's where it had come from. The buck was running down the slope, away from the top. Nothing in sight, so Ben started sliding backward on his belly, keeping his eyes glued to the ridge line. He stayed as low in the leaves as he could get. He made it to where the slope dropped off into the ravine where the interstate ran. The mass of small cedars and sweet gum trees shielded him from any driver's view. The root he grabbed with one hand as he dropped the rest of his body over the side of the ravine, stopped his backward slide.

A head was the first thing he saw. Moving slowly. Looking all around. Then the binoculars came up and that's when Ben lowered his head into the ground. He knew that the next few minutes would be critical. He just hoped this man couldn't tune in to the memories the way the buck could.

The feet were coming down the slope and Ben raised his head slowly. He knew this wasn't a hunter because he didn't have on the orange vest, and he didn't carry a rifle or bow. So he must be scouting before the season began. Ben hoped he hadn't seen his big buck.

He might not have seen him but he sure saw where he had been feeding. The man stopped and knelt among the acorns and saw where the buck had gorged himself. He stood up and looked down the slope and smiled. Ben felt sick. So he would now be coming to these woods to hunt. Something must have happened. No one had ever hunted here before. Somebody must have bought or leased the land.

Ben now knew that he and the buck were in trouble, unless he could get the deer to cross the interstate to where he lived. But he knew he could never get the buck to enter the tunnel he used.

The man turned once when he got to the top of the slope and looked back toward where Ben lay. But Ben had not moved. He was too smart for that. The buck was probably standing in a thick stand of bushes watching, also. He would never move either, Ben knew.

When he was sure the man was gone, he released his hold on the root and started slowly sliding down the rock and cedar bush covered slope to the gulch below. There was a bare spot on the slope, but he would wait until he heard no cars on the highway before crossing it. Then when he got to the bottom, he would be out of sight of the speeding cars on the interstate. He could then run to his tunnel and cross under to the other side. If he could just get the deer to follow.

But then, maybe the buck was like him. A loner. An outcast. One who hid from memories.

Chapter 2

Dave Warren was a loner, too. He had much rather walk the woods or sit in the shade of one of the last of the big elms in this part of the country. That was a lot more fun than walking the mall or sitting on one of the benches with thousands of people scurrying by on senseless missions.

But the most fun was trying to find where the big bucks lived. Where they ate. Where they rubbed their antlers. Where they fought, leaving large bare areas in the ground as a tribute to the magnificence of the struggle.

This farm he was now scouting for deer had almost fallen into his lap. As if it was meant to be. When he saw the car with Nashville tags pull up in front of the Lewiston Sheriff's Department a week ago, he had wanted to head for the back when the fancy dude in the three piece suit got out. That's what he usually did when he saw lawyers coming in. Let the sheriff handle them.

But the sheriff wasn't in so he had asked the guy if he could help him. Dave had stood in the front entrance to the jail as three piece suit opened the door.

"Detective Dave Warren. Can I help you?"

"My name is Franklin Hanes. I need to see the sheriff." No hands were offered between lawyer and law officer.

"The sheriff isn't in at the moment. Can I be of assistance?"

"Is there someplace we can talk?"

Dave pointed toward the office where he had been killing time. The man walked in and sat down in the chair usually reserved for suspects. He reached in his inner pocket and pulled out a blue covered document. It was a deed. He pointed to his name on the front and then opened it to the description on the first page.

"As you can see, I have acquired a farm in this county. Two hundred and fifty acres off Green's Road, just west of I-65."

"Is that what we call the Garrett Place?" Dave asked.

"I believe that was the name used by the realty company."

"Then I know where it is."

"Good. I want to let you know that I own the property and request someone to check on it occasionally to make sure no one is trespassing."

"Mr. Hanes. Naturally we will patrol the area and do our routine job of checking, but let me make you a better offer."

The eyebrows came up and the lawyer's skepticism rose with his voice. "What is that?"

"If you'll give me exclusive hunting rights to the property, I'll post it with no hunting signs. I'll make sure no one is out there messing around. I'll fix whatever fences need repairing, and you can call me anytime, day or night, and I'll let you know what's going on around there."

"You'll be the only one who hunts there."

"Absolutely! I don't go in for large parties."

"How long would this agreement be for?"

"You can terminate at any time."

Dave could see his mind working. He knew he was trying to figure out if there was a catch somewhere. If this old country boy was trying to who-do him.

"And you want nothing more than a place to deer hunt?"

"That's right. An exclusive place to deer hunt without people around."

Three piece suit got up suddenly. "You've got a deal. I'll draw up a contract and send it to you. If you like it, sign it and make a copy and send it back."

Dave stuck out his hand this time. The lawyer shook it and left.

Standing in the woods just over the hill from where Ben's buck stood listening, Dave patted his pocket. He had a feeling that this was going to be the best deer season ever. Especially if he got a shot at the deer that made the big tracks under that oak tree back over the slope.

What he couldn't figure out was what else had been over that slope. He had smelled it and it was nothing like he had ever smelled before. A damp, earthy wet dog kind of smell. And he thought he knew all the smells in these hardwood forests.

Dave leaped the trickling creek that started at the spring near the base of the hill he had just descended. He was on the backside of the slope, away from the interstate. Away from the oak tree where he had seen the sign of a deer feeding, and from where he had smelled the strange smell. He tucked that odor away in his memory. He would try later to recall if he had ever known it.

He crossed the marshy area where several wet weather springs surfaced and kept the ground spongy. On the other side was the only structure he could find on this old farm. A fallen down barn that had a milk shed attached to it. The milk shed was still standing. Dave stepped inside and saw the six wooden stanchions where the cows had stood with their heads caught, as the farmer and his wife milked them. The smells in here were wonderful. Hay. Grain. Old cow pies, hard as rock. Mice and mold. Dave loved them all. Sometimes he thought he had been born with the wrong nose. He had an animal nose. When he was a little boy they had made fun of him because he was always smelling things that nobody else smelled. His daddy had once said that he had such a good smeller that he could "sniff out a poot in a windstorm."

Dave knew it wasn't the nose. It was the brain that interpreted the smells. Just like sight. Everybody had eyes, but not everybody saw. In fact, his favorite expression had to do with eyes. He had used it at times when people said something about his nose. "None are so blind as they who will not see."

His four wheel drive Dodge truck was parked under the hedge apple tree that grew beside the milk shed. When he reached it, he opened the door and sat on the ledge beside the seat and pulled out a plug of Bloodhound. He sliced off a corner of the square of tobacco with the razor sharp Hen and Rooster knife he kept in his pocket. He looked around. The Garrett Place. He had been eyeing this place for years. He had wanted to hunt here but had not been able to get permission. The old couple who owned it had been unable to work it, and it had grown up over the years. Now three piece suit had bought it and Dave had the paper in his pocket to prove he was the only one who could hunt here.

Now, if he could find out who owned the nine hundred acres on the other side of the interstate, he would have a hunter's paradise. But he wasn't going to hunt there without permission. The last one who had tried it came back to his truck after a day of hunting to find all four tires cut. The windows smashed. The seat covers slashed, and even one door twisted half off.

Dave had laughed. "Serves him right. He knew better." The only thing nobody could figure was, "Who had done it?"

The place was owned by someone in New York. At least, that's what everybody said. Nobody really knew who owned it. Just that it had belonged to Minnie Hill who had lived on it until she had finally given up in her eighty-fifth year and had gone to live with her niece in New York. The niece had been killed jay walking on the streets of Manhattan and Minnie had died in a nursing home. Everyone said some of her heirs owned the farm.

Dave just knew he lusted after it. It was across I-65 from the Garrett Place, but he knew he would never go over there without permission.

****

No such strings were on Ben. He could come and go as he pleased. That's because he had no truck to be smashed. He smashed. Or tires to slash. He slashed. He loved to wreck and smash what he called the opulence of society. Especially when he found it intruding on him. He had been hiding when the hunter had come back to his truck to find it torn all to pieces. He watched in glee as the man almost cried at the devastation to his truck. Then the memories came flooding back. "To think that a man could cry over a wrecked truck when they had laughed at him over his wrecked life," he thought.

Now, as he crouched in the tunnel under the interstate and waited for dark, he thought about what must have happened to the property where his buck lived. There had been no one on it for years. Now a hunter was there. Ben had heard the man's truck, so the hunter had driven through the gates. He wasn't sneaking. He wasn't like Ben, but he was going to ruin everything, unless Ben could stop him.

Ben never used the word "I" anymore. Plus he never talked. Only in his mind, and he never moved his lips. He simply referred to himself as Ben. He thought as if his brain was detached from his body. At one time it had almost become so. Now it was just the memories that were detached, and they kept trying to rejoin themselves to his brain.

If he wasn't careful, they were going to ruin his awareness. Make him vulnerable to the synthetic devices used by humans. Like binoculars and spot lights.

The tunnel shook ever so slightly as a huge truck roared over head. Ben blinked. He had dozed. Without even knowing it. Now it was dusk. He could leave without being seen if he flitted from bush to bush until he got to the woods on the other side of the open field outside the tunnel. Then he would be on his property. The small open field went with his buck's property, but no one realized it. Since it was on his side, everyone assumed it was his. He would never tell. He had sealed his lips when he had seared off the memories.

****

Dave pulled onto the gravel road that bordered the interstate. Green's Road. It was the only access to the Garrett Place. For an instant his head lights were shining directly across the four lanes of super highway into the open field dotted with cedar bushes. Moving cedar bushes? At least, it had appeared that one of them had. He backed up quickly and pointed the truck lights over that way again, but whatever he had seen was gone. If he had seen anything. Nothing was moving there, now. Maybe it was a late feeding deer. He headed back toward town. He would be back early Saturday morning. He wanted to see the morning habits of the animals of the Garrett Place, now that he had seen the evening ways. Unless Betty Lou had something planned for him on his Saturday off. Sometimes she made plans for him until she realized that the time right before deer season was just as important as the actual season. That's when he made all his scouting runs. That's when he saw the things he needed to see. And smelled the smells.

CHAPTER 3

Ben couldn't believe it. He had almost let that man, the intruding hunter, see him. He had felt the lights seeking him out and had frozen behind a bush while the man backed up, looked again, then drove off. Ben then waited until it was pitch black dark before moving again. He had gone too many years undetected to get caught now.

The path he was now on, he would never travel in daylight. But he often used it at night. Because to go through woods and over the ridge to get to his house would take too long in the dark. The only problem with this deer and cow path was it circled over property that wasn't his. Property that he had thought was his until he had seen the little pink plastic strips tied to trees and bushes where a surveyor had marked off a plot of ground. He had gone back and searched his map and description and had found that the area was not his. It was a narrow rectangle of land that jutted into his nine hundred acres, coming perilously close to his house.

Then the trucks had pulled in and workers had begun building a house. Ben had watched the progress of the house, especially late in the evening when a young couple would come out and sweep up sawdust and small pieces of wood.

The house was now complete. It was a country style house with rough sawn board siding and a huge rock chimney. But what Ben hated about the house was the large, black dog on a chain in the back yard. The dog knew every time he used the path. He would begin barking and lunging at his chain. The path was about a hundred and fifty yards from the back of the house so Ben knew he couldn't be seen. He crouched down anyway. He wanted to watch the man come out and try to calm the dog. He didn't, but the woman did.

"What's the matter, boy? Something out there? Probably just a coyote or a skunk. I'll bet you would like to get loose so you could find out, wouldn't you?" The dog continued to leap at the darkness. He then turned and ran back to the woman and whined and look up at her.

Ben crouched and watched the woman. Then he turned his head and stood up and walked slowly up the path. He couldn't look at her and keep the memories at bay. It hadn't been a problem until one day he heard the man call her name. Natalie! Something about the name hurtling at him across the open area behind the house, sent him into spasms. He had fallen backward onto the ground behind the mass of honeysuckles where he had been crouched. The name bounced around inside his head like a caroming pinball.

The dog knew he was moving because he started another barking frenzy. Ben started loping. He would run until he got to his house. He had to get away before the woman's name started cartwheeling inside his head .

Now on this night, Ben followed the path until it came to the fence the people had erected around their property. Three strands of barbed wire on metal posts. Ben couldn't figure why the people wanted a fence. The only animal they had was a dog. Ben hit the ground on his belly and slid under the bottom strand. If it had been daylight he would have jumped it. Like a deer.

The path entered the woods on his property and wound its way up the thickly wooded hill to the ridge overlooking his house. When he got to the top of the ridge he turned right and headed west along the path. When he got directly behind his house he dropped off the path and found his way down through the woods toward his wood framed house. He was halfway down the slope when he saw the light. It was bobbing and weaving and moving directly toward his house. He heard voices and then the bark of a dog.

Ben didn't panic but he turned and sprinted back up the hill as fast as he could in the dark. As he reached the top of the ridge he heard the hollow sound of footsteps on wood and knew that whoever it was had stepped upon his porch.

He turned left at the top of the ridge and continued as if he had never dropped off the path. His eyes constantly flicking down the slope toward the house. They were inside, now. He could see the light reflecting off the old window panes. He gritted his teeth and moaned softly. Then he smiled to himself at the thought of the huge rock he would find and heave through the window of the truck.

If they had come in from the east, which it appeared they had, there were only two places they could have parked. He headed for the first one. It was a place where the bull dozers had come one day and made a place for the school bus to turn around. Ben had thought they were going to push down his fence and come on his property, but they hadn't. But it made a great place for coon hunters to park at night and let out their dogs.

Ben ran along his fence beside the gravel road. He could see the limestone shining faintly white in the darkness. At first he thought the hunters must be at the other spot. There was no truck in the bus turn around. But as he started down the fence toward the curve in the road where the shoulder was wide enough to pull off, he happened to look over in the woods across the road from the turn around. He saw the gleam of chrome.

He froze. There could be someone left with the truck. He had to get across the fence and find out, except this wasn't a barbed wire fence. It was a net wire fence.

Ben eased down the wire until he came to a place where a cedar shielded him from the truck, and climbed. He then darted across the gravel and melted into the fence row on the other side. As he got close to the truck, he could see that the fence had been cut so the truck could be backed into the woods and hidden. The fury rose in him. Even though the truck wasn't on his property, the men had committed the unpardonable before coming onto his property. They had cut a farmer's fence.

His foot hit a rock and he stooped to pick it up. It weighed about fifteen pounds. As he approached the truck on the passenger side, he raised the rock over his head. Two steps and he heaved it with all his might. It smashed the glass and landed on the seat. He found two more rocks and smashed the driver side window and then the windshield. It wouldn't cave in, but splintered into a thousand pieces.

He took out his knife and went to work on the tires. The truck slowly settled down as the air whooshed out of the slashed rubber.

The seats were next, and when he got through with them, they were ribbons. He opened the glove box and threw the contents out into the woods. He then fumbled under the hood and found the latch that released it. With his knife he cut every belt and hose he could find. He removed the radiator and oil filler caps and flung them into the ditch. By this time he was in a frenzied sweat. He started making the little animal sounds that he had made that time so long ago. The time he didn't like to think about. The time of the memories.

The laughter was the only thing that warned him. Otherwise, he would have been caught. He spun and ran into the trees behind the truck. The only thing was, he was not on his property now. He would have to cross the road to get back. The coon hunters would be up and down the road, cursing and yelling. That would bring him back to his frenzy. The last scene he could remember in the other world was filled with cursing and yelling. That's why he hated that world. The people in it were so crude and ugly.

He put his fingers to his ears when the men got to the truck. He didn't want their curses and yells to bring him back to the brink of the other world. He was vulnerable then. He still had to escape.

Ben concentrated on moving quietly as he crept away from the shattered truck. Suddenly a gunshot blasted the night. It brought him up short. Had they seen him? No! They couldn't have. No one had ever done that.

He looked back through the trees and could see a light moving erratically up the road. It was the man with the carbide light on his head. He was screaming and yelling curses into the night air. Ben's mind shut them out, and he moved down the fence toward the curve in the road. He could cross now. The man's loud mouth would mask any sounds Ben might make. He darted across when he saw the light pointed in the other direction.

The house. He had to get there. Had to see if they had found anything that showed his presence. Or had seen anything to indicate that the house had a sometimes inhabitant.

Chapter 4

Chief Investigator Dave Warren listened as Butch Gibson told his sad tale about coming back to his truck and finding it smashed to bits. Dave would occasionally write something in the comments section of the report he was filling out. He didn't really care about Gibson's truck. He didn't care about Gibson, either. He was the kind of slob who gave all hunters a bad name. Cutting fences and hunting without permission.

What interested Dave was the way the truck had been smashed. Just like one a couple of years back.

"You crossed the fence onto the old Minnie Hill Place? Is that right?"

"Well, we didn't really know where we was. We just followed the dogs."

"That's a net wire fence all along that road. You had to know you were climbing a fence."

"Well, yeah, but we didn't know we wasn't supposed to hunt over there."

"I'll bet you know it, now."

"That ain't the point! What are you going to do about catching whoever ruined my truck?"

"I'm not going to do anything. You're the one in the wrong. You cut a fence and trespassed on private property."

"We didn't cut that fence. It was already cut."

"You're a liar, Gibson, and you know it!"

Gibson leaped up at the accusation and opened his mouth to say something. He thought better of it when Dave came up out of his chair with him and looked him in the eye. He just grabbed the bill of his cap and jerked it down over his eyes and stalked out.

Dave leaned back in his chair and closed his eyes. The images of the Garrett Place and his truck sitting under that hedge apple tree, still fresh in his mind. What would he do if he came back and found every window in the old Dodge broken? Try to figure out who, that's what. He knew the why. Hunting without permission on the Minnie Hill Place.

"Somebody doesn't want anyone hunting on the Hill Place. Or even trespassing. Now, who is that somebody?" he mused.

Dave mulled over in his mind everybody he knew who lived on the roads that bordered the nine hundred acres. One of them had to be the one. One of them was keeping an eye on the property for whoever owned it. That had to be it. The owner in New York, or wherever, was paying someone to keep people off the property.

"A man will think twice about going back out there. That's for sure," Dave said with a slight grin. He got up from his desk and walked out to the dispatcher's desk.

"I'm going to do some scouting around about this truck smashing thing. I'll be in the car most of the time."

"10-4, good looking."

Dave grinned and headed for his patrol car. If Betty Lou saw the way that new dispatcher flirted with him, she would have a fit.

"Blonde hair and blue eyes," Dave said to himself as he pulled away from the jail. "That'll get 'em every time."

Dave knew where the truck smashing had taken place. His pal, Leon Fleming, who worked night patrol, had taken the call last night and had gone out and done the initial report. He told Dave that Gibson had cut the fence on old man Barron's side of the road.

When Dave got to the spot on the gravel road, an old man in a faded pair of overalls was at the gap in the wire, pulling and patching and cussing and spitting. Trying to suppress a grin, Dave walked up to him as he struggled with the wire.

"Having problems, there, Mr. Barron?"

"None that I wouldn't have if them coon hunters wouldn't cut my fences!" the old man swore.

"It's that Gibson fellow. He's the only one that does stuff like this."

The old man stood up straight and wiped his forehead as he removed his straw hat with the green eye shade built into the brim. His tobacco stained mouth parted in a toothless grin as he looked at Dave. "And he won't be back unless he wants his truck tore to hell again."

"You got any idea who wrecked his truck?"

The old man dropped his grin and looked at Dave with pure evil in his eye. "Nope! But if I'd a' caught him, I'd done it myself."

"You ever see anybody on the Hill place, Mr. Barron?"

"Nope. I hardly ever come back here on this side of my place. Unless it's to fix a fence like this."

"Who keeps an eye on the place? You got any idea?"

The old man stopped his pulling and looked at Dave. "You're asking a lot of questions about that place. You wanting to go coon hunting over there?"

"I'd like to go deer hunting, if I could get permission."

"Well, you can forget that! And you better stay off that place if you don't want your truck to wind up like that Gibson fellers."

"You ever go over there, Mr. Barron?"

The old man's watery eyes narrowed and he spat a stream of juice at the center of the dusty road. He stood looking across the gravel toward the thickly wooded and grown up Hill Place. Dave thought he wasn't going to speak, but then he finally did. "Ten years ago I went over there. But I won't never set foot on it no more."

"Why? Did something happen?"

"Every time I'd come down this road I'd jump the biggest covey of bob whites you ever did see. But they'd fly over the fence into that Hill Place. One day I decided to go over there and thin them birds out. I took Sally, my little bitch Pointer. One minute she was hunting up through a little patch of sage next to some woods. The next minute she was gone. I hollered and looked for her for over an hour before leaving."

"Did you ever find her?"

"When I got back home I did."

"So she had come back home?"

"Not exactly. Somebody brought her home."

"I bet you were glad to see her."

"She had a wire around her neck and she was hanging from the ceiling light in the kitchen. Her belly was ripped open and her guts was lying all over the eating table."

Dave looked at the old man. His toothless mouth was closed as tight as it could get. His chin was jutting out and Dave could see he was fighting back tears. Dave couldn't speak. The story both revolted him and scared the life out of him.

"Me and Clella Mae was married for forty eight years. She give me that pup for our last anniversary."

"And you got no idea who done it?"

"The same one who done this," he said, pointing to the bits of glass lying at his feet.

Dave walked back to his car, leaving the old man in a dream like state, standing next to his cut fence. His mind began working as he drove along the edges of the Hill Place.

"Somebody is hunting on that place and doesn't want anybody else around. Either that or they've got a still up there and are afraid someone will find it. Or maybe a pot patch is more like it. But it's got to be somebody who lives right around here. People would notice a strange vehicle."

Dave drove the borders of the Hill Place for two hours. He stopped and talked to several people who lived on the roads around it. No one knew anything. No one had ever seen anyone in the last ten years on the place. It was almost unbelievable. Here was nine hundred acres of wilderness in the middle of McCord County, just ten miles from Lewiston, and nobody had ever set foot on it without getting their dog killed or truck wrecked.

As he headed back to town he looked at himself in the rear view mirror. He spoke to the blue eyed, blonde image. "Somebody knows more than they're saying. Whoever owns that place is paying one of these people to keep everybody off. I'm going to find out who that is. I just hope I don't wind up with my guts on old man Barron's eating table."

Chapter 5

Ben sat in the fork of the silver maple tree that grew on a little rise about three hundred yards from the spot where he had wrecked the truck last night. He watched the old man fix the fence on his side of the road. When the patrol car pulled up, he squinted his eyes, trying to get a better look at the driver. He couldn't tell but it looked a lot like the deer hunter he had seen late yesterday evening on the Garrett Place. Surely he wasn't a cop, also. What if he was looking for Ben? No! Everybody thought he was dead, didn't they? Had they sent somebody to look for him after all these years?

Ben felt the panic. He hadn't felt it in years. He had felt so secure, now a cop was looking for him. He scrambled down from the tree and headed for the top of the ridge above his house. From there he could see most of the road that bordered his property. He ran the ridge for two hours watching the cop in the patrol car cruise and stop at each house along the road and talk to people.

Maybe the old man told him about the dog. Now, the second truck smashed. He's just guessing, Ben thought. He doesn't really know Ben's here. Just like the coon hunters who went in the house last night. They were just curious about the house sitting there abandoned. So they went in.

When Ben had returned to his house last night, he had gone to his spot on the hill behind the house to sleep. He didn't dare go in the house in the dark. He wanted to wait for daylight so he could see where they had walked. He wanted to see if they had gone into the basement, although he doubted it.

So, the next morning he had gone in the front door, something he rarely did, and followed the foot prints in the dust around the house until they had ended up at the basement door. He could imagine the one with the light looking at the yawning hole at his feet. No steps leading down. No way to negotiate the ten foot drop. Unless he did just that. Drop. Then, there was no way back up unless he had a rope around his waist like the one Ben always carried.

Ben uncoiled his rope and threw it over the beam that spanned the hole. He grabbed the two dangling ends and swung into space. He slid down into the dark hole and then pulled the rope after him. As he coiled the rope around his waist, he groped his way across the dirt floor of the smelly old basement. He put one hand out so he wouldn't run into the back wall. When he touched the shelves where Minnie Hill's mother had stored her preserves, he stopped. He knelt on the right side of the shelves and worked his fingers in the crack between the back and the dirt wall. He pulled gently and the shelves moved as a unit away from the wall. He didn't need much room to squeeze his body in behind the shelves since the hole he had made ten years ago in the dirt wall was still there. He knelt inside the hole and reached into the basement and pulled the shelves flush with the wall.

He was now in his tunnel. When he felt his knees cross the rock foundation, he knew he could stand up. He had crawled into the old storm cellar that had been built years ago just to the rear of this old original Hill house. The doorway from the basement to the cellar had collapsed some time ago and Ben had fixed the small hole in the wall to crawl through. He had then covered it with the shelves. It had taken him over a year of hauling dirt in buckets, and carrying rocks in his bare hands to cover the outer entrance and disguise it as a rock and dirt pile. The opening was small and faced the wooded slope just behind the house, and he could slither down the hill and creep into the rock pile like a snake.

He felt along the wall until he came to the shelf he had attached to the cellar wall. It held his precious candles and the matches he stole from time to time out of cars or buildings. But the candles were what he cherished the most. He was getting low and must soon find some more.

The match flared and he stuck it to the candlewick. When it was burning brightly, he walked over and sat in the old reclining chair he had hauled down before he closed up the outer entrance.

He looked around his underground world. The cot he slept on. The box beside the chair where he kept his Bible. Then the brief case. His eye always fell on it. He used to look through it years ago. The last time had sent him into crying fits. Now he sometimes took it in his lap and looked at the brass clasps, but he never opened it. The memories and images and sights and sounds that rushed out were too much for him to bear. They made him think about what he had become, or worse, what he had been. He couldn't handle that.

His stomach growled and reminded him that he hadn't eaten in a long time. He reached into the basket beside the chair and got an apple. The last of the ones he had gotten off the trees of the man who ran the bull dozer. The name on the truck door said Pruitt Excavating. The truck that hauled the long trailer that the bull dozer rode on.

Ben had gotten a ham or two out of the big smoke house Pruitt had behind his main house until the big pad lock appeared on the door. He must have missed the hams. Ben was careful around Pruitt's house after that.

Ben munched the apple and wondered about the cop. Was he really looking for him? Was he the same man he had seen on the Garrett Place? Was Ben foolish to believe that nobody would ever get suspicious about the Hill Place? It had been ten years. How much longer could he go on living here without being sought?

The sleep last night on the ground had been fitful. He slept best in the daytime on his cot. He walked over and blew out the candle and then laid down. He would go out tonight and try to find some more candles and maybe some cans of food, if he could take them without alerting anyone. The old houses where elderly people lived, old country people, were his best bet. But somehow he knew that he would be drawn to the house where Natalie lived. The name haunted him. Her face. He wanted to look at it. The dog he wanted to kill.

Chapter 6

Natalie Dunn watched the sun slide behind the ridge that ran down the backbone of the large tract of land behind her house. She knew that the interstate was on the other side of the rock and tree covered crest. She could see a high point in the center of the ridge and she suspected that from a spot up there one could see for miles around.

"I'm going to hike up there one day," she said to the big, black dog that stood beside her, his heavy tail thumping against her leg. He looked up at her and whined.

"I'll take you with me, Butler. You know I wouldn't leave you here. We may just go up there tomorrow. Jeff won't be back until tomorrow night." She knelt and hugged the Lab and he tried to lick her head off. The attention excited him.

She walked back toward the house. The dog followed until his chain stopped him. He then ambled back to his dog house and flopped down in the doorway by the water dish.

Natalie loved the nights when Jeff was away in Louisiana. The days were okay too, but she liked to feel the darkness creep in around her. Sealing her off from the things she didn't want to look at. She was just glad Butler was out there. He wouldn't let anything get close to the house. She could see him lying in the door of his house, looking at her as she stood at the kitchen sink, cutting up a tomato for her salad. The square of light from the window brightened as the gloom deepened. The dogs eyes gleamed yellow as he watched her through the glass.

Suddenly he was up. Out of the little house and facing toward the ridge. She could hear his low growl and see the hair on his back standing straight up. He moved toward the darkness and disappeared, leaving just a gleaming taut chain pointing into the void.

Natalie dropped the knife and ran to the back door. She jerked it open and ran out into the splash of light from the window just as Butler started barking. The sudden sound startled her, but she ran toward the leaping dog who turned on her as she came up behind him. When he saw it was her, he turned back to his frenzied barking into the darkness.

"What is it, boy? What's out there?" She knelt and tried to hold the dog but he was beside himself with fear and excitement. He almost knocked her down with his jumping and leaping. Natalie stood up and moved away from Butler, out into the yard and the darkness. Something was out there and she intended to find out what it was. She stopped beside the tiller that Jeff had left at the end of the garden spot he was preparing. Something made her want to yell into the dark. "Who's out there? Go away and leave us alone!" She could see the black mass of honeysuckle vines growing in a clump by the fence, and started toward it. "If you are behind those weeds, I'm going to find you."

She stopped just short of the vines as headlights swept the back yard. She spun and watched a car drive up beside the house and a man get out. He left the motor and lights on. When he crossed in front of the car the light beams showed her his uniform and she then saw the light bar on top of the car.

Butler, his attention diverted from the dark to the light, began barking at the man as he walked toward the back door. Natalie called to him as he raised his fist to knock.

"I'm back here." She knelt beside Butler to quiet him as the man in uniform turned toward the sound.

"It's okay, Butler," she said as the man walked toward them.

"Mrs. Dunn?" he inquired.

"I'm Natalie Dunn."

"My name is Dave Warren with the Sheriff's Department. I hate to bother you this late but I've stopped a couple of times and you weren't home."

"That's okay," she said, rising to stand beside Butler.

"That's a beautiful dog, Mrs. Dunn." He put his hand out for Butler to sniff. Natalie watched as the man ran his hand along Butler's jaw and then up to the top of his head and began scratching his ears. Butler liked it but not to the point he dropped his guard. He kept his eyes on the man just in case.

"I've been investigating a case of malicious destruction. A man had his truck vandalized down the road a ways last night, and I was wondering if you had seen anyone around here that didn't belong in the area?"

"No, I haven't seen anything other than the normal traffic past the house."

"What about back there on the Hill Place? Have you seen anybody there since you've been living here?"

"We haven't seen anything there, but Butler here evidently has. That's what I was doing just now. Butler was barking at something that gets him excited every night or so."

"What do you think it is?"

"I don't know, but it has Butler all shook up. I don't think he saw anything but he must have smelled it."

"Why do you say that?" Dave said, the mention of smell getting his curiosity up.

"I was back there by that patch of vines and I smelled whatever it was and it nearly gagged me."

Now Dave was really curious. "What did it smell like?"

"I couldn't describe it. Maybe like an old sour dish cloth stuffed inside a pair of smelly tennis shoes."

"And you think it was coming from whatever is back there?" Dave tried to see if his mind would put the smell he had in there with the description Mrs. Dunn had given him.

"That's odd," he said.

"What's odd?"

"I smelled the same smell the other day when I was scouting for deer on the other side of the interstate. Maybe that's all it is. A smelly old deer."

"Either that or a rotten skunk."

"Well, if you see anything just give me a call down at the Sheriff's Department," the deputy said, handing her a card with his name and number on it.

Natalie watched the man in uniform walk back toward the patrol car. She wished Jeff was here, now. She wasn't normally afraid at night, but the barking of Butler and the visit of the deputy had gotten her nervous.

She quickly filled Butler's water dish and hurried inside and locked the back door. She went around to the rest of the doors and windows and made sure all were secure.

As she stood at the sink looking out into the darkened backyard, she could still see Butler standing beside his house looking toward the back. "What if somebody really is out there?" she thought. "What would I do if they tried to get in here?" That was one aspect of life she hadn't thought about. She would have been shocked at the primitive world of Ben right outside her back door.

Ben lay in the tall grass behind the mass of honeysuckle vines and watched the cop and Natalie talk. He watched the man rub the head of the dog. The distance was too great for him to hear what they were saying, but he felt like sinking into the ground when Natalie turned and pointed right at him. Had she seen him? It was too dark. There was no way she could have known he was here. Except for the barking of the dog.

He wondered what the cop was asking her. What had he asked all the people he had visited today? Ben wished he could hear. But then he wondered if he would know what the words meant. It had been so long since he had heard real words from people up close. He wanted to get close to Natalie so he could hear her talk. To see if it sounded the same as it had so many years ago.

The sounds came to his lips before he knew it, and the dog began his low growl. Ben buried his face in the grass to keep the sounds away from the dog, but it was too late. The big dog was straining at his chain, pulling in Ben's direction. Ben touched the knife in its sheath. If the chain broke he would need it. He thought about the point entering the smooth, soft belly of the dog. That would stop the barking.

Ben started crawling. He had to get to the front of the house, away from the dog. Away from the light in the back. He wanted to see the face of Natalie up close.

Natalie looked closely at her face. The tiny lines were starting around the eyes and mouth. She used to tell Jeff that if she was going to have a baby, it would have to be soon. Now, she never mentioned it. She had reached the point where she knew that now she didn't want a baby. Not with Jeff.

There was still no sign of gray in the dark hair. She checked that every night when she brushed her one hundred strokes.

She got up from the dressing table she had insisted on putting in the large bathroom. That was one thing she was not going to put up with if she could help it. A tiny bathroom. She slipped a robe over her gown as she headed down the hall to the kitchen and den.

Butler's chain was stretched tight. It would have hummed if she could have strummed it. She stood by the sink and idly thought about the sound it would make until it dawned on her that something was wrong. She lowered the glass in her hand to the counter. Her hand shook so badly that the glass chattered as she sat it down.

The chain was long enough to allow Butler to disappear around the side of the house. Toward the front. The front! Whatever was out there was now in the front of the house. She could hear Butler's low growling.

Natalie spun away from the sink and ran across the large room. As she passed the fireplace she grabbed a poker. The window at the front of the den! She had failed to close the blinds on it. And the one in the corner beside the fireplace. She had forgotten that one also. She grabbed the cord on the window blind beside the fireplace and pulled, dropping the poker to the floor. As the blind rattled down, she turned to the other window and stooped to pick up the poker. Her head coming back up froze in the shock position. The wildest pair of eyes, sunk back into the gauntest face she had ever seen, locked onto hers. For how long she didn't know. It seemed like forever.

Her right leg started to cramp, otherwise she couldn't have moved. When it collapsed and she fell to the side, breaking the eye contact, the face in the window disappeared. Natalie wanted to scream, but she couldn't. She crawled to the window and grabbed the cord and pulled. The blind came down and she grabbed the poker and stood up. Where was he now? Was he trying to get in one of the other windows? Or the door?

She swung the poker around in front of her as she spun to the middle of the den and looked frantically from one opening to the other.

"Stop it!" she screamed. The sound calmed her. She ran to the phone on the wall by the back door and punched the buttons for the Sheriff's Department off the deputy's card she had placed over the phone. The deep, commanding voice that answered, made her realize that she didn't know what to say. She tried to speak but her mouth wouldn't work until the voice spoke again.

"Dave!" She almost yelled the word. "I need to speak to the officer named Dave. He was out at my house about an hour ago."

"Dave Warren, ma'am?"

"Yes! That's his name. I need to talk to him."

"He's off duty, ma'am. Could someone else help you?"

"No! Get him! There's someone out here trying to get in my house!"

"Ma'am, you'll have to tell me who you are and where you live."

"Natalie Dunn! He was just out here! Please tell him to hurry."

The rattle of Butler's chain startled her. She slammed the phone into its receiver and ran to the kitchen window. Butler was now straining the chain toward the back again.

"Now it's in the back again!" she screamed. "Whoever or whatever it is!"

Her mind suddenly realized that it didn't know which. Was the face in the window really a man? Could it have been just a reflection? Maybe her face looked like that to other people. Maybe she was just seeing herself as others saw her. She didn't know how long she stood there.

The lights sweeping the house brought her out of her daze. Then the noise of the car sliding on the gravel as it came to a stop, reassured her. The man in the uniform was going to make everything all right.

Butler growled at him, but the man's voice stopped Butler in his tracks. "Easy boy," he said as he walked by the kitchen window toward the door.

Natalie wanted to collapse into his arms but instead she just opened the door for him. His shirt tail was out and a big black revolver was in his hand. His eyes were looking everywhere but at Natalie. They probed into the house, past her head, looking for something amiss.

"I got a call as I was heading home that somebody was here. What's wrong, Mrs. Dunn?"

Natalie's words came gushing as she felt the relief that rescue brings. "I saw a face in the window. A wild face. With a beard. He was looking right at me."

"Now, Mrs. Dunn, just calm down. Where did you see this face?"

"At that front window by the corner. He was looking right at me."

Dave walked over and pulled the blind back up and looked out. He could see little with the lights reflecting in the glass.

"He's not there, now. He ran when I saw him."

"I know. I'm going outside and look around."

Dave walked past Natalie and went outside to his car and got a flash light. He walked around to the front of the house and looked at the ground in front of the window. It was mulched with bark chips all along the front.

"No tracks here," he muttered as he looked into the window. He saw Natalie at the sink, looking out the window toward the back. He walked along the front of the house toward the other end, away from the driveway. As he rounded the corner he caught a whiff of something. He stopped and stepped back. Was that it? Was that the same smell he had picked up across the interstate? The same one Natalie had smelled earlier? He sniffed the air but couldn't find the odor again.

When he got around to the back door, Natalie was standing there looking at Butler's chain. It was stretched into the darkness.

"Show me exactly where the face was, Mrs. Dunn."

Natalie walked across the room to the lower pane on the left and pointed. "Just about my height," Dave muttered.

"Do you think he's gone?"

"I would say whatever was out there is long gone by now. It was probably just a peeping tom. I've got an idea who it is. We've had trouble with him before. All he does is look. He's harmless."

Natalie watched Dave walk toward the back door. He had the flashlight in one hand but he had put the big gun in its holster. When she realized what he was doing, she almost panicked.

"You're not leaving, are you?" she gasped.

"Yes, ma'am. Every thing looks all right around here, now."

"What if he comes back?"

"Have you got a gun, Mrs. Dunn?"

"A gun?"

"Yes, ma'am. A firearm."

"No. My husband has one but he keeps it with him."

"Well then, all I can tell you is to lock your doors and windows and call us if he shows back up."

"You've got to protect me. You can't just leave with that man still out there."

The irritation rose quickly in Dave and he spoke hastily. "You want me to move in with you, Ma'am? If you want twenty four hour protection, you'll have to hire a body guard."

It had been years since Dave's face had been slapped. Natalie's open hand landed with suddenness. He staggered backward two steps and then simply turned and walked to his car. He wanted to be mad, but he realized that it was embarrassment he was suffering. He shouldn't have said what he did, but these urbanites, as he called them, who moved out into the middle of nowhere and then expected to be coddled every minute, just irritated the hell out of him.

He eased the car in reverse and backed out of the drive, never giving Natalie another look. She stood by the door, looking at the car disappear around the curve in the road. When she realized she was alone, she acted quickly. She ran to Butler and unsnapped his chain.

"Come on, boy. You're going to spend the night inside tonight. I'd like to see whoever is out there try to get past you."

Ben watched Natalie slap the cop's face and then lead the dog inside. He was confused. She had waved at him earlier in the day when he left. Now she slapped his face. But taking the dog inside? Who was she afraid of? The cop? Afraid he would come back? Maybe she was afraid of Ben. No! She couldn't be. But was that fear in her eyes when she saw him in the window? Or recognition? Ben's Natalie? Was she becoming that? Like the deer could sense Ben's presence, maybe Natalie could tell when the memories were upon him. Could feel the air become alive with people and happenings as they surrounded him and tried to take him away. Up, away from here. Away from his nine hundred acres and the peace he pulled in around him. Take him back under the roadblock, back into the seething turmoil he had run away from those thousands of years ago.

Ben's steps were drawn to the area where the purple flowers grew. Minnie Hill had planted them years ago, right after she and Walter had built the antebellum style house they lived in until Walter died and she moved to New York. Ben had burned the grand old house soon after arriving on the place because he knew that if anyone ever returned to the 900 acres, the house would be the first place they would go. He then moved into the smaller house that had been abandoned by Minnie and Walter when they built the new one. It was in the middle of the farm and the area around it was covered in weeds and thorns. Now all that was left of the three story mansion was one of the three chimneys, and the Iris that grew in profusion.

How did Ben know that his Natalie loved flowers? Had he taken them to her before? His mind told him he had. But it had been long ago. On the other side of the roadblock.

****

She screamed. So sudden was the shock that she couldn't stifle the cry of surprise that escaped her lips. Butler leaped past her as she opened the door, letting in the warm sunshine. Leaped past the old fruit jar that held the purple Iris.

Natalie trembled, but her hands going to her mouth, suppressed another scream. Then it hit her. He had been back! Her eyes quickly swept the yard, looking for him. Butler was already doing that. He was off his chain now and he was inspecting every area that he couldn't reach when he was tied. He was running, his nose to the ground, sniffing every place the man had stepped. He ended back at the door with Natalie, looking at the flowers in the jar.

So harmless. So beautiful. So full of fear. Why had she screamed at flowers? She now realized that whoever was out there was simply lonely. So what if he was a peeping tom? The flowers suddenly told her everything she needed to know about him. They were his apology for looking at her. For scaring her. A pervert or a man bent on violence would never do such a thing.

She patted Butler's head. He looked at her, the flowers now a small barrier between them. A peace offering from one whom he must guard against. One who put off powerful signals and odors. One who was trying to get past him to Natalie. He would seek him out the first chance he got. His flesh would feel good between his teeth.

Natalie raised her eyes to the back. To the high ridge that rose behind the house. To the dense woods and thickets. She wondered if the man was watching her. She raised her hand, almost in a gesture of welcome. She was no longer afraid.

Chapter 7

Ben was there before daylight. Lying in the leaves on the slope below the ridge where he knew his deer would come to feed. He usually didn't come across the interstate in the morning. He was afraid of being caught over here all day. But today was different. He didn't want to see Natalie when she found the flowers. The last time he had given her flowers, in the other life and the other world, she had screamed at him and flung them in his face. He had stood stoically as the water and petals fell from his head to his feet, and then had squinted as the vase shattered into a million pieces as it hit the wall beside him.

He heard the harsh, guttural grunt of the buck before he saw him. He was coming through the blackberry and buck bushes toward the oak tree. To the acorns and breakfast. Ben watched him come through the briars, the huge rack held high to keep from getting tangled. It was barely enough light for Ben to see the brown coat of his buck. The brown that would soon be a dark gray now that winter was coming on.

The sun began to peep over the ridge behind Ben's back. The ridge that rose behind his house. The sun would already be coming through the windows of the old house. Ben's eyes were on the buck as he ambled toward the oak tree, when suddenly something caught in the corner of his eye.

A flash! Up high in a tree at the top of the slope. Ben froze. His head on the buck, his eyes trying to search the tree without moving his head. The buck hadn't seen it. Animals don't look up. They never expect danger from above. Ben usually did, except for this morning. His mind had been on Natalie, and he had allowed himself to be pinned down early in the morning on the wrong side of the interstate by somebody in a tree with a pair of binoculars.

Ben slowly, inch by inch, began moving his head toward the tree where the flash had come from. It had to be the same one who was here earlier in the week. Ben wanted to see if he and the cop were one and the same.

The legs dangling down were what gave him away, otherwise Ben would never have seen him. But that was all he could see. The thick leaves covered the rest of him.

Ben lowered his head into the ground and prepared to wait. He knew the man wouldn't climb down until the buck left. And that could be an hour or more.

He must have dozed because suddenly he felt footsteps, and they weren't his buck's. The leaves rustled and Ben felt the feet coming closer. He dare not raise his head because the movement would surely cause him to be seen. He was glad he was burrowed into the leaves. He always did that to keep the deer from seeing him. He just hoped the man didn't step on him.

The feet came close, but then went on down the slope. Ben heard the man sniff as he went by. These early mornings must have given him a cold. When the man was well down the slope, Ben raised his head and looked after him. He was too far away to tell if he was the cop, but one thing was certain. Ben would have to quit coming over here. The man was too good. This was twice he had almost caught him. Ben would have to find another deer. One closer to home and on his side of the interstate.

****

Dave Warren slowly made his way back to his truck. He had seen the big buck on his first morning of scouting. And he had smelled the smell again. He just couldn't figure out what it was. He had never smelled anything like it. Deer didn't smell that way. Unless the buck had an injury that was infected. Maybe that was it. But he hadn't noticed anything odd about the buck. He would have to look at him more closely. He didn't want to kill a diseased or injured deer.

Betty Lou had rolled over this morning when he had gotten up early. But it was Saturday and he always got up long before daylight.

"What are you going to do today?" she asked him. Mumbled was more like it.

"Gonna scout the Garrett Place. There's a big buck out there that I want to get a look at."

"Did you ever think about looking at your wife on Saturday?"

"I should be back by noon. I'll be your slave all afternoon."

"Funny," she mumbled as she turned over and went back to sleep.

Dave felt guilty as he got ready to leave the house. Betty Lou had struck a nerve when she mentioned looking at his wife. Natalie Dunn had been on his mind for the past few days and he had been thinking about looking at her, not Betty Lou. Then he thought about the other night. The smell had been at Natalie's house, so it couldn't be the deer. It had to be a human smell, but even old Joe Mooney didn't smell that bad. At least, the last time Dave had smelled him, he didn't. He was unable to find him at his usual drinking places, but Dave was sure that old Joe was the one Natalie had seen looking in her house. Mrs. Pruitt had caught him looking in her window and called Dave. When he had gone by Joe's house, or what he called a house, the smell had almost gagged him.

Old Joe Mooney lived in a shack without water or lights, across the highway from the Hill place. When Joe had opened the door at Dave's knock last year, the smell coming out had almost knocked him off the porch. But he couldn't remember it as the same smell that he had detected at Natalie's or the Garrett Place.

"Well," Dave said as he put his binoculars in the seat of his truck. "I just might go by and see old Joe this morning. He's probably sleeping one off, if he pulled his usual Friday night and got drunk at the County Line Beer Joint."

When Dave pulled onto the Columbia Highway from Green Road, he saw a pile of rags lying under the overpass bridge where I-65 spanned the Columbia-Lewiston Highway. He pulled over on the shoulder in the shadow of the concrete over head and walked across the highway to what his nose told him was old Joe. The rumble coming from the rags told him that the drunk had never made it home. He had slept the night under the interstate bridge.

Dave aimed his lightweight Browning boot at Joe's butt and grinned as the pile of rags grunted when the toe struck home.

"Get up, you stinking old pig!" Dave said as Joe rolled over and squinted up at him.

When Joe saw who it was who had kicked him, he scrambled up and got to his feet. He knew Dave would kick him until he did.

"I hate to stink up my truck but I guess I'll carry you home. I sure ain't going to put you in jail and have the whole place infected."

Dave pointed toward his truck as Joe staggered across the highway and got in the passenger door. Dave immediately rolled his window down and got his face into the fresh air as he started driving. It was either that or puke inside the truck.

If he hadn't been thinking of Natalie, he would never have thought of it. He was going to question Joe when he got him home, but as he approached the Hill Road, he suddenly turned right and headed toward Natalie's house.

"Hey! I live on the other side of the highway. Why you turning here?"

"I've got to see somebody. I'll get you out of here as quick as possible. I ain't enjoying this anymore than you."

Dave pulled his truck all the way up Natalie's driveway and when he got even with the back of the house, he looked over past Joe's slumping head and saw Natalie sitting on the back steps lacing up a pair of hiking boots.

"Wait here," he said to Joe as he got out and walked around the front of the truck. Dave noticed she had on a pair of green shorts and a butt pack around her waist.

Natalie finished tying the last boot and stood up as Dave approached her. He thought about apologizing for the other night, but decided that he couldn't pull it off without causing more damage.

"Mrs. Dunn, I want you to look at the man in the truck and tell me if he looks like the man you saw in your window the other night."

Natalie looked past Dave's shoulder at Joe just as he raised his head. She stared at him for a good five seconds, and then turned back to Dave.

"No, that's not him. This man's face is too fat. The man I saw had a thin face. And a black beard, not gray."

"Well, I guess that rules out one suspect. I'll keep trying. Have you seen anything else since that night?"

"Not a thing. I've had Butler inside with me, though. Nobody's going to bother me with him around."

"Will your husband be back soon, Mrs. Dunn?"

"He should be in tonight."

"That's good. I've been worried about you out here alone. I'll rest easier, now." That was as close to an apology as Dave could come. It seemed to be all right with Natalie.

"Well, thank you. I appreciate you checking on me. I'll tell Jeff what a good job you've done."

"You're not going mountain climbing are you, Mrs. Dunn?" Dave said, pointing down at Natalie's hiking boots.

"Not unless you call that little hill back there a mountain," she said, pointing at the ridge behind the house.

"You're not going to climb that ridge?" the incredulity apparent in Dave's voice.

"If I can make it, I am. Jeff and I have crossed the divide at Pawnee Pass in the Rockies in Colorado. So that shouldn't be too bad."

"You know that ridge is on the Hill Place, don't you, Mrs. Dunn?"

"Nobody lives back there, do they?"

"No, but I don't think it's a good idea for you to go back there alone."

"I'm taking Butler with me. He'll protect me."

"Mrs. Dunn, you seem to think that dog is superman or something. There are some people in this world who are not afraid of a dog."

"Why don't you make a move toward me and see what he does. If you're not scared." She took a step back and looked at Butler who was lying with his head on his paws, his eyes on Dave.

"Mrs. Butler, I mean, Dunn. I am just trying to make sure you're safe."

"Are you sure you're not trying to move in with me?"

Dave started to speak, but instead spun on his foot and walked back to his truck. "Smart aleck woman," he muttered under his breath as he got into the truck with the now welcome smell of Joe. He ground the starter before he realized that he had left the truck running. He cursed as the Bendix tried to kick into the spinning flywheel. He watched Natalie as she knelt and undid Butler's chain and started across the back yard toward the field that lay behind her house.

"Something about her just irritates the crap out of me!" he said under his breath. As he watched her walk across the yard, the sun gleaming off her bare legs, he also felt the guilt rise in him. He realized that he was looking at another woman for the first time in his married life. A woman who irritated him and intrigued him at the same time. A woman so totally different from Betty Lou, that the thought of being with her sent chills up his spine. A woman who could mesmerize him in such a way that even Joe could see the pictures in his brain oozing out into the heavy air inside the truck cab.

"Gottcha a' girl friend, ain't you, deputy. I'll bet your wife don't know about that cute little thing. Gimme' five dollars and I won't tell her."

"Shut up, you old drunk. She ain't my girlfriend. She's been having trouble with a prowler."

"Yeah. If she ain't careful, you'll be the one prowling around here."

Chapter 8

One of the biggest thrills in Natalie Dunn's life had been when she and Jeff had flown to Denver to go hiking in the Rocky Mountains with Jeff's college roommate and his wife. The scenes from the trip were still etched in her mind. They had started early one morning at a place called Long Lake near Boulder. Jeff had carried a forty pound pack and she had carried a smaller twenty pounder.

The trail up was awesome. Winding through snow fields, then plunging into pines, then back up toward the top and a snow covered expanse to be traversed before reaching the divide and Pawnee Pass.

She still felt the exhilaration of standing at the summit, beside the sign that said the elevation was over ten thousand feet. Then they started down the other side, through a series of switch backs, to a beautiful lake, also called Pawnee.

She and Jeff had lain in their sleeping bags and looked up at the unbelievably clear night sky. She could still remember the sudden feeling that descended upon her as the enormous expanse of sky seemed to develop into a giant funnel with its rims each mountain top that surrounded her. Then the tiny, swirling vortex that began in the center with the twinkling of a single star, became a peephole that only she could put her eye to. But when she did, the whole world unfolded before her, and she was looking at the expanse of time from the topside. Only then did she understand why the ancients had thought the world flat. It was simply incomprehensible for a human to look at a round, spinning globe and understand how people could stand on the underside and not fall off. Or get dizzy.

She got dizzy just trying to imagine the spinning part. Or the insignificance of her tiny self lying on a mountain surrounded by millions of acres of land and trillions of square miles of sky.

Then she was spinning. As if some giant had reached down and inserted his finger inside the front of her shorts and jerked her skyward, her arms flinging backward, reaching for Jeff. Then, watching him fall away as she arched upward, looking back over the top of her head toward the earth. The insignificant little earth now. The higher she got, the bigger she felt. The more she could see, the larger grew her field of view. Until she could see it all. But the one quick glance was all she got. The finger released and she was suddenly back beside Jeff in her tiny sleeping bag, wondering what it all meant. Why was she chosen to be transported? To be given the opportunity to see all? To see the larger expanse, the wider view, the overall picture?

Natalie had never felt the same since that night. Her steps for the next three days had been exaggerated. Taken with such precise placement that Jeff had started wondering what was wrong with her. How could she tell him that she was walking from millions of miles up? That it was a long way from the top of the universe to the bottoms of her feet. And that the thousands of people who were hanging on to her every step, were depending on her to tread gently and lightly so as not to jar them from their perches.

That night came back to her at various times. Like now, as she started toward the ridge behind her house. A little hill that was nothing compared to the peaks in the Rockies. But then she was nothing compared to the ridge, and Butler was nothing compared to her. And she had treated Dave Warren's feelings as if they were nothing.

She felt bad about smarting off to the deputy. He had seemed concerned about her and she had used his line back at him. Tit for Tat. She thought she had outgrown that. The night at the top of the universe had taught her better. She just forgot sometimes. She made herself a note to apologize to him.

"Let's go, Butler." The dog was circling the honey suckle pile for the tenth time. He hesitated, then left the dense foliage as she started under the three strands of barbed wire Jeff had strung around their property. She stood up on the other side. She was now on the Hill Place, as everybody called it. She looked toward the ridge that now seemed much closer. It wasn't so tall. She figured she could be up to the top and back at the house by noon.

Three hours later, which was noon, she was about halfway there. The ability of the earth to grow thistles, briars, brambles, and small thorny trees was unbelievable. She had lost track of the times she had gotten halfway through a patch of briars and had to turn around and go back and try to find another way.

Butler could go through or around, the briars not bothering him. But her legs were becoming a mass of cuts and scratches. At one time she had been close to panic. A patch of unusually tall blackberry canes had almost seemed to reach out and grab her. Every movement she made just brought more tall canes bending down to wrap her around the head and shoulders.

When she finally got free of the almost alive briars, she found a tree with a large rock under it, and sat down to take a drink from the bottle in her pack. She gave Butler a bite of the cheese sandwich. Half of it was a good bite for Butler. She then watched him run off towards a patch of woods that grew about a hundred yards from where she sat. He came back once to lick her face, and she leaned back against the tree trunk and thought about Jeff and the life they were living.

They were just going through the motions of being man and wife. As the time drew nearer for him to return from the oil rig in Louisiana, she found herself wishing that something would happen and he would simply not show up.

The silence got to her at first. Even though the world is small compared to the universe, it is still a large place filled with billions of people and animals. But it is amazing how quiet a secluded spot on this planet can be. Especially when noises are expected.

Natalie opened her eyes and looked around. Nothing. She looked at her watch. She had been asleep, or out, for about a half hour.

"Butler!" She said the name more as a way to create some noise among the quiet, than as a call for him to come.

She looked toward the woods where he had disappeared. There was a waist high briar field between them and her. She got up and plunged into it. She called his name several times as she made her way through the patches of thorns.

In the woods the underbrush was thin and she could move around better. She ran through the trees, calling Butler's name again and again. It wasn't like him to disappear like this. Maybe she should have put him on a chain, but he would have pulled her to death. She had tried that before, while walking him. He was simply too big and strong for her. And to think that the deputy imagined there were people who weren't afraid of Butler.

The trees began to thin and Natalie could see the clearing up ahead. She ran toward it, still calling her dog's name. It was an opening between the woods and the trees that grew at the base of the ridge she was wanting to climb. Only now, all she could think of was finding Butler. Or him finding her. The clearing was full of blackberries and she cringed at the thought of going through them. She turned and looked back into the woods. Where was Butler? Maybe he had gotten lost and gone back home. She turned and looked once more at the ridge. Then she turned and looked down at her legs sticking out of the shorts. How stupid she had been to wear shorts. Her legs were bleeding from dozens of scratches. And she still had to get back home. The universe had suddenly gotten smaller. It had compressed itself into a few square acres of thorns and honey locust trees. She couldn't even raise herself up enough to see if there was a path through the thorns.

"That's it," she muttered. "If I could get up high, I could see if there is a path that animals use. In the Rockies, Jeff kept pointing out trails that animals used. He said they always take the path of least resistance."

She looked around for a tree to climb, but none had branches low enough for her to grab and pull up. She slowly made her way back through the woods to the edge where she had just struggled through, and felt the despair well in her. She wanted to cry but knew that nothing would be accomplished by that.

She walked along the edge of the woods looking for a path into the briars. She found none. So she simply plunged into the mass of nature's little daggers. After about ten minutes she lost her sense of direction and had to constantly keep turning and looking at the ridge that was now behind her. It was the only thing that kept her headed in the right direction. She simply kept it at her back.

"Butler!" Her cries for the dog were weaker, now. Her legs were getting spongy. Her body was giving in to the constant pulling and scratching of the briars and thorns. She was almost to the point of giving up. She was long past desperation. When she got to the edge of another patch of blackberry, she looked back at the ridge to make sure she was headed right. The sun was low in the sky over the top of the unreached destination.

"It must be late! Oh, Lord! What if I can't get back by night? Butler!" Her eyes grew wide and she felt herself losing all control. Her scratched hands came up to stifle a scream and that's when she saw the roof of her house. Then she saw the barbed wire fence about fifty yards in front of her.

"Oh! Oh! Oh!" She settled the scream back down inside her with the little sobbing sounds. She began trotting toward the fence. It caught her back as she crawled under but she never felt it. What was one more scratch? The short, smooth, green grass of the back yard was like heaven. No thorns. No briars. Nothing grabbing at her legs. All she could think of was getting the boots off and turning the water hose with its cool, cleansing water onto her burning and bleeding legs. The end of the hose was lying on the rock patio that Jeff had built. Right next to the cedar picnic table that he had bought from one of the neighbors up the road, who made them to sell at flea markets.

She turned on the hose, then sat down on the seat of the table and took off her boots. When the cool water hit her bare legs, she almost fainted with relief. She brought the hose all the way up to her waist, getting her shorts wet. She didn't care. All she wanted was relief from the burning cuts.

The arms were next. As she played the stream over her arm, she idly looked at her watch. "Three thirty! I've been gone over six hours!" She jumped to her feet to turn off the water, and that's when she saw Butler. Sleeping, right on the back door step.

"Of all things, Butler," she said, dropping the hose and running over to him. "Leave me in the woods so you can come home and take a nap." She wanted to be mad at him, but she was too glad to see him.

Natalie knelt down to grab his big head in her hands, and that's when she put her knee right in the middle of his intestines. The shock. The smell. The squishy feel of the guts on her leg sent her upward and reeling back ward.

"Nooo! she screamed, raising her hands to her mouth. "No! No! No!" Her hands went to her stomach, her heart, back to her mouth. She looked at the dog. Lying so peaceful, so quiet, so horribly dead with his guts spilled out on the step.

"Please, somebody! Help me!" she screamed. "Please, somebody! Come help me!" She ran toward the end of the house. She couldn't go in the back door over Butler. The walk in door beside the garage door was open but the door into the house was locked.

"The car! I'll go get somebody!" She was talking to herself now. Anything to break the silence of the dead dog. "The keys. I left them inside on the table. I can't get to them, now."

She ran into the back yard. Her bicycle was leaning against the large tree that Jeff had insisted be left standing when the house was built. She ran it down the drive and leaped onto it and started up the gravel road toward Mr. Barron's house. She had spoken to him once out at the mailbox, but the old man didn't seem all that friendly.

He was sitting on his front porch when she came pedaling into the yard. He looked idly at her as she leaped off the bicycle and let it drop in the dust in front of the steps.

"Mr. Barron!" was all she could get out. Her breath was coming in huge gasps. "My dog, Mr. Barron. Somebody killed...my dog! I've got to call the Sheriff."

"Lotta' damn good that will do," the old man muttered, never even getting up from his seat.

"Mr. Barron, can I use your telephone?" Natalie was getting desperate. The panic was rising in her again.

"Help yourself. It's right inside the door on the table."

Natalie jerked open the screen door and stepped into the dark front hall. She could see the phone on the table. It was one of the old black rotary dial jobs. She was thankful she remembered the number because there was no book. She dialed the number and thought the round finger hole dialer would take forever to come back from each digit.

"Sheriff's Department."

"Dave Warren, please."

"He's off today. Can somebody else help you?"

"No, I need him! Can you give me his home number?"

"I can't do that, ma'am. We've got another deputy on duty. Can I get him to help you?"

"No! I need Dave. Please call him at home and tell him Natalie Dunn needs him. My dog has been killed. He's got to come. Please!"

"I'll try, ma'am, but if I can't get him, tell me where you live so I can send somebody else."

"No! I don't want anybody else. He knows what's going on out here. Please, get him." Her voice trailed off as she took the receiver away from her ear and gently placed it back onto its resting place.

Her panic was gone. It was as if nothing mattered. If Dave didn't come she would just lie down beside Butler and put her head in his guts and go to sleep. She just didn't care anymore. Then when she got up tomorrow morning she would start packing. She wouldn't spend another night in that house.

She walked back onto the porch and the old man spoke.

"Did you get 'um?"

"Yes. He's coming. Thank you." She felt like a zombie. She must look like a wreck. She looked down at herself. No shoes. Legs scratched as if she had been fighting a mountain lion. Shorts wet. Hair damp and stringy, hanging down in her face. If she thought it mattered, she would apologize or explain. She did neither. The old man didn't care.

"Who killed your dog?"

"I don't know. I went hiking with him. He got lost and when I got back home he was on the step, dead."

"Was his guts lying all over the place?"

She turned toward the old man. Slowly, the awareness crept in. He had killed Butler. Her eyes narrowed and the old man saw the set of her jaw and the way she turned her body toward him, getting ready for the kill. He laughed.

"I didn't kill your dog, if that's what you're thinking. But I could have told you that's what would happen if you went on the Hill Place with one."

"How did you know?"

"The same thing happened to mine, only her guts wound up on the eatin' table."

Natalie's mind was going. She didn't know how she was going to tell Jeff, but the resolve she could feel, the empty calmness in her stomach, the complete detachment from life and living, was going to cause him no end of suffering. She would have to leave, and there was going to be nothing he could do or say to keep her.

She stepped off the porch and mumbled something to Mr. Barron as she picked up the bicycle and pushed it out of the yard. She was out of sight of him before she got on it and started pedaling. The driveway was empty when she got home, but she didn't care. She let the bicycle fall and walked over to where Butler lay. She sat down beside his head and began rubbing it. She said a few words to him, but that was only to let him know she wasn't mad at him for running off. She leaned her head back against the door and started crying. A good old fashioned, cleansing cry. She had to get it out, get it over with so she could start again.

When she opened her eyes it was to a different world. It was still spinning, it just had a different axis. Her. And Dave Warren was standing there looking at her. Actually, he was spinning around her.

"What happened, Mrs. Dunn?"

"I wish you would call me Natalie. You make me feel a hundred years old."

"I'm sorry. What happened, Natalie?"

"He killed Butler."

"Who?"

"The same one who killed Mr. Barron's dog."

"How did you know about that?"

"He told me. He said he could have told me what would happen if I took a dog on the Hill Place. Could you have told me the same thing?"

"I guess so. I knew his dog had been killed over there."

"Thanks for warning me. My dog's dead because you didn't care enough to tell me what would happen."

"Mrs. Dunn. One thing I've found out. People as stupid and bull headed as you don't take advice. They have to find out the hard way. Now, do you want me to bury this dog for you or are you still convinced that he can protect you?"

Natalie pushed off the door with her head, stood up beside the dead dog and faced Dave. She clenched her fists into the sides of her thighs. She wondered what it would be like to punch Dave right in the mouth. She knew her words would hurt more.

"You arrogant sonofa…! You think you know everything, don't you? You're one of these big, tough, macho outdoorsmen who goes around killing defenseless little animals and then hanging them on your wall, thinking that looks manly. Well, let me tell you one thing. I wouldn't let you touch this dog, much less bury him. It wouldn't surprise me if you are the one who killed Butler, thinking you could then move in with me."

"Lady, I figure that when I die, I'll end up in hell. Why would I want to move in with you and spend any time here on earth, in hell?"

Dave got great satisfaction from his words. He smiled at her. He had found out that smiling at a mad woman was a lot better than arguing with one.

Natalie opened her mouth to speak, but his back was already turned and he was walking toward his truck. He surprised her by turning in mid stride and walking backwards, looking at her. He opened his mouth, a smile still on his lips.

"I know it's going to be hard on you, but don't bother to call me anymore. I won't come. If you need anything, there's a mental health clinic in town."

She opened her mouth again to speak, but again he had turned his back to her and was getting into his truck. Leaving. Just like a man. That's the way they handled confrontation with women.

The green flies had begun to blow Butler. She knelt beside him. She had to pick him up and carry him to where she wanted to bury him. But the guts? What was she going do about the guts? She couldn't pick them up. She couldn't pick Butler up and have his insides stringing all across the yard. What was she going to do? She grabbed the thick fur behind his head and leaned forward and buried her head in his neck. The tears wouldn't come. She was dry. She just sobbed in great heaves and clinched her fists tighter in his fur.

That was the position she was in when Jeff found her two hours later. She didn't know him. She never had.

Chapter 9

Ben had sworn, had even promised his mother's grave, that he would kill every dog he could get his hands on. It didn't matter if they yipped with a high pitched bark or snarled with a deep, throaty roar. He would kill them all if he got the chance. He could still remember the two police dogs that had come at him. One had leaped at his throat but of course, had taken the arm thrown up in defense. The other had sunk his teeth into his thigh. The two cops who had then stood and laughed as he was being chewed up, had become almost as hated as the dogs.

Ben had watched from his spot at the edge of the field on the other side of the barbed wire fence as the cop drove up to his Natalie's house. He was too far away to hear the words but he knew she was mad when she stood up and yelled at him. Ben wanted to laugh when the cop left, but he didn't know how. Then he wanted to cry when his scratched and bleeding Natalie knelt over the dog and didn't get up. He knew how to cry, but didn't want to cry for the dog.

He couldn't understand how she could love something like that dog, when he hated it so much. He knew that the dog would have never let him get close to her. He wondered what it would be like to be able to put his arms around her shoulders and lead her back to his house. Would she like living under the ground with him?

When the man she called Jeff came home and put his arms around her, Ben wanted to strangle him like he had done the dog. He wondered if he could lure Jeff under the tree in much the same way. And then drop the rope around his neck when he was looking up at him. A quick snatch was all it took to break the neck. Ben still didn't know why he slit the belly open and spilled the guts. Maybe he just liked to hear the knife slide through the skin, making the little tearing sounds as it parted flesh.

As it got fully dark and the lights came on inside the house, Ben knew that he could go to one of the windows and look at his Natalie. He was glad the black dog wouldn't be there to growl at him and make Natalie nervous and afraid.

The blinds at the front of the house had been lowered but the one right across from where Natalie was sitting still had about an inch of space at the bottom. As Ben stood in the darkness at the front of the house and put his eyes to the crack, his mind suddenly took him back to the other time. To the time in the other world when he had looked through a window similar to this and seen his Natalie with that man. Had seen the things she had been forced to do. Had seen the man bend over her and put the needle in her arm. Just like Jeff was doing to Natalie now!

"No!" Ben wanted to cry out and warn her, but he hadn't spoken in years. Only in his mind.

But as he watched, he realized that Jeff wasn't hurting her. He was wiping cream on the cuts on her arms and legs. Ben was glad he wasn't doing those other things to her. He would hate to have to kill Jeff the way he had killed the dog. But then Jeff wouldn't run all over the place, sniffing, smelling, scratching, looking in every hiding place of Ben's. That's the reason Ben hated dogs. They were tattletales. Little blackmailers. Everything they saw or heard, they pointed their noses at and yipped and yapped and told the whole world about it.

Ben still remembered the old man's dog. The bird hunter. He had come at him, barking and snapping, as if Ben were the one trespassing. But killing the dog was all it took to keep the old man off his property. Then Ben felt sad because he knew that Natalie would never come back because he had killed her dog. But he could always come to her.

The struggle she had gone through trying to get to the ridge was heart breaking to Ben. He had watched his Natalie in the other life go through a similar struggle. Pushing into the scratching, clawing mass of jostling people, her arms high above her head.

In the other life, Ben had been up high, just like in the tree this afternoon, watching her struggle through the grabbing blackberry canes. But in the other life, they weren't canes, they were arms. And he wasn't in a tree, he was in a glass enclosed balcony, Sealed off from the screaming and yelling masses. Separated from the noise that surrounded her, but able to see the reaching, grabbing arms. He had smiled then. Proud of her and the way she moved through the crowd, being the best at what she did.

When someone had opened the glass doors, he could remember the shock wave of sound that hit him, causing him to recoil in fright. Just like today when the dog suddenly burst through the bushes and ran to the base of the tree where he was sitting about halfway up, watching his Natalie fight and gouge her way through the thorns. The incessant barking had almost caused him to temporarily go insane. The way he had done in the other life.

But he had quickly snapped out of it and grabbed for the rope around his waist. When the loop settled over the dog's head and the barking was quickly cut off to a strangled yerp, Ben watched grimly as the dog's feet flayed the air as his brain died from lack of oxygen.

Ben wondered if the dog would have behaved differently if he had been smart enough to know that his actions would lead to such a horrible death. Probably not. People were smart and they did much the same thing. Even his own Natalie, who had framed certificates attesting to her intelligence, had inserted her head into a noose, similar to the way the dog had. And Ben had been unable to help her once her mind had been altered by the scratching, clawing thorns.

That's what Ben must do. Get Natalie away. Before the blank look on her face and the stare in her eyes became fixed. The way it had done on his other Natalie.

Chapter 10

Dave Warren was now a believer. He had wanted Joe Mooney to be the one who had been looking in Natalie's window. After seeing the dead Butler on Natalie's doorstep, he knew that smelly Joe wasn't the one. He had also wanted to get a good look at the butcher job on Butler, but his verbal battle with Natalie had cut that off short.

"I almost feel like I'm married to the woman. The way we fight every time we get together." Dave was sitting in his office at the jail. He was writing down every thing he knew about the strange happenings at the Hill Place. Beginning with Mr. Barron's, then Butch Gibson's encounter. He wanted to mention his smell across the interstate and the fleeting shadow in the field, but he knew the Sheriff would want something more substantial than that.

The two butchered dogs were significant, Dave thought. He used them to show that he thought it was an experienced outdoorsman who was doing the intimidating of trespassers of the Hill Place. What he wanted was the Sheriff's blessing and support for a full length investigation of the property.

"This isn't enough to get a warrant on, Dave," the Sheriff said when he read the report.

"I know it isn't, Sheriff. But what I need is your permission to get that guy at the airport to fly me over the place. Maybe I can spot a pot field or something else that looks suspicious."

"So you think somebody's growing marijuana out there?"

"You've been reading about these pot growers out west running people out of the parks? Well, somebody is running people off this place. He's killed two dogs and smashed up two pickups. He hasn't hurt anyone yet, but that may be next."

"Who actually owns this place?"

"I can't find that out. The deed in the courthouse is still registered to Minnie Hill. Of course, she died and left the place to something or somebody. Either that or she sold it before she died. But whoever owns it hasn't registered the deed."

"Who pays the taxes?"

Dave's face went blank. Why hadn't he thought of that? Somebody had to be paying the taxes or the county would foreclose on it and sell it.

"I hadn't thought of that, Sheriff. I'll check on that and let you know."

"That's why two heads are better than one, Dave. One will think of something that the other doesn't. But you may have something here. If somebody is doing something illegal out there, it looks like he's been doing it for some years, so he's not likely to quit anytime soon. You do a little checking and then let me know what you come up with. If you need to take a little airplane ride, do it. We've got some money in the drug fund. Do you know what pot looks like from the air?"

"Yeah, I rode with that state trooper who spots all the dope for them. He pointed out to me the difference between pot and corn."

The Sheriff stood up. Dave knew he had gotten to first base with him. Now, all he had to do was find something just a little more tangible and he could have that warrant. That permission to get on the Hill Place. He would start in the Trustee's office, where property taxes were paid.

****

"And that's all it says? Just the name and under it, Trust Officer?"

"That's it. And the return address is not even the bank. It's a post office box in New York."

"So a trust officer at City Bank in New York writes the check and mails it to somebody else who in turn mails it to you?"

"That's what it looks like."

"Do you remember what the name is on the return address?"

"I knew you were going to ask that," the lady in the Trustee's Office said. She turned to the other woman in the office. "Francis, do you remember what that return says on the check that comes for the Hill property taxes?"

"It's the address that we mail the tax bill to. I can look it up for you."

"Would you, please," Dave said.

Dave had his notebook out and was writing when Francis found the address. "G&S Services, P.O. Box 144926, New York."

"Thank you. You ladies have been a big help." Dave closed his note book and walked out. At least he had a start.

Except there were ten G&S Services in New York. And he didn't have a street address, only a p.o. box. He never knew if he talked to the right one. All he knew was that none of them would tell him anything. Except a couple of them who were plumbers. The one he suspected of being the one he wanted, only told him that they dealt with clients who wished to remain anonymous, and unless he wanted to take advantage of their services, there was nothing she could tell him.

After she had explained several of those services, Dave said, "In other words, you're a mail drop."

"We have been called that, Sir, but that is not our only function."

"Well," Dave drawled, doing so intentionally to the New York girl, "If your clients are anonymous, how do you identify them?"

"Some by number, some by name, but we are the only ones who know. We simply identify them by the correspondence that we receive."

"So if a bank sent you a check to pay some property taxes in Tennessee, you would just have to know what to do with the money. Is that right?"

"You're getting close to asking confidential questions. If you were a client of ours, you wouldn't want people asking such questions of your affairs, would you?"

"Thank you, ma'am," Dave said as he hung up.

He got much the same answers from the City Bank, Trust Department. There was nothing about a trust account they could tell him unless it was an account with his name as administrator.

Dave got up and walked over to the wall map of McCord County. He followed the Columbia Highway west out of town until it came to I-65, which was six miles out. He then dropped his finger south and traced the outline of the area south of the highway and east of I-65.

"A man could grow pot out there, harvest it and have it on the interstate, moving toward the cities without ever getting on a county road," he mused as he looked the property over. "That's got to be it. But who? Nobody ever sees anyone out there who doesn't belong. That means it's somebody who lives right around there. Old man

Barron? Naw. Mr. Pruitt? The bulldozer man? Nope. Jeff Dunn? Hmm? Mystery man. Works out of state. Nobody ever sees him. Comes in late on weekends. Leaves early on Monday. Maybe he's not going anywhere. Maybe he's just driving down the road, pulling into the Hill Place and harvesting pot all week."

Dave snapped his fingers and walked away from the wall map, pleased that he had come up with a likely suspect. Now to find out more about the man. Then something hit him.

"The Dunns haven't been there ten years. Old Man Barron's dog was killed ten years ago." His excitement dropped, then came back. "Maybe they lived close around here. He could have been coming here from somewhere else. Anyway, I'm going to start with him. He's as good a suspect as any."

Dave wouldn't let his mind accept the fact that Natalie might be involved in anything illegal. If it was her husband, she had nothing to do with it. He just hoped Betty Lou couldn't read his mind as he defended Natalie. She wouldn't understand.

Chapter 11

Natalie couldn't understand. Could Jeff not see? It was over. Nothing that had taken place in her life, up to now, mattered. Everything was beginning from here. Jeff was new. He wasn't the one, either. He just didn't know it. He kept trying to talk to her, find out what happened, console her about Butler. She was having none of it.

"Just leave me alone, Jeff. I don't want to talk about it."

"Don't want to talk about it!" Jeff exploded. "Our dog is killed. You're cut to pieces. Somebody has been prowling around the house while I'm gone and you don't want to talk about it? Well, think again, Missy! You'll talk about it if I have to squeeze it out of you."

Natalie narrowed her eyes to slits as she looked up at Jeff as he stood in the middle of the room, his fists on his hips, looking at her as if she were a school girl.

"I'm leaving you, Jeff. Tomorrow, as soon as I can get packed, I'm leaving. Don't ask me why, because I don't know. I just know I can't stay here anymore. Not at this place. Not with you."

"I knew it! I knew it! Leave you alone for a while and you find somebody else. You little cheater! Prowlers! You just made that up in case I discovered that some man has been around here. I can hear it now. 'Who's underwear is this behind the bed, honey? Oh, I guess the prowler left it.' "

"You call me a cheater!" Natalie stood up on her burning legs to face Jeff who had stalked over to glare down at her, a haughty look on his face. "Don't try to act like you've never taken any of those bar girls home on your little secret trips into New Orleans."

She had hit it. She could tell by the look on his face that he was stunned for a moment by her accusation. Now it was her time to be haughty. The match book she had discovered in his car had tipped her off. That and the case of crabs he had given her, that she hadn't told him about. She laughed in his face.

"Don't look so surprised. Word gets back. You thought nobody saw you down there, didn't you?" She really had him now and she knew it. He began swallowing and stammering.

"I don't know who, I mean what, or anything you're talking about." Jeff's voice was lower now. He wasn't so sure of himself. Natalie didn't even want to gloat over her victory. She just wanted out. If she could leave tonight, she would.

She knew she would sleep in this chair tonight so she might as well get used to it. She eased herself back into it. When her eyes came even with the window across the room, they locked onto the round orbs she could see through the gap at the bottom of the blind. He was back! She screamed! Butler wasn't here to warn her.

"It's him!" She fell back in the chair, pointing.

Jeff looked toward the window and then spun and ran out the back door. He started around the corner of the house toward the garage, but then stopped and reversed his course and headed toward the other end of the house. The dark end. The end toward the fields and the Hill Place.

"I'll catch you, you peeping sob!" he cursed under his breath as he rounded the corner. The last six months of working on the oil rigs had toughened him. And he'd had a few fights with various local toughs when they would go ashore. But none had fought as savagely as the man he encountered as he rounded the darkened corner of his house.

The man was moving fast, because when they collided in the side yard, Jeff was knocked off his feet immediately. He yelled in surprise.

"Hey, you!" Jeff bellowed as the dark form plowed into him. He was up quickly and grabbed the figure before it could scramble to it's feet and get away. It was the wrong thing to do. The peeper he'd caught began swinging his arms and legs wildly and the guttural sounds that came from its mouth reminded Jeff of some wild animal.

He only had his hands on the man for a few seconds before he fought his way out of his grasp and sprinted across the yard, leaping the three strands of barbed wire, and disappearing into the field at the end of the house. But in those few seconds Jeff knew that he had a wild thing in his arms. The stench was over powering. He had never smelled anything like it.

As he watched the dark form race away into the night, he raised his hands to his nose and sniffed.

"Damn!" he swore. "That's the stinkingest thing I've ever smelled. That guy hasn't had a bath in years."

Jeff knew it was no use chasing the man in the dark. But when tomorrow came he would see what he could find in the way of a trail the man might have left.

Natalie was at the back door when he got back around into the arc of the porch light. He raised his hands to her nose when he got close to her.

"Whew! What is that?" she squealed, jerking her head away.

"That's your prowler. He smells like a dead goat."

"That's the same smell I caught a whiff of by those bushes across the fence," Natalie said. She almost got into a conversation with Jeff until she realized she hated him. She walked to her chair and sat down.

"Anybody that smells like that should be easy to track. I'll find out tomorrow when I follow him onto that Hill Place. That's where he headed."

"You won't get far. That's where I got all these cuts. That place is like a jungle," Natalie said.

"Well, he's going to have an old jungle stalker on his trail. I didn't go through Army basic training for nothing."

"Don't yell for me if you get in trouble back there. I won't be here."

"You're still saying you're going to leave me?"

"If I'd been unfaithful to you, wouldn't you leave me?"

Chapter 12

Ben raced through the night. Frantic. Scared. Stumbling and bumping into things, skirting the thorn thickets that had ensnared Natalie. Finding the grass tunnel he had made through the honey locusts and slithering through until he came out on the other side next to the woods. He found the faint trail and then ran like he had in the other time. Only that time it was people he was bumping into. And he could hear the footsteps pounding the pavement in pursuit. This time nobody was chasing, but it took him a few minutes to realize it. When he finally could hear that the man who had grabbed him was not running after him, he slowed to a walk. He wished he could talk out loud to himself. He remembered doing that before to calm himself. But that had been years ago when he still knew how to talk.

When he finally got under control and on the path that led to the top of the ridge behind his house, he began to think about what had happened. He had almost been caught. But worse than that, he had been seen. And touched. Over the years Ben had become so paranoid that he believed every one in the world was looking for him, and knew that he existed on this place. Now he was certain the man would have an army looking for him when it got daylight.

Ben stopped when he got to the spot on the ridge where he dropped off to his house. His mind was in a quandary. He didn't know what to do. He didn't know how soon the man called Jeff would come after him. Natalie didn't like Jeff, Ben could tell. He yelled at her and she didn't like that. She didn't like the cop, either, but she had yelled at him. Ben would never yell at her.

Maybe Natalie could keep the man from coming after him. It had been so long that Ben couldn't remember how men and women talked to each other. He only knew that it got ugly sometimes.

And then his mind saw a man preparing for battle. Getting the gun out and checking it. Putting on the dark clothes for night warfare. It was then he knew that she would never be able to keep her man from coming after him. She hadn't been able to in the other world. And she wouldn't be able to do it here in this world.

There was one difference. Here was Ben's world. Before it had been the other man's world. Ben would remain out in the open. In his element, where he could fight, run, and hide. He had yet to fight in this world, but he knew it was coming. He had been preparing.

Ten years ago when he had first come to this place he had noticed the neat little stacks of rocks that someone had placed at various locations around the farm. It had taken him days to finally figure out that there was no significance to the piles. It had simply been someone's way of picking up rocks and getting them out of the fields, without hauling them off. They weren't cairns leading the follower to the veiled waterfall through which passage to Shangri-La was made.

So Ben had begun making his own piles of rocks. Only his rocks were fist sized. Ideal for throwing. And he had put them at strategic locations where he could ambush walkers on trails. Could throw his rocks from high up, and whoever was down below would never know where they were coming from.

But the spears were what he enjoyed making. He had sat for hours under the cover of the trees at the top of the ridge, and had skinned the bark off the hickory saplings. Then he had whittled the ends to make the sharp points. When all the sap was dried out of them, they became very hard. And they flew beautifully when thrown. Ben would practice for hours until he could hit a man sized target at one hundred feet. But a man hadn't come after him, yet.

As Ben stood at the top of the trail, he knew that was about to change. He could feel inside that the man would come. He would try to hide from him, but in the end he knew he would have to fight. All because he wanted to look at his Natalie one more time.

And then his skin began to crawl. Before, when the man had come looking for him, he had done so only after Natalie had been killed. Had been reduced to a pile of broken bones and bleeding flesh. He surely wouldn't be so foolish to harm this Natalie. Not after what Ben had done to the other man. In the other world, on the other side of the barricades.

Ben wondered if the man still remembered him. If he thought about him as he lay on his bed unable to move. Unable to do anything but wonder if Ben was still alive. And if he was, where was he?

Then Ben smiled. He didn't know he had done so, until it was gone. And then he didn't know whether it was a lip smile or a mind smile. He only knew that it brought back the pleasure of the moment when he did to the man what that man had done to Natalie. Only he had left the man alive. So he could think about what he had done for the rest of his life. And the last thing the man saw was Ben's smiling face. Right before Ben punched out his eyes.

Chapter 13

Natalie looked out the kitchen window and watched Jeff lace up his boots as he sat at the picnic table. He was actually going back there after the man he had grappled with.

Natalie didn't care about that man anymore. She was leaving and she didn't care if he lived or died. But last night Jeff had insisted on telling her again and again about the fleeting instance when he had the "stinking sob" in his hands.

"What makes you so sure that he will be back there? He may have just circled around and walked in from there. Maybe he lives somewhere else," she said.

"Nope, not this guy. He lives back there. He's an old hermit living back there somewhere, and he thinks he can come to our house and look at you through the window. I'm gonna' show him what it feels like to have a number eleven hiking boot shoved up his butt."

Natalie had simply gotten up and gone to bed. Jeff acted so snotty at times. She would just let him sleep on the couch. She had made a loud noise as she slammed the bedroom door. He knew better than to try to come in.

The next morning he had acted like nothing was wrong between them. He never mentioned her leaving him. Even when she told him again that she wouldn't be home when he got back from his hike. He had just looked at her, leered was probably a better word, and said in his avoid confrontation at any cost voice, "I'm not worried about you. Just call me when you get tired of sleeping by yourself."

Now as she looked at him through the window, she shuddered to think he had slept with her after being with those whores in New Orleans. When he stood up from lacing his boots, he caught her looking at him through the window. He winked at her before she jerked her head back. She swore at herself as she squatted down below the sink. "He truly is an arrogant bastard."

When she looked up again, he was striding across the back yard toward the fence at the edge of their property. She watched him push down the top strand and swing one leg then the other over to the other side. She breathed a sigh of relief. She would pack a few things and be settled into the motel in town before Jeff got to the first thorn patch. She had called the little out dated tourist court in town. She wanted one of those little isolated cabins that were only rented to secret lovers.

An hour later she was still trying to pack everything she thought she would need. "I can always come back next week when Jeff is not here and get the rest of my things," she said to herself. She then thought of Jeff back on the Hill Place. "What if he breaks a leg?" She then put it out of her mind. He was a big boy. He didn't seem to think there was anything he couldn't handle. She would like to see him fighting his way through those acres of blackberry bushes. She could see him now. Cursing and swinging his fists at those "sticking sobs!"

****

From where he lay Ben could see the back of Natalie's house. It was a long way off but he could tell if anybody left the house and came his way. When he saw Jeff push down on the barbed wire fence and step across, he knew he had been right. He was coming. Onto his property. Breaking his laws. Subjecting himself to the punishment Ben deemed necessary.

Ben wondered if Jeff would try to make it to the top of the ridge the way Natalie had. The absence of the dog and the presence of the thorns had stopped her. That was the way Jeff was headed and Ben saw him pause ever so slightly as he crossed the faint trail that skirted the first mass of thorns. Halfway to the large patch, he stopped. He looked up at the ridge and then looked back at the spot where the path was. Ben knew then that he was going back to the trail, even though it headed in the wrong direction.

Several times over the years Ben had watched people come on his property. He had always stayed in front of them. Anticipating where they would go. Capturing and killing the dog if there was one. But always staying ahead of them, readying himself for the time when he would have to fight and defend.

Usually the people were just hunting or blackberry picking. The hunters he dealt with. The blackberry pickers always seemed poor and pitiful, so he just left them alone. They usually didn't come very far onto his land. Just far enough to fill their buckets with the juicy blackberries.

Jeff was the first one who had come with the specific intent of looking for Ben. As Ben watched him take the path that led into the woods, he wondered if he would just wander aimlessly about, or would he turn back toward the ridge once he got into the trees. It was always easier walking in the woods since the trees kept the thick undergrowth sparse. Natalie hadn't known that. Jeff did.

The trail petered out in the woods, but Jeff turned and headed toward the heart of Ben's acres. As soon as Ben saw him emerge from the woods, he left his observation point and ran toward the bluff he knew Jeff would have to pass under. He got in position at the top. Right next to the two large rocks he had placed there earlier. Maybe a rock slide would deter the man. Natalie hadn't been able to stop him.

As Ben sat above the trail, he wondered if Natalie would bury her head in Jeff's hair and cry over him the way she had cried over the dog. She wouldn't have to if Jeff went back home after the first "accident" he had. Ben tried to make everything he did look like an accident. Except for the truck smashings. But something told him that those could always be attributed to vandals, since they were never on his property.

It had been that way on the street outside the last place he had lived in the other world. There was always a car smashed by vandals. And he had smashed the car of the man who had taken Natalie away from him.

Ben had then laughed his insane, high pitched laugh when the man had come back and found it wrecked. The man had looked up at the roof where he knew Ben was hiding and cursed him with the vilest string of oaths Ben had ever heard. He had a feeling Jeff would do the same.

The shuffling feet. That's how Ben could hear Jeff coming. They all shuffled their feet in the woods. Kicking rocks and breaking twigs. Ben would never be caught like that. He knew how to move silently. He caught a quick flash of Jeff's shirt through the foliage and heaved the big rock he had raised above his head. He saw it disappear through the leaves in the direction of Jeff. He was hoping it would hit on the slope just before it got to him and cause others to start sliding toward the walking man.

Nothing. He heard absolutely nothing. He surely didn't hit him in the head and knock him out cold, did he? Ben crouched on the bluff high above the trail and listened for sounds of the man. Either moving away or moving upward toward him, but all was silent. He would have to see what he had done. He must have thrown the rock out too far over the trail and it had hit the man and either injured him or killed him. Ben wasn't sure how he would handle a dead man. It had been a long time since he had killed a man. He could still see his face. And the face of the one whose eyes he had punched out. The son he had killed because he had taken his Natalie. The father he tortured because he was the one who brought the sharp things Natalie stuck in her arms.

He was down. Ben could see the blue of the shirt lying in the leaves beside the trail. The rock must have hit him. Well, it didn't matter. Either way, the man didn't have any business coming on his property.

Ben eased off the rock ledge beside the trail and stepped in his crouching walk over toward the prone figure. This was as close to a real human as he had been in a long time. He eyed the boots. He could use those. The ones he had were beginning to come apart. He had stolen them almost three years ago. But he would come back after dark. He didn't want to do anything in daylight except to look at the man's face. Something inside made him want to look at another human being.

He walked around to the head of Jeff and bent down to look. That's when Jeff's hands came up and grabbed his arms. Ben's startled eyes looked right into the wide open face of Jeff as he yelled, "Gottcha', you snooper!"

The only thing that saved Ben was the rotten shirt. As he flung himself violently backward, the seams in the shoulders of the shirt parted and Jeff was left holding nothing but the two shirt sleeves. He came off the ground but Ben was already scrambling down the slope away from the trail, running for his life. Jeff came hard after him, stumbling and lurching, not used to running on the loose dirt of the forest floor.

By the time he got to the bottom of the slope, Ben was disappearing into a clump of thick locust saplings. Jeff stopped, breathing heavily. He looked down at the two sleeves. He started to bring them up to his nose, but he didn't have to. He could smell them where they were. It was awful. But he held on to them. He wanted to show Natalie that the man was really here. She didn't believe him, he could tell. He headed back to the house. He turned and looked at the clump of locust where the man had disappeared.

"I'll be back, and I'll get you then, you stinking peeper."

****

Ben watched the man. He was sick to his stomach. He had never been sicker unless it had been when he had watched Natalie walk the streets of the slum where she went to be alone. Why wouldn't they leave him alone? What was it about the world that hated a man who simply wanted to be alone? Why did they keep coming after him? And why would this one come back? Which was what Ben was sure he would do. And what would be the next trick he would use to try to catch Ben? Ben hoped he would get another dog. He would love to show him what he could do to another dog.

****

Jeff caught Natalie just as she was leaving. The back seat of the car was piled with clothes.

"You're really leaving, aren't you?" He hadn't actually believed it.

"I told you I was."

"Look!" he said, holding up the sleeves. "He's back there. I almost got him. Smell this crap."

"Get that away from me!" she yelled as Jeff stuck the stinking sleeves toward her face.

Jeff stepped back and looked at her. "Come on, Natalie. What is it going to take to get you to stay? You want me to tell you I'm sorry about New Orleans? You want to have a baby? Let's take a vacation. Go on a cruise. What do you say? Go on a second honeymoon. That should bring the romance back."

Natalie looked at him. He had no idea what went on in a woman's body or mind. He thought just saying he was sorry would wipe out the little whore house excursion in New Orleans. He had no idea that she could never trust him again. Maybe he didn't care. Maybe his conscience ended at the base of his belly. Whatever, she just knew that it was over. And the last thing she wanted was a son like him, or a daughter who adored him.

She put the car in reverse. As it started slowly backward, Jeff began walking along side. He put his hand on the door. He braced his feet against the ground, trying to hold the car back.

"I'm leaving, Jeff. That's all I can tell you. Now let go."

"Come on, Natalie! I need you. Who's gonna cook and wash around here?"

"Why don't you bring one of those whores from New Orleans up here?" she said as she spun the tires in the gravel, sending the car backward away from him.

"Then go to the devil!" he yelled, ramming his middle finger in the air. Natalie looked at him as the car slid to a stop at the end of the drive. She couldn't believe she had put up with it this long. The picture of Jeff, the obscene gesture in the air, the look of contempt on his face, she would keep with her forever. Just in case she was ever tempted to come back.

She put the car in drive and pulled away. The motel man had told her she could stay as long as she liked. She might have to stay until she settled with Jeff. Then she would get a job and an apartment. That sounded nice. Then she could be alone. That's all she really wanted.

Chapter 14

Ben couldn't hear the movement anymore. He knew he was out there. He just couldn't hear him. He had made all kinds of noise getting up the slope. Now it had stopped. Maybe he had fallen and hit his head on a rock and was out. Maybe Ben had been out. He knew he had dozed two or three times. He had let his head slip down onto the rock where he was lying. And he didn't know how long he had slept, he only knew the sound of the man coming up the slope had awakened him. His senses had been right when they told him the man called Jeff would be coming back this night.

Now the man was no longer crashing and stumbling. He was either moving quietly or was simply sitting still. Suddenly, something moved off to Ben's left. He spun at the noise and his boot scraped the shaley rock on top of the slab jutting out over the slope. The beam of light stabbing through the pitch black night, caught Ben exposed on the ledge.

The light was terrifying for Ben. He was like a mouse caught in a corner, his big eyes bulging, his legs quivering, waiting for the cat to pounce. If the light had never wavered, never left his eyes, Ben would have been caught then and there. But the man carrying the light stumbled and the light shifted away from Ben's face and he saw the legs and body of the man carrying the light, and that's when he came out of his trance.

Ben rolled off the ledge and fell down the slope into the night. Blinded, he fell, knowing that anything was better that capture by the man. His fall was broken by a sassafras sapling. The top of the little tree bent under his weight and he landed on his back, stunned. He looked down at his legs to see if they were broken. He raised them up just to see if he could. That's when he realized that the light still had him pinned, exposed to the world as if it was broad daylight.

Scrambling to his feet, Ben looked up the slope and saw the light was coming toward him in a rapid bobble. He turned and fled down the hill, slipping and sliding in the leaves and small rocks that littered the ground. But the light still held him.

When Ben got to the bottom, he turned to his right and ran along a faint trail that he used to get to the top of the ridge. His breath was coming short now. He had used up precious air in his excitement and panic at being pinned to the ledge by the light. Now he was breathing harder than he ever had. But the light wouldn't leave him. It helped him see the trail better as it ebbed and flowed around him and lit up the trees ahead of him, but it never once dropped back or away.

The leaning, hollow truee. He had to get to it. But it was up over the top. Ben had never expected to get caught down the slope, away from the top. He hadn't prepared any weapon caches down here.

Suddenly, the light behind him flashed upward. The man must have stumbled. Ben darted to his right, up the slope, cutting in behind a hollow locust that had fallen across the trail and had caught in the top of an oak. He was halfway up the slope before the man figured out where he was.

The light caught him again, but he had a lead now. And he knew where he was going. But the man behind was good. He began making up ground on Ben, even up hill. Ben could feel the light coming closer as the shadows it threw grew larger. That's when the animal cry rose in Ben's chest. He felt the fear and with it came the extra adrenalin needed to get him quickly to the top.

The cry came again as he turned left at the top and headed down the trail. He had to get to the hollow tree. It was now his only hope. He must take talons. He must become the one he hated. The thing that he dreaded becoming. The evil one returned to take vengeance on his tormentor.

He found the tree. He almost missed it in the dark. The light from behind flickered over him just as he grabbed the trunk and swung in behind it. He didn't know whether the man had seen him or not. He just knew that one of the spears nestled in the hollow tree, came easily to his hand.

The man was pounding down the trail toward Ben. How close was he? Ben had to judge quickly and then step out at the right moment and throw. He judged wrong. Jeff was almost upon him when he stepped out with the spear cocked over his shoulder. All he had time to do was bring the slender hickory shaft down and point it toward the running man with the light.

The speed of the man surprised Ben. He thought he was a fast runner but this man was lightning. He crashed into Ben before he could get out of the way. His head smashed into Ben's face, knocking him over backward, stunning him, sending him spinning into the leaves.

Pain, eyes watering, something warm running down from his nose into his mouth. Ben tried to get up but his eyes felt as if they wouldn't open. His face felt numb and he raised his hand to his nose, but he couldn't feel it. Then he knew it was blood coming from his nose. He could see it on his hand through his teary eyes. Then he froze. The man must have him spotted, the light was shining on him, unwavering. Ben slowly rolled his head to look toward the light. It was low on the ground. The man was lying there, holding the light on Ben. Why didn't he get up and come toward him? Now was the time while Ben was stunned.

Ben lay there long enough to realize that something was wrong. The man didn't move, either. That meant he was stunned also. Ben got up slowly and eased down the trail away from the man, out of the glare of the light. It didn't follow him as before.

Ben dropped to his hands and knees and worked his way back toward the light. As he got closer, he saw that the man appeared to be propped up on his elbow. The way Natalie used to read on the floor in front of the fireplace. It was so strange. The man couldn't be reading here in the dark. The light wasn't even pointing at the book. Except it wasn't a book in the man's hands. It was the end of Ben's spear. The back end. It was sticking out of his chest. The long end coming out of his back was what had him propped up.

Ben stepped around the man and picked up the light that was pointing off into the night. As he brought it back to the man's face, he saw that his eyes were open. Glazed, but open. His hands had a death grip on the end of the spear, but he had grabbed it too late. It had already gone three quarters of the way through him.

Jeff looked at Ben, unable to move. His eyes followed Ben as he squatted and looked at him. He blinked and Ben could tell that it was hard for him to get his eyelids back up once they went down. Ben had time. He would wait for the last closing. Unless the man died the way the other one had. With his eyes open.

The mouth opened and the words came out just like before. "Tell Natalie I love her." The animal sound came to Ben's lips just as before. How many would he have to kill before they stopped loving his Natalie? Stopped taking her away from him.

The fury rose in him and he almost did to this one what he had done to the other one, now so long ago. But he held back. Something told him this one was different. And Natalie was different, also. Anyway, the man was about to die. Ben could tell that his eyes had closed for the last time. But why was he not enjoying watching this one die? Had the years mellowed him? Or was he just aware that this one was dying for different reasons?

Bubbles suddenly appeared at the man's mouth and the sound startled Ben. He realized that he had been staring at the dead man, letting him transport him to another world. One in which he no longer lived. But one that still lived in him.

His world came back and he knew that now he had a difficult task in front of him. He had to get the man off his property. Somewhere so nobody would know that he had died here. There was no alley filled with garbage to dump him in, as he had done before. No street full of derelicts for the police to patrol each morning to see how many had died in the night.

But there was a huge difference that suddenly filled him with joy. Natalie! This time Natalie was still alive. Would be there for him when he came back from his grisly task. He hoped she would be propped up on her elbow, reading in front of the fireplace.

Chapter 15

Dave Warren had wanted to be in law enforcement from the first day he had picked up a pistol. Something about guns and law enforcement went together in his mind. His dad had given him an old Colt Woodsman, and he had spent hours with the little .22 pistol. It had been his sixteenth birthday and he would never forget what his dad had told him when he presented him with the gun.

"Son, a lot of boys get a car on their sixteenth birthday, but I can't afford that. Instead, I'm giving you something better. Something that takes a lot more skill to operate than a car. Something that can teach you more about yourself than a car ever could."

When he brought the gun out from behind his back, Dave's eyes brightened. The gun had been behind the glass counter at Will Hardison's Hardware. It was used, but in perfect shape. It still was. After twenty years Dave still got the gun out and went into the woods with it. Every time he looked at it, he thought of his dad. He had been partially disappointed when he didn't get a car, but now he was very glad that he had gotten the gun. He could give it to his son, if he ever had one. If his dad, dead now for ten years, had given him a car, it would be long wrecked. Long forgotten. This little Colt Woodsman would last several lifetimes.

And it had taught him several lessons. The first one had been, "mistakes can be serious." Dave had practiced loading and unloading the pistol. He would fill the magazine with long rifle cartridges, insert the magazine in the butt of the gun and then pull back the slide to chamber a live round. Then reverse the procedure to unload. The day came when he forgot.

He had brought the gun into the house and went to his room. He took the magazine out but forgot to pull back the slide to empty the chamber. He accidentally pulled the trigger while wiping the gun with an oily rag. The muzzle flash in front of his face sent particles of powder into his eyes. The bullet narrowly missed his head and buried itself in a book on the shelf. He still had the book with the bullet in it. He wanted to remember that little piece of stupidity.

The other lesson the pistol had taught him was, "patience and perseverance pay off." Once he had learned to shoot the Woodsman well, he began to hunt with it. He started with rabbits and then graduated to squirrels. He spent hour upon hour stalking rabbits, finding them sitting, and then slowly bringing the gun up to eye level and squeezing off the killing head shot. Squirrels had been little different, except there had been a lot of sitting under the huge oaks, waiting for the feisty little bushy tails to come out on a limb.

When Dave began deer hunting, the little Woodsman went with him in an old leather shoulder holster that he had gotten at the Army-Navy surplus store in Nashville. It rode up under his left arm, snug and out of sight when he had a jacket on.

Dave spent most of Monday mornings thinking about his weekend. He had scouted for the big buck on Sunday, but his mind had been on Natalie Dunn's dog. Something strange had risen in him on Saturday evening when the dispatcher had called him at home and told him that a Mrs. Dunn needed him out at her house. He had made sure that Betty Lou heard it as Mrs. Dunn, not Natalie. She needled him about his love affair with Natalie Wood and his sorrow at her death six years ago. If she had heard the name Natalie, she would have been suspicious at his going to her on his off time.

But it was the dog's death that had him worried. Whoever was doing this to dogs to keep people off the Hill Place, would have to resort to doing the same thing to people sooner or later. He just hoped it wasn't Natalie that got the first treatment.

He had dreamed about her last night. He still shook when he thought about it. In his dream he had pulled back the covers to get in bed with Betty Lou, who was sleeping peacefully. Instead, it had been Natalie and her guts were all over the bed. Radiating out from her split open belly, covering the area where he had to lie down. And a smiling Natalie had beckoned him to come to her, waving her arm over the gory mess in the bed.

Thankfully, he hadn't gotten that far. He had flung himself off the bed, almost waking up Betty Lou.

When the Sheriff pushed open the door to Dave's office at seven o'clock to see if he was in there, the squeaking awoke him again. He had dozed in his chair, his head in his hands.

"Boy, you got here early, didn't you? Katy said you were in here at five. Anything going on?"

"Nothing other than another strange incident out at the Hill Place." Dave proceeded to tell the Sheriff about Mrs. Dunn's dog.

"Why don't you take that plane ride today and see if you can see something. If you want, I'll see if I can get the state trooper who specializes in marijuana spotting."

"If I don't find anything, we'll try him. Let me see what I can find first."

"Sure thing. Let me know what you come up with."

Dave sat looking at his notes. There was a pattern and it was bizarre, in a way. But only if you believed something was going on out there. Otherwise, it just looked like some random acts of violence. "Maybe it's just a kid who gets his kicks out of smashing cars and killing dogs," Dave thought. But then he remembered the ten year span and knew that a kid would have outgrown it.

He heard the dispatcher's excited, high pitched voice and knew immediately that something was up. He almost ran into the Sheriff as he rushed out of his office and started down the hall to the front.

"What's up, Sheriff?"

"Just got a call that Jerry Wakefield at the Gulf Station down at the interstate found a body in a trash can behind his place."

"A body? Let me go get my kit. You want me to ride with you?"

"No! You go on. I'll make sure the ambulance and coroner are called."

Dave grabbed the black bag he kept ready for calls like this and ran out the front door to his car. He smoked the tires as he raced up the hill to the Lewiston square. He didn't turn on his siren and blue lights since traffic was light. He was around the square and headed out the four lane toward the interstate quick enough without them. If it was a body, there was no great rush anyway.

Lewiston was about six miles east of I-65. Dave was at the Gulf station, which was on the southeast corner of the Lewiston exit, in less than five minutes. When he pulled into the station he saw a few of the local boys standing in a semi circle about ten feet from the trash area at the side.

Dave got out of his car and immediately saw the trash can, which was a fifty gallon drum, and the legs of a man sticking out of it. Evidently the top half of the man was over in the drum. It was as if someone had leaned over into the drum to get something and had gotten stuck. Except he wasn't moving.

"That's the way I found him this morning when I come around here to throw something away. I thought it was somebody who had just fallen in. But when I grabbed him, I knew he was dead. He's stiff as a board."

"Are you the only one who's touched him, Jerry?" Dave asked.

"Hell yes! And I wouldn't of done that if I had of known he was dead."

"Does anyone here know him?" Dave knew that was a dumb question as soon as he asked it.

"Yeah, I recognized his butt from our high school picture," some wise guy said. Dave just grinned. He didn't acknowledge the remark. He knew he deserved that answer.

He made his own remark. "Fairly new hiking boots. Not brogans like people around here wear. No billfold in his back pocket. You guys haven't seen a billfold anywhere, have you?"

"Not unless it's fallen out and down in the can," Jerry said. "We ain't touched him."

Dave decided not to touch him either until the Sheriff or the coroner got here. And that didn't take long. The Sheriff pulled up as they spoke.

"Anybody we know, detective?"

"No sir. Not yet, anyway."

"Well, let's get him out and on the ground. It's not going to hurt to move him, now."

The man's body had already set in a curved shape, the way he had been hanging over the barrel rim. When Dave and the Sheriff laid him on his back on the pavement, his knees remained up in the air. As the two uniformed men stood up, the group of men moved in as a unit and leaned over to look at the face of the dead man.

Jerry was the first to speak. "That's that fellow that works on the oil rigs in Louisiana. He stops in here and fills up whenever he's heading back down there. Name's Dunn. Reason I remember it is, it's the same name as the governor we used to have."

Dave had been gently patting the pockets of the dead man to see if there was anything in them. He froze as the name Dunn came out. For an instant, then he went back to patting. Why did he not want them to know he recognized the name?

He finished his patting and then slowly stood up and looked down at the face below him. So this was Natalie's husband. The one he had envied. The unseen man who kept him from thinking about her in that delicious, forbidden way. Now he was dead and there was nothing to keep Dave from rushing to her and breaking the news, then having her collapse in his arms. Nothing other than his marriage to Betty Lou, and the fact that he and Natalie were as different as any two people could be. Plus, she evidently hated him.

The Sheriff must have seen something in Dave's face. Or his actions. He spoke, never taking his eyes off of his detective. "You know him, Dave?"

Dave narrowed his eyes, trying to fool the sheriff into thinking that he had been in the process of jogging his memory. He spoke as if recalling pages from a note pad. "I've been to a Mrs. Dunn's house a couple of times. She's the one who had the dog killed I told you about. But I never saw her husband. She said he worked out of town."

"Soon as the coroner and the ambulance gets here, we'll take him to the hospital. I'll notify you if we get a positive ID. In the meantime, why don't you see if this woman is home and can come to the hospital. It wouldn't hurt if you had another woman with you. This Dunn woman will probably be hysterical when she finds out her husband is dead. Is there a neighbor close by who could help?"

"I'll see." Dave headed to his car. He didn't know what to think. Natalie's husband dead. He made it all the way back from Louisiana only to be robbed and killed a few miles from home? How would Natalie react? Calmly or hysterically? He had this strange feeling that she wouldn't be at all upset at the death of her husband. She was probably one of those types who got more upset over a dead dog than a dead husband.

As he pulled away from the station, he looked back at the small knot of men huddled around the body on the pavement. With his windows up, the men were silent to him. Their gestures and motions seemed like pantomime, and he the only observer to a secret play. He felt like he had stumbled through the jungle until he came to a clearing deep in the woods. There a ritual was being carried out. The ritual of the uncaring and uninvolved standing around looking at the body of the village idiot. Wondering how he died. One now turning and pointing up the cliff, saying perhaps he fell from there. Another pointing to the trash can, the one who had made the remark to Dave, and asking how he got in there headfirst. Then one pushing the first for his stupidity, sending him toward the dead man with his knees still up in the air.

The pushed, stupid one leaped when he realized that he had almost stepped on a dead man. Into the air he went, pirouetting over the slain one, his foot coming down in a puddle of oil, sending him into a split, one foot going forward, the other still behind on the asphalt.

Dave watched, fascinated by the performance, as the man struggled to retain his balance in his split position. Then wanting to applaud, as the struggle became hopeless and he fell over, like the Swan, his hands coming up over his head.

There was no curtain, only wise guys rushing over to yell "safe", their only stage the little league park, their only antagonists, the parents of others.

Dave pulled away, his mind going to Natalie and what he would say to her. Should he try to fool her and say that he was only hurt? Maybe Jerry was wrong. Maybe it wasn't her husband. He couldn't tell her it was until he had been officially identified. No. He would just tell her that a man was at the hospital without any identification, and could she come tell them if it was her husband or not. He just wanted to be close by when it came time for weeping and consoling. He wanted his shoulder to be the closest one.

Chapter 16

All Dave's rehearsing was for nothing. Natalie wasn't home. Nobody was home. The house wasn't locked. The back door opened easily as he tried the knob after knocking several times. He knew he shouldn't, but he stepped in.

"Mrs. Dunn!" he yelled one more time. No answer.

The big room he stepped into was empty. The kitchen was to his right, a bar with stools separating it from the great room. Then a door out to the garage. He crossed quickly to the door and opened it. One car was in there. One oil spot for the other.

Quickly back into the big room and across to the hall that led to the west end of the house. Past a locked door. He tried the knob, then moved on. Then the bedroom. Where Natalie slept. He looked at the bed and saw only one head hole on one pillow. Only one person had slept here last night. The cover was only pulled down on one side.

He turned and saw the open closet doors. The empty racks. No ladies shoes on the floor. He stepped over to the huge bathroom and saw the void. Where the bottles and rows of makeup and lotions should be. Nothing. The woman of this house was gone. And if Jerry was right, so was the man.

Dave had seen enough. He quickly went to the back door and stepped out onto the patio and pulled the door closed behind him. He had almost made it to his car when he heard the gravel sound out on the dirt road. He stood and looked over the top of his unit as a car pulled into the drive. He had never seen Natalie's car, it had always been in the garage. But it was her. He saw her through the windshield. He could tell that she hadn't expected him.

Her window was down and she began talking as soon as she pulled even with his car. "I should have known that when you said you wouldn't come when I called, that you would come when I didn't call."

Dave couldn't believe that she had started on him already. But he couldn't let her get to him. He had resolved to take her abuse.

"Good morning, Mrs. Dunn. Where have you been this lovely morning?"

"Is that any of your business?"

"No, ma'am, I guess it isn't," Dave said as he walked around the back of his patrol car toward her. "Actually, I'm here on official business."

"Well, state it and then get on with your other duties. I've got things to do."

"Mrs. Dunn," he began. He kept hoping she would correct him again and tell him to call her Natalie, but she didn't. "There's been an accident. I need for you to come to the hospital with me and tell us if the man we have is your husband."

"What's wrong with him? Is he hurt bad?"

Dave could tell there wasn't a lot of emotion there.

"I'll have to let the doctor tell you that. Do you have anyone here in town who could meet you out there? Any family?"

"No. I don't have any relatives anywhere that I know of. Why? He must be bad. Why don't you just come right out and say it. Is he dead?" It looked like she wasn't going to let him be diplomatic about the affair so he just came out with what he had. "Mrs. Dunn, we have a body but there is no identification on it. The man who found it said he thought his name was Dunn, but he wasn't sure." Dave watched her, looking for the emotion, the breakdown, the hands coming up to conceal the quivering lips. He saw nothing. "Do you want to follow me out there?" He was sure she wouldn't want to ride with him.

"Can I ride with you?"

"Well, sure. And I'll bring you back." He almost stumbled as he started back toward the driver side of the car. Natalie had reached for the door and was already in.

When they got on the highway, he wanted to ask her where she spent the night, but thought better of it. He wanted her to volunteer some sort of information, but she kept quiet. He looked once at her, but she was staring out the side window, no expression or sign of emotion on her face.

He parked beside the Sheriff's car and they both went in the emergency room doors. The Sheriff was standing beside a cubicle with the curtains drawn. Dave could see several pairs of legs around the bed inside.

"Sheriff, this is Mrs. Dunn."

"Nice to meet you, Mrs. Dunn. I hope we are wrong and it's not your husband in there."

Something made Dave believe that she was hoping just the opposite. Maybe it was the way she parted the curtain and stepped over to the bed and said in as calm a voice as he had ever heard, "That's my husband. That's Jeff Dunn."

Dave looked at her as she turned and walked out. His shoulder was ready but she had no intention of using it. He looked at the Sheriff as she repeated the statement to him.

"Mrs. Dunn, at your earliest connivence you need to come down to the department and give us a statement. You can let Detective Warren here know when you want to come."

"I'll do that, Sheriff. Now I would like to go home. I need to be alone."

"Some arrangements need to be made for the body, Mrs. Dunn," the Sheriff said.

"I'll call his parents and tell them. I'm sure they will handle it. I don't know if I can bring myself to do the necessary things."

She turned and walked out. Dave followed her, looking back at the Sheriff who stood dumbfounded, watching her leave.

"What kind of woman is this?" Dave asked himself as he watched her get in his car. The questions he would have to ask her were growing into a long list. Some of them he knew would never get asked. He knew he would dread the answer. She still hadn't spoken when he pulled up in her driveway.

"Are you going to be all right, Mrs. Dunn? Do you need me to do anything, or call anybody?"

"No, I just need to be alone for a while." He kept waiting for her voice to break, for something to show him that she wasn't made of stone. She simply got of the car and walked around the front of it and strode briskly toward the back door. She didn't look back at Dave. If she had she would have seen the same thing that Stinking Joe had seen. His eyes following her every move.

He didn't know why, but when he got to the highway, he turned left, toward the interstate, instead of toward town, and pulled off the highway into a hay field and turned around and stopped just inside the bushy fence row. He could see the end of Barron Road. Natalie's road. In exactly three minutes he saw her.

"I guess three minutes is a while," he said as he watched her turn toward town. He let her get a half mile ahead, then pulled out behind her. She was easy to follow. He could tell that she never once checked her rear view mirror.

At the top of the hill, just inside the city limits, she turned right, and as he passed, he saw her pull into the back of the Cabin Motel. He drove on by and turned one street down. He came back around the block and parked on a side street where he could watch the small cabin out back where she had parked her car.

He watched her make several trips from the cabin to the car, carrying clothes and a suitcase. On the last trip she wasted no time leaping into the car and backing out and heading back out of town. He followed for a way, but when he saw her turn on Barron Road, he knew she was going back home. The only question was, "What was going on, and why?"

****

A strangeness, a feeling like she had never experienced, came over Natalie. When she left the house yesterday, she told herself that she would never come back. She would send someone to get whatever she needed from the house. But she would never go back in. Now that Jeff was dead, she felt this unquenchable urge to get back into the house.

She worked feverishly to get her belongings out of the car and back into her house. It was almost as if she didn't want anyone to know that she had not been here when Jeff died. Or was killed. She realized that she didn't know how he died. Had someone shot him? Pushed him over a cliff? Why hadn't she asked the deputy how he died? The answer was not pleasant, but it was the truth. She said it out loud so there would be no possibility that she was fooling herself. "I guess I just don't give a crap."

Natalie picked up the phone to call Jeff's parents in Nashville, but knew she couldn't do that. So she called his sister in Franklin, just south of Nashville. The sister went to pieces and dropped the phone and Natalie waited for several minutes before she picked it up again. She tried to give her some of the vital information but knew she wasn't getting it. So she hung up and waited for the parents to get the word and call. She prepared her voice to sound distraught, then began to feel guilty at not being upset. Two years ago she would have been, but something had happened in the last few months and she had felt herself becoming detached from Jeff. Detached from every thing, actually.

At one time she had felt herself anchored. Sure and steadfast in life. Now, all of a sudden, she was drifting. Not lost, just drifting away from the people she had been tied to. She felt as if her life was a boat that was suddenly free from its moorings, and she was moving out into the main channel. She could look back and see Jeff in the shallow water, the calm water, and she didn't care that he needed her. Didn't care that he wanted her to come back. She had upped anchor and she was getting the hell outta' Dodge, to use the expression he always thought so cute.

The phone rang and she started sniffing, trying to get something in the way of a teary sounding voice. It was Jeff's father. She used the phrases "I don't know" and "what am I going to do?" so many times that Jeff's father finally said he would handle every thing. That's all she wanted. She knew she could never do anything like pick out a casket or talk about burial plots.

She was exhausted when she finally hung up. He would get back to her when everything was done. She knew that this hurdle would be hard, but in a few days it would be over and she would be free. She looked down at her hands. Why did she feel as if she had killed Jeff? Why was she checking her hands for blood? Why did she feel guilty because she was not sorry? That's one of the things she would have to work on. She should feel sorry for Jeff, whether she loved him or not.

As she moved over to the back door and looked out over the great expanse of rough country at the rear of the house, she suddenly knew why she felt guilty. It was because she knew that Jeff was going to die when he left yesterday. She could see him now, striding arrogantly through the grass, heading toward the Hill Place. The man who had run from him, had fled his grasp here in this yard and also when he had jerked his sleeves off, would not run forever. A strange feeling had come over her yesterday, but she couldn't tell exactly what it was. Now she knew. The man back there was just like her. Willing to drift as long as people left him alone. But when Jeff pushed, he would react.

She had started to yell to Jeff when she was pulling out of the driveway yesterday, to tell him what was about to happen, but had stopped. A vision of death had floated before her. What was about to happen had already happened. It was past. There was nothing she could do to stop it. Just like she and Jeff. It was already over. Even though it hadn't come about, her body and mind, just like that night in the Rockies, had leaped ahead of her and she had watched the events unfold.

The man back there suddenly became real. A man with whom she could identify. Someone with all the things she wanted. A life without hassle. A life alone. A life so totally without direction that the only goal became the aimlessness. The only successes marked by the passing of each undisturbed hour.

Then she remembered his eyes in the narrow slit under the blind. They were haunting her, seeking her out, wishing to be with her. But afraid. Afraid of the risk involved.

Then Natalie cried. She knew then that she was afraid. She didn't want anyone to come close to her because of the risk. Just like the man back there. That's why she had never given herself completely to Jeff. Oh, sure, she had given him what he wanted often enough, but herself? Never! She could see her eyes in the reflection of the glass. They were just like the ones under the shade.

Not like the merry blue eyes of the detective, Dave Warren. That's why she hated him so. He was so open, so eager to be a friend, so disgustingly simple and straight forward in his approach to life. That's why she had tried to hurt him. To show him the risks involved in closeness. To make him aware that friendship doesn't come cheap. It extracted a heavy price. One she was not willing to pay. A heart and a soul.

Chapter 17

"That cold-hearted woman killed her husband!" the Sheriff exploded. "Now, I don't know why you're trying to cover for her, but you better not be setting yourself up with her."

"Wait a minute! What are you trying to say? That I had something to do with his death?"

"I'm saying this is the strangest looking murder I've ever seen, and it looks like you've gone sweet on the prime suspect."

"Just because I said that I could understand her not being torn all to pieces over her husband getting killed? You call that being sweet?" Dave yelled back, his anger flaring.

"Well, I'm thinking of taking you off this case. It looks like you've made up your mind that she's innocent."

"That's a whole lot better than making up my mind that she's guilty, like you've apparently done. I thought we were supposed to let the facts make the conclusion, not make the facts fit our conclusion. Is that what you want me to do? Go out and find some evidence that proves her guilty, whether she is or not?"

"Oh, come on, Deputy. You wouldn't believe her guilty if she walked in and confessed."

"And you wouldn't believe anybody else who walked in and confessed. You'd accuse them of lying to cover for her. You've made up your mind that she's guilty and anything else be damned. Well, I'll find out who killed him. But I'm not going to decide before hand who that person is, like you apparently have."

"You might not, Hot Shot. As of right now, you're off the case."

"Good!" Dave yelled, jumping to his feet. "I've got two weeks vacation coming. I think I'll take it right now. Got a little deer hunting to do."

"Just make sure you stay away from that woman. She's a suspect in a murder. A murder you've been ordered off of."

"What I do on my own time is my business, Sheriff," Dave said, putting his hand on the door knob and jerking the door open.

"What you do on a murder case I've taken you off of is my business," the Sheriff said, standing up and looking Dave in the eye.

Dave was so mad he couldn't see straight. As he walked by the dispatcher's desk, he said suddenly, "I'm going on two weeks vacation. You can send someone to my house to pick up the car." He finished the words as the front door closed behind him.

****

Dave jerked his tie off and flung it against the wall. He hooked the toe of his left foot on the heel of his right shoe and jerked the shoe off. It hit the wall with a thud as he kicked it with all his might. He sat down and took the other one off. He held the shoe in his hand and looked at it.

"Get out of my life, Natalie Dunn!" he screamed, as he threw the shoe against the wall. The shoe bounced off the paneling and fell to the floor to lie with the other. Two black marks on the wall testified to the violence of the separate impacts.

Dave lowered his head. He felt better now. He looked at the wall where the shoes had hit. The pictures on the wall that Betty Lou had hung, were still there. He would be in deep trouble if he had broken those. He stood up and walked over and picked up the shoes and then walked slowly through the house, down the hall to the bedroom. He took off his duty belt and hung the assembly over the bedpost, the butt of the revolver he carried on duty, jutting out into the room. He then stripped off his uniform and walked into the bathroom. He closed the door and looked at himself in the full length mirror Betty Lou had him put on the back of the door.

He recited from his folder at the jail. "Five foot ten. One seventy five. Blonde hair blue eyes." He pinched a few inches around his middle. The one seventy five was more like one ninety five now, he knew.

"Crap! I've got to lose a few pounds. This is getting too much to carry around," he said as he looked at the small roll around his waist. He then ran his hand over his chest. The big, full, deep chest that still had the look of the weight lifter. Even to the point of no chest hair. When other boys had begun getting body hair, Dave had remained hairless. Even to this day, his light skinned body was devoid of chest and leg hair.

"Wonder if Natalie would like that?" he said out loud, then slapped his face in mock shame. He couldn't believe he was thinking about another woman after all these years of being married to Betty Lou. Especially another woman who, apparently, hated the sight of him. And he didn't especially care for her attitude. But then, what was it? What made him think of her to the point that he got mad at himself when he realized that she was on his mind so much?

"Just forget about her, you big dummy," he said to the mirror as he pulled off his shorts and jumped into the shower. When he came out he felt better. He went to the closet and got a fresh set of camos. He quickly put them on and then got his Vietnam Jungle Boots out and laced them on. Next was the Bianchi shoulder holster, and then the Colt Government Model .45 that King's Gun Works in California had done a Combat Special on.

"The Sheriff said to take a plane ride, so I better do that before he changes his mind." Dave grinned. He knew the Sheriff would be furious when he found out that Dave had gone up in the plane. "But he'll get over it. He's been mad at me before."

****

Dave looked back at the runway. It always amazed him how quickly a small plane left the ground. They didn't appear to be going that fast, but when he looked back at the ground, the runway got tiny, fast.

He looked at the pilot. Clay Downing ran the flying service that was based at the City of Lewiston Airport. He had his headphones on and was watching his gages and instruments as the single engine Sundowner clawed its way into the sky.

Dave had explained to him where he wanted to go. He told Clay he wanted to start at the Gulf station at the interstate, then fly east toward Lewiston, keeping the Hill Place on Dave's right the whole time. He wanted it spread out beside him. Then when they had circled the entire property, he wanted to fly in toward the center and then do the same thing again. He figured about four circles would do it.

From the air the place looked so neat and pristine. The huge section of trees seemed to be surrounded by nice, clean areas of open space. But Dave was not fooled. He knew the open looking areas only appeared that way from the air. They were head high in thistles and thorns.

The second circle took them over Natalie's house. Dave had not realized that the piece of property that the house sat on was inserted into the Hill Place like a puzzle piece. He saw the house coming up and could see immediately that Natalie's property cut up into the rugged Hill Place. The road made a curve into the property there, also.

Dave suddenly realized that Natalie was outside, in the back yard, on her hands and knees digging next to the propane gas tank. He put his binoculars quickly to his eyes and focused them. A small black box was on the ground beside her, and from the size of the hole she had started, it was apparent she was going to bury the box. She never looked up as the plane swept over. Dave looked back at her small figure receding in the distance and wondered if she would ever be very far from his mind.

He wanted to push from his mind the thought that kept creeping in. "What if she had killed him?" No! She couldn't have! "What was she burying?" Evidence? No! Whatever it was, she had a perfectly good reason for doing so. It was then that Dave began to realize what had been forming in his mind. He would quit the Sheriff's Department before he uncovered anything that would prove her guilty of murder.

"Why in the world would you want to protect her?" he said out loud. Clay looked sharply at him. Dave grinned. He didn't realize his thoughts had come through his mouth so loud.

"Just talking to myself," Dave shouted at Clay over the din of the engine. He put the binoculars back to his eyes and went back to looking at the Hill Place. He had told Clay that he was looking for a field of marijuana, which indeed he was. He could see no other reason for someone keeping people off the property.

On the last circle he saw the house. The tin roof glimmered dully through the leaves. Dave threw up the binoculars and studied the house. A front porch supported by six posts. Six or eight steps leading up to it. That meant it was high on the front side and the back was practically buried in the hillside behind. There was no activity around the house. The yard was literally head high in weeds.

The plane suddenly lurched and Dave quickly looked at Clay, who in turn looked at him. "Updraft," he yelled. "Coming up the slope to the top of that ridge."

Dave looked down. They were over the house now, circling at the top of the ridge behind it. He could see a faint trail running along the top of the ridge behind the house. He would have never seen it if he hadn't lowered the glasses and looked directly down through the trees. He filed that away. It was probably only a deer path, but who knows? Maybe a human made it.

"Did you ever see anything?" Clay yelled as he closed up the last circle at the top of the ridge.

"Nope! Nothing that looks like pot. Looks like a wasted run." Dave lowered his binoculars and settled back in the seat as Clay lifted a wing and banked toward the airport. The flight path took them directly over Natalie's house again. She wasn't in the yard and Dave's mind brought up all that he had been trying to suppress. The fact that she hadn't been in the house the night her husband had been killed. Why did she try to conceal that? But the Sheriff didn't know about that. What had frosted the Sheriff's cods was the way she had reacted to the news of her husband's death. No crying and no hysteria as he had predicted. When she walked out of that hospital and told him to contact the next of kin, he had pronounced her guilty of murder. And when the Sheriff said "guilty", he didn't intend for anyone to object.

The three car caravan turned off the main highway onto the gravel road leading to Natalie's house, and the dust cloud that rose behind each car sent a signal to Dave's brain. It just took a while for it to penetrate the deep layers of thought that were shrouding his skull.

Clay saw them too. "Where in the devil are they going? Must be a raid. That's the Sheriff's car in the lead. I can tell it because it's solid white. The others have the green stripe."

"Swing back, Clay!" Dave yelled. "Let's see where they're going."

The right wing dropped and the Sundowner banked sharply. Dave was looking directly down at the ground as he was flipped up on his side in the tiny cockpit. But he never took his eyes off the cars. He knew before it happened where they would turn. Right into Natalie's driveway.

Like dominoes falling, the doors, all six of them, opened in succession. As each car pulled to a stop, a door on each side opened and six men in uniform got out and headed for the back of the house.

"What are they doing?" Dave yelled into the cockpit, lurching against his shoulder harness, trying to release himself from the confines of the plane so he could go to the rescue of his beloved Natalie.

"They're your people. Don't ask me what's going on," Clay yelled. "Looks like a dope raid to me."

Dave knew. It was a Natalie raid. A Terry King raid. Terry would be the one who the Sheriff would have given the case to when he took Dave off. And Terry would have convinced the Sheriff that he needed a warrant immediately to go look for evidence before the suspect had a chance to destroy it.

"Get me back to the airport! Now! Pour the coal to this thing." Dave figured that since small planes left the ground quickly, they would return in the same manner. He was wrong. He believed that he could have flown himself quicker than the Sundowner was pulling the ground toward them. His feet were already running when the plane taxied up to the hanger. He leaped from the door before the prop stopped turning.

"Send the bill to the Sheriff's Department!" he yelled at Clay as he ran toward his old Dodge truck. He didn't know what he would do, but he knew that he had to get to Natalie as quickly as possible.

Except he wasn't quick enough. The driveway was empty. The door was locked. An official paper was attached to it. "These premises have been sealed under order from the county sheriff."

Dave slowly turned away from the door. Natalie was gone. Surely they hadn't arrested her. But she wouldn't have gone with them voluntarily. Terry King would do anything to make a name for himself. Of that Dave was sure.

He drove slowly back to town. He had to think. His first impulse was to charge into the jail and demand to see on what grounds Natalie had been arrested. But something kept telling him that wouldn't look too good. The Sheriff was already angry at him. Had taken him off the case. He couldn't let them think he had a "thing" for Natalie. But he had to see what they had charged her with. See the evidence.

The car from the radio station was already there. Terry King was holding court in the front lobby of the jail when Dave walked in. He grinned at Dave and kept on talking to the radio reporter and several others who were standing around. "We have arrested a Natalie Dunn and charged her with the murder of her husband, Jeff Dunn. We obtained a warrant this morning and conducted a search of her house and found sufficient evidence to charge her. We also found a small amount of marijuana and the...murder weapon."

Dave was stunned. Terry had purposely left that last part hanging to see how Dave would react. To tease him and then slap him in the face with it. He wanted to turn and run back through the front doors and keep on running until his legs collapsed from exhaustion. Instead, he pushed through the crowd and went through the doors behind Terry into the cell area. He knew where Natalie would be. The only cell available for a female.

She was standing at the bars. She heard him come through the door at the end of the corridor and was looking, her head cocked sideways so she could see down the hall. As he got closer and she saw who he was, she drew back.

"What do you want?"

Dave stepped close to the bars and looked at her. He could tell she had been crying, but she was over it now. Mad had taken its place.

"How did they charge you with murder, Natalie?"

"You ought to know, you traitor! Why didn't you come with them? Too ashamed to look me in the eye?"

"Natalie! I've been taken off the case. I am on vacation. I didn't even know this was going down."

"Likely story. You've probably been sent back here to try to get me to confess. Well, it won't work. I know how you cops play the good guy, bad guy routine. Well, bow out. I don't believe you. You might as well send in the bad guy to work me over for awhile."

Dave looked at her. She never ceased to amaze him. Nothing he said ever came out right. She looked so small and forlorn in the dirty cell. Even after berating him, he still wanted to put his arms around her and hold her until she stopped crying. His shoulder was still available.

"Are you her lawyer, Warren?" Dave hadn't even heard the door open. He jumped and looked down the hall. The Sheriff was standing there, his large frame filling the doorway.

Dave looked from him to Natalie. He knew what she was thinking. There was nothing he could say. She said it.

"Can I call them or can I call them?" She smiled at him. Not the kind he wanted. It was a sick, kind of know it all smile. He started to try to tell her it wasn't the way it seemed, but she wouldn't let him.

"How tough on me will he be? Will he make me want to collapse in your arms and tell you all about how I killed dear old hubby so I could be with you the rest of my life?"

"Natalie?"

"Leave me alone, creep! You people make me sick." She turned and walked to the bunk at the back of the cell and sat down.

"Well, are you coming, Detective, or am I going to have to drag you out of here?"

Dave walked toward the Sheriff. The man stood aside and let him through the door. "I thought you were on vacation, Warren?"

"I am, Sheriff. I just came in to see what you had on her. I was investigating a prowler out there, you know." The Sheriff slammed the door behind him. "Yeah, well, we think that prowler business is just a bunch of hokey. A smoke screen for her to hide behind so she could murder her husband and blame it on a mysterious prowler."

Dave turned and looked at the Sheriff. He had seen him this way before. When he made up his mind, there was nothing anyone could do to change it. And he only got mad at people who disagreed with him. He took a difference of opinion personally. Dave tried to keep his voice noncommittal as he spoke. "What kind of evidence did you find at her house?"

The Sheriff looked at him, almost as if he was trying to decide if he could be trusted or not. Then he spoke with an assurance that the facts he possessed could sway anyone's opinion.

"The best kind. Good old hard evidence. We even found the murder weapon. It's got traces of something that looks like blood. We found an insurance policy that had just been taken out on him. And a letter to her sister telling how desperate she was to get rid of her husband. She tried to destroy that right there in front of us. We caught her in the middle of packing, too. Evidently she was getting ready to run out. You have any idea where she would be trying to go?"

"None, whatsoever. All I know is she said she has no relatives that she knows of. But what was the murder weapon? I thought we assumed he was shot."

"That's where she tried to fool us. The coroner called after you left and said that after examining the wound and finding pieces of wood and bark inside the body, he had come to the conclusion that the man had been stabbed with a sharp stick or piece of wood."

"And you found that stick?"

"Yep, right under the kitchen sink. Evidently she tried to wash it off. If she had just thrown it in the fire and burned it, we would never have known what she killed him with."

"And she had just taken out a big insurance policy on him?"

"That's right, the dumb slut. Well, we don't know who took the policy out, but she was sitting at the kitchen table looking it over when we came in."

Dave was getting sicker by the minute. But he couldn't let the Sheriff see that he was concerned about Natalie. That it was tearing his guts to hear what the Sheriff was telling him. And he didn't know why. He couldn't tell himself what it was about Natalie Dunn that pulled at him. That made him want to jump up in the Sheriff's face and scream at the top of his lungs, "Liar!"

Instead he calmed himself and asked another question. The Sheriff seemed eager enough to tell him everything, as long as it seemed he was agreeing with him. "Can I see the letter she wrote? So she hadn't gotten a chance to mail it?"

"That's right. It was lying open on the table. It's in my office. You'll see what kind of mean, cold woman she is when you read this letter." He walked down the back hall toward his office. Dave followed, still dazed by what he had heard.

The Sheriff handed him a piece of paper. "That's a copy. The original is sealed in my safe. Read 'em and weep. That's one cold hearted babe."

Dave tried to keep his hand from shaking as he took the letter. He never saw the greeting to someone named Joan. The letter was for him. It had to be. His eyes started to mist as he let himself slip inside of Natalie, seeing not the mean, evil woman the Sheriff saw, but a sad, hurt and disappointed little girl who had sought comfort and security in a marriage with a man whom she had at one time loved. But now, as he read the lines and also read between them, he could see she was desperate to end the relationship that had failed to bring her the warmth and understanding she needed. He couldn't see murder in the word "desperate", the way the sheriff had. He couldn't see evil in her heart when she used the word "hate" to describe her feeling for her husband. The Sheriff did.

Dave saw an anxious plea from a broken hearted woman to her friend for understanding. The Sheriff saw a motive for murder when she told this Joan that she was expecting to receive a lot of money in the near future.

The Sheriff's eyes bored into his when he looked up. He wanted, now more than ever, to go back to Natalie and hold her in his arms and let her tell him everything that had ever troubled her soul.

The Sheriff laughed. "I just wonder if she thought she could get by with it. She acted like we would just let her collect her money for killing her husband, and then go on about her business."

"Has she posted bond?"

The Sheriff laughed again. "It doesn't look like anybody is going to go it. We listened when she called her sister in law and she told her that her husband wouldn't let her put any money out on her. And then she had the gall to call her husband's father. He told her to go to hell."

"That's too bad," Dave said sadly, before he thought.

"Bad! She can rot back there for all I care."

Chapter 18

Natalie looked down at her legs. The cuts and scratches from two days ago were still there. She brought her legs from under the bunk and swung them straight out in front of her. Smooth, slim, brown, hard muscled legs. From bicycling, walking, jogging. Anything she could do alone, without the jostling, scratching and clawing from others. She had almost gone crazy when the six men in uniform had burst through the back door of her house.

And that tall, skinny deputy named King who had arrogantly walked over and slapped the search warrant down on the table in front of her. Him, she hated. Especially the way he came out of her bedroom with her overnight case that she hadn't unpacked and said in his nauseating, nasal, "Were you going somewhere, Miss Dunn?"

She kept her cool and didn't said a word. She had simply looked at him in the most unpleasant way she could conjure up. When he came back from a short consultation with the Sheriff and began reading to her from the little card in his pocket, she stood up beside the table and cut him off with her voice. "What would a snotty nose punk like you know about anyone's rights?"

Sitting on the bunk in the cell, she laughed when she thought about the look on the deputy's face when she had called him what he was. But he had gotten even.

"Put the cuffs on her!" he yelled right in her face, as if he was a drill sergeant and she a raw recruit. But she had smiled at him, infuriating him further. When he pushed her from behind, she turned and sweetly said to him, "My, my. We seem to have a mean streak when it comes to abusing women, don't we?"

But what had ticked her off was the absence of Dave Warren. Did he really think she would believe his story about not knowing what was going on? And then to try the good cop, bad cop routine on her? "Come on, fellas. Give me a little credit. I've seen a few cop shows on TV," she said out loud.

The door at the end of the corridor opened and she ran over to the bars and pressed her face against the steel so as to see who was coming. It was the old man who had booked her. He had been nice. Had told one of the deputies to take the handcuffs off. Had even yelled at that snotty nose King when he kept sticking his face through the door of the booking area. "I'm handling this operation! You get back up front!"

"I thought you'd like to know," he began. "That you are going to have to spend the night in here."

"Why? Just because nobody will go my bail. What about a bail bondsman? Aren't there any of those around here?"

"Seems like someone told all of them that you were a runner."

"Jogger, actually, but what does that have to do with anything?"

"I'm talking about someone who is likely to skip bail. Run out on them."

"What is going on around here? I've got money in the bank. I can go the bail."

"You got twenty five thousand dollars?"

"No! Is my bail that high?"

"That's just what it would take to get you out. The Sheriff convinced the judge to set the bail at two hundred and fifty thousand."

"That sonofa…!" Natalie could see the old man recoil at her language. She was going to have to watch it. This might be the only friend she had in here. "I'm sorry," she said hastily. "I just can't believe this is happening to me."

The old man just looked at her. He was one of those people who kept a perpetual grin on their face. It didn't mean they were always happy. It just meant that they laughed a lot more than they frowned. But he wasn't laughing now. He was serious.

"You will be arraigned tomorrow. The judge will probably lower the bail. He'll ask you if you have a lawyer then, too."

"I don't know any lawyers."

"He'll appoint you one if you can't afford one."

"Yeah, I know what kind those are. The ones who can't do anything else."

****

Dave left the jail by the front door after talking to the Sheriff. He walked toward his Dodge, but suddenly turned around the corner of the jail and jogged down the alley to the back. Two inmates were washing the Sheriff's car by the back door. He barely glanced at them as he went up the steps to the door that was never locked in the daytime. It opened into the short hallway that ended at the jailer's area where the booking took place. Nobody was around so he stepped through the door that led to the cell area where Natalie was. He started to jump back when he saw someone in front of her cell, but relaxed when he saw it was only old Clarence. He walked down the hall toward them.

"What's going on with her, Clarence?"

"I was telling her that her bail has been set at two and a half bills. And that she would have to stay the night in here."

"What about bail bondsmen?" Dave asked, same as Natalie had.

"They've all been informed that she is a risk to run."

"Sonofa…!"

"That's what she said."

"I've got money in the bank," Natalie broke in.

"How much?" Dave asked.

"About five thousand."

"Not enough, but maybe enough to hire a lawyer. I'm going to go see a friend of mine. He's just started practice, but he'll take this case if I ask him."

Natalie looked at Dave. He had barely spoken to her. He had done all his talking to the old jailer. Almost as if it wasn't any of her concern. As if she didn't exist.

"Do I get any say so in any of these plans? Or am I just a bystander?" she suddenly asked.

Dave turned toward her but kept his eyes on old Clarence. He couldn't quiet bring himself to look at her standing there in the cell, behind the bars, so close to him but separated by yet another barrier. And he knew that at the first opportunity he would not be able to restrain himself from taking her in his arms and covering her face, her neck, her whole body with kisses. Instead he shot back.

"Lady! In spite of you and your smart mouth, it looks like I'm going to have to try and help you."

"Oh, it's lady, now. Well, don't do me any favors. You people have helped me enough, already."

Dave looked at her and opened his mouth to speak, but then turned on his heel and left. He would have slammed the door but it would have brought the Sheriff running. So he eased it closed and disappeared.

"You two been enemies long?" Clarence asked.

"Long enough to know that he's an arrogant ba...boy." Natalie caught herself before she called Dave a bad word. She could tell Clarence didn't like to hear women curse.

"He may be the only friend you've got. The Sheriff took him off your husband's case because he accused Dave of having a thing for you. I could hear them yelling all the way up the hall."

"Well, he's got a funny way of showing it. He starts something every time he sees me."

"A while ago he was talking about getting you out of jail and you started on him, is the way I remember it. You ever hear the old saying about catching more flies with honey than vinegar? You ought to try it."

Natalie watched the old man walk down the corridor, his head down, going from side to side. When the door closed, she felt as if everything she had ever loved, every dream she had ever had, was simply sucked up into a great vacuum. Pulled from her like the insides of the deer Jeff had hung up in the back yard. She had walked out of the house just as he had grabbed a hand full of guts and jerked. She had grabbed her stomach and run back in the house, feeling the terrible twisting feeling all the way down to the base of her stomach.

Now she spun away from the bars and grabbed her stomach, feeling the terrible emptiness inside. He whole life had been one empty feeling. A void with nothing to fill it. No hope of ever finding anyone who could come inside her and help bring her life and feelings to the surface.

Natalie had this horrible, reoccurring dream that always brought her from her sleep in a state of breathless sweat. A man would enter her from below, his whole body going in. And the pain was unbearable as she fought the intrusion. But he kept coming and she could feel him moving up through her insides. Then her air became cut off as he neared her heart and lungs, and before he could finish his ascent, she awoke. Breathing hard and clutching herself in a desperate effort to crush the intruder who had dared get inside her.

She raised her head when she realized she had been doubled over in the middle of the cell. When her face came into view, it was in the polished stainless mirror. Her brown hair, cut short to spite her mother, was unkempt where she had been running her hands through it. But her face was what grabbed her. It was if she was seeing a stranger. The dark brown eyes were deep pools on an amber sea. Her cheeks were sunken, little hollows in the centers, reminding her of the forced diets her mother had put her on, so she could be thin for the beauty contests she was determined Natalie was going to win.

The brown eyes suddenly blazed at the thought of her mother. She advanced on the mirror. Daring it to reveal the Natalie behind the scowl. Behind the pain and tearless eyes. She pursed her lips that had been taught to curse and smile. The curse from the heart, the smile from the first layer of epidermis only.

Natalie hated herself for being beautiful. Until the darkness of her eyes grew into shadows that etched a storm cloud of lines over her brow. Then down to the cheeks, pulled hollow by the mouth that no longer smiled. No longer pled for votes from the judges.

Her fingertips fluttered to the cheeks, then to the brows that had been allowed to grow bushy. Her mother would have hated it. But something now made her want to thin them, brush some color to the cheeks. What was it the old jailer had said. Something about a "thing" for her. He must have been mistaken. Dave Warren might have a "thing", but it wasn't for her.

"Yum, yum! Ain't we a pretty thing? Especially from the rear end."

Natalie spun at the intrusion. She had been leaning over the sink, searching her face in the mirror. She didn't hear the door at the end of the corridor open. It was the deputy, King. His eyes never left her totally, but they travelled her completely. He jangled the large key ring in his hand and raised it toward the lock on the cell door.

"Did we do a body search on you, Miss Dunn? I meant to have our female jailer do that before she left. Looks like I'll have to do it myself, now that she's gone." He stepped into the cell and pulled the door shut behind him.

Natalie panicked. Not since her mother's boy friend had grabbed her when she was fourteen had she felt such a rush of fear. But her face didn't show it. She stood by the bunk and watched King as he came toward her. The smile came back. Along with the curse. It was a low whisper, barely audible over the sound of two beating hearts. Both beating at the same level, but at opposite ends of the sexual pendulum.

"That's right, you punk. Come on. I've got something for you, too."

Chapter 19

The McCord County Courthouse sat in the middle of Lewiston's town square. The bronze Confederate soldier on his pedestal looked at Dave as if he was reminding him of the cold and heartless statue he had left in the cell down at the jail.

"That's what she might as well be, for all the feeling she's got," Dave said as he passed under the stare of the soldier. He ran up the steps to the courthouse. He would check the Register of Deeds Office first. That's where he knew he might find Ritchie Osborne. A young, struggling lawyer spent a lot of time searching titles to property. Nobody trusted him to do much else. He would have to prove himself before he got the juicy divorce cases. Or the big shot DUI cases. The ones that were never settled in court. Always in the judges chambers, or in the alley outside. That's where the cash money changed hands.

Dave and Ritchie had gone to high school together. "Crap! Has it been fifteen years?" Dave thought as he headed down the hall on the second floor of the courthouse. Ritchie had gone to college on a ROTC scholarship and then had spent three years in the Air Force before ejecting from his flamed out F-4 over the Mojave. A cracked vertebrae in his neck had rendered his head about forty percent immobile. The only thing it hadn't done any damage to was his jawbone. He could talk a mile a minute.

So the Air Force had released him and he had gone to Law School at the University of Tennessee in Knoxville. A year ago he put up his shingle in a renovated house on the west side of the square. If he was making any money, it didn't show. The old station wagon he drove was new when they graduated from high school.

Dave stuck his head inside the deed office and asked Bree if she had seen Ritchie. "He was here about an hour ago but I think he went to his office."

"Thanks," Dave said, and went down the hall sticking his head into other doors, looking for the gregarious lawyer who usually visited every office on the second floor when he came to the courthouse.

When he was satisfied that his friend wasn't around, he went down the steps to the ground floor and turned toward the west side of the square and pointed himself at the little house that was Ritchie's law office.

"I didn't do it, Ossifer. Don't arrest me. I got a large wife and family to feed."

"Ritchie, you're still as full of crap as ever," Dave said, a mock look of disgust on his face as the big, hulking lawyer stood behind his desk with his hands up in the air. His secretary was shaking her head and walking back to the reception area where she had greeted Dave.

"Hey! When you spend your days stuffing ten pounds of do-do into a five pound bag, a little of it is bound to spill out on the stuffer. So, what's going on, Big Dave? You come to take me out to dinner?"

"Dinner? It's three o'clock in the afternoon!"

"Man, I can eat anytime," Ritchie said, slapping the stomach that protruded over his belt buckle.

"I've done a little too much of that, myself," Dave said, grinning. "No, what I came to see you about was ah, uh, kinda'...well, like a friend of mine is in jail and uh, well, she kinda' needs a lawyer and..."

"She?"

"Come on, Ritchie! She's not my girlfriend or anything like that. She's just a woman in trouble and she doesn't have anybody to go on her bond."

"No husband?"

"Up until this morning she did."

"What happened to him?"

"She is accused of killing him."

Ritchie eased himself back down in his chair. He motioned for Dave to do the same in the chair behind him. He leaned back and put his fingertips together in front of his face in the classic pose of the lawyer listening to a client.

"This is the way they told us to do it in law school," he said. "Now, start from the beginning, Dave, and tell Uncle Ritchie all about it."

Dave started with the first call to Natalie's house when he was checking on the truck smashing. Then to the prowler in the window, and the cut open Butler on the doorstep. Next came the discovery of the body of her husband and her subsequent arrest for murder while Dave was on vacation. He included his disagreement with the Sheriff and then his visit with Natalie when he sneaked in the back door of the jail.

"You never saw this woman's husband alive, did you Dave?"

"Well, no, but..."

"Just the facts, ma'am."

"No. She kept talking about him coming in, but I never saw him."

"So, she could have been setting you up to provide her with a perfect scenario of prowlers, dog killers, and then finally a murder?"

"That's possible, Ritchie! But that doesn't explain the dog killing from ten years ago, or the truck smashing."

"Could be pure coincidence."

"Horse hockey, Ritchie! This woman didn't kill her husband and stuff him head first in a garbage can. Anybody that knows her can see that."

"You've got a thing for her, don't you, Dave?"

Dave leaped to his feet, temper gone wild. "You sob! Why does everybody think I've got one on for this woman?"

"Dave, Dave, Dave, take it easy!" Ritchie laughed, remaining seated as Dave leaped about. "I was just checking to see how much you believed in this woman's innocence."

"I would believe she would kill her husband before I would believe she would kill her own dog and slit his belly open."

"What's the Sheriff going to say when he finds out you're helping defend this woman?"

"You're going to help her?"

"I'm going to go talk to her. You want to go with me?"

"You know what the Sheriff's going to say. I'll wait here."

****

Sheriff's Deputy Terry King knew that if he didn't get to a doctor soon he could lose his left eye. In fact, it might be gone anyway. The only thing he knew was, he couldn't tell anyone the truth about how it happened. But he had to tell them something. The blood was already streaming down his face and dripping onto his uniform shirt.

With his left hand clamped over the eye, he ran out of Natalie's cell, never even attempting to close the door. When he got to the jailer's desk in the hallway outside the corridor, he threw the keys at the peg on the wall and reached into his pocket and pulled out his three blade Case knife. He pulled the hand away from his injured eye and opened the longest blade. With it in his hand and the bloody eye dripping through his fingers, he pushed open the door to the front of the jail.

"What happened to you?" the dispatcher yelled.

"Cut myself with my own knife!" Terry wailed. "Somebody get me to the hospital."

"Good thing the Sheriff's gone. He'd have a fit, you bleeding all over the floor."

"Get Hobbs to drive me out there. He in his office?"

"I think so." The dispatcher got up and ran over to the office of the bookkeeper who always kept his door shut. The carryingson of the jail didn't interest him in the least.

When he came ambling out behind the dispatcher, King shouted at him that he was dying and for him to get his lazy butt moving and drive him to the hospital. Hobbs just grinned and headed out the front door, King sidling behind him, urging him to break into something other than a slow shuffle. They almost collided with Ritchie Osborne on his way in.

"Trouble with a prisoner?" Ritchie said to the dispatcher who had returned to her position behind the desk.

"No, the idiot cut himself with his own knife. What can I do for you?"

"I need to see a client of mine who is being held here. A Mrs. Dunn." Ritchie started around the desk before the dispatcher had a chance to speak. He pointed to the door at her back. "She in the cell where you always keep women?"

"Yeah, but I'm not sure you can go back there. The Sheriff didn't say anything about her having a lawyer."

"Hey! Everybody who is anybody these days has a lawyer. You don't want the Civil Liberties Union down on you, do you?"

"I guess not. The jailer had to leave early and the night man hasn't come on yet. Just go on back."

"Thank you, dear lady," Ritchie said, bowing briskly from the waist toward the dispatcher who was helpless in the face of his bull.

"Dave was right. I am full of it," he said to himself as he stepped through the door to the back of the jail. He turned left and opened the door to the cell area where women were kept. The first thing he saw was a startled and scared looking woman standing in the corridor beside an open cell door.

"You must be Natalie Dunn. I've heard so much about you from one of your admirers that I just had to come down here and meet you. My name is Ritchie Osborne."

"If you're not a lawyer, you missed your calling. And if you think Deputy Warren is an admirer of mine, then I have a bridge in Brooklyn I'd like to sell you."

"Well, he was right in one thing he said about you."

"And what might that be?"

"He said you had a smart mouth."

"Are you here to help or insult me? Or are you like the last one that left? Here to do a body search?"

"Is that how Deputy King cut his eye? Doing a body search on you?" Ritchie said, grinning at the defiant Natalie standing in the corridor with her hands on her hips.

"I have no idea. I just know he left here holding his eye."

"And evidently forgot to lock the cell doors."

"He lost interest in me quickly."

"Remind me later to ask what you did to him. Right now I would like to talk to you about going with me on a cruise to the sunny Caribbean." Then Ritchie's voice changed and he grabbed his belly with one hand and he put the other arm up in front of him as if it were around the shoulders of a dance partner. He spun once in the dark corridor and ended up facing Natalie. "We could make such beautiful music together," he said in his impersonation of a Latin lover.

Natalie laughed. It started deep in her stomach and rose through her body like the tremor in a young walnut tree as the summer evening breeze starts it twisting and shivering right before a rain storm. It ended as a mellow, soothing, delightfully soft ringing sound much like the light tapping of fingernails on a hollow gourd. Her head shook from side to side. Her dark eyes brightened for the first time in a long time and she looked at the large, over stuffed lawyer who was still standing in front of her in his frozen dance step. His head cocked to one side as if awaiting an answer to his proposal.

"Did anybody ever tell you that you were full of bull?"

"About ten minutes ago. Other than that, never."

"Well, Mister Lawyer, you get me out of this mess and I'll go to the moon with you."

"I'll settle for a run down to the Bungalow Club. Now, what is a beautiful lady like yourself doing in a dump like this?"

Just like that. Serious. No bull. Natalie could tell that he had cut it off. She didn't have to ask. She knew. That's because he had a defense mechanism just like she did. Only his was light hearted bull crap. Hers was smart mouth.

"It's a long story, but they've accused me of killing my husband."

"I've got a long time."

"I can't talk about it in here. Can you please get me out of here?" Her eyes were begging. Something she didn't do often.

"May I assume that you are retaining my services as your legal counsel?" Ritchie asked, no trace of laughter.

"Yes. I've got some money in the bank. About five thousand dollars. Is that enough?"

"More than enough, dear lady. Do I call you Mrs. Dunn?"

"You do and I'll kill you. It's Natalie."

They both froze. He began slowly shaking his head. He raised his finger in front of her face and slowly shook it back and forth. "No, No, No. Don't ever say that again. Not even in jest."

"I'm sorry. So, how do I get out?"

"I've got a feeling that the sheriff has purposely made himself unavailable. I'm going to call the DA. And the judge if I have to. Now, you get back in that cell before they accuse you of jailbreaking. And me as an accessory."

Natalie stepped back inside the cell and pulled the door shut. She watched Ritchie move quickly through the door leading back to the jailers quarters. He was gone about ten minutes. When he came back she could tell that he did not have good news. He wasn't crestfallen, but close. Her spirits sagged with his.

"I guess I can unpack my bags, can't I?"

"It doesn't look good. You're probably going to have to spend the night in here."

"Why?"

"The DA and the Sheriff have the authority to set bond in cases like this until the accused can be arraigned. You won't be arraigned until tomorrow. It'll be before Judge Heartburn."

"Heartburn?"

"Mashburn, really. But we call him Heartburn. He'll give it to you if you're not careful."

"Wait until he gets a load of these beautiful legs. That ought to change his mind." Natalie stepped back and stuck out one of her scratched and cut legs.

"I've been meaning to ask what happened to your legs?"

"I went hiking through the blackberry patches on Saturday. The day my dog was killed." Her eyes dropped and the sadness returned. It was as if it had suddenly hit her that she was in jail and all hope was gone. She turned from the door and faced the wall. Her arms went around her waist and then moved up to her shoulders, vainly trying to stop the wracking sobs that had enveloped her body. The tears rolled from her eyes and she knew that she could no longer face what was happening to her. She didn't want the lawyer to see her like this.

Ritchie didn't know what to do. He opened the cell door and stepped up behind Natalie. He wanted to put his hands on her shoulders to console her, but somehow knew that would not be the thing to do. He was glad he hadn't when he felt the hands on his own shoulders.

"What kinda' crap is going on back here?" the voice behind him snarled.

Ritchie turned to see the man he knew to be the night shift jailer standing behind him. He felt Natalie move away from him, going deeper into the cell.

"I was just consulting with my client, Mrs. Dunn."

"With the door open? How did you manage that?"

Natalie spoke. "Deputy King left it open. He said there was no need for me to be cooped up in this little cell. He said I could have the run of the hall."

"King said that?" the jailer asked, incredulously.

"How else do you think it got open?" Ritchie asked. "I sure don't have a set of keys to it."

The jailer shook his head and walked back down the hall. "That King is losing his mind."

Natalie looked at Ritchie and grinned through her tears. Then the laughter came back and she pointed at the door the jailer had gone through. "When King gets back he's going to come apart when that guy tells him I'm loose back here."

"Speaking of King, what did you do to him?" Ritchie asked.

Natalie raised her hand in front of her, making a fist. Her thumb came out between the forefinger and middle finger. The thumb nail, which had a sharp, downward curve, looked like a small dagger. Her voice was a steady, even, steel-drawn sound.

"His eye had a gleam in it. That's what I aimed for."

Ritchie walked out of the cell. He stopped, turned, and with his hand on the door, said slowly, "Natalie, we're going to have to spend a lot of time rehearsing our lines."

"What do you mean?"

"I'm going to have a hell of a time convincing a jury that you're not capable of murder."

****

Dave leaped to his feet when Ritchie came through the door. The secretary had already gone. Dave had dozed in the chair in the hour that his big lawyer friend had been gone to the jail.

"You didn't bring her?" he asked, crestfallen when Natalie didn't appear with Ritchie.

"Looks like she's going to have to spend the night in jail. Neither the judge nor DA will budge."

"What did you think of her? No way she killed him, did she?"

"Does Betty Lou know you're in love with this woman, Dave?"

Dave swallowed hard and looked at Ritchie for any sign of amusement. There was none. He jerked his mouth open, a hot denial rising from his depths. Ritchie raised his hand, pointed his finger, and said as he looked Dave in the eye.

"Wait a minute, Pal. Remember? I'm an old bull shooter. And there's one thing you can't do. And that's shoot me a load of bull."

The quietness of the room. The presence of one from whom he had nothing to hide, nothing to fear in reprisal, nothing but a willing ear, brought Dave to the truth, even the things he knew to be true that he had been hiding from his conscious self. His voice, devoid of all emotion, quietly broke softly from his lips.

"I've never felt anything like this in my life, Ritchie. When I see her, something inside me starts singing, even when she makes me angry by cutting me down, it keeps on lifting me up. I know what it means now when somebody says they would sell their very soul for something. I would for her."

"And you don't do a very good job of hiding it, either. It's written all over your face."

"What am I going to do?" Dave implored, looking helplessly at Ritchie.

"The same thing I'm going to do. Work your butt off to get her out of this mess. Then worry about your feelings later."

Chapter 20

Ben climbed into the tall pin oak tree for the fifth time since Natalie had been gone. It was now the third day since the cops had carried her away, and she still was not back. He looked intently toward the back of her house for any sign of activity. There was none. He had wandered in the darkness around the house last night, looking for something to remind him of her. There was nothing. He wanted desperately to go there in daylight in hopes that he might see something that he could pick up. Something that had belonged to her. That was the one thing he regretted from his other life. There was nothing but the memories to remind him of his Natalie. But that was the way he had wanted it when he left. He had brought nothing but his briefcase with him. He had purposely avoided anything to remind him of Natalie. Now, he wished he had something of hers he could hold in his hand and look at. Sometimes he had trouble remembering her. That's why he came to look at this Natalie.

The memories of Natalie being carried away came rushing back at him three days ago as he watched the cops walk Natalie out of her house. The only difference was, before they had picked her body up off the street. Then he had also been up high. Only he had been in an empty apartment across the street from the horrible scene of her death.

Ben's mouth dropped open in amazement. He knew he shouldn't have remembered the street where he had seen Natalie's body. He had to grab the trunk of the oak to keep from falling. The trembles hit him that hard as the memories of he and Natalie and her apartment where she was suddenly alive again, all came back. He had to get down from the tree before his eyes rolled back in his head, searching for the pictures stored there. Then he would be unable to function. Unable even to hold onto the tree trunk.

The tire on gravel sound came to him faintly on the breeze. It was blowing from the house toward him. He gritted his teeth and forced himself to focus on Natalie's house. The front end of a car, not Natalie's, came into view at the side of the house.

She was back! Her dark hair. Her slim brown legs, the way she swung her arms, he still remembered that from watching her come toward him in the woods, all jolted him from his trance-like journey back in time.

Natalie was now. Except she had someone with her. Not the cop she hated. This man dressed the way Ben used to dress. It was strange. He hadn't seen anyone dressed like this in a long time. The dark suit with the vest. No! Don't remember buttoning the vest, then going back and leaving the bottom button undone. Or climbing the steps to Natalie's apartment, hoping this time she would see him. And would love him instead of Van. Ben fingered the knife at this waist. If the big man with her put his arms around her, he would consider cutting his throat.

He watched them intently, looking for any sign to indicate that she was in trouble. Might possibly need Ben. There was none. She hugged her arms to herself then flung an arm toward Ben. Without looking, she indicated his position. They both turned and looked toward him. Surely they hadn't seen him. No. They went back to talking. Then the tall man turned and walked toward his car. He said something to Natalie and she laughed. The man watched her get her keys from her bag, then rip the paper off the door. The paper the cops had put there.

When she went inside, he got in his car and left. Ben slid down from the tree and walked slowly toward his house. He needed to be alone. No more memories of Natalie today. As he walked he looked down at his boots. That's what he really needed. He had wanted to take the boots from Jeff, but had decided that would look strange.

As he walked along he thought about the man Jeff. He was glad he had killed him. Natalie appeared to be happy. He was afraid she would miss him and want him back, but it seemed that she was doing well without him. And for some reason he could tell that this new man, the big one with the vest, was not a replacement for Jeff. The cop wasn't either. Ben could tell that Natalie hated him. That was good. That left only Ben.

Ben kept to the trees and woods when he was out in daylight. He knew that it was too easy to be seen out in the open. He had almost been in the open three days ago when the small airplane had suddenly appeared over the ridge, flying low. Then had started circling like one of the angry wasps from the big nest in the ceiling of the kitchen of his house.

But boots were what he needed. He had to get his mind back to his existence. He had not had any trouble focusing on his daily needs until Natalie came back and moved into the new house. Now she crept into his every thought. Kept him from being what he wanted. Alone. Alone in his thoughts. Alone in his life. Alone in his memory. Remembering only what he needed for survival. Now, her memory not only kept him from being what he wanted. It kept taking him back to what he had been.

The last boots he had gotten had belonged to a hunter. He had taken them out of the back of a truck parked all night down at the Gulf station. Before that he had taken the boots of the old man with the bird dog. They had been on the front porch where he had forgotten and left them overnight.

Ben headed for the house where he had gotten the shirt after Natalie's man Jeff had ripped the sleeves out of the one he was wearing when Jeff had faked the injury and had grabbed Ben. If the man had boots that fit as well as this shirt, he would be lucky.

He lay on his stomach in the tall weeds behind the house and watched the child swing. He could remember sitting on a bench in the park and watching children swing. His child? No! There were no memories of that. But why did this child look so much like something that was creeping in? An image from the past that swung, like the pendulum of the clock he used to have in the hall, into his present life and then, like an old movie going out of focus, trailed off into nothingness as the child swung behind a cloud.

The house was red brick and fairly new, and the tract of land it sat on was a small plot that had been sold off a larger farm that joined Ben's. The dense field of weeds, sage grass, and thistles had been cleared just enough for the house. The back yard was small and Ben could crawl almost to within touching distance of the house.

As the child swung, Ben could see the mother's face in the kitchen window, watching. Ben was disappointed. There were no clothes on the line. He had planned to get another pair of pants if he couldn't find any boots.

Ben started to crawl away when he heard the telephone ring. The small window was up and the sound came through sharp and clear. The child also heard the sound. Her little face came up and she looked toward the house. Then she slowed the swing and got off. Ben watched as she came toward him. He was glad now that he had made a path through the weeds. He was going to have to move fast to keep the child from seeing him.

He started moving backward in a scuttling crawl as the child parted the first of the brown sage that bordered the back yard. Her freckled nose wrinkled as she moved toward him.

Ben's path through the field was almost like a tunnel in places. He had purposely pulled some of the taller weeds and thistles over the trail so that it wouldn't appear that there was a regularly used path in the field. A person walking wouldn't have noticed anything amiss, but a small child, toddling, was just the right height to see the intriguing opening in the sage and thistles.

Suddenly Ben knew how old she was. Three! How did he know? Could he have a memory of her, too. Like he did of Natalie? All he could think of was getting away. He could hear the little girl talking and jabbering to herself. She hadn't seen him yet, but any minute she would round one of the little bends and catch him crawling away from her. She seemed to have an easy time with the path. If Ben had been making it for a three year old, he couldn't have made it any easier.

When she laughed, he panicked. She had seen him and thought he was playing a game with her, crawling backward the way he was. Their eyes locked and she pointed at him, her mouth wide with delight.

They were almost to the woods that were on Ben's property. There was no fence at this point, just the demarcation between field and trees. Suddenly a scream pierced the air. An ear jarring screech that left no doubt that the person behind the scream was scared literally to death.

"Amanda!" was the name the woman squalled out as soon as her panic stricken scream died on the air. Ben could tell she was out of breath and running, because the next scream seemed to come from a different place. But he had no time to think. No time to ridicule the woman in his mind for her foolish behavior. The girl had him. Just as he left the tunnel at the edge of the field and started to raise up to run into the woods, she grabbed his shirt tail.

If her mother had been listening instead of screaming, she might have heard the little girl's giggling laugh. Ben froze. He knew he should disappear into the darkness of the woods. Be gone before someone came for the girl. But when he looked back toward the house, now about a hundred yards away across the field, he knew that the woman didn't even know where her daughter was. He could hear the woman screaming and the sound was coming from the front of the house. He caught a glimpse of her running down the road.

He looked down at the girl, standing there looking up at him. There was no fear in her eyes, only wonderment at the sight of him. Ben was trapped. He couldn't leave her here and run into the woods, but he couldn't just stand here with the child holding onto his shirt tail. So he reached down and picked her up.

"You stink," were the first words Ben had heard from a female in ten years. It felt so natural holding the child that Ben wondered if he had ever done it before. He looked toward the house and knew that the little girl would never make it back there on her own. He also knew that soon there was going to be a lot of people looking for this child.

So he ran. Deeper into the woods. The little girl holding tight around him and laughing as if the game she had started was continuing. He didn't go toward his house. Somehow he knew that he couldn't take her there. But he couldn't just leave her in the woods. He had to get her to someone, but he couldn't give her to a stranger.

Ben circled to his left, staying in the woods, but paralleling the road. He wanted to hear how much traffic the girl's disappearance would cause. At a spot where the woods came down close to the road, Ben paused and walked, the girl still in his arms, near the edge and looked toward the fence row that bordered the road. Suddenly a huge column of dust came billowing up from where the road rounded a hill. A white car with red flashing lights on top came roaring down the road. Ben watched as it disappeared around the curve just before the house where the little girl in his arms, lived.

The faint animal sound came to his throat as he wheeled and ran back into the darker part of the woods. He mustn't let the cops see him with the little girl. Amanda. Her mother had called that name and he liked it. He could remember it.

Now he stopped. What was he to do? The cops would soon be swarming over this road and the fields around it, looking for the little girl.

Suddenly he knew. He headed for the path that would let him circle the series of hills that lay behind the woods. Once around them he only had one low ridge before he was back into the valley that lay behind the ridge where his house was. Then only the woods and thickets that lay between he and Natalie. He would take the girl to Natalie.

He stopped twice to put the girl down so he could rest his arms. She never once cried or seemed to be scared. To her it was still a game. Ben running through the woods with her in his arms. Several times she put her fingers to his face, feeling the thick beard. Ben's dark eyes would dart to her face, seeking the reason behind the probes. There was only curiosity. After several minutes of being on the ground she turned to him and held up her arms and said, "Go, go."

Ben then picked her up and resumed his running trot through the woods. After the second stop he felt her head droop to his shoulder and her little hands go slack on his chest. She was asleep in his arms. And he running through the woods like a wild animal. He felt his own arms hug her tighter. It felt like something he had done before. The animal sounds came but they were soothing, gentle, not the harsh guttural cries of fright.

When he got to the fence behind Natalie's house, he stepped over the top strand and then cradled Amanda's head in the crook of his elbow and bent over. Stooped over and moving slowly, he headed for the back yard. It was still daylight and he never moved away from the woods while the sun was still up, but he had to get his precious cargo to Natalie. It was a chance, but he had to take it. He circled to his right and got the big silver gas tank between himself and the kitchen window where Natalie might be standing. When he got to the mowed part of the lawn, he dropped to his knees and started crawling, holding Amanda with one arm.

He made it to the tank without being seen. Amanda was starting to wake up and he stood her in front of him, his back leaning against the tank. She stood between his outstretched legs and looked at him. Ben raised his hand to her face and touched the softness of her cheek. She brought her dimpled hand up to touch the warm spot on his face where the first tears he had shed in ten years were starting to collect.

Ben knew then, without even thinking about it, that he had known this little girl back then. Had sat in the grass with her before him and dried her tears and then had watched her run off to play, leaving that tremendous longing in his heart as she left him, never to return. He must get her to Natalie. Before the urge to keep her brought him out of his world and forced him to accept a place in the one in which she belonged.

He looked around the end of the tank. Natalie was nowhere in sight. He took Amanda by the hand and guided her to the spot where she could see the house. He pointed toward the back door and said, "Mommy." Amanda looked at him. She had no way of knowing it was the first word he had spoken in ten years. It came out so naturally that at first Ben didn't realize he had said it. For the first time Amanda was startled. The look on Ben's face frightened her. She turned from him and ran in her little stiff legged run toward the house saying, "Mommy, Mommy!"

Ben crawled slowly toward the higher grass at the side yard and was making his way toward the fence when he heard the back door slam. He burrowed into the grass and turned toward the house. He saw Natalie come out the back door and stand there, looking down in amazement at the little girl running toward her.

****

Another five minutes and she would have been asleep. She had just raised the foot rest on the recliner when she heard the tiny cry from the little voice in the back yard. At first she thought it was a bird. But then she knew it was a child. Natalie got up and looked out the back door and saw the child by the picnic table. When she saw Natalie at the door she started toward her calling "Mommy."

Natalie stepped outside in time to bend down and gather the child up as she ran to her. She noticed the strange smell but dismissed it as just lingering in the air.

"Well, where did you come from, little Cutie Pie? Is your mother back there somewhere picking blackberries?" Natalie looked around the back field but saw nothing. She started, the girl in her arms, toward the end of the house. "Maybe she's parked in the driveway and I didn't hear her," she said, her voice going to the sing-song way that people talk to small children.

Natalie stopped at the end of the house and said again to the child, "Not here. Wonder where she is?" Before she could start back she heard a car coming up the gravel road. "Maybe that's her." She paused as the car came in sight. "No. It's just Mr. Barron. No need to wave at him. He won't wave back." She turned with the child in her arms and walked back toward the picnic table and sat down.

"Dink," Amanda said, her little face looking up at Natalie.

"Are you thirsty? I'll get us some nice cold milk. You wait right here." Natalie got up and ran to the back door. She looked back once at the little girl before going in the house and returning soon with a glass of milk. She watched as the little girl drank, milk spilling out of both sides of the glass.

"My, my! You were thirsty, weren't you?"

Amanda nodded. She handed the glass back to Natalie. Natalie stood up and looked down at the little girl sitting on the picnic table, her legs kicking back and forth, first one then the other.

"Okay, now, tell me your name so I can call somebody and tell them I have a little visitor that I don't know what to do with. Can you tell me your name?" Natalie bent down and peered into the eyes of the red faced and sweating child.

"Manda. My kitty name Dolly."

Natalie leaned back and laughed. "How wonderful," she thought. "To be a child and have such an innocent view of the world."

"Well, Manda, let's go inside and call someone and tell them that a little girl misses her kitty and wants to go home and see her." She reached for the child and she came easily into her arms. Natalie had taken but two steps toward her back door when a high pitched, shrill voice brought her up short.

"Freeze! Bitch!" As if the word "bitch" was a command also. She slowly turned, Amanda held close to her breast, to see what could be yelling at her so stridently. She saw the white eye patch that could only belong to Deputy King. The other eye was looking at her down the top of the barrel of a bright, shiny gun.

Natalie shrank from the sight. She clutched Amanda closer to her as she took a step back. Her eyes couldn't tear themselves away from the stare of the one eye of King superposed over the deadly eye of the gun barrel.

"Take another step and I'll kill you!" The "you" could only be her. The way he drug out the "you" sent chills up her backbone. The eyes looking at her, both unwavering, grasped her as firmly as she did Amanda.

"Down!" he screamed again. "Put the girl down!" Natalie saw him go into a slight crouch, the left hand coming off the gun to point at her. His voice also rose another octave.

Natalie slowly bent over and set Amanda down on the brown sandstone rocks of the patio. Amanda immediately began crying and holding up her hands toward Natalie. King, moving forward now, ignored the little girl, his eyes never leaving Natalie.

"Move away from her! Now!" Natalie took two steps sideways and King rushed forward, his hip striking Amanda, knocking her to the rocks.

Then he was on Natalie, his left elbow coming forward in a sweeping arc, catching her on the shoulder, spinning her backward. Then he grabbed the back of her hair and continued his charge until his momentum was stopped when Natalie's face came in contact with the rough siding of the house.

Natalie screamed but before she could even react to King's sudden move, he grabbed her under her right armpit and slung her back away from the house. He stuck his foot out as she came by and using her own falling momentum, propelled her head first onto the patio. Her head made a sickening, thudding sound as he then leaped astride her triumphantly. His breathing was quick and excited as he fumbled with the handcuffs in the pouch on his belt. When he had her hands secured, he jumped up, breathing hard.

He leaned over and picked up the revolver lying beside Natalie's head. It was still cocked and he forced his nervous, trembling hands to lower the hammer before he holstered the weapon.

King then ran around the end of the house and headed toward his car which was parked down at the road by the end of the driveway. He had not wanted to alert Natalie to his coming. He jumped in the car and cranked the engine. When it caught, he jerked the shift lever down into drive and floored the accelerator. The car came roaring up the gravel drive, fishtailing and throwing rocks to both sides as it swung violently back and forth. When the car slid to a stop, he leaped out and made sure that Natalie was still where he had left her, and then leaned back into the car and grabbed the mike lying on the seat.

"Twenty-two to Station One."

"Station One."

"I've got her!" he screamed into the mike. "Tell the Sheriff I've got her!" He had lost all semblance of control. He started to throw the mike back on the seat when the dispatcher came back at him.

"Twenty- two, what's your position?"

King rammed the mike back into his face and yelled into the dispatcher's ear. "The Dunn woman! She's the one who had the little girl. I got her. Call the Sheriff and..." He threw the mike down and ran toward Natalie who was attempting to struggle to her feet.

"Oh no you don't!" He yelled, sending Natalie sprawling with a kick to the small of her back. With her hands behind her back, the only thing to break her fall was the side of her head. She rolled over, blood starting to pour from a cut over her eye, and looked at the grinning man looming over her. He was standing spraddle-legged, and without thinking, she arched her back, using her manacled hands for leverage, and kicked upward, her foot striking home between his legs.

King sprang backward, too late. The look on his face was one of disbelief as he doubled over and fell heavily to the patio, landing on his rump. He rolled over, drawing his knees up to his chest as his hands went to the aching in his loins.

The scuffing Natalie made trying to regain her feet again, brought him out of it. Despite the pain, he lurched quickly to a standing position as Natalie came up onto her knees. He drove his own knee into her face, sending her over backward. She screamed in agony as her ankle was caught under her, the popping sound it made, audible over the sounds of the struggle. Deputy King leaped astride her as she twisted to get her weight off her hands in the small of her back. He brought his right fist upward, his high school ring flashing bright in the sunlight, and then smashed her in the face above the left eye. His own eye glazed over as he thought of Natalie coming at him with the thumbnail, and he again started the fist down toward her face. His arm was almost wrenched out of the shoulder socket as a stronger hand grabbed his forearm.

"You yellow sob!" King turned just in time to see the fist coming at his face. He didn't have time to react and the meaty fist caught him flush on the nose, sending him over backward in a mist of red spray. The next part of Dave Warren's body that contacted King was the booted toe. It drove into his rectum as far as Dave could get it, and King screamed in agony. Dave drew back to kick again when the Sheriff grabbed him from behind and slung him around, away from the fallen King.

"Enough!" roared the Sheriff. "What is going on here?"

The Sheriff had reacted to King's frantic calls over the radio as quickly as he could. He had been at the house of the missing girl, talking to the distraught mother when he heard King say that the Dunn woman had the little girl. He had been in sight of the Dunn house when he saw Dave Warren's Dodge truck go sliding in a shower of gravel into the driveway of the house. Evidently he was monitoring the police channel and heard King's breathless ravings.

The punch thrown at King's face was a good one. But not as good as the one the Sheriff saw King throw at the defenseless woman's face. He looked down at her. She looked a mess. Blood from a cut over her eye. The side of her face had numerous scratches and bruises. And there was blood coming from her mouth. He looked at King. He was still sitting on the ground holding his nose. It was pouring blood. One thing for sure, Dave Warren could punch. He had power in those shoulders.

"King, I don't know what's been going on, but you've sure made a mess of this woman. Come on Dave, let's get her cleaned up before someone sees her."

Dave looked up at him from his position of kneeling beside Natalie. He had almost cried when he had first knelt beside her and seen the face he loved, covered in blood. When he realized what the Sheriff was saying, he slowly stood up and faced him. The thing riding inside him was about to break out into the open, and it didn't look like there was anything he could do about it.

His voice remained low and even. His eyes locked onto the Sheriff's. "Let me tell you one thing, Sheriff. If you try to cover up anything that scumbag King has done, I'll fight you from here to the jail. He beat this woman up with her hands cuffed behind her, and that better be the way it's reported."

The Sheriff took one step toward Dave and grabbed his green Army shirt by the front. Dave's heavy forearm came up quickly and knocked the Sheriff's arm aside. He then stood with his fists clenched, waiting for the next move from the Sheriff. It was only words.

"Warren, I've taken you off this case and you're on vacation, anyway. I want you in your truck and gone from here in less than a minute. If not, you'll be arrested for interfering with a lawful investigation. Now move!"

Before either could do or say another thing, the clicking sound froze them in their tracks. Men who live around guns know the sound, and it is frightening. Except this time they were both fooled for a split second. The sound was coming from a camera. The third click was when Dave realized that it wasn't a gun being cocked.

Both men whirled toward the sound and saw the reporter from the Lewiston Gazette lower the camera from his face and look sheepishly at them. His skinny face broke into a grin but quickly changed into a scowl when the Sheriff took a step toward him.

"Get outta' here with that camera!" he bellowed. "We're trying to conduct an investigation and you're interfering." The reporter dodged around the Sheriff and took several steps out into the back yard. He held his ground in the face of the Sheriff. Dave liked that. "Now, look here, Sheriff. I am not interfering. I'm just covering this story. I'll stay out of the way." "That's right, Sheriff. If a man wants to take pictures of a woman that Deputy King has beaten up with her hands handcuffed behind her, that's his business."

The Sheriff turned on Dave, his face a mask of fury. As soon as his back was to him, the reporter raised the camera and began snapping again. The sound went unheard as the Sheriff roared at Dave. "By golly, Deputy, you've gone too far! I expect loyalty from my people and it looks like I ain't getting it from you. So don't bother coming back to work when you get off vacation, 'cause I'm firing you right now."

King came off the ground, still holding his nose, but that didn't stop his mouth. "That's right," he sneered. "You get the hell outta' here. We'll handle this. We don't need no help from a butt licker like you."

Dave's right hand came from nowhere and caught King in the teeth. He dropped like a rock. The camera clicked. Along with the revolver the Sheriff had drawn. It was aimed at Dave's belly. "You're in serious trouble, Warren. Striking an officer. Obstructing an investigation. You better leave while you can. And remember what I said. Don't come back." The Sheriff was smiling. He had it under control, now.

Dave slowly began edging away from the Sheriff. He looked at Natalie who was still lying on the patio. Her eyes were on him. She had been watching him. Dave's hand slowly came up, the fingers reaching for Natalie, then curling gently inward, hoping to draw her to him. The way he was drawn to her.

"I'll come for you. I'll follow you to town. Nothing else will happen." Dave's voice was low. He started backing away, down the patio, toward his truck. He never looked at the Sheriff. His eyes remained locked on Natalie.

Suddenly a high pitched screaming voice broke the silence, and Dave whirled as a woman came running around the side of the house. "My baby! Where's my baby?"

Dave spun back to the Sheriff. Their eyes both had the same question. "The little girl? King said he had her. Where is she?" King was struggling to his feet as the Sheriff was yelling at him.

"Where's the girl, King? You said you had her!"

"She was here a while ago," King slurred through his shattered teeth. Dave took a quick scan of the back yard and then turned and ran around toward the front of the house. As soon as he turned the corner he saw the little figure huddled under a bush near the front porch. She was trembling as he picked her up and ran with her back to the rear of the house. He ran into her mother as he rounded the corner.

The reporter knew exactly which shot he wanted because he was following the woman. He snapped as Dave handed the child to her. He grinned at Dave as he lowered the camera. Over the voice of the woman crying, "My baby! My baby!" repeatedly, he spoke. "Seems you and the Sheriff have a difference of opinion over how to arrest a woman. Give me a call if you have anything to say."

"I'll do it, George. Right now I better leave. Before I get the same thing Natalie got."

"I think you can handle yourself a little better than she can. I'll follow her to the jail, if you want. He's not going to do anything else to her with me around."

"You'll wind up out of the loop."

"When he sees the pictures I took and the story I'm going to write, I'll be lucky not to wind up with a loop around my neck."

"You mean you're not going to run just what the Sheriff tells you, like you did on the story about her arrest for murder?"

"Hey, what else did I have? You want to give me something else on it, I'll listen. You know how you people treat reporters. Throw us a little bone here and there. And then get mad when you get the slightest bit of criticism."

Dave grinned at him. A sick little I guess you got me there, sort of grin. He looked at George Emmons, reporter, photographer, and errand boy for the Lewiston Gazette. The man had always treated him straight, even when he didn't agree with all he reported. He opened his mouth to be straight with him, when the Sheriff and King came by, holding Natalie between them.

George and Dave were standing in the shadow of the house by the garage when they went by. From the back, the sight of the shackled Natalie between the two men in uniform, her head forced down as her elbows were used as leverage points, was pitiful indeed. George raised his camera and, just as Natalie stumbled, he snapped.

As she twisted, Dave saw her face from the side. The side with the scratches and bruises. He also saw something else. And he knew it would haunt him forever.

It was the face of a lamb being led away to stand before judgment, bleeding and whipped, but still able to look the accuser in the eye and to hear the voice of the faithful whisper in undying love. Whisper, unable just yet to raise the cry. Believing, but afraid to speak too loudly lest anyone should hear and point and say, "Weren't you one of the ones?"

Dave whispered, slowly and softly. Because that's the way he felt, not because he was afraid. "That woman never murdered anyone. And she didn't kidnap that little girl."

He turned to George and the man knew he meant what he said. "And that is what I better read in the paper."

Chapter 21

Ritchie Osborne was waiting for the Sheriff and Natalie when they got to the jail. George Emmons was trailing the Sheriff's car and got quickly out of his car and ran toward Ritchie, who was standing by the front door of the jail. Ritchie stuck out his hand toward George, but never took his eyes off of the car bearing Natalie and the Sheriff.

"George, how's it going?"

"Good, Rich. You here because of this woman?"

"Yeah. Dave Warren called me and said I should get down here quickly. Said they beat her up. I can't believe they'd do such a thing to a woman."

"He must have gone in her house and phoned. But he's right. Wait'll you see her."

The Sheriff had other ideas. He got out of the car at the curb and stood there until King had pulled up beside him in his car. When King got out and looked at the Sheriff over the top of his car, the Sheriff said in a loud voice, "Deputy! Clear this area! I don't want anybody threatening this dangerous prisoner I'll be bringing in."

"Yes, Sir!" King ran forward, pointing his left finger at first George, then Ritchie. His right hand was on the bouncing gun butt at his side.

"You two! Move! Now!" He stopped about ten feet in front of the two men who were standing on the low step in front of the jail door.

Ritchie moved first. To his left. To George he said, "Okay, George. You clear out that way. I'll take this side."

George, picking up quickly on Ritchie's move, chimed in. "Gottcha' there, Ritchie. I'll clear out this side. Everything clear on your side?" He backed up the hill away from Ritchie, sweeping his hands behind him in a paddling motion.

"Clear over here, Boss!" Ritchie yelled, throughly enjoying himself, now.

George turned to King, who was still standing in the middle of the sidewalk leading to the front door. "We got it clear around here, Deputy. You can tell the Sheriff that he can bring his dangerous prisoner in now." He raised his camera that had been dangling around his neck. He brought it up in front of his chin and then said to King, "I'm all ready. We're waiting on you."

"You couple of smart alecks! King! I want these two clowns out of here, now!"

King started toward Ritchie, still pointing with the left hand, the right still on the butt of the gun.

"Okay, lawyer puke! You heard the Sheriff. Move!" George was the one who moved. He saw his chance with the two men focusing on Ritchie. He was around behind the Sheriff and snapped two pictures of Natalie in the back seat of the car before the Sheriff knew what was happening. When he heard the second shutter click, he whirled on George who brought the camera up and snapped it in the Sheriff's direction before turning and darting away up the hill toward the square.

"You don't have to clear that far, George," Ritchie yelled.

"You do if someone is after you," George yelled back.

"Well, I guess that means I can go and talk to my client here in the car, doesn't it?" Ritchie retorted, moving toward the car as King and the Sheriff stepped toward George. At his words both whirled and headed toward him. He stopped and held up his hands in mock surrender. "Hey, guys. Just kidding." He stopped and backed away again.

The Sheriff, tiring of the game and trying to seize control of the situation, grabbed the door handle of the car and jerked it open. He yelled at King. "Keep them back, Deputy. I'm going to take the prisoner inside." He reached in the back seat and grabbed Natalie by the elbow and pulled. She came out head first, before she could get her feet out. The Sheriff stopped when he realized that she was going to fall out of the car on her head. He spun around and looked at George who was snapping away.

When Natalie had her feet out of the car and bunched under her, he pulled again on her elbow. She came out this time and he shielded her with his body as best he could.

George scurried to the front of the car so he could get a head on shot of the couple. He forgot about King. Until he felt his hands on his arm, pulling the camera away from his eye.

"Put the camera down! Didn't you hear the Sheriff?"

George jerked his elbow out of the grasp of King, but by then the Sheriff was past him, moving quickly, propelling the helpless Natalie toward the front door of the jail. Ritchie saw his chance and stepped toward the hustling pair.

"Natalie! Dave called me and told me what they had done to you. Don't worry. We'll be right out here. They won't do anything else to you. We'll make sure of that."

Then she was gone. With Deputy King trailing in her wake, walking backward, covering the rear, pointing at each of the men on the sidewalk, keeping them at bay. He felt for the door without ever turning around, as if George and Ritchie were two desperadoes who bore such scrutiny. And then, he too, was gone. "We're pretty good together, aren't we? It was Ritchie who spoke. "Of course, we didn't gain any friends at the Sheriff's Department by our little performance, did we?"

"The way I look at it, I didn't have any friends here to start with," George said.

"If you're on Natalie Dunn's side, you've got one."

"Who's that?"

"Dave Warren."

"He doesn't work here anymore."

"Since when?" Ritchie turned to George, surprise registering in his voice.

"Since the Sheriff fired him out at this woman's house when he stood up for her."

"He didn't mention that when he called me. But he did tell me he had slugged King in the nose. I wanted to say something to King about it, but never got the chance."

"What happened to his eye?" George asked.

"Natalie did that."

"When?"

Ritchie looked at him, then at his watch. Then at the jail door. Then back to George. "Tell you what. I've got forty five minutes before

I have to see another client. Why don't you come to my office and I'll tell you all I know about Natalie Dunn. Then when Dave comes by, which I'm sure he will, he can tell you the rest. Whattayasay?"

"Lead on, Boss. You clear the way and I'll bring up the rear."

If anyone other than Deputy King had been watching, they would have laughed at Ritchie walking up the hill toward the square, waving his hands in front of him as if clearing a path through tall, heavy saw grass. And George Emmons, crouched, walking backwards, swinging his camera from side to side, warding off attacking savages.

Deputy King, standing at the door of the jail, was not amused nor impressed.

"Look at those two nut jobs," he muttered through swelling lips. "All they need is Warren and they'd be the Three Stooges."

****

Dave Warren was not a snoop. He stood before the closed and locked spare bedroom door in Natalie's house for a full two minutes. Trying to decide. Trying to convince himself that he shouldn't try to open the door so he could see what was inside the room. Then he convinced himself that what was in there could be of help to Natalie in her desperate situation. And if it was something that would harm her? He would get rid of it.

He looked at the door knob. It had one of those little holes in it that took a flat key. He had a screw driver in his truck that would do nicely. He needed to look around outside, anyway.

When he got back inside the house, he locked the back door. He didn't want anyone coming in on him. He bolted the latch. That way even Natalie, if they let her out and she came back, would have to knock.

The door opened quickly when he slipped the tiny screw driver into the hole. He stepped into the room. It was like most spare bedrooms. Used for storage. There was an ironing board with one of Natalie's shirts on it. Dave laid his hand on it as he stepped past it to look around.

There was a sewing machine that didn't show much use and a desk in the corner by the window that was piled high with papers. On a little shelf that pulled out from the desk, sat a typewriter.

Dave went over and sat down in the chair in front of the desk. He put his hand on a stack of papers and idly thumbed through them. Nothing interesting there. He pulled open the shallow middle drawer. Nothing there but pens, clips, rubber bands. The usual. He then pulled open the large drawers down the side. Nothing but paper, envelopes. Even the short middle. Short drawer? Something in his mind clicked. He quickly pulled out the middle drawer again. It was shorter than the other two, and it stopped so he couldn't pull it all the way out.

Dave quickly pushed the chair out of the way and dropped to his knees in front of the desk. He ran his hand to the rear of the drawer and felt the stop that had been nailed to the side. He got the screwdriver out of his pocket and pried it off. The drawer came out into the floor when he pulled this time, and he sat down and looked into the space behind. A box with a file folder on top. A box that had once held a ream of typing paper. He put both hands into the hole and gently removed the box and sat it in front of him on the floor.

He raised the lid off the box. He got the same effect as if he had rubbed Aladdin's lamp. He felt the presence of Natalie. He watched as the cloud that hid her life rose before him. Through the cloud, dimly, he could see etchings of lead colored words slithering down a milky page. Moving as if they were being written by a liquid brush stroke of hot linotype dipped in silvery paint. But so hot they burned their way through from the back side of the sterling plates.

Dave became lost. Inside her being. Flowing through her pores until he was completely immersed in the creature that inhabited the body of Natalie Dunn. A fellowship arose, sort of a co-existence. Partly because of the secret he now shared. The secret he had stolen like a lover creeping into a room at night to partake of the musky, sweet forbidden fruit of one unknown, but remembered by the soft gasps and fluttering sighs.

The mist swirled before Dave's eyes. Covering, then uncovering her life. A pouring out, such as had never been seen, until the molten, liquid words had covered the entire span of her years from inception, in her own mind, down through a dark tunnel of eternity, and then up through a startling, stark, unnaturally bleak semi-arid expanse of blazing hot reality which explored her conscious mind, peeling away any covering which might have shielded her inner most thoughts, exposing them to even the most casual of passersby, making her, not the secret lover of dreams, but the most callous of whores, conveying her treasures to each and every one, making each feel special until each notices the line behind him stretching as far as the eye can see.

Dave's eyes misted with the words, which became not only words but minutes, days, and years in Natalie's life. A sudden plop, almost a sizzle, as a large tear fell onto the page, startled him into sound. "Oh, Natalie!" he cried, brushing the other tears away before they too, fell and struck the sacred pages of her life. The light had become so dim that with the obstruction of tears, he could barely see. When he finally finished and looked up toward the light of the window, he realized there was no more light, no more sunshine to pour through the jagged opening he had ripped in Natalie's shroud.

He now knew. Without a doubt, he knew how a woman felt after being raped. Not so much the physical pain, but the mental anguish that comes from knowing that a man has violently, and without consent, taken something that is truly valuable, priceless beyond all earthly standards, and spat upon it, defecated upon it, and then stomped it, hog like in his attempt to destroy that which is beautiful, and which he doesn't understand. Dave Warren had just raped Natalie Dunn. Only he hadn't done it to destroy. He had done it out of pure desire. Selfish lust, unable to be suppressed. With the first words, he knew he should have stopped, but like the heart that burns with an unconscionable yearning, he drove forward until he was spent. Until his desire was sated, but at the expense of someone's virginity. Natalie's.

The shame he felt burned the back of his neck as he quickly returned her soul to the box and placed it, along with the hurriedly read file folder, in the hidden recess. He could feel her presence in the room as he ashamedly fixed the stop so the drawer would not come all the way out of its slide.

And then like a thief sneaking away from a burgled house, he tiptoed out of the room and locked the door. Standing in the darkened hall, he looked toward the other bedroom, the one where Natalie slept. The longing returned with the thought of her there on bed, but he quickly turned his back on the imagined sight and walked with stiff legs toward the den and the back door. He pulled the door open and with an unnatural motion, raised his watch toward the faint light left in the sky.

"Three hours!" he yelled to the sky. And then he felt the regret. It was over. The three most glorious hours he had ever spent in his life. A man normally spends precious little time inside the soul of the woman he loves. He had just spent three hours inside Natalie's. And it was a sensual and tumultuous upheaval.

Standing on the patio in the surreal part of evening, just before light becomes dark, when objects start to fade from the seen to the unseen, the ones near the earth, dark, the ones close to the sky, merely an outline against the light, Dave realized that part of his life had ended. It was only now that he recognized that he had a life of parts. Before he had thought, albeit subconsciously, that his living was a single thing. The waking, eating, sleeping and laughing all blended into one. Now all those parts, which were the life he knew, had ended. And Betty Lou? She was simply one of the other parts. In there with the eating and sleeping. Nothing more. She had become a slice of bread not eaten, or a dream never remembered. Maybe even a small, amusing thought that never made it to laughter. But as a part, she had died. As a member she had atrophied and dropped off. Replaced with a vibrant, new shoot. A new growth that had literally pushed aside all other limbs and entwined itself around the main trunk, crowding out the other living things, taking their water, food and sunshine.

In this dream like state, Dave walked toward his truck, his boots making no sound on the sandstone rocks of the patio. His eyes were still focused on the soft dreams that he had evicted from Natalie's soul.

If he had looked, he would not have believed his eyes. The apparition that rose in front of him was simply not of this world. He stood helpless before the wild, hairy thing that bore quickly down on him, running from behind the shambles that had once been his Dodge truck. The sounds, low, animal noises that came from the creature were the sounds that could have come from Natalie as he pressed his conquest of her.

But the smell. Not from her. The stench that preceded the sudden movement of the animal-like charge, lifted the veil that Natalie's hand had dropped over him. And the last light, the only light left, seemed to gather at the point of the spear. The part that had been sharpened, stripped of all bark, leaving just the shiny, hard penetrating thrusting end. The end seeking to take his life as he had taken Natalie's with his desire.

Dave's left hand came across his body as he spun to his right. The point started to enter the skin but his swiveling body and the slapping hand caused it to simply cut a furrow along his belly under a couple of layers of skin, not the deep penetration like he had imposed on Natalie. And then the stinking body smashed him, following the thrust, hoping to drive home the deadly weapon.

Dave came out of his reverie. The palm slap and turn had been reflex. The burning pain in his belly and the smashing, stinking body slamming him backward onto the rocks of the patio, were real. He landed heavily on his right elbow and shoulder, but rolled quickly to his left and came up in a crouch. The spear had clattered to the rocks and Dave's fingers searched for it as the sound told his mind it was nearby. But his eyes were on the thing that had attacked him. It had gone by him after its mad charge had sent him sprawling. Now it was faintly silhouetted against the western sky, and was coming back toward him.

As Dave's fingers found the shaft of the spear, he felt the things foot find it also. He tightened his grip on the haft end, but the thing quickly bent and grabbed the sharp end and a deadly game of tug-of-war began. Dave thought he was strong but the man, he knew that's what it now was, was a good match. He snatched suddenly on the spear and almost caught Dave off guard. He lurched toward the bushy haired, bearded man and then the direction of the spear was suddenly reversed and Dave found himself caught halfway. He almost lost his grip on the haft but recovered, grabbed the wood with his left hand and threw himself to the side. The sudden weight shift caused the man to lose his balance and Dave saw him pitch to one side, falling next to the picnic table.

Then he saw him no more. He heard the thudding footsteps across the back yard, but the trees blocked the lightness in the sky and the man simply disappeared into the dark. Dave was up quickly with the spear in his hand, but there was nothing left. It was as if the struggle had been a microcosm, set down suddenly in the midst of modern man. Then the framer of this small world had stepped back and said, "This is what it once was like. And the time may yet come again when man will strive with wooden spears. For, after all, how far have you come?"

Dave felt the words in his head as he tried to put the last few moments on hold, then play them back in his mind. It had happened so quickly and suddenly that it didn't even seem real. But the smell. That was the key. It brought it all back. From day one when he had first smelled it. To Natalie's comment about smelling it back by the honeysuckle. That smell was on him. He pulled the front of his shirt up to his nose and sniffed. It was in his clothes. Then he felt the tear in the front of his shirt. He ran his hand inside and felt the blood trickling down his skin. His fingers felt the path the point had travelled, and he knew that he had come within two inches of death.

It was then he knew. He looked down at the wooden weapon in his hand and felt what Jeff Dunn had felt as the creature rushed at him out of the night. Except that Jeff hadn't seen the point coming at him. Dave shivered to imagine what it had felt like going through.

When he got to his truck, he also knew what Butch Gibson had felt. Something was odd about the truck. It was sitting too low on the ground. He couldn't believe it. His truck was smashed just like the others. This stinking, wild thing was the one. The truck smasher. But why did he do Dave's? Dave hadn't been hunting on the Hill Place. He had just been in Natalie's house.

Dave walked around his truck. Sick. Not so much for the truck, but for what he was going to do for a ride now that the truck was ruined. It would take weeks to get it running again if the man had done to it what he usually did.

But right now he had to get back to town, and he couldn't call Betty Lou and tell her to come get him at Natalie's house. He was glad he hadn't locked the back door. He went inside and turned on the light. Her keys were on the counter by the sink. He could take her car. In fact, there were two in the garage. Hers and Jeff's. No. That wouldn't be right. To take without asking. He would call Ritchie. He might as well get them both out of trouble. He and Natalie, that is. He surprised himself. Thinking of he and Natalie together.

After Ritchie said he would come and get him, Dave walked outside and got the spear that he had leaned against the side of the house. He went to the access door that led to the crawl space under the house. He slid the spear under the house and then laid down on his back. He felt with his hands until he found a wire strung through the floor joists. He then laid one end of the spear upon the wire and rested the other on the block foundation. It nestled there out of sight. He didn't want anyone to see it just yet. He didn't think anyone would believe him. Not even Ritchie. In fact, he found it hard to believe himself. But the smell. That was the thing that made it real for him. But then, he had always been a smell guy.

Chapter 22

Ritchie Osborne lived alone. His wife had gotten tired of Ritchie's bullcrap about two years ago and had taken the two children and left. Gone back to Mama. When asked about his wife, Ritchie would say, "I sent that caddy back to the clubhouse." The clubhouse was in the Texas panhandle. That's where he had met her. Her daddy owned the oil field where Ritchie was working. He had taken a two year sabbatical after two years of law school. Two years was a long time for Ritchie, and after his second year of law school on the GI Bill, a buddy who was also not doing too well in the grade department, talked him into going to Texas and working in the oil fields. The buddy lasted three months. Ritchie stayed and married Gwendolyn Stearns, the boss's daughter.

They had two kids. It happened so quick it made his head swim. But the interfering mother of Gwen, Sybil, "Sib to all my friends, darling," she would say, was what drove Ritchie, with Gwen and the kids in tow, back to Knoxville to finish law school. And in another year he did finish. Everything. Law school. His marriage. His role as father to two kids.

Sib and Rob came and got Gwen and the kids. He still couldn't believe he had actually married a Gwendolyn. They came during finals, got her and the kids and every stick of furniture in the apartment. When he got home that evening after stopping and having a couple with some of the guys to celebrate victory over the final course, he walked into a bone bare apartment.

There was no note, no word left as to where they had gone. Of course, he knew. When big, blustering Robert, "Rob to his friends," had yelled at Ritchie over the phone one day that he better "quit treating his little Gwen like a dog," Ritchie had suspected that something was up. Gwen must have been telling them that he was treating her bad. The problem was, she just wanted to go back home to Mama.

So the immediate surprise of coming into the empty apartment was short lived. He had taken his clothes that had been thrown into a corner of a closet, stuffed them into paper sacks, she had even taken all the suitcases, and moved into the apartment with his buddy, Travis Gillium.

They had stayed in Knoxville, studied for the bar exam, laughed at the private investigator that Rob had sent to spy on him, signed the papers giving Gwen everything she wanted, and then after taking the bar exam, had gotten roaring drunk and, together, called Gwen and given her one more reason to hate his guts.

Ritchie had not known how much Travis had despised Gwen until they had gotten drunk that night. He also didn't realize how thankful he was to be rid of her. Except for the kids. He knew that he might as well forget about little Rob and Sarah. By the time Gwen and her parents got through with them, they would not even know he existed.

Ritchie walked back into his office on Lewiston's square after watching Dave Warren drive off. He couldn't believe what had happened to Dave's truck. Dave hadn't seemed too upset about it. He seemed more worried about what he was going to tell his wife. And he seemed extremely upset about Natalie having to spend another night in jail, and the fact that he didn't have any wheels to enable him to go down there and check on her. So Ritchie had loaned him the old Chrysler he had acquired for six hundred dollars because he thought it was a good deal. Also, because that's what the man who owned it had owed him for legal services.

It was a good old car. Ritchie kept it parked in the alley behind his office. He watched Dave back it out, and thought about Gwen. He didn't know why. Just because he knew how much she would have hated something like that old car. Of course, the letter from her lawyer was on his mind.

They had been divorced for over a year and this was the first he had heard from her since it was final. But it wasn't unexpected. This latest thing was something he knew Rob and Sib would do sooner than later. Get the kids.

The letter was the first of the legal steps Gwen was taking to have her new husband adopt the kids. Ritchie sat back in the chair he bought from Blackburn's Used Furniture Store and looked out the window at the teenagers who were beginning to gather on the inner circle of the square. He wondered if his kids would do the same sort of thing when they got to be teenagers. One thing for sure. He would never know. Gwen would have them completely severed from him by then.

"What the crap!" he said suddenly. He knew then that he would sign the kids away. Fighting, and then losing, with the likes of Gwen and her parents was not something he wanted to do, regardless of the stakes.

He had more important things to attend to. Like getting Natalie Dunn out of jail. If this latest thing with the missing girl was any indication of her luck, she had better pack it in. A jury would probably flip a coin with a "heads I win, tails you lose," attitude, and it would come up tails for Natalie every time.

Ritchie didn't know whether Natalie had done what she was charged with, but one thing he did know. He was going to burn Deputy King, and the Sheriff with him, if he insisted on defending King. He knew he wouldn't win any friends down at the jail, but what King had done to Natalie was inexcusable. And it was so evident that a fool could see that he had struck her several times in the face. George's pictures would show all that, and his story in the paper would attest to it. And if something wasn't done about it, he would get the Civil Liberties Union down here, as he had mentioned to the dispatcher.

"This might be the big case that puts my name on everyone's lips," Ritchie said aloud. He had been a lawyer for over a year now, and it was just beginning to feel comfortable. Like this was where he belonged.

He looked back on his life and thought about all the things he had tried to become. He ticked them off on his fingers. "An Air Force pilot, an oil well driller, a husband and father. I've failed at everything I've tried to do. Let's just hope I don't fail to keep an innocent person out of jail."

But there was one person who was going to have to spend another night in jail. Natalie. He had gotten the judge to lower the bail when he had convinced him that Natalie was not going to run. But that was on the murder charge. When he had called him about the new charge of kidnapping, the judge had exploded over the phone.

"You convinced me to lower her bail so she could get out, Ritchie. Now, she's gone and kidnapped a child? And you want it to be lower still? Get serious!"

"Judge, ah, Mashburn," Ritchie said. He always had to pause before he said the man's last name to make sure he wasn't going to say Heartburn. "I think once you see the evidence in this so-called kidnapping, you'll agree that there is no way this woman kidnapped that child."

"She was caught with the child in her arms after being seen getting out of her car with the little girl. It seems open and shut to me."

Ritchie's mouth came open but he clamped his lips shut to keep from saying it. He almost forgot he wasn't talking to the Sheriff. But from the sound of it, the Sheriff had already done some serious talking to the judge. He was already convinced of Natalie's guilt. Just like the Sheriff was.

"Would she be able to get out of jail to go to the funeral of her husband?" Ritchie asked, his voice dropping into monotone, trying to strip the emotion from his words.

"The way I understand it, his family might not be too happy with her there. It's not appropriate for the murderer to show up at the funeral of the victim, now is it, Ritchie?"

"No more inappropriate than an accused showing up before a judge who's already convicted her of murder before the trial even starts."

There was a long pause at the other end of the line before the judge spoke. Ritchie's heart began pounding. He felt Natalie's chances dwindling, all because of his smart mouth.

"How long do you plan on practicing law here in Lewiston, Ritchie?" the judge asked, casually.

"The rest of my life. Why?"

"I was just wondering if you knew about the rules that keep a lawyer from trying to influence a judge's decision?"

"I sure do. But it looks like the Sheriff has already formed your opinion for you, so nothing I say will matter, anyway."

The line suddenly went dead. And it was a few seconds before Ritchie realized that the judge had just hung up on him. Ritchie gently put his own receiver back in its slot and lowered his head to his desk top. The question the judge had asked him kept ringing through his head. "How long do you plan to practice law in Lewiston?"

He knew he had answered the question wrong. He should have said, "Evidently, not long, if staying here means I have to get in bed with unscrupulous people like you and the Sheriff."

Ritchie felt his stomach knotting as he thought of what could happen to his career if he made an enemy of the judge, in who's courtroom his whole professional life would be spent. It was not a pleasant thought. But neither was the image of an innocent person going to jail. If indeed, Natalie was innocent.

"That's what I have to prove, isn't it?" he said as he got up from his desk and walked over to the window that looked out over the square and the courthouse. He looked past the three story building that housed the county government to the jail sitting just down the hill on the northeast corner of the square. He laughed when he thought of him and George "clearing out" around the jail.

The phone ringing startled him. He spun and grabbed the receiver. It was Dave Warren. Ritchie could tell he was with his wife.

"Any news on that prisoner?"

Ritchie grinned at Dave's words. He could see Dave sitting at home with his wife trying to act nonchalant about the "prisoner" he was talking about.

"Have you told your wife that you've been fired over this prisoner, Dave?"

"Who told you that?" Dave asked quickly.

"George Emmons said the Sheriff fired you out at Natalie's house when they arrested her."

"Well, I don't think he can make it stick. Rules have to be followed, you know."

"Are you Civil Service, Dave?"

"That's right. They protect people from things such as that."

"Do you think you are being vague enough to keep your wife in the dark, Dave?"

Dave laughed a nervous little ha, ha into the mouth piece. "Yeah, I guess so. We wouldn't want them to find out, would we?"

"About the firing or about the prisoner you're concerned with?"

"Neither."

"How did you explain the truck?"

"Vandals."

"How do you explain Natalie having the child in her arms?"

The air exploded out of Dave and whooshed into the phone, making a ringing in Ritchie's ear. He jerked the thing away from the side of his head and looked at it. He knew Betty Lou must be giving Dave some awful looks by now. He put his mouth back to the phone.

"I'm waiting for my answer, Dave."

"I'll see you tomorrow. I'll show you all the evidence I've gathered. Then you can decide whether you want to go ahead with this thing. See you, Rich."

The second one to hang up on him. In the space of about ten minutes. He thought about Dave sitting there in his house with a woman he didn't love. He had been in that boat, although his woman had been easy to not love. Dave's only problem was he loved another woman. Ritchie didn't have another woman. After Gwen he didn't want one. Just yet, anyway. He preferred stopping at the Dairy Queen and getting a sack of gut bombs instead of going home to a meal cooked by a Gwen. He could eat in silence. Not so with Gwen.

He shook his head violently. He had to quit thinking about her. It would ruin his whole day. The question he had to think about was how did the child get in Natalie's arms. There was no defending her until it was answered. And only she could answer it.

He turned away from the window and quickly left the office. He would go by the jail and try to see her. If they would let him. If the Sheriff and King were gone, he could bluff his way past the dispatcher and jailer.

Luck was with him. The jailer had run up the street to the Blue Bird Cafe to get some supper for himself and the dispatcher. The dispatcher on duty was the same one from the night before last. Ritchie walked right by her toward the back.

"Got to see my client, Mrs. Dunn. She still in the same cell?" The dispatcher pointed but Ritchie just waved at her and said, "Don't get up. I can find my way."

He was through the door before she could respond. He did see her reach for the phone before the door closed her off from view. He knew he had about ten minutes.

Natalie was on the bunk lying down, her back to the cell, her face buried in the crack between the bunk and wall. Ritchie stopped before the bars and looked at her. She hadn't heard him. From what little he knew of her, he suspected she wouldn't want him looking at her in this position, and feeling sorry for her. He tapped on the bars with his pen.

"Mrs. Dunn," he called softly.

She spun, violently throwing off the blanket covering her. She was off the bunk in one quick movement and walking toward him, her eyes asking the question, "Am I getting out?"

Ritchie slowly shook his head. "The judge says no. Another night in here. I'm truly sorry, Mrs. Dunn."

"I told you it's Natalie. I've told Dave Warren that, too. Do I look like a Mrs.?" She put her hand over her swollen eye.

"No, Natalie. Can I ask you a very important question?"

"I'm not going anywhere."

"How did you get the child?"

"I was in the house and heard it crying in the back yard. I went out and there it was."

"And you have no idea how it got a mile and a half from its house?"

"I have an idea, but no way of proving it."

"Let me hear it."

"My prowler brought it to me. He brought me flowers one time. And he looked at me through the window of the den. And I guess he's the one who killed Butler."

"Your husband?"

"No, my dog. But now that you mention it, I guess he's the one who killed Jeff, too. I hadn't even thought about who killed him. I just know I didn't."

"So this mysterious prowler is the one who's done everything from killing your husband to kidnapping the little girl?" Ritchie said, doubt creeping into his voice.

Natalie turned away from the bars and walked back to the bunk and sat down. She pulled the blanket over legs and then laid down and rolled over to face the wall.

"Good night, Counselor. Come back when you're not so skeptical."

"And to think Dave Warren's in love with this woman," Ritchie said under his breath. He turned away from the cell and headed back down the corridor. He was tempted to slam the door at the end, but didn't. He was glad he hadn't when he considered Natalie's plight. Alone. Jailed for the second time in as many days. He forgave her immediately for her words.

When he got to the front, he thanked the dispatcher profusely, but could tell by the way she kept watching the front door that she was expecting someone any minute. Ritchie jumped in his car and headed east, away from the jail and the square. He saw the Sheriff's car pull in just as he turned the corner by the VFW building. He had just enough time to get a sack full of gut bombs and get to his apartment in time to catch "Matlock". He never lost a case. So he and Ritchie had something in common. Ritchie had never won one.

Chapter 23

George Emmons felt himself getting dizzy. Not from a lack of sleep. He had been in the darkroom just behind his office until midnight. He had developed two rolls of film and printed a couple of the shots of Natalie he thought were especially dramatic. He had left them hanging over the darkroom sink, dripping their little drops of fixer into the drain.

He had been so on edge that he hadn't gotten to sleep until two. But that wasn't what was causing him to have to grab on to Mr. Endsley's desk this morning to keep from falling. It was the words that Mr. Endsley, Editor of the Lewiston Gazette, had just spoken to him, that caused him to reel.

"We won't be running the pictures or the story in this form, George." He was holding the rough draft of George's story in his hand. He looked up at his only reporter and photographer. He smiled at the look on his face.

"But Mr. Endsley. The pictures! They beat her up. I don't understand. This is a big story." George could hardly control his shaking. His hands gripped the edge of the desk as he leaned in toward Mr. Endsley. The sparse blonde hair on his head seemed to brighten as his face grew red with emotion.

"We're not running your story, George. And the pictures are just not right for a family paper." Foster Endsley stood up and moved around the desk toward George, who had all the appearance of becoming disoriented.

George was still leaning over the desk, looking at his story lying there where Mr. Endsley had left it. His hand slowly reached for it, but Endsley's large hand clamped on his arm.

"My story. My pictures. It's mine, Mr. Endsley," George said, his voice coming hollow-like, almost detached from his body.

"They belong to the paper, George. And the decision is not to run them. The McCord County Art Guild is having a big art show on the court house lawn. I want you to get some pictures of that. It will be our lead story this week."

George Emmons walked slowly from the office of the editor. The owner. The business manager. It was his paper. Mr. Endsley ran it all. George just worked for him. He felt his hand on his shoulder give him a gentle pat as he headed across the hall to his office. Or his desk in the big office. The large room he shared with the advertising girl and the classified woman.

He didn't know how long he had been sitting at his desk before he started coming out of the shock that had settled over him. He threw himself violently backward in his chair, the rollers on the legs sending it into the wall behind him. He stalked into the dark room and saw the blank clothes pins holding nothing, whereas last night they held his dreams. If ever a calling inspired dreams, it was the newspaper business. To George, there was something sacred about a newspaper. It was the gospel call that brought men to the truth. The fervor and missionary-like zeal that had filled him last night as he worked in the darkness, rose like bile to his throat, almost choking him on its bitterness. His mouth opened and worked silently, the hot, scalding words wanting to come, but the shock still sufficient to keep the mind from forming them properly.

He waved his hand under the clothes pins, wanting to make absolutely sure that the negatives weren't still hanging like little black pig tails down toward the sink. He put his hand down in the sweet smelling pan of fixer where he had developed the two shots of Natalie, one in the back of the police car, the other of her being led away from her house.

Nothing. A big fat zero. That's what he felt like. He turned and slowly walked out of the darkroom and plopped down at his desk. His mind was still trying to comprehend what had happened. His story. His big shot. With pictures and everything. Now nothing, because somebody said it wasn't suitable for a family newspaper.

"What's the matter, honey?" Carol Russell, the advertising girl said after watching George for a few moments.

George snapped his head up, trying to shake the dull depression that was beginning to take hold of him. "Nothing," he mumbled and got up quickly from his desk and grabbed his camera by the strap. He snapped a drawer open and grabbed two rolls of film and stuffed them in the pocket of the old sport coat he wore because he knew it said, "newspaper".

"Nothing! Gotta' do a story on the Art Guild," he said as he headed for the back door. He knew he had to get out of the building before he got mad. It wouldn't do to kick the trash can by his desk. But the one around the corner of the building in the back alley was fair game. With one well placed kick he sent it reeling and rolling across the greasy alley and into the bushes.

He wanted to cuss but he was trying to break himself of the habit. In college he cussed all the time. That was the big thing. See who could cuss the best. In fact, he and his roommate would sit around the University of Tennessee Daily Beacon office at night and think up new cuss words. Change some by putting -ing on the end, or change a couple of letters in a real ugly one, like the f-word. Or add an r. Rs went well in cuss words. His roommate would write headlines for the paper using the mock cuss words. They would get drunk and laugh their cans off at what they thought was the funniest thing they had ever done.

Well, his roommate now had a job with the Nashville Tennessean, but George had elected to come back to his hometown and go to work for Mr. Endsley at the Gazette.

"Suck City!" George exploded at the warm fall air as he walked across the back parking lot and down the alley toward Council Street. He decided to cross Council and continue on down the alley toward the jail. He stopped in the shadows just inside the alley and watched. He loaded a roll of black and white Tri-X in the camera while he stood in the shade of the buildings. The brick of the old structures were cool to the touch. He was studying one of the mortar joints that had a green growth forming along it when he heard the gravel crunch behind him. He spun, his heart leaping into his throat, and had to catch a flopping camera to keep it from slamming into the wall.

"George! Don't be so jumpy. You got a guilty conscience?" Dave Warren grinned.

"You scared me, Dave. I thought it was my boss sneaking up on me. I'm supposed to be at the Art Guild on the square."

"Art Guild? When you've got a red hot story here at the jail?"

"There won't be any story or pictures on the arrest of Natalie Dunn in the Lewiston Gazette."

"What?" Dave asked, whipping his head around to look at George.

"Mr. Endsley said that kind of story doesn't belong in a family newspaper."

"Well, somebody will run those pictures. We'll send them to Nashville."

"You'll have to take them away from Mr. Endsley. He's got them now. Took them right out of the dark room."

Dave peered into the sad looking face of George Emmons. There was no mistaking the dejection. "You're not kidding, are you?"

"I wish I was."

"Family newspaper, huh?"

"That's what he said."

"Damn!" Dave suddenly blurted. "Crap! Why didn't I remember that in time?"

"What?"

"The family connection between Mr. Endsley and the Sheriff. Endsley's wife is the Sheriff's aunt."

"Undoubtedly, he is her favorite nephew."

"Only nephew," Dave said.

"Well, that's not talked about at the paper office."

"But it sure explains a lot, doesn't it?"

George's sick grin was answer enough. He turned and looked toward the jail. There was little activity this early in the morning. He looked back at Dave who was staring through hooded eyes at the building where Natalie Dunn had spent the night. "So, what are we going to do now?"

The muscle in the side of Dave's cheek tightened and stood out. He turned to George, his eyes gleaming with determination. Even in the dim alley, the light blue of Dave's eyes picked up color and sent sparkle radiating out in every direction. George took a step back as the pale blue orbs stabbed at him. He knew at that moment that he didn't want Dave Warren for an enemy. The eyes had gone from soft, blue and friendly to hard, steely and mean.

"I've got a story to tell. I told Ritchie Osborne that I would come by this morning and talk to him. You might as well come hear it, too. I don't have to worry about it coming out in the paper now, do I?"

George laughed, "No, but I've got a friend at the Tennessean who will come down and do some real reporting, if I asked him."

"Let's go see this big, slobby lawyer. Maybe he can give us some good news this morning. I don't need any more bad."

****

Ritchie Osborne listened in disbelief to Dave Warren's theory about the strange intruder who lived on the Hill Place. Dave told how he speculated that it was he who had killed the two dogs and wrecked the pickup trucks parked along the road, including his own. He told about the smell and how he and Natalie had smelled the same thing.

Ritchie snuck a glance at George to see it he was believing the story. George was too shocked to write any notes. He was just sitting with his mouth open. The story was just too unbelievable. People didn't live like that in this modern world of 1988. But people did fall in love and do things they wouldn't ordinarily do. Like make up preposterous stories to protect a lover. Ritchie had a sneaking suspicion that Dave Warren was the one who left the flowers on Natalie's doorstep. She thought the intruder left them. But could Dave have taken the child to her? And why would he do that?

"How did the little girl get a mile and a half from her house to Natalie's?" Ritchie asked suddenly. He wanted to see if Dave's story matched Natalie's. He knew they had talked after she was arrested for murder, but they hadn't been near each other since.

"Boy, now that's a hard one. I've thought about that all night. Either the mother's lying and took the little girl into the woods, hoping to get rid of her, or the man who lives on the Hill Place picked her up and carried her to Natalie."

"Like he did the flowers?"

"What flowers?"

"Natalie told me that one morning after she had seen this man at her window, she found a jar of flowers on her doorstep."

Dave rose from his chair in the corner away from the window that looked out onto the square. He walked over and looked at the people starting to browse through the art exhibits set up under the shade trees on the south side of the court house.

"So close and yet, so far," he muttered, his eyes taking in the scene but not really registering what was happening. His mind was on the tangled jungle that was the Hill Place and the man who ran the woods and ridges.

"So, Natalie knows he's there. She never mentioned the flowers to me. Of course, she had no reason to." He turned away from the window and looked at George who had said nothing through the whole conversation about the man in the woods.

"What do you think about all this, George?" Dave asked.

"I don't know what to think. I guess I'm still a little shocked about my story and pictures, and now you start talking about a wild man living here in the county, killing dogs and kidnapping little girls and bringing flowers to ladies. I don't know what to think."

"Think it'll make a good story?"

"If it's true, it will. But from what I've heard, no one has actually seen this man."

"Jeff Dunn did!" Dave said, wheeling away from the window and striding to the middle of the room.

"Can he tell us about it?" Ritchie asked, smiling.

"Do we even know that this mystery man is the one who killed him? This is the first I've heard about that," George said.

"Oh, he killed him, all right," Dave said, his voice going quiet and low.

"How do you know that?" Ritchie asked.

Dave slowly pulled his shirt tail from his pants and pulled the front up, exposing his smooth, rounded, hairless belly. The red, open gash that began near his navel and travelled around to his right side, leaped out at the two men as if it were the garish lips of a down and out hooker in a late night bar.

"Because he just missed doing me in the same way."

Chapter 24

Betty Lou heard it from one of her friends. The wife of one of the deputies who worked with her in Pencil Pack Department at Venus Pencil Company. She tried to hide the shock and fear that the words brought to her. The embarrassment, also. She didn't do a good job of hiding any of it. She could tell by the way the other women looked at her that they had also heard it. She was the last to know.

So, by the time she heard Dave pull into the driveway at five o'clock that afternoon, she was good and mad. Furious would be more like it. But she was going to try to be calm about the whole matter. Maybe he had a good reason for not telling her, although she could not imagine what it would be.

She was sitting on the couch in the den that had once been a garage they had converted when they bought the house ten years ago. Dave walked by her and went into the kitchen, mumbling only a "Hey, Betty Lou," as he went by.

"Wrong!" she thought. "He's not starting off right."

She got up and followed him. "How many more vacation days do you have coming, Dave?" she asked him.

"I'm not sure. Maybe about eight more. I'm not sure."

"And then you're going back to work?"

"Don't know anything else to do."

"What's the Sheriff going to say when a man he fired shows up at work?"

Dave turned from the refrigerator where he was standing, trying to decide if he wanted something to snack on. He looked at his wife. "Who have you been talking to?"

"It's for sure not you. Everybody in town knows but me."

"Well, I didn't want to worry you. I don't think he can fire me. He doesn't have a reason."

"Messing around with a female prisoner is not a good reason?"

"Who said that?" Dave yelled, whirling toward Betty Lou, his eyes flaring wide.

"They told me you fought Terry King over her," she yelled back at him.

"That's a lie! He was beating her up and I pulled him off." Dave's heart was racing. He didn't know how he was going to talk about Natalie in front of Betty Lou.

"If she's as mean as they say she is, maybe she needed beating up. She killed her husband, didn't she?" Betty Lou asked tauntingly. "And then kidnapped a little girl?"

"She did no such thing!" Dave yelled. "Natalie's not that kind of person."

A pause, a look, a knowing look from Betty Lou. Her voice lowered to a pleasing tone. "Natalie? Is that her name? Natalie is her name, Dave?"

"That's right. Is something wrong with her being named that?"

"Oh, no. It just makes everything a little clearer. I seem to remember you making a few trips out to a Mrs. Dunn's house. But I didn't know her name was Natalie. Natalie Dunn. So she's the one, huh?"

"What's that supposed to mean?" Dave shot back at her.

"So now she's a grieving widow who's got the head detective of the Sheriff's Department on her side?"

"What are you talking about?" Dave whispered, dreading where this conversation was going.

"They said at work that you refused to arrest her. Terry King had to go do it."

"Who is this "they" who seems to know everything that goes on down there?" Dave was getting mad and Betty Lou kept boring in.

"Just somebody who will tell me what you won't. Was your truck parked at her house when it was vandalized?"

"Well, yes, but I was investigating this kidnapping."

"And didn't hear your truck being wrecked?"

"I was, uh, looking through the woods, trying to find out how the little girl got to Natal- uh, Mrs. Dunn's."

"You can say Natalie in front of me, Dave. I understand. I've known for a long time now that you've had somebody else. I just didn't know who."

"That's a lie!" Dave yelled. The kitchen was getting smaller. The air was closing in on him and getting stuffy.

"Do you want a divorce, Dave?" Betty Lou's voice was even.

Dave looked at her and opened his mouth to deny he wanted any such thing. To say so would be to admit that he was in love with Natalie. But there it was. Right what he wanted. Divorce. Betty Lou had said it. He hadn't had to. But still, he couldn't let her know what he felt.

"Well, no. No! I don't want a divorce. What makes you think I would?"

Betty Lou smiled at him in the sweetest way. She knew that everything was falling apart, but she wasn't going to let Dave know that she cared if it was or not. And she especially wasn't going to let him know that he was hurting her.

"Dave, you're not very convincing. But don't think it's going to be easy. I don't believe that home wreckers like her, and people like you who fall for them, should be allowed an easy road. It should be hard. So get ready for it. You want to move out or do you want me to?"

"Betty Lou! I don't know how you came up with all this so sudden. You're talking crazy!" Dave was coming apart. He couldn't believe that this had all happened in the last ten minutes. But the question remained. Was Betty Lou bluffing or did she know something? She couldn't know anything. He didn't even know it all himself. But was it that obvious that he didn't love her anymore? Had he been that poor at hiding the way he felt? He felt himself staring past Betty Lou at a point fixed in space, his mind focused on Natalie in the cell, her face turned toward him, the snapping brown eyes going soft as she sought for his help, needing his strength to sustain her.

Betty Lou waved her hand in front of his eyes. Then snapped her fingers as she said, "You can come back to earth now."

Dave blinked and turned toward her, still seeing Natalie, unwilling to return to reality, to Betty Lou. His mind slowly cleared Natalie out, but he still could not speak. He was too unsure of what he would say. But he was also sure that his silence was just as damning to his cause. He wanted to tell Betty Lou how much he loved Natalie. He had this urge to pour out his heart to her, not to hurt her, as he was sure it would do, but to simply be able to confess his love of Natalie to her in the way he had never been able to do to Betty Lou herself.

He couldn't help it. He was going to do it, knowing all along that it would damn him to hell for doing Betty Lou this way.

She beat him to it. She wouldn't let him speak the words he wanted. Betty Lou was smarter than she looked.

"I don't want any confessions from you, Dave. Because I know that you would tell me all of it. You love her, don't you?" She threw her hand up in front of his face again. "Don't even answer that! I couldn't stand to hear you say something about her that you haven't said to me in ages."

She whirled away from him as tears began to form in her eyes. She had taken three steps into the den before it hit her. She didn't have to take this. Spinning back to face him, the tears slinging bitter spray into the room as they left her eyes at the speed of sound, she brought her finger up to point at him as he stood by the refrigerator.

"You rotten piece of crap! You're really in love with her, aren't you? Did you help her kill her husband? I'll bet you did! I can't believe this is happening to me." She was going crazy, now. She was fighting to keep from crying. Her pride wouldn't let her be sad, so she got mad. She wanted to beg him to stay, to say it wasn't so. To tell her that he loved only her, not this devil woman in jail.

Dave didn't know what to do. He couldn't fight with Betty Lou over Natalie. His mind raced, looking for something to say. There was nothing. He simply stood and looked at her. He didn't even know it, but some words came out of his mouth. He couldn't have repeated them under threat of death.

"Betty Lou, I'm sorry." He turned and walked down the hall to the bedroom. He couldn't tell if she was coming along behind him, or not. The shades were drawn and the room was dark. He walked over to the waterbed and laid down. The soft rocking soon had him transported to Natalie's arms. Arms that had never held him. To her lips. Lips that had never kissed him. To the soft words she had never spoken, soothing his ear as they moved gently up from his mouth to his cheek. The cheek that had only received a slap.

The slap came back, only it was a click. A rolling sort of click, sounding for all the world like the click of the Model 25 Smith and Wesson hanging on the bed post above his head. He looked up and saw the empty holster hanging there, the gun hanging out in space in front of him. Sharp and defined. In the dim light, every corner and curve outlined, as the shiny blue surface reflected all available light back into Dave's eyes. Then as if on a zooming lens, his eyes seemed to shoot out on stems, reaching back behind the gun to the face of Betty Lou.

The grim, uncaring, damn you to hell face of a scorned and rejected woman. The woman he had been married to for fifteen years. The woman who had stood with him, unwavering, just as the heavy frame revolver never wavered in her hands. Never moved an iota in the white knuckled grip of Betty Lou.

The hollow point Winchester Silver Tips nestled in the cylinder peeked at Dave around each side of the barrel. But it was the one that he couldn't see that had him worried. The one on top, right behind the barrel, right in front of the poised and cocked hammer with the snaggle toothed firing pin, waiting to pop the primer.

"I could kill you. I really could." Betty Lou's voice was cold and detached. It was almost like it was coming from a robot. The monotone, hollow sounding voice, devoid of all caring and emotion. Dave heard the words but his eyes were still riveted on the two silver eyes that stared at him around the four inch nose of the Smith and Wesson.

"But then they might put me in the same cell with that…that… Natalie. I might catch syphilis, or something from her." Betty Lou paused and lowered the gun. Dave waited for the clicking sound that said she had uncocked it. He heard nothing. Betty Lou's eyes never left him. She continued to stare a hole through him.

Dave opened his mouth to try to speak, but she cut him off. She raised the gun and pointed it at his heart. She smiled. A cold, icy fingered smile that Dave knew he, by his actions, had been instrumental in putting there. "I could do it, Dave! I really could. For that I thank you. Now, you can leave me alone and not worry. I'll have this." She brought both hands back to the revolver and lowered the hammer with the gun pointing at the ceiling. She then backed away toward the door, the gun still pointing up at the ceiling. "I'm going to keep this. It's not the department's gun, is it? I remember you buying this on your own. I'm now going into the spare bedroom and shut the door. I have a few things to think about. When I come out in about thirty minutes, I don't want to see you. I might mistake you for a prowler. We wouldn't want that, now would we?"

Dave heard the bedroom door click. It seemed like the last few minutes had been nothing but a series of clicks. Each triggering something different. Eyes popping open. Heart leaping into sudden motion. Now feet swinging off toward the floor.

He almost fell as he stood up. Most of the blood had left his head, and the sudden movement made him dizzy. He stood in the middle of the dark room, his leg pressed against the side of the jiggling water bed, the motion he had caused when he sprang up, pushing at him. He stooped suddenly and reached under the bed and pulled out the black bag he carried when he went to the police academy. In five minutes he had everything in it he thought he would need until he could get back in the house.

He didn't know about Betty Lou's thirty minutes. She might miscalculate and come out early. He didn't doubt for one minute that she could kill him. And he sure as hell didn't want to be here to find out how good her aim was.

Ritchie's old Chrysler cranked on the first turn. He backed into the street and looked toward the house. A shadow crossed the window in the spare bedroom. Startled, Dave dropped the shift lever into drive and gunned the old car. As he pointed it toward the apartment of its owner, he knew no where else to go, he looked into his rear view mirror. Betty Lou's words came back to him. He spoke softly, hoping she wouldn't hear. "You know. I really am a rotten piece of crap."

Chapter 25

Judge Clifton Mashburn not only gave other people heartburn, he gave it to himself. And it was the constant changing that did it. One minute he was a tower of strength, making judicial decisions with the rock-hard firmness of a Supreme Court member. He could still hear his stinging words to that young lawyer, Osborne. The one who had yet to come around to his way of operating a court room.

"The decision of this court, Mr. Osborne, is to not grant bail. The accused has proven herself to be a risk when out on bail. Kidnapping on top of murder? Come now, Mr. Osborne. Let's be reasonable. Society deserves some sort of protection, does it not?"

Now two weeks after that piece of swift and sure justice, he was quivering around the mouth, dabbing at the corners to try to stem the flow of the saliva that dribbled down on his tie when he was nervous. He had made sure that the party on the other end of the phone line had hung up before he slammed his receiver down.

"I hate these liberal Jews!" He was referring to Gloria Fishbien of the American Civil Liberties Union. She had called him from Nashville in reference to Natalie Dunn and his denial of bail to her. She had gently reminded him that never had a bail denial case been turned down if it was appealed to Federal Judge Freeman's court. "And that includes excessive bail, also, your honor," she had sweetly reminded him.

Mashburn grabbed a pen while he jabbed at the corners of his mouth with a fore finger stuck inside a white handkerchief. He wrote furiously, mumbling the whole time about the Jews and the women taking over the world.

He jerked open his office door and flung the paper down on the desk of his clerk. "Get that typed up and down to the Sheriff! I'm taking the day off. I've got some reading to catch up on." He then stalked out the door and down the hall to the steps that led out of the courthouse.

The clerk looked at the note and whistled. "Well, I'll be a monkey's uncle! Look at this!" He turned to the secretary who had her eyes still on the door that the judge had slammed. "He's letting that Dunn woman out of jail on her own recognizance."

****

"I know I had some money in here!" Natalie said. She turned around to go back to the jail, then stopped. She had been so surprised when the jailer had come back and told her she was getting out that she hadn't thought to check the brown paper sack with her possessions in it. She was halfway across the street when she stopped and turned back. Then she thought. "I don't really want to go back in there." She turned and headed toward the square. "I'll just go to the bank and get some money out of my savings."

But that wasn't a pleasant experience either. The teller might as well have dropped a bomb on her. She just stood at the window looking at her. She had just told her that there was no money in the account. In fact, had been closed out.

Natalie gave a nervous little laugh. "You're kidding, aren't you?"

"No, ma'am. It says right here. Jeff Dunn withdrew all money and closed the account on October 25."

"But it wasn't his money! It was mine! It wasn't even his account. It was in my name!"

"He had the book, Ma'am."

"I don't care what he had! It was my money!" She was becoming dangerously agitated. She pushed herself away from the window, hoping to get control of herself before she was tempted to reach through the opening and strangle the teller. She then felt someone beside her.

"What seems to be the problem, here?"

"I came to get my money and it seems that it has been given to someone else," Natalie said to the tall, dark haired man with the long sleeved white shirt and tie.

"Let me see that book," the man said to the teller. She passed him the book and he studied it for a few seconds.

"Is that your husband's signature, Mrs. Dunn?" the man asked, pointing to the book.

"I don't know and I don't give a crap. I just know it's not mine." Her hand moved with lightning speed and she quickly snatched the book from the man. She had had enough. She spun away from the counter and headed for the door. She was out into the November sun before the man and the teller could react.

"Can she do that?" the girl said to the man.

"Looks like she just did," he replied.

****

Dave Warren wasn't especially happy about living with Ritchie Osborne. Not that he missed Betty Lou. He had only been with Ritchie a week and a half. He had gone back to his house the day after leaving, when Betty Lou was at work, to get some of his things. The locks had been changed on the doors and there were several boxes sitting beside the house. A note was taped to one of them. "This is all your stuff. Everything left in the house is mine. Don't try to get inside. Mr. Lovelace is watching you."

Dave had whirled and looked up the hill to the house next door. The old man was sitting in a lawn chair in his side yard, watching Dave. He didn't smile or wave. Dave had just picked up the boxes and put them in the back of the old Chrysler.

So this was it. Everything he had in this world was in those boxes in Ritchie's apartment. He pulled clothes out of them as he needed them. All he had worn so far was the same pair of camos. He'd washed them a couple of times so they weren't stinking or anything. But he sure would have dressed better if he had known that he was going to pick up the woman he was in love with.

He almost ran over her. She ran right out in front of him as he was coming around the square in front of the bank. At first he didn't recognize her as Natalie. But when he did, he slammed on the brakes and jammed the shift lever up in park. Right there on the busy street. He leaped out as she dodged around the front of the car and ran on across the street toward the courthouse which sat inside the inner circle of the square.

"Natalie!" he screamed. He hadn't meant to yell so loud, but he was so shocked and surprised to see her that he almost didn't recognize her. She looked so pale and wan. Her hair was a mess and there were streaks down her cheeks where it looked like she had been crying. And the bruise was still by her eye.

She stopped when she heard her name. A car screeched to a halt in the other lane as she almost ran into its path. She turned and looked toward Dave standing beside the beat up Chrysler. The car blew its horn at her and she simply looked at the driver and then started walking slowly toward Dave. She walked up to him, keeping the open door he was standing behind, between her and him.

"Natalie, I didn't know…" the car behind him began blowing its horn. Dave looked back and then looked at Natalie. He had to have her. Had to get her in the car. Oh, please get in, Natalie. "Natalie, get in. Let's get away from this traffic."

She took two steps back, then turned and ran around the front of the car and opened the big passenger door and fell inside. Dave quickly got behind the wheel and started off with a jerk. He smelled her when she got inside. She had a slight odor. But he knew it was from the wonderful facilities at the jail. Especially for women. A pan of water and a cloth. That had been the extent of her bath for the last two weeks, he knew.

But to Dave it was a wonderful odor. He wrinkled his nose to bring more of the Natalie smell in. He looked over at her as she slouched in the seat, her knees drawn up to her face, her feet on the dash. She was looking at him. She frowned.

"I stink, don't I?"

"You smell wonderful," Dave said. He then blushed and looked back at the road. He couldn't believe he had said that. He wanted to look back at her but he could tell she was still looking at him. So he just drove, heading west, straight out of town. When he got to the by-pass he looked at his watch. It said ten thirty. He looked at her. She was staring out the window.

"Are you hungry, Natalie?"

"About to starve. I haven't had anything since yesterday morning."

"You mean they haven't been feeding you?"

"King enjoyed bringing me a plate of food and then throwing it on the floor. That's what he did yesterday."

"That sonofa..." Dave quickly looked at Natalie as he cut off the oath.

"Of a what?" she asked, laughing at his look of shock. "Come on Dave. You know old smart mouth Natalie by now, don't you? Isn't that what you told Ritchie Osborne I was?"

Dave blushed again. He tried to speak but his tongue wouldn't work. He had to change the subject. "How did you get out of jail? Ritchie told me yesterday that he didn't think you would ever get bail."

"I have no idea. I just know I didn't argue when the jailer came and got me and said I was being released. There was nobody there. They just pointed me to the door and said bye."

"Strange. Hey! Is this hamburger place good enough? They have a car hop so we don't have to go in."

"What's the matter? You ashamed to take me in?"

Dave turned quickly toward her, dreading the old Natalie. The old game of taunting and baiting. Instead he saw a softening. A look of laughter around the eyes. Not anything that anyone else would notice. Only him. He had seen the other. The hard glint. The defense mechanism kicking in. That's what he expected now, especially after having spent two weeks in that rat hole of a jail. He grinned at her and she almost smiled back. "No, it's just that I'm ashamed that this is the best I can offer you. You deserve Champaign and lobster after what you've been through."

A soft murmured thank you and a lowering of the head to acknowledge the question of "is a double cheese and fries okay?" was her response. "I don't have any money. They took it at the jail," was offered in a low voice.

"I could have told you that," Dave said as he handed a five through the window.

"Like you could have told me about my dog?"

"Yes, and like you could have told your husband about the man running loose back in the woods behind your house?"

Natalie sat up quickly. "You know about him?"

"He's your prowler, isn't he?"

"Yes, and Jeff knew about him. He almost caught him one night outside the house. He had his hands on him."

Dave reached down and pulled the camo tee shirt up from the waist. "This is how close I came to him."

Natalie reached over and put her finger on the long red gash running around Dave's belly. "Did he do that?"

"Yep. Probably with the same spear he killed your husband with."

"Where were you? Did you go back there after him?"

"No. It was right in your back yard. I'd gone back out there to look around after you were arrested the second time, and he came at me. Almost got me, too."

The car hop handed Dave a sack through the window and he passed it to Natalie. Dave then backed out and gunned the old Chrysler down the bypass. "Where to now?" he asked.

"I'd like to go home and take a bath. I feel like I'm starting to smell like Jeff said the prowler smelled."

"That's got to be it!" Dave said excitedly. "When he came at me I smelled him almost before I saw him. It's a powerful odor. Whoever he is, he's gone for years without a bath."

"What would he be doing back there? Why would anyone want to live like that?"

"Why would anyone want to live in this world as we know it?" Dave asked, looking over at Natalie as she wolfed down the burger.

"I guess you're right. I'd swap with him right now, if I could."

"Yeah. Look at me," Dave said. "No job. No house. A borrowed piece of junk car. A broken marriage."

"Broken marriage? You?"

"Yep. We split. I'm living with Ritchie."

"What happened?"

"Oh, it's been a long time coming. She just got tired of me and kicked me out."

"I can understand that," Natalie said, turning to Dave and giving him a big grin. "How's that for a smart mouth return? And a smile to go with it."

"I guess it's better than some I've gotten from you."

"Just take me home, James. I don't have the energy to argue with you."

Natalie nodded, her head falling back against the seat as Dave wheeled the old car out the road toward her house. Her mouth dropped open as she slept and Dave kept stealing glances at her. No makeup. Dirty streaks down her cheek. Hair tangled and stringy. Lips dry and cracked. Legs still showing the scratches from the thorns behind the house. She was beautiful. He wanted to stop the car and slide over to her, putting his arms around her and covering her face with kisses.

He resisted the temptation until he pulled into her drive. When the car fell silent and the movement stopped, he felt himself drawn to her in much the same way he had been in her secret room when he had invaded her soul hidden inside the desk. And she responded.

From her drowsy condition, relaxed and drifting in another world, a world away from the hell of the last two weeks, she felt the gentle pressure of the arms around her and the warm breath on her cheek. She subconsciously suppressed the desire to awake and face reality. The dream was much better. It felt so good to feel warmth and softness replacing the steel and filth. Her breath drew in quickly and she felt almost violated as wet lips sought hers, and a moist, darting tongue entered her mouth. It had been so long since she had felt the delicious sensation of being caressed and stimulated. She squeezed her eyes shut as the lips left hers and travelled upward, over her eyelids, then down to her ear, the quick tongue darting in that orifice also, then down to her neck and around her chin and back to the lips where it had begun.

This time she returned the kiss, pushing her lips against his until the pressure she was exerting startled her and she opened her eyes.

"What are you doing?" she said slowly as she pulled away from Dave. She watched his eyes flutter open. She searched them for the look of conquest. She saw only the things she felt. A deep pool of emotion that yearned for release. A wanting to give with no barriers to leap, no games to play.

Dave felt the things inside that only come once in a life. Suppress them and they die. Release them and they sometimes kill another someone. But one or the other must be done. He felt his heart moving his lips, forming words he had never spoken, detaching themselves from his body and moving along an umbilical cord to Natalie. Entering her in a way he had never entered a woman. Discovering that the other entering was so base, so secondary, so inconsequential that it no longer mattered if it was ever done again. But this entering of Natalie was life itself. The other he could do without. But like the other he must do it quickly before the feeling wilted. Before the desire became localized and the emotions funneled themselves to one orifice and exited the body in a rush, leaving nothing behind but unspoken words and a feeling of bewilderment. With his emotions strong and his head empty of reasoning, he spoke.

"Natalie, if it ever happens again, if the world ends tonight and I never see you anymore, I'll be happy knowing one thing. That I didn't let this moment pass without filling it with every thing I am feeling inside about you. I'm not very good with words, but I'm not holding back any that happen to come. Because they are the only real, true words I guess I have ever spoken to anyone, other than myself. And the things I just did to you, I have no apology for. I couldn't have stopped myself if I had wanted to. And I didn't. And I would do it again." Natalie kept her eyes glued to Dave's. She wanted nothing to break the spell. She didn't know how she would react to the words coming from him, but she wanted to hear them. All of them. And she wanted them coming just as they were. Not filtered through some shrewdness or cloaked in some phallic shroud. And the eyes held the key. As long as they were clouded with the haze of intense emotion and not the glaze of desire, she was content.

So she held his gaze and willed him to continue. She felt the power and knew that she could get anything she wanted from him. In any way. She only wanted his words. Real words. He continued.

"I want to apologize for all the mean things I said to you. I think what it was, I could feel myself being drawn to you, and then subconsciously trying to push you away. I felt the only way to do that was to bite at you like a dog."

Natalie's eyes started to droop. Dave's soft words were putting her to sleep. She wanted a bath and then a soft bed. And then her mind drifted to the bed with Dave in it with her. She wondered what it would be like. There was a small confusion inside her. The brash, macho deputy striding away from her, then wheeling and hurling bitter words at her as she wept over her dog.

Then from nowhere, much like a silent ship nosing out of a fog bank, he appears at her side, whispering things she could only imagine a polished, professional lover would say. But there was no polish. Just the rough edges of a tender heart that lies buried inside many a man, but covered with all the rubble of Marlboro, Gusto, and vicious linebacker hits.

Jeff would have died before he would ever let anyone see a little tenderness from him. She could tell that Dave was having a struggle, but he wasn't fighting to keep it in. He was simply wading through the surf toward the shore, leaving behind the boiling, roiling, smothering waves. Resisting the temptation to turn and fight, instead, looking toward the cool haven of palms, searching the shadows for the arms that were waiting for his return. Not as a conqueror of men, but as one who has conquered self. One who has risen above the terribly small and misconceived limitations of the social mind.

She had never seen the process, but could tell that it was a difficult undertaking. Natalie knew that her own struggle would be equally as hard, so it was time for her to speak. Not that the silence in the car was overpowering. Just that Dave had bared his soul to her, had thrust it at her, unashamedly and without reservation. Now she must do something to preserve the tenderness, to keep it from being withdrawn into its hard shell of pride. She must show him that the tender conqueror, thrusting with the fervent heart, is much desired over the warrior, the one who vanquishes with the hard thrusts of sexual fervor.

Natalie began with her arms. She slowly raised them to Dave and encircled his body. He had turned in the seat to face her and she gently pulled him to her. This time her lips sought his, thrusting at him, wishing to give back all that had been given, and more.

The wetness surprised her and she pulled away. The salty taste of tears flushing across her lips as they spilled down Dave's cheeks. She went back for more, scooping tears with her lips, then spreading them over his face with her kisses.

"I'm overwhelmed, Dave. You've caught me completely off guard. I'm not good at saying what I feel, unless it's a cutting remark, and I guess you've heard enough of those from me. But I feel so good about being with you. Before I thought you were just another macho, big shot womanizing cop out to get all he could."

She recoiled at the way he drew back from her words. "Oh, I've got such a long way to go when it comes to talking proper. I'm sorry, Dave. Please overlook my smart mouth. I'll try to correct it along with the trash mouth."

"I'm just not used to hearing women talk the way you do," Dave said, smiling at her embarrassment.

"I don't think anyone really is. I guess I do it to shock people. To see their reaction. I'll try to do better."

"Please do, dear lady."

"Oh, it's dear lady, now. The last time it was just lady. Do you remember that?"

"Yeah, I guess I wasn't too nice."

"Well, you feel awful nice to me," she said, reaching for him again. He fell into her arms, seeking her face with his lips. The dried tears on his cheeks making little crinkly sounds as the skin moved against hers. His mind raced backwards to the times he had looked at her and wondered what it would be like to be in her arms. It was every bit as good as he thought it would be. And more. He could tell that she had been holding feelings inside, the same as he had been, for a long time. He dreamed now of the nights they could lie together and whisper those inner thoughts to each other, knowing that each word would be treasured by the other.

His mind took over and he relaxed his body. Natalie felt him going slack in her arms, and felt him no longer return her kisses. She gently pulled away and opened her eyes to view the change in him. She saw his sagging cheeks and lips partially opened. His hand fluttered in her lap, resting on her bare thigh. She had no urge to grab the hand to keep it from touching her. For the first time in her life she felt no fear, no trace of apprehension, no mental scrambling in an attempt to head off the next onslaught on her body.

Natalie watched Dave's face, searching it for clues to his feelings, closely watching his eyeballs skitter behind the closed lids. Like a child sleeping, the rapid movement indicating dreams. She saw awareness slowly creep in and he jerked his hand off her leg, the sudden movement making her jump. She saw his eyes grow still and knew that he was awakening behind the lids. She prepared for the opening. Wanted to see his eyes appear. Wanted to see the life in them. The joy they danced with, the deep flecks of dark blue scattered throughout their robin's egg color. She wasn't disappointed.

"Kinda' disappointing to open your eyes and see only me, isn't it?" she whispered, knowing he would disagree.

"It's the most, ah, uh..." Here he twitched his shoulders. His fingertips came to her, touching, drawing strength from her, hoping to find words to help him express the oneness he felt when he was with her. "Fabulous is the only word I can think of and it isn't enough. I told you I wasn't good with words."

"You do fine. Just keep it up."

He paused and looked deep into her eyes. "Do you want me to be this way with you, Natalie?"

She opened her mouth to speak, but stopped. She knew what he was asking. He was asking for her permission to give away his heart. And it wasn't a trick question. It was still coming from the honest Dave. Now, she didn't know what to say. She knew she couldn't commit. But she also couldn't be vague or flippant.

"I wish you had stopped after the me. Then I would have known how to answer. I would have simply said, 'Yes, right after I have a bath.' " She put her finger to his lips which were parted in a smile. "You're laughing at me."

"I am not," he said, letting the smile spread out into a genuine grin. "I was just letting myself feel how nice it is to be with you. And you don't have to answer the rest of the question. I like the way you answered the first part. Deep down inside, I'm still a dirty old man."

It was her time to grin. "You are not! You are the most unusual man I've ever met. It's just that my life has been so torn up the past two weeks that I don't know which way I'm going. Let me get a hot bath and a good night's sleep and tomorrow about noon when I wake up, I'll be ready to answer any question you can throw at me."

"You got it!" Dave said. He gave her one last quick kiss and opened his door and got out. He ran around the front of the car to meet her as she got out with the paper sack in her hand that held all she had when she went to jail.

Dave froze when he saw the door. It had been smashed in. It was partially hanging on its hinges. He dashed back to the car and got the old Army .45 Auto from under the front seat and was back at Natalie's side within ten seconds. His left arm went around her as he edged toward the broken and battered door. He could feel her shaking. Her voice trembled as she spoke.

"They've broken in my house."

Dave released her at the door and reached inside the opening and flipped the light switch he knew was right inside on the wall. The room was flooded with light and they saw that no one was in the big room. Dave quickly leaped through the opening, the Colt sweeping the room. He felt Natalie behind him, her hand on his shoulder. They quickly searched the rest of the house, turning on all the lights. They found no one.

"There's a lot of stuff missing," Natalie said, no emotion in her voice. He had watched her unlock the spare bedroom with a small key over the lentil. The bedroom where she kept her naked soul. She came out at peace. Evidently it was still there.

"Can you tell what is missing?"

"It appears to be mostly Jeff's stuff. All his clothes are gone. Some of the furniture that was his before we married."

It was then that Dave saw the piece of paper propped up on the kitchen counter. Held there by a can of black pepper. He walked over and picked it up. Natalie stayed with him. She read it over his shoulder. He felt her breath suck in. Her words didn't surprise him.

"Those rotten sonsa...!" She turned and walked to the center of the big room. She looked around her. What was left was hers. It was better than nothing. She looked at Dave. He was better than anything she had ever had. She was content.

"What the crap!" she said. "I guess they felt like they needed something of his. They also wanted to hurt me. Well, they can't. I won't let them. And I'll bet that Deputy King enjoyed kicking down that door to let them in to raid the place." She walked toward Dave, her eyes flashing, her stride purposeful. She put her arms on his big shoulders and clasped her hands behind his neck.

"Well, guess what, Dave Warren?"

"What?"

"I don't care that Deputy King let Jeff's parents in to get anything they wanted. They didn't get the main thing. You know what that is?"

"You?" he guessed.

"That's right! Me! The whole time I was married to him, they tried to take me down. And he was just like them. Cut Natalie down. Make her feel small. Well, I hated them for it. But I didn't let them get to me then, and I'm not going to…" Her words were cut off by lips pressing to hers. She tried to pull away. She wasn't through. And she wasn't going to let Dave Warren shut her up. But then she ceased to resist. This was better than talking, anyway. She relaxed in his arms and felt the gentle pressure of his body, sending tingling sensations down her length. She brought her arms down and then back up under his, encircling his broad back, pulling him to her. The kiss seemed to last for two lifetimes. When the pressure subsided, she felt the warmth slowly come over her. The warmth she knew she wanted after the bath was over.

"Are you going to wake up in my arms tomorrow, Dave Warren?"

"Are you trying to seduce me, Natalie Dunn?"

"I think it's the other way around. You're the one with all the charms. All I've got is a smart mouth. Remember?"

"I know that I want you more than I've ever wanted anything in my life. But to answer your question, no, I'm not going to wake up in your arms tomorrow, Natalie."

She drew back slightly. She could tell that he was serious. He had withdrawn the smile. "Why?" she asked quickly. Almost letting him see the hurt.

"I'm afraid I would ruin it. Don't you see how close we are to something wonderful. I can't take a chance on doing something to make it go sour. I lo--, uh, I just can't take that chance."

"And you're going to let me stay here by myself?"

"No! You can't stay here alone. Especially with the door smashed in. No way to lock it. I've got to get that fixed."

"And I've got to have a bath."

"Tell you what. You take a long and steamy bath while I see if I can fix the door. Then we'll go back to town and try to talk to Ritchie. We've still got a half day. Then we'll talk about waking up tomorrow." She brought her arms from around his neck and placed them on his chest. Her dark blue eyes looked into his. The incongruity of her and Dave leaped out at her. She knew deep down that something was out of step. Her physical self wanted Dave Warren. She hadn't got the mental to chime in yet. She had a feeling it would be discordant.

Natalie grinned at Dave. She had to break away. She brought her fingertips to his lips. "You fix the door. I'll take a bath. Then I can think better. We'll decide what to do then."

Dave watched her walk away, disappearing down the hall to the bedroom at the end of the house. Where the big bath room was. The one he had pictured her in. Bathing, powdering. Doing all the things women did in a bathroom. The sound of the water brought him out of it. He shoved the Colt into the waistband of his pants behind his right hip bone and went over to inspect the door. Something told him he didn't really want to fix it. Not by tonight, anyway. He wanted to be with Natalie. His excuse of not wanting to ruin the relationship didn't seem to be of much import. "It might ruin it if I don't stay with her," he thought to himself.

He straightened up from inspecting the door jam and looked out across the back yard to the imposing presence of the Hill Place. The place he had inspected from the air. Suddenly Dave knew that whatever happened to Natalie would happen to him. And that it all had to happen right back there. On the Hill Place. The place that had drawn him even before he had known Natalie. The place that was even now, drawing him ever closer.

He stepped out of the shattered opening and in a trancelike state started across the backyard toward the thorn infested nine hundred acres. Dave felt helpless in the face of the force pulling him. Halfway across the yard he saw a veil descend. The force became two. And like a tornado that suddenly picks up massive amounts of dust, the twin forces became visible.

Parallel, one on top of the other, they came from the veil. Their dark, piercing eyes directed at Dave as he walked toward them. And then he saw what he knew Jeff Dunn had not seen. That the sucking, swirling funnels of force were emanating from two sources behind the veil. And that anything drawn into the funnels would be either sucked upward or slammed downward.

Dave smiled as he walked. He would never have guessed that it would be this easy. The upper tunnel was the one to chose. To be drawn into. Why had Jeff not seen it? It was so simple.

As he neared the two sucking ends he relaxed, allowing himself to be drawn ever closer to the upper tunnel. Then it happened. Like two flexible corkscrews turning in opposite directions, suddenly coming together down their length, the tunnels meshed. The ends flailing each other as they whipsawed back and forth, undulating like two twisting, fighting serpents. The upper tunnel now below. No! Now it was above! Which one? Where was the right one?

Dave panicked. He flung himself backward, twisting away from the violent forces drawing and pulling at him. The thud of his back hitting the ground shocked him into reality. He was stunned for a moment. Then the gouging pain of the pistol in his back caused him to roll over. He came to his knees and slowly brought his head up to look at the Hill Place. The funnels were gone. But they were imprinted on his brain. The memory would be there forever. Because he now knew that he had seen the ending. Or was it the beginning? He suddenly didn't know. Were the openings of the funnels the ends or the beginnings?

Dave staggered to his feet. He didn't dare look at the Hill Place. He knew that the apparent serenity of the innocent looking forests and fields would try to lure him into its trap.

Natalie! He had to be with her. Only she could help him find the end. In a stumbling trot, his lips muttering her name, he headed back to the house. Where she was, he cared not. Only one thing he knew. Only she could save him from the death that awaited at the end of one of the funnels.

Chapter 26

The short, round, white haired man with the weak eyes looked at Dave and started to smile, but then thought better of it. The intently reading Dave might look up and see him smiling at him and think him funny. Him being an old bachelor and all.

The elderly little man, Clyde Patton, was affectionately known as the McCord County Historian. That's all he really wanted to talk about. He studied it night and day. The only friends he had were county history buffs. Or antique collectors. The two went hand in hand.

Earlier when Clyde had looked through the leaded glass panels beside his front door and seen the blonde haired, camouflaged ex-deputy standing on his front porch, he had started not to open it. Clyde not only knew the history of the county, going back to 1813, he knew the most current events. He called it that instead of gossip. But he knew the Sheriff had fired Dave Warren for interfering with an investigation. That was odd to begin with. But the rumor was Dave had a thing for a woman prisoner. The one who's husband was killed on the Hill Place. That place was history. That interested Clyde. He opened the door.

Now he watched Dave read. His eyes darted behind the thick, frameless lenses. He looked over at the stack of boxes beside Dave. Each one had material in it about the Hill Place. Most of Clyde's history was categorized by sections or communities in the county. The Hill Place documents were scattered through the boxes marked Barron Hollow. When Dave had told him he was interested in the history of the Hill Place, Clyde had started dragging boxes with the Barron markings over beside the chair he had made Dave sit in. Clyde didn't like people to stand in his house. He was short and anyone standing made him nervous.

But he knew that he couldn't stand much more of Dave sitting there reading. He wanted to talk. He could tell the man what he wanted to know, if he would just ask. He didn't have to read it. Clyde could read it to him. From memory.

"What exactly are you looking for, Mr. Warren?"

"Well, really, uh, the last owners of the Hill Place and what happened to them."

"Then why are you reading the diary of Captain Isaiah Hill? He was the original Hill. He was given the land by Congress after a distinguished career in the US Navy. He was notable for a naval victory in the War of 1812."

"I guess Minnie Hill is the one I'm looking for," Dave said sheepishly.

"Minnie Hill never married. She was the last Hill to live on the place."

"Who did she leave the place to?" Dave asked, closing the diary and looking up into the twinkling eyes behind the thick lenses.

"Ah ha! Current events! You're wanting to know who owns it now. Is that it?" the little man said triumphantly.

"Well, I guess so."

Gossip or history. Clyde didn't care which. History was his passion, gossip his hobby. Although in later years he found himself preferring gossip. His peers were dying off and the interest in history was dying with them. But there was always someone interested in gossip. Or current events, as he liked to call it.

He leaped from his seat across from Dave and floundered through the boxes stacked around the history room of his house and wound up over at a large, wall to ceiling bookcase. He pulled a stack of newspapers down from a top shelf and walked over to Dave. "In here someplace is the New York Daily News. There's a story in there about Minnie Hill's niece being run over on a downtown street. Just a small item, but I circled it. A friend of mine in New York sent it to me. He's a McCord County expatriate."

Dave found several Daily News papers but none had a circled item. Until the bottom of the stack. Almost the last one. It was dated September 19, 1978. It was on the business page and he almost missed it. Even the small headline would have made him miss it if he hadn't of been looking just for it.

"Wall Street Broker Killed in Traffic Accident."

The word killed was what drew Dave to the headline. That and the faint, faded circle around the story that Clyde had drawn. But the name of the broker who was found lying in the street, apparently run over by a hit and run driver, was what caught at Dave's throat. His eyes continued reading the short item. The lack of witnesses. No one saw the car hit the broker. It had apparently happened at night. The body was found in a pool of congealed blood, lying against the curb where it had been flung by the speeding car, the head crushed by a tire.

Dave's eyes got to the end of the story but he had to swallow several times before he could make them go back to the first sentence.

Maybe he had read it wrong. Maybe it would be changed by the time he got back up there. But no! The words may have faded slightly in the thousand years it took him to read the item and then force himself back to the beginning. But they hadn't changed.

"Natalie Hill!" He almost choked as he unknowingly said the name out loud.

"Did you know her?" Clyde's eyes brightened. Maybe this ex-deputy could add to the Hill history. Because as far as Clyde could find out, the Hill name had died with her and Minnie. Natalie first, unexpectedly, and then Minnie in a nursing home.

"No! I, ah, didn't know her. I just got choked." Dave coughed. A dry, unproductive cough. One that made Clyde look at him with suspicion.

"Maybe you went to church with Natalie. How old are you?"

"Thirty-three. But I don't remember a Natalie Hill."

"Natalie was five years old when she left her in nineteen sixty three. Her mother, Minnie Hill's sister, took her to New York so she could become a famous model and actress. But Natalie disappointed her and went into the stock market. The way I hear it, the woman died in an asylum telling everyone that her daughter was a famous actress."

"What was her name?" Dave asked. He reached in his pocket and pulled his notebook and pen out. He flipped to a blank page and wrote Hill at the top. When Clyde said the name "Rebecca Hill", Dave wrote it down and beside it he wrote, "Natalie Hill's mother." He looked at it and then raised his head.

Clyde was waiting for his question. "If she was a Hill, Minnie's sister, how come her daughter...?"

"Was named Hill, also?" Clyde finished. "That's because no one but Rebecca knew who Natalie's father was. And if she named her after the father, then everyone would know who he was." Clyde paused, watching Dave for effect. Dave only nodded, the new things he was hearing sinking in.

Clyde continued. "Rebecca and Minnie were old maids. They both lived with their mother and father right there on the Hill Place until the two old people died. Both on the same day, about eight hours apart."

"That's unusual," Dave said.

"What's unusual is how Rebecca ever got pregnant. As far as anyone could ever find out, there was never a man on the place. And those girls never went anywhere. How Rebecca Hill got one of her eggs fertilized is a mystery to this day."

"So how and why did Rebecca move to New York when Natalie was five years old?"

"Evidently Rebecca took the money from the inheritance and left Minnie with the land. The stigma of the child with no father was just too much for her. That, plus she always did have visions of grandeur. When hers didn't turn out, she evidently shifted them to her daughter." Clyde was getting into the story now. His remembrances were fascinating to Dave. And he could tell that the little man enjoyed the spicier side of the people who made the history he so much loved to talk about.

"Did you keep up with the Hills in New York?"

"A little. My friend kept me informed whenever he found out anything."

"Is he still alive?"

"No, he died a few years ago. But his wife still lives there. He has some boxes of papers and books for me that I'm supposed to go up there and get, but I've never gone. And I don't guess I ever will."

"Why?"

Clyde took off his glasses and polished them on a handkerchief he pulled from his back pocket. He hooked the wire pieces behind each ear and adjusted the nose pieces with his forefinger and thumb before he spoke again.

"Do I look like New York City? Do I look like Manhattan? I've never been out of Tennessee, and I never intend to go. The McCord County line is the farthest I ever want to travel."

"If you'll tell me his name and address, I'll go get them for you, if you want me to."

"You're going to New York?"

"Sooner or later, it looks like," Dave said with an exasperated tone to his voice.

Dave spent another hour milking the historian for every thing he knew about the Hill Place and the Hill family. As he told the friendly man goodbye, with the New York address and a letter of introduction to the widow of his friend, he looked around him. The front porch they were on ran the length of the old house and two thirds down one side. Dave listened idly as the man told him the history of the house, and how at one time this part of town was the thriving center. Looking around the neighborhood, Dave could tell that time had passed it by. Most of the houses around Clyde's were small, unpainted. A few looked deserted. Dave's mind drifted as Clyde talked. Back to the conversation in Ritchie Osborne's office that led him to Clyde in the first place.

His mind sucked free of any and all distractions by the twin funnels on the Hill Place, Dave had walked back into Natalie's house. As soon as she was through with her bath, they had driven to Ritchie's apartment. Ritchie had seen immediately the single purpose that was driving Dave, and had cut off the bull before it got started. The intensity of the two telling the story, left no doubt in Ritchie's mind of the existence of a strange being on the Hill Place. And that he was the one who had killed Jeff Dunn.

And Natalie wasn't stupid. She didn't kidnap the child. But she was quiet. Not as outspoken as Dave. Not as vehement in her denial of guilt or as sharp in her criticism of the Sheriff and deputy King.

Ritchie could see something in her eye as she looked at Dave when he rose to his feet to angrily denounce anyone who would dare to accuse or abuse Natalie.

Something had captured Dave. Something had crept inside him and replaced his easy going, carefree manner of living with a bone hard, single purpose drive. He could have had a banner across his chest with the words "Free Natalie Dunn" and he wouldn't have looked out of character.

Ritchie caught a slight, almost imperceptible twist of Natalie's head when Dave stood up and smashed his fist into his palm and said that he was going to find out everything he could about the Hill Place, even if it meant going to New York, or to the ends of the earth.

Dave would have never thought about the county historian, Clyde Patton, if Ritchie had not suggested he begin there. Dave thought more in the official channels of investigation. Court house, deeds, wills, that sort of thing. Ritchie had talked with Clyde on several occasions. They both had the same gift of gab.

Dave thought of Ritchie as he stood on Clyde's front porch and listened to the little man ramble. He could see his big lawyer friend following the same interests and pursuits.

He blinked and nodded when Clyde turned, pointed and asked a question that Dave thought a mumbled "uh, huh" would fit as answer. He looked at his watch and shuffled his feet.

"Well, Mr. Patton, it's been so good to talk to you. I'll let you know if I decide to go to New York." He hustled down the sidewalk before anymore talk could continue. He looked at the little man on the big front porch as he drove away. He thought how awful it must be to only have the interest of people dead a hundred years as one's main concern. But maybe that was a whole lot simpler. It would be a lot easier than the search for the man on the Hill Place. The search that he and Natalie, they were one now in his mind, had before them.

The funnels that he had seen reaching for him, their tentacles waving at him like the arms of the sensuous dancer on the dark floor of the bar in Casablanca where he and his Navy buddies went on leave while he was stationed in Morocco, made him aware that the search must begin and end on the Hill Place.

Something Clyde said had just been idle prattle at the time. Gossip. But then Dave realized that sometimes gossip was the real history. "George Washington slept here," may have been gossip, but it was the stuff of history. Clyde knew this. Dave was realizing it.

It kept coming back to him as he drove. Something Clyde had said. The little mystery within the large deception that had puzzled Clyde. Now it not only puzzled Dave, it was growing into something huge. Maybe it was the answer to the whole ball of wax. The statement that Clyde had made about as far as anyone knew, there had never been a man on the Hill Place. Well, Dave knew there was a man on the Hill Place. And he knew how Rebecca Hill got pregnant. The only question was, who? Could Natalie Hill's father and Jeff Dunn's murderer be one and the same man?

Chapter 27

Natalie hadn't really wanted to come to Ritchie's apartment, but Dave had insisted. And she was too tired to resist. She slept about three hours in the bed that Dave had been sleeping in since he had been staying with Ritchie. The clicking of the front door had awakened her. It was probably Dave coming back. He was going to do some research on the Hill Place, both at the county historian's, whoever he was, and at the courthouse.

A strange feeling came over her as she heard the footfalls coming down the hall. What if it wasn't Dave? What if it was Jeff's killer coming for her? How could that be? How could she even think that way? But she wasn't scared. She realized that after all that had happened to her, she would never be afraid again.

It was Dave. He stopped at the door and looked in at her. She had the strangest feeling. How could she sort out her feelings about this man? How could she make herself evaluate him fairly? The times she had seen him when he was a deputy, he had seemed to her the epitome of everything she hated. Now he seemed to be a decent, kind, caring person.

When he came toward her and sat on the bed beside her, she didn't cringe like something inside her told her she should. Like she had with every man she had ever known.

"Did you rest okay?"

Of her, always of her. She smiled at him. Not like the smile she used to have just for the judges. But a natural smile. One she didn't have to think about, or hold for an unnaturally long period of time. But it still caused the old feelings to creep from the crevices. She used every trick to push them back, down inside the mental holes where she had buried them. Covering them with green algae to keep them from coming back and ruining her life again. She looked at Dave. His face seemed to soften when he was with her. She knew it was real. As real as he was. She dreaded the day when he would make the mistake, say the wrong thing that would bring her temper to the surface. To see that would change the look on his face.

"Ritchie must have given you the best bed in the house. I slept like a log. What time is it?"

"Five o'clock. You hungry?"

"Starved. Are we going to eat again?"

"Whenever you're ready." Dave paused. He wanted to tell Natalie about what he had found. About his theory on the killer. But he didn't want to raise her hopes, only to be dashed if his theory was wrong. He told her anyway.

"Guess what? I may have discovered the identity of Jeff's killer." The change wrought in Natalie was enormous. It took ever fiber in her being to keep Dave from seeing the profound shock that his words caused. He felt a slight tightening of her body at his words, but attributed it to the excitement of hearing of proof of her innocence.

"Who?" she forced herself to blurt, her eyes coming wide open with apprehension.

"Well, I don't know his name, but I don't think that's important. It's just his existence I have to prove to get you cleared. Anyway, approximately thirty years ago, an illegitimate child was born on the Hill Place to one of the sisters who owned it. Rebecca Hill. I think that the father of that child, who was named Natalie Hill, and Jeff's killer are one and the same man. He's been there the whole time. Living like a hermit.

"That's unbelievable!"

"I know. But now I know what I have to do. In fact, two things."

"Knowing you, you will do them in reverse order," she teased. "So what's the last thing to do?"

"Go out in those woods behind your house and find that man. Bring him into the courtroom to prove you didn't kill Jeff."

"What's the first?"

"Go to New York and find out everything I can about Rebecca and Natalie Hill."

Her arms flew up, flailing the air. Dave just happened to be close enough that the soft brown arms went around his neck. Her mouth came open, a dark, soft hole surrounded by delicious white teeth. His mouth closed on hers as he bent to meet her. A passion suddenly surfaced, one that must have been seething just below the soft skin of Natalie. It enveloped Dave. He could feel it coming out of her, grabbing him with such tenuous hooks that he knew escape was futile. Never could he have dreamed of such a reckless and wild pleasurable feeling that came over him. The smoothness of Dave's skin excited Natalie because of its unexpectedness, just as the expected smoothness of hers sent Dave reeling with tiny shivers cascading over his body and mind. He seemed to find himself caught in the folds of her gray matter.

Natalie drew Dave to her. Except this time the feeling was not suffocating. It was like simply scooting over to make room for someone in the back seat. Someone to ride with. Someone to lean against, to fall asleep upon. To be able to turn to and drowsily ask if lovemaking is a possibility. Knowing that a murmured acceptance is forthcoming, even before the proposition is placed.

Natalie discovered love. How to give it. How to receive it. The realization softened her. Made her slowly aware of the man next to her who had guided her to the discovery. Was it an accident? Undoubtedly. In no other way had it ever been discovered. The real secret lay in realizing it, and then holding it and keeping it. Keeping it clean. Pure. Safe from the past. Away from the lesser and baser humans who would try to take it from them. This Natalie knew would be the hardest task. The impossible one for her. If only the man beside her knew how. Then it might be safe. Otherwise, she would lose it. With the first word spoken in anger.

"What have we done?" It was Dave speaking. Realizing instantly that, indeed, something had happened. It was a question longing for an answer. One that she wasn't sure she could give. Unless she could keep her outer self from taking the question away from her.

"We have done what nobody has ever done before. We have given to each other, and have not taken anything."

"I feel myself becoming a part of you." Dave paused and looked at Natalie. Her eyes were closed and a faint trace of a smile was on her face. "I hope that doesn't sound too corny. I'm not much of a romantic."

She turned her head toward him, picking up the words he spoke. Her smile became larger as she brought fond words to her lips. "Oh, you're doing fine. I feel like I've known you forever. Like I was born with you inside me and I've just gone through a long period of labor, and now here you are. All fresh and newborn, lying beside me."

Dave's eyes grew wide with wonderment. To hear someone speak to him like this, was unreal. He had lived with another woman for fifteen years and never felt anything like the things he had felt in the last thirty minutes. He knew now why people left mates and ran off with others. For the very things he was feeling at this moment. It was happening to him. He wondered if Betty Lou was suffering. He gritted his teeth. He mustn't think of her. Not in the same bed with Natalie.

"I love you, Natalie Dunn." Dave spoke the words as he reached over and pulled her to him. She came to him and he put his arms around her. There was nothing greedy or vulgar in his touches. Just a simple desire to know and remember what it felt like to hold her. He ended up at her face, his hands holding her head still so he could look into her eyes. Searching for the soul, the unquenchable spirit he had seen in the secret drawer of her house. It was there, hidden behind the dark, blue eyes. Dave had seen her fury. He also knew that her passion could match it in intensity. But her quest, her search. That's what he was unknowingly looking for. Desperately trying to find out if his own path, which lay behind him like a jet contrail, pointing toward Natalie, would intersect with hers. He knew from what he had seen in her drawer in the room, that the spirit of Natalie was volatile, unsettled. But when it did come to rest, it would be secure. And it would cling to the haven it had found. Dave desperately wanted that to be him.

Natalie's eyes still held their secret. Her heart wanted to let it out, but her mind still held sway, telling her that it was not time. There were things in the way before the goal was reached. The path was not clear enough for her to see whether Dave Warren was an obstacle in that path, or if he was part of the goal at the end of it. She brought her arms up and clasped him around his broad back.

"I can't tell you the same thing in return, Dave. There are some things I have to work out in my mind before I can even think about falling in love. And I don't want to think about you suffering for me during this trial coming up."

"Natalie! I love you! Knowing you've got troubles ahead doesn't change that. Look at the things I don't know about you. Maybe there's something behind you that ought to make me not love you. But it won't. I don't even know where you were born. When you were born. How old you are. How you met Jeff. Did you go to college. Nothing! I know absolutely nothing about you. Except that I love you."

"And you want me to tell you all of that before we go any further?"

"No, not really. It doesn't matter. I'd like to know some of it, but it's not important. There is one question I'd like to ask, though."

"Ask it. I may not can answer it."

"Did you ever love Jeff?"

She waited a long time. She looked into his eyes. The light blue eyes that were almost clear enough for her to see her reflection in them. She would answer this question honestly. Others she might not.

"No. I never did. So, I guess I better answer the question of why I married him. In a way, I don't know why I married him. It might take me a life time to explain why, but I guess the best and simplest reason would be, I was running away from something and he was the first thing I came to."

"Do you know that you wouldn't have been arrested if you had cried and gone to pieces when you discovered he was dead."

"If I had it to do over, I would do the same thing. Who does that Sheriff think he is to judge me on something like that?"

"And you wouldn't pretend that you loved him to escape what you've been through?"

"No!" Her eyes flared and she arched her back and pushed away from him. "Are you suggesting that I should have?"

Dave grinned at her anger. His heart loved the way she got mad, the way she let her emotions go. He wished he could let go in the way she did. He tried to kiss her but she pulled away. He knew his actions were getting to her, but he didn't care.

"If you had acted any other way, you wouldn't have been Natalie. I knew you wouldn't be upset when you came out from identifying him. I knew you didn't love him."

"How could you have known that, then?"

"I can read animal sign in the woods. I can feel things that other people are thinking. I discovered quickly that you reacted honestly to things and people. You didn't hide what you felt. You got mad at me and let me know it. I could see nothing in your eyes when your husband's name was mentioned. It was like he didn't even exist."

"I didn't know I was so easy to read. What else do you know about me?"

"That you love me, but you won't come out and say it."

She opened her mouth to speak. He cut her off.

"And that's what confuses me about you. At times you let your emotions completely take over. Then at others, you stop and let your head decide." He smiled at the look on her face. It was one of confusion and helplessness.

"What are you, Dave Warren? You keep me off guard more than anyone I've ever known. You're not a redneck deputy sheriff and you don't belong down there. But you know that, don't you? So, what are you going to do now?"

"I don't know. I just know I don't want that job back. I've decided that I don't even want to fight them over it. I'm not even going to fight Betty Lou over the house or anything. She can have it all."

"I knew you wouldn't."

"Now, how did you know that? You been taking lessons from me?" he said, grinning at her.

"No. It's just that as different as we appear to be on the surface, deep down inside we're pretty much the same."

"Except for one thing, Natalie."

"What's that, old wise one?"

"You keep running away, and I have this terrible feeling that I'm not going to be able to keep you."

Natalie grabbed Dave with both arms and buried herself in his arms. She pushed at him, wanting him to hold her and never let go. To do anything to keep her from escaping from the bonds she wanted around her. "Oh, Dave. Please love me. Even if I never love you, I want you to love me. And if I try to go, don't let me. Hold me. Do anything to keep me from leaving. But most of all, love me. Please!" Her arms pulled. Her legs begged and entwined. Her heart pled. And her body joined with his in an effort to prove to him what her lips could never say.

Her passion reached new heights, and Dave rode the crest and felt every ripple of her body and mind. He knew that she was trying to tell him things in a language he had never heard spoken before. Almost like a sign language with the words not only coming off the fingertips, but oozing out of the pores of the skin, and being driven into his soul as she pressed and pushed with every part of her body. Her lips, her hands, even the heels of her feet, pushing into him the things she wanted to tell him. But not one coming through the larynx.

"You can't say it, can you?" he whispered harshly.

"No!" she screamed. She arched upward, finishing her silent speech, her body's passionate plea for help ending in a climax of physical and emotional release.

The scream was real, though. At first Dave though he hadn't really heard it. Just imagined it. But then the stunning push she gave him with her body, dumping him aside as she leaped upward and off the bed, sent the sound of the scream echoing through his head. The next one came on top of the first.

"No! No!" she screamed again and again. "Why can't you take no for an answer?" She flung herself into the corner by the bed, her arms pressed out beside her, holding onto both walls as if trying to keep them from closing in on her. "You want me to tell you that I love you? Well, I'm not going to do it! No! How's that for an answer? I don't love anybody!"

Dave came off the bed and walked toward his Natalie who was pressed into the corner, her wide eyes trembling with fright. As Dave approached her, the panic stricken eyes of Natalie darted around the room, looking for an escape, a place to go. She saw there was none. When Dave got to within arm's length of her, she lashed out at him with both hands. He simply walked through her flailing fists and enveloped her in his arms. She opened her mouth to scream at him but he simply closed it with his. She tried to twist away but her head was pushed back into the corner and she could go nowhere. He didn't release her until her arms had dropped to her sides and her breathing had become calm.

"Natalie," he said, softly and calmly. "I don't want you to say anything to me. I just want to be with you to help you and love you. I'll do whatever I can to help you through this." Her eyes grew soft and liquid. Tears starting to form in the corners as she looked up into Dave's face. "I'm sorry I went off like that. I didn't want you to see me in that condition." She allowed him to lead her back to the bed where she collapsed in his arms, soft sobs making her body tremble like that of a purring, contented cat.

Dave held her head under his chin and pressed her face into his chest. The strangest feeling came over him. He felt like he was holding a shadow, a fleeting glimpse. He ran his hands over her back to make sure she was real. The feeling only enhanced the terrible specter of emptiness that was slowly coming up on his horizon.

He suddenly realized that he had been right when he had told her earlier that he knew nothing about the woman in his arms. The woman he loved. The one he had left a wife of fifteen years for. He spoke to the wall. Natalie heard.

"You know something, Natalie? If I were to wake up tomorrow and find you gone, I wouldn't have any idea in the world where to start looking for you."

Chapter 28

The Holland Tunnel sent Dave's mind reeling back to the only other time he had been through this highway under the Hudson River. He had been leaving New York on a 650 Triumph Bonneville that he had acquired on his year and a half U.S. Navy tour of duty in Morocco. There had really been no need of a Second Class Petty Officer with a rating of Shore Patrol at a tiny Naval Communications Station in the town of Sidi Yahia just outside of the port city of Kenitra, but that's where his orders sent him. His duties were minimal so he had spent most of his free time riding the Triumph 650 all over the country.

From Tangier in the north on the Mediterranean, to Marrakech in the south on the edge of the Sahara, to Casablanca in the middle, to Fez in the east, he had made his tour enjoyable with his travels. Then when it was time to leave after his year and a half, he was given the option of going back to the states on the Italian Liner Raffaello. He chose that because he could take his motorcycle. He left New York by way of the Holland Tunnel, which was scary on a motorcycle, and travelled south to Fort Bragg, North Carolina to visit with his old high school buddy who was stationed there. From there he rode the

Bonneville to Lewiston, Tennessee, stayed a few days and then on to Millington Navy Base in Memphis to be discharged from the Navy.

These memories came flooding back as Dave exited the tunnel and spent the next hour trying to find the police precinct nearest to the street address where Natalie Hill had been killed. It took another hour of waiting inside the busy precinct lobby to get anyone to talk to him. He had given the desk sergeant a slip of paper with the name of Natalie Hill on it, and the date of her death. He told the man he would appreciate any information they could give him on the matter. The man had seemed intimidated when Dave had used the words please and thank you.

As Dave sat and waited, he thought about the last few days. And one night. One night with Natalie. It was almost a relief to be away. She seemed driven by a need that was both physical and emotional. But he wanted her to come with him to New York, but Ritchie had nixed the idea. The terms of her release forbade it. She couldn't leave the county.

She had tried to hide it, but Dave had seen the relief in her eyes when Ritchie had said she couldn't go to New York. Maybe she wanted a few nights without him, also. But Dave had convinced himself that he needed to come to this city where Rebecca Hill had fled with her daughter. Somehow the man in the woods behind Natalie Dunn's house was tied to the Hills of New York.

Natalie Dunn! The name excited Dave. He said it to himself over and over. Natalie Smith didn't sound as good. That was Natalie's name before she married. Tears came to Dave's eyes as he thought about the words from the deposition that Natalie had given to Ritchie. Natalie had insisted that Dave leave the room when she started answering the questions Ritchie asked her. But Dave asked that he be allowed to read the deposition after it was typed. He had to know everything about her, to be able to help her.

Dave had literally cried in front of Ritchie when he had read the answers Natalie gave to the questions. It all came back to him in a jumble of words and emotions.

Born in North Carolina in 1958. That made her thirty years old. Abandoned at the door of an orphanage. Raised by a Smith family whose name she took. Met Jeff Dunn while he was in college and she was a waitress in a diner. Married after two weeks of courtship. Moved to Tennessee after Jeff got the job on the oil rig in Louisiana. Found the piece of property in McCord County and built a house on it. They wanted close to I-65 so Jeff could have easy access to the route south.

The rest of it Dave knew. He had been a part of most of it. He could have almost guessed at a lot of the other. The part of her being an orphan. It fit. The way she trusted no one. Loved no one. But Dave knew he could change all that. Just by loving her and trusting her.

The short, fat legs and the huge stomach were the first things he saw out of the corner of his eye. The legs had walked up beside him. The deep, gravelly voice that sounded like rocks being poured out of a bucket, was speaking to him.

"You the one wanting to talk about this note?"

"Yes, Sir!" Dave leaped to his feet and found himself looking into the eyes of a cop. The man could have been nothing else. Bullet shaped head, covered with closely cut GI hair, pig eyes set back into a fleshy face, lips pulled down over clenched teeth, and the dead cigar between those teeth to round out the appearance.

"You don't have to sir me," the man said as he turned and waved for Dave to follow him down a hallway to a small office.

"Yes Sir...I mean, OK," Dave stammered. The man walked around behind a cluttered desk as Dave stepped inside the office. A chair was sitting against the open door, so evidently the man didn't mean for Dave to close it.

"Detective Joncik," the man said. "What can I do for you?"

Dave reached for his wallet and flipped the badge out that the Sheriff hadn't taken from him, yet. "Sheriff's Detective Dave Warren of McCord County, Tennessee." He held the badge up in front of the man's eyes so he could see it was an authentic badge. He hoped the man wouldn't ask for a phone number so he could call the Sheriff. If he did, Dave would just have to tell the truth and hope the man believed him.

"I'm investigating a murder in McCord County that took place on the property that belonged to this woman, Natalie Hill. Somehow her death and this murder are connected. I've got to find out how." Dave decided to get straight to the point and not try to hide anything. The man's attitude didn't invite beating around the bush.

Detective Joncik sat down and motioned for Dave to do the same. He took the dead cigar from his mouth and looked at it. "All this crap about no smoking forced the Chief to ban smoking in all offices. That's why this thing ain't lit." He leaned back in his chair, satisfied now that he had explained the dead cigar. He picked up a file from the pull-out shelf beside him and opened it. He looked at Dave over the top of it. "Now, tell me what Natalie Hill, deceased, has to with your murder."

Dave's fingers itched. He would give anything to look at that file. Maybe if he was convincing enough, the detective would let him see it. He leaned forward, his elbows on his knees. "Natalie Hill was born on this property in McCord County thirty years ago. Illegitimate, father unknown. Her mother brought her to New York when she was five. Wanted to make her an actress. Left behind on the property was Minnie Hill, Natalie's old maid aunt. When Rebecca Hill, Natalie's mother, died in a mental institution, Minnie came to New York to live with Natalie. But then Natalie was killed in an accident and Minnie died in a nursing home. That leaves the property in limbo. Nobody knows who owns it. The taxes are paid by a forwarding service here in New York."

Dave watched the heavy detective flip pages in the file. There were several clippings from a newspaper. The pig eyes looked up at the silence. Dave leaned back and continued.

"So what does all this have to do with my murder? I think that the murderer and Natalie Hill's father are one and the same. He's living on this property, and has been for thirty years, and the only person to see him, he killed."

"Whoa! Right there! How in the hell can a man hide for thirty years and nobody see him?"

"This place is unbelievable, Detective. It hasn't been touched in thirty years. Not a bush or a tree cut. It is completely grown up in thorns and weeds. It's 900 acres of wilderness that is virtually impassable."

"What's the land worth?"

"At a thousand dollars an acre, almost a million."

"Worth killing someone over, I guess," Joncik said.

"Most definitely."

"I investigated Natalie Hill's accident ten years ago," Joncik went on. "I wanted to upgrade it to homicide since it was hit and run, but I was overruled. There was something about it that bothered me. But we were covered with other cases, and it got pushed aside."

"What was it that bothered you?" Dave asked.

"The fact that we could find out very little about the woman. We didn't even have a picture of her, and her face was virtually destroyed in the accident. So we had nothing. It was like somebody wiped out her past. She had a few co-workers at the stock exchange, but they hardly knew her. A man who said he was a friend, identified her body. A Ben Jamison."

"Where did she live?"

Detective Joncik flipped back to the first page and read the address to Dave. It went into the little book in his shirt pocket. Also printed indelibly on his mind.

"And this Jamison man who identified her?"

"I've looked for him since, but he has disappeared."

"So you think she was murdered, not just run over in an accident?"

"Did I say that?" Joncik asked, his little eyes glittering in the folds of flesh that was his face.

"Not in so many words," Dave grinned.

"And what about your murder? Was it made to look like an accident?"

"Oh, no. The man who was killed had gone onto the Hill farm to try to capture this man who is living there. He had fought with him earlier when he caught him around his house at night."

"You said earlier that this man was possibly Natalie Hill's father? That right?" Joncik said, getting up and walking around behind the desk.

"That was my theory," Dave said defensively.

"So, if Natalie was dead, he could claim the property, or at least nobody would be alive who could claim it. Right?"

"I guess so. But how could he have gotten to New York to kill Natalie Hill?" Dave asked.

"The same way you did."

"Then all he would have to do would be to follow her around and wait for the chance to run over her."

"You country boys ain't all dumb. You got it! Makes sense, don't it?"

"Except for one thing," Dave said.

"What's that?"

"How did he get the property in his name if Natalie was dead and Minnie was in a nursing home?"

"You ever hear of forgery?" Joncik asked sarcastically. Then he grinned. "If he's crazy, he's probably smart, too. Most of them are, I've found."

"You said you didn't have a picture of Natalie Hill. Do you have a description?"

"I've got the coroner's description. It's kind of gruesome, but it will have to do. You want a copy?"

"Please, Sir."

"You country boys say please and sir a lot, don't you?" Joncik said as he walked around Dave and out the door to the copy machine in the hall. When he came back, he laid two pieces of paper on Dave's lap. The fact sheet he had on Natalie. Dave scanned it. It had the address of the nursing home where Minnie Hill had died. That was the only other address he needed. He rose to go. He stuck out his hand.

"Well, Detective Joncik, you have helped me tremendously, and I appreciate it."

"You may have helped me, Detective Warren. I might get this case reopened. Might solve a murder here while you solve one in Tennessee. Give me something. Where I can get in touch with you." He held out his hand to Dave. Dave fished in his pocket for one of his cards that he had brought to New York for this purpose. As he handed it to Joncik, he decided to tell the truth.

"I haven't gotten a place to stay here, yet. And if you call the Sheriff and ask him about me, he'll tell you that I am no longer one of his people."

Joncik's eyebrows came up and he stopped in mid-stride. "You better explain that."

"The Sheriff refuses to believe that this man lives on this Hill Place. He has arrested another person for this murder. All he wants out of it is a conviction. He doesn't care if he has the right person or not."

"You telling me the truth, boy?"

"Yes, Sir!"

"And this person who is accused of murder. You working for them?"

"Yes, sir."

"Who is it?"

"The wife of the murder victim."

Joncik's eyes got even more recessed in his fat head. He looked at Dave, doubt beginning to show in his face. He opened his mouth but Dave answered the question before it was asked.

"I'm in love with her. We got something going."

****

The building at 235 East 73rd Street was beginning to be run down. The apartment number that Dave had, indicated the Hills once lived on the third floor. He hoped to find someone around who had lived there when Natalie Hill was alive.

Dave sat in his car, actually Natalie Dunn's car, and studied the building. He thought it ironic that one Natalie could hold the key to the freedom of the other. A dead Natalie could set free the very much alive Natalie.

His eyes brightened as the front door to the building opened and an old woman stepped out, pulling a small cart. She headed up the street toward the market Dave had seen about three blocks away. Dave got out of the car and locked the doors. He ran across the street and approached the woman from the rear. He let his feet scuff noisily, as he didn't want to frighten her. He had his billfold with the badge showing in his hand.

"Pardon me, Ma'am. I'm Detective Dave Warren," he said, holding the badge up toward the woman. He saw no need to tell her that he was not on the New York Police Department.

"Oh, officer! You scared me. I thought I was going to get mugged again."

"Again?"

"For the fifth time. You don't know how horrible it is getting around here. Why, just yesterday I saw the most loathsome creature loitering around our building. Officer, it's getting so..."

"You don't mind if I walk to the market with you, do you? Here, let me carry the cart." Dave cut the woman off and reached for the handle on the two wheeled cart.

"Oh, not at all. Why just the other day..." the voice blended into the street noise and the abstract thoughts and voices running through Dave's brain. He walked with the woman who never stopped talking. He followed her into the market and pulled the cart while she shopped. She talked to the produce, the shelves, the floor, the fish. Anything that would listen, she talked to it. And Dave prayed.

Prayed that she had lived in the building when Natalie Hill was there. Prayed that if she had, she would talk about her the same way she talked about everything else.

Dave pulled the cart back toward the apartment building, heavier now with its load of groceries. As they neared the front door, Dave knew that he had to broach the subject soon. If he could find an open spot in the stream of words that flowed out of the old woman's mouth. She drew in a breath and Dave cut in.

"I'm interested in a woman named Natalie Hill. Were you living in this building when she lived here?"

"You're not from here, are you?"

"No, ma'am. I'm not."

"Does Detective Joncik know you are snooping around here?"

"Yes, ma'am, as a matter of fact, he does. I've talked to him today."

"Where are you from, young man?"

"Tennessee."

"And you're interested in Natalie Hill?"

"That's where she was originally from. Before she moved to New York."

"I wish to the Lord she had stayed there. You don't know the trouble that woman caused in this building. Why, just the other day…"

"Ma'am, could we go inside and talk about this. You can call Detective Joncik and he'll tell you I'm all right."

"I'm going to call him from the lobby. You wait right here." The woman inserted the key to the front door and quickly stepped through the heavy door as it slammed behind her. Dave stood on the sidewalk and looked down at the cart of groceries. He looked around at his surroundings. On the streets of New York. He couldn't believe that he was here trying to solve a murder in Tennessee by solving one in New York that happened ten years ago."

"Bring that cart in. Al says you are okay."

"Al?"

"Al Joncik. He says you are to call him as soon as you find out anything."

"Have you talked to Joncik about Natalie Hill?" Dave asked as he followed her to the elevator.

"I did ten years ago when she was killed. That's the last anybody's asked me anything about it, until now."

The universal silence of elevators that no one dared break, held sway over the old woman. But it was short lived as her mouth started again when the doors opened on the third floor.

"Al said for me to call him when you left and for you to come back by the precinct when you left. To protect you."

Dave looked up and down the hall as they walked to her door.

"Which apartment did Natalie Hill live in?"

"Number 302. Down there on the left."

As the little old woman that Dave didn't even know the name of inserted her key in the apartment across from the elevator, Dave saw that she would have had a clear view of 302's door from her apartment. And she was right across from the elevator so she could see anyone coming and going on this floor.

Dave pulled the cart into the apartment as the woman held the door for him, and then shut and bolted it behind him. Her mouth began again once she was safely within the confines of her abode and Dave just listened, hoping she would answer his questions without them being asked. As he walked by the telephone table he looked down at the phone bill lying next to the old black telephone. "Gloria Schuburt" was the name on the front of the envelope.

Evidently Natalie Hill had been the subject of much concern to Gloria. And the object of much scorn. Dave wanted to call her name to see if he had it right.

"Mrs. Schuburt, did Natalie Hill ever talk about a farm in Tennessee?"

"That woman never talked to me, period. She yelled at her mother and then her Aunt Minnie. But, she never talked to me. I knew too much about all her shenanigans."

"Oh, she was a rounder, huh?"

"I don't know what that is, but she drove her poor mother crazy. Wouldn't do a thing the woman wanted. They weren't relatives of yours, were they?"

"Oh, no ma'am. I didn't know them. I'm just trying to find out what happened to the farm in Tennessee."

"Well, I wish they had stayed in Tennessee and fought there instead of coming up here to fight. A girl who had the talent she had, and then to throw it away so she could be a business woman, ought to be ashamed. And then to drive her mother to an early grave like she did. Sinful, that's what it is. Sinful."

"What talent did she have?"

"Acting. She could have been the most famous actress this city ever had. Her mother had books full of pictures showing the awards and contests she had won, but she threw it all away and drove her poor mother crazy."

"Did you talk to Rebecca Hill?"

"Every day of her life until they carried her away and put her in that place for crazy people." Gloria Schuburt talked as she worked, putting in cabinets the things she had bought. She grunted and strained as she reached and stretched, but she never stopped talking.

Dave looked for something to do to help her, but she bustled around and never seemed to need any help.

"Why, just the other day, I was saying to my poor departed Leonard, God rest his soul, that I was glad he had left this world and didn't have to see how that girl treated her poor mother. He died before I moved in this building thirteen years ago."

"Did Rebecca ever give you a picture of Natalie?"

"Oh, heavens, no! Everything she had of Natalie's was sacred to her. She had awards and pictures and ribbons and clippings about all the things Natalie had done. When she came over here, she always brought her picture album but she never took anything out of it."

"What happened to all the things?"

"Gone. Trashed. Everything burned. That girl got rid of everything when poor Mrs. Hill died."

"Mrs. Hill?"

"She was a widow. I never met her husband. She said her poor Isaiah died and left her like my Leonard did me. She's probably turning over in her grave thinking about her daughter burning everything she ever owned in this world."

"And she got rid of all her mother's effects when she died?"

"I watched the trash man carry out six barrels of her mother's things. Six, mind you. Everything the poor woman treasured, she took out and burned. But by then she was on dope, so nothing she did surprised me."

"Dope? Natalie used drugs?" Dave asked.

"When all your friends are dope heads, what do you expect? She overdosed once and somebody called the police and they came and got her. I'm just glad her poor mother, God rest her soul, was gone and didn't have to see it."

"She overdosed on drugs?"

"Her boyfriend was with her but he left before the police got here. I saw him sneaking out of the apartment. He must have called the police. You want me to make you some coffee? I'm going to have some anyway, so you might as well."

Dave watched her start the coffee. He grinned to himself at the chubby little woman. He felt like he was performing a good deed, giving her a chance to talk to someone. Evidently, no one else would listen.

"Did you tell Detective Joncik all this?"

"Heaven knows I tried, but he wouldn't listen. I tried to tell him she was a dope head, but he said no drugs were found in her body when she was killed, so she must have kicked the habit. I figured her boy friend just hadn't brought her any dope the night she was killed."

"What was his name?"

"I heard her call him Van. He wound up dead in an alley. Then when her weird friend Ben came and told her, she went crazy."

"Natalie went crazy?"

"As a Cossack. She screamed and threw things at the poor man. Then she left here screaming and him chasing her. He must have chased her into the path of a car because she never came back. I peeked out my door when I heard the yelling and running. If her mother, God rest her soul, could have seen her in those tacky cut off jeans and halter top, she would have screamed."

"Maybe that was the whole problem."

"What?"

"Her mother screaming at her."

"Let me tell you something, young man. That woman, God rest her soul, lived for that girl. She wanted nothing but the best for her.

She spent her whole life trying to get that Natalie to be something, and what did she do? Thumbed her nose at her and got herself run over because she was too doped up to get out of the way of a car."

"I thought you said Joncik said no drugs were found in her body?"

"Well, the body that left here that night was so high she could hardly walk."

"Did the police call you to identify the body?"

"Detective Joncik showed me a picture of her on the table, all laid out and dead. It almost made me sick. Her head had been run over and all. But it was her all right. Al showed me the locket she had been wearing when she was killed. It belonged to her mother and had poor Rebecca's picture in it, God rest her soul." The old woman paused as if remembering something strange. And it was. "But that's what is so strange. She hated her mother, God rest her soul, and then was wearing one of her lockets when she died."

"She probably felt bad about the way she treated her when she was alive."

"I hope the poor girl repented before she went to her grave. Otherwise, she'll wind up in the devil's hell."

Before Dave realized it, Mrs. Schuburt was putting pots on the stove and pans in the oven and the smell of cooking starting permeating the kitchen where he was sitting. He stood up, starting to protest the effort she was making on his behalf, but she stopped him before he spoke.

"My Leonard, God rest his soul, wanted me to cook a hot meal every night, and I still do, in his memory. Then I eat what's left over the next day. Are you tired, young man? Your eyes are drooping."

"I haven't had much sleep in the last few days," Dave said. He grinned at Mrs. Schuburt. He wondered if poor departed Leonard had ever gone to sleep while she was talking. He had probably been dead for several days before she ever noticed. If her talking made him as tired as it made Dave, he probably ate many a meal in the same sort of trance that Dave ate in. Eating and nodding and grunting a few words here and there.

When it was finally over and time for him to go, he promised her that he would call her and write her and visit her and do anything else she wanted. If she would just please let him get away. She made him promise to go back by the precinct and see Detective Joncik.

It was late when Dave walked up the steps to the police building and went in. The duty sergeant said he thought Joncik was still in his office. He heard Joncik's voice telling him to come on back. He had the most wicked grin on his face when Dave walked into his office.

"Tell me everything Mrs. Schuburt told you about Natalie Hill," Joncik said as he leaned back in his chair and lit the cigar between his teeth.

"I thought you weren't supposed to smoke in here," Dave said as he sat down.

"Chief's gone. You gonna tell him I lit up?"

"Oh, no. You might punish me by making me go live with Mrs. Schuburt."

The throaty, cigar smoke infested laugh rumbled from Joncik's chest. Dave wondered how often the man laughed. Probably not often, judging by the head that popped in the door and asked, "You all right? I heard a strange sound coming from in here."

"Get outta' here, Neuman. Can't you see I'm busy," Joncik yelled at the head, picking up a paperweight to throw at the heckler.

"That woman is something else, isn't she? But she was my only source for any background on Natalie Hill. And all she could tell me about her was she lived across the hall from her. She knew nothing about her past."

"I don't suppose anybody does, now," Dave said. He decided not to tell Joncik anything that Mrs. Schuburt had told him. If he wanted to know, he could suffer through it the way he had. The only thing he wanted from Joncik was a look at the picture of Natalie Hill that he had showed the poor Mrs. Schuburt. Joncik pitched it across the desk when he asked for it. It was horrible. A naked, dead woman on a table in the morgue. Her head crushed in by the tire of an automobile.

Then his head began to spin. What was it? What made the woman on the table look like his Natalie back home? The vision of Natalie lying beside him on Ritchie's bed came back to him. It transposed itself over the picture of Natalie Hill on the slab. His fingers trembled. He quickly threw the picture back to Joncik before he got sick and threw up.

"You any closer to finding the man who killed her and who killed your man in Tennessee?" Joncik asked as he blew a billowing cloud of blue smoke toward the ceiling.

"What about her boyfriend, Van? Mrs. Schuburt said he was found dead in an alley. That right?"

Joncik's eyes narrowed. He gave Dave a questioning look. "There was a man killed that same night, but no one told us he was Natalie Hill's boyfriend. It appeared to be a drug killing and it was soon forgotten. We never IDed the man because he had no identification on him."

"Mrs. Schuburt told me she had heard Natalie call him Van and he was killed the same night Natalie was. Maybe somebody was eliminating anyone and everyone who knew or had dealings with Natalie Hill," Dave said. "Tell me, Detective. How would I go about finding out what happened to Minnie Hill's estate after she died? I think if I can find out what happened to the property, see her will, if it had ever been probated, find out who the property went to when she died, we'll find out who killed Natalie Hill. And maybe Van, too."

"That's it!" Joncik exploded, slapping his hand down hard on the desk. Dave heard feet scramble in the big room outside as the sudden noise echoed from Joncik's office. "Why didn't I think of that?" He lumbered to the door of the office and yelled at one of men outside. "Neuman! Get in here!"

The heckler appeared at the door, breathless. He must be the new man on the force, Dave thought.

"Neuman! A woman dies in a nursing home. Two months later her only heir dies in a car accident. What happens to everything they owned?" Joncik turned to Dave with a rare grin and said, "Neuman's our hot-shot lawyer turned cop. We ask him everything. That right, Neuman?"

"Right. Did she have a will?"

"Don't know. I haven't touched this angle before. I'm working on a ten year old murder. This woman died two months after her mother died."

"You'll have to start in probate court, trace her will, find out if she had any property, request..."

"Whoa, Neuman! Not me! You! I want you to start on it in the morning."

"It will take a while."

"An innocent woman's life hangs in the balance, Neuman. You want to be responsible for that?"

"What's her name, Joncik? I'll start tomorrow." Neuman held out his hand for the file Joncik was pushing his way.

"Now, what were you asking about how you could find out something around here?" Joncik said as he lowered himself back into his chair.

"How long do you think it will take?" Dave asked.

"About a third of the time it would take you if you tried to get anything out of the public servants in this city."

"I don't doubt that," Dave said as he rose form his chair. "Now, I've got to find a cheap place to spend the night, and a telephone."

"You can use that phone right there," Joncik said as he stood up.

"I have to call Tennessee."

"If it has to do with this case, I can log it in as an expense."

Dave walked around the desk and picked up the phone and dialed Ritchie's office number. Joncik reached over and punched the speaker button. Dave knew that the conversation coming up would be Joncik's way of checking his credentials. They better be good. Ritchie's secretary answered.

"Osborne Law Office."

"Pat, this is Dave Warren. Is Ritchie in?"

"Oh, oh yes! Where have you been? Just a minute."

Dave grinned at Joncik. "Kinda' excited, wasn't she?"

"Dave! Where have you been?" Ritchie's voice came on high and nervous sounding.

"Ritchie! You don't drive to New York in a couple of hours. I was on the road all day yesterday and last night. I've been up all day tracing Natalie Hill. What are you so excited about?"

"The trial is starting tomorrow. We picked the jury today."

"What happened? It wasn't scheduled before three weeks when I left."

"The Sheriff pushed the judge to move it up. He must have known you left town. And you know Heartburn."

"Oh no, Ritchie! We're nowhere near ready. They can't do this! It'll take me a week to track down that guy in the woods."

"It'll be over by then. Heartburn said he was going to allow three days for the trial. No more."

"Three days? It'll take me a day to get home!"

"Have you found out anything?" Ritchie asked anxiously.

"I just got here, Pal. But the police have been helpful. They're going to trace Minnie Hill's property disposal for me. Save me a lot of time. But I've got to get back. I can't wait. I can't even do anything else. I've got to get on the road now." Dave's voice quivered as he thought about the urgency of the task in front of him. Ritchie must have caught the note of despair.

"Take heart, Dave. We got three women on the jury. That's something in our favor."

"Did you try to get Heartburn to delay starting the trial, Ritchie?"

"I told him you were in New York following up on an extremely important lead, and that the results could be crucial to our case."

"What did he say?"

"Said he couldn't allow a wild goose chase to postpone this trial."

"That idiot!" Dave exploded. He looked over at Joncik who was listening intently to the conversation that was filling the room.

"The Sheriff told the judge that he had enough evidence to convict, no matter what we came up with. He said it was the most open and shut murder case he had ever seen," Ritchie went on.

"If I could lead that wild man in front of the jury, it would be open and shut," Dave said.

"You just get back down here and find him," Ritchie pled.

"I'm on my way. See you tomorrow. I'll drive all night." Dave hung up. He looked over at Joncik. He had his brow furrowed. The folds of fat on his forehead etching deep lines above his eyes. He looked at Dave as the phone clicked down into its receiver.

"What makes you so sure this man is in the woods on this property?" he asked Dave.

Dave jerked his shirt up and snatched his tee shirt out of his pants. His smooth, hairless belly shone in the fluorescent light in the office. The healing red gash around his middle leaped out at Joncik's eyes, and they got big with wonder.

"Because he almost got me the same way he did this woman's husband."

"Dear mother! What did he use on you?"

"A six foot long spear. Just like a wild man from the jungles of New Guinea."

"Or the streets of New York," Joncik said, shaking his head in disbelief.

Chapter 29

Dave was dead. His mind had ceased to function. He had almost killed himself and twelve or seventeen other people. He couldn't remember, or care. All he knew was he had to get home. To Natalie. When Ritchie said the trial was starting the next day, Dave slowly felt himself going numb. The hours with Mrs. Schuburt had started the deadening, like body blows softening up a fighter. Then the word from Ritchie that the trial had been moved up, was like the left hook to the head.

Dave's head dropped forward onto his chest. The sudden snapping action brought him out of it. He jerked the car back from the shoulder into the right hand lane.

"Damn!" he screamed into the windshield. He slapped himself viciously on the side of the face. He had actually been asleep for several seconds. He looked at his watch. He still had three hours to Nashville, and he was going to have to pull over and nap one more time. Then he could drive on in. But the first day of the trial would be over. And he had wasted three days on the road, to and from New York, and hadn't discovered a cotton picking thing. Three days he could have been tracking down the man in the woods behind

Natalie's house. But maybe Detective Joncik would discover something. Dave couldn't believe how helpful the man had been. He had been expecting the New York police to treat him like a red headed step child. Just ignore him. But he did have a little to offer them. He might have helped them solve a ten year old murder.

Natalie Hill. He thought of her. He had wanted to visit her old haunts. See the things she had seen. Walk some of the halls she had walked, and talk to someone who had known her. But Judge Heartburn had brought an abrupt halt to that.

****

Natalie stared at Judge Mashburn with eyes that wished to kill. And she would have if she could have gotten by with it. The judge had, for the third time, brought an abrupt halt to Ritchie's objection to the opening remarks of the prosecutor. This time he slammed the gavel as he roared at Ritchie.

"Counselor! I told you that you can't object to the opening remarks. Now sit down and let the prosecution finish."

"But Your Honor. The remarks are inflammatory and completely unfounded. He's simply trying to rile up the jury."

"Overruled! Osborne, one more word out of you and I'll hold you in contempt!"

Ritchie sat down and smiled at the jury, then rose half way from his seat and bowed slightly to Judge Mashburn.

"Thank you, Your Honor," he said in the sweetest voice he could summon.

"Thank you, Your Honor," the assistant district attorney said to the judge while smiling sweetly at Ritchie. "Now, I will continue." He turned to the jury.

"As I was saying, we will prove beyond a shadow of a doubt that this vicious and sadistic woman murdered her husband and then took this stick, which she had sharpened on both ends, and ran it through his body in an attempt to make it look like an accident." He picked up a three foot long hickory stick and waved it over his head.

Ritchie turned to Natalie and put his hand on her arm. "What about cold blooded and heartless? He didn't mention those two attributes of yours."

Natalie looked at him and dead panned back. "Yes, and he forgot merciless and contemptible."

George Emmons was sitting in the first row of seats, just behind the rail that separated the spectators from the participants of the trial. He was close to the table where Ritchie and Natalie were sitting. He heard the exchange. He leaned forward and said to Ritchie, "Don't forget hardhearted and ruthless."

Judge Mashburn's gavel pounded the bench in front of him. "Quiet back there or I'll clear the courtroom." George sat quickly back in his seat and buried his head in his notebook, writing furiously.

"Ritchie did his half rise and bow to the bench. "We're sorry, Your Honor. We were just discussing our opening remarks. Trying to come up with some colorful adjectives to compete with the prosecutor's choice of words."

Judge Mashburn raised his gavel, but then slowly dropped it. He didn't know what to make of Ritchie's statement. He turned to the prosecutor and opened his mouth, but the little short, fat assistant DA was standing close to Ritchie and Natalie, so Ritchie spoke quickly to him.

"You may continue, counselor. I believe we've got you down for merciless and ruthless next."

The man turned to the jury and smiled his sweet smile. "The defense seems to think that this trial is all one big joke. Something funny. But I can assure you ladies and gentlemen of the jury, that this is no joke. A murder has been committed, and we intend to prove that this woman did, willfully and with malice, kill her husband."

He turned and pointed at Natalie who fixed him with the stare that she had reserved for the judge. She just switched it to him. His words seemed to fade in and out, coming from a distant place, one she could never visit. Could never hope to put on her itinerary, since the people of that place were imaginary and the words they spoke were fabrications and lies.

Natalie suddenly lurched forward in her chair. The movement was so swift and noticeable that every eye in the courtroom looked in her direction. But she was already past the recognition stage. She shut her eyes to the world around her and moved into her inner self. She picked up the yellow pencil in front of her and bent over the pad before her. The pencil moved quickly from line to line as the words she wanted so desperately to say flowed down from the graphite core inside the cedar stick onto the stark white pages. Like blood flowing from a puncture wound, the words came from her, some of them completely unrecognizable even to her. But they were her. They told her story better than any pair of lips ever could. And the droning of the prosecutor's voice seemed to enhance the quality of the sentences coming from her. Making an overriding barrier to shield her from the harsh realities of the world.

The words of the assistant DA were real. The stuff of her world. From the time she was a child, somebody had been trying to hurt her. With words, with emotions, with other instruments of destruction they had been thrusting at her. Before, she had always taken as much as she possibly could, and then had just walked or run away. She had never been able to fight back, until recently. With Jeff. And lastly with Dave. But she had discovered that the best and most efficient way for her to fight, was with her fingers. Wrapped around a pen or pencil. Or pounding on a typewriter. She could slap the face of an opponent as her fingers punished the battered keys of her typewriter. The scene when she had slapped Dave Warren's face came floating back to her, and she smiled. It must have been an appropriate time, because the court room erupted in laughter at that very moment.

Natalie raised her head and gazed around, but the moment was lost on her, and she quickly bent back to the task that was pressing her for completion. Like a funnel full of sand, she had to empty herself. If something stuck inside the spout where the words were flowing out, a kick or a tap on the side would dislodge the blockage and start the flow again. Because the sense of nonfulfillment was such that Natalie could not bear to stop short of the emptying of the funnel, she pressed herself onto the paper in an effort to squeeze the last drop of blood from her soul. The pages flipped themselves as they became full of Natalie. When the ordeal was finally over, a drop of sweat glistened on the end of her nose and she raised the hand that held the pencil to wipe it away.

Ritchie was leaning forward on his folded arms, his head turned toward her, watching her face, not the paper. Her eyes came to rest on his as she felt the fever of the past few minutes recede. Felt the slow reawakening of her physical body, coming out of the cocoon that her mind had wrapped around her.

"What are you staring at?" she quietly asked him.

"I don't know. I simply don't know," he said, almost absentmindedly.

"I was out of it for a few minutes," she softly said. She took her hand and turned the pad over so that the words she had written could not be seen.

"What were you writing?"

"Nothing. Well, just my reflections on the proceedings of the day. Just mind wanderings. Nothing important."

"Well, what's coming up is important. I am going to give our opening statement. At the moment I am consulting with you." Ritchie lowered his voice. "Remember, everyone in this courtroom is looking at us. So I want you to smile. Look happy. When I get up to talk to the jury, I want you to follow me with your eyes. Then look at each member of the jury in a pleasant way. These people are your friends. Remember that."

Ritchie stood up and strolled over to the jury box. It was on a platform, elevated about a foot off the floor. The jurors were looking down at him, especially the ones in the back rows.

"Ladies and gentlemen of the jury," Ritchie began. This was his first trial and a lot of his performance was going to have to come directly from his training and from his viewing of Perry Mason and Matlock.

"See that woman there at the defense table?" He turned and pointed at Natalie. All eyes of the jurors were on Natalie. Her own dark eyes glistened as she watched Ritchie, just as he had told her to do. The pale pink dress with the blue and red flowers scattered through it, seemed to set off her brown hair. Red highlights flickered through it as she moved her head, following Ritchie around the room. The dress, long sleeved with lace at the cuffs and neck, had been chosen by Ritchie. He had found out her size and gone to the dress shop and bought it himself. He wanted to emphasize her beauty and femininity, not her power and athletic ability. It worked for Ritchie. To him she looked charming and petite. He just hoped the jury thought the same. All he needed was for one of the men to fall in love with her.

"That woman was arrested for murder simply because she was born an orphan."

"Objection!" the prosecutor screamed, leaping to his feet. Judge Mashburn slammed his gavel and growled, "Counselor, confine your remarks to the facts of the case!"

"That's precisely my contention in making the statement I just made. There are no facts in this case. There is no evidence, whatsoever, to show that Mrs. Dunn killed her husband. She was arrested because she was born into this world a homeless orphan."

"Objection again, Your Honor!"

"Osborne, I'm warning you. The facts of the case."

"Your Honor, I'm making this fact of Mrs. Dunn's birth an issue in this case. There is no other explanation of why she was arrested. Furthermore, the prosecutor has no basis for objecting to my opening remarks. His were based purely on speculation and rumor."

"Objection and objection, Your Honor," the DA said, more subdued this time.

Ritchie then turned his back on Judge Mashburn and the prosecutor and leaned on the rail in front of the jury box. He lowered his voice and quietly said, "Do you get the impression that someone is trying to railroad the defendant? Maybe trying to make a name for themselves on a big murder case?" Ritchie nodded his head as he looked from one end of the box to the other.

"Speak up, Osborne. You must speak to the whole courtroom."

"I'm waiting for you to make a ruling on the prosecution's objection,

Your Honor," Ritchie said as he turned and leaned against the railing. He smiled at the judge. He had decided last night that he was going to make the judge mad at him. Do everything he could to antagonize him. Take the attention away from Natalie and focus it on himself. And in the process, maybe the jury would see how that his contention of Natalie being railroaded was valid. Especially after they saw how the judge was going to railroad him.

"Sustained!" Heartburn roared. It hadn't taken long. Ritchie smiled. He had already gotten to him.

"Thank you, Your Honor. No more mention will be made of Mrs. Dunn being born an orphan." Ritchie turned to the jury and bowed. "We will now talk about the evidence that the prosecution has against Mrs. Dunn." Ritchie stood in front of the jury and folded his arms. He shifted his weight from one foot to the other. He then put one elbow in the palm of his hand and rested his chin in the palm of the other. He let his shoulders hunch forward and his brow go furrowed as if in deep thought. He brought the hand that his chin had been resting in up to his head and scratched his going bald cranium. He turned to the bench with a quizzical look on his face and then turned back to the jury. A tittering of laughter started out in the spectator area and Ritchie could feel it coming toward the jury box. Before he could say anything to the jury, the judge broke the silence.

"Osborne! You are making a mockery of this proceeding. I am going to find you in contempt if you continue in this manner." Ritchie turned to the judge, the quizzical look coming back. He turned to the jury and opened his mouth and pointed his finger at the gaping hole. They laughed. Ritchie knew then, that he had them. They were on his side. He had succeeded in showing them that the judge was against him even when he didn't say anything. So he knew he had gone far enough. It was time to get serious.

"Your Honor, I apologize. I was simply trying to recall the evidence against Mrs. Dunn. I remember now. An insurance policy and a stick."

The rest of Ritchie's opening statement was general in tone. About how a 115 pound woman could not have possibly carried a 225 pound man the distance involved. And there was no evidence of the body being dragged.

Natalie sat through it all, her slim arms propped up, her hands under her chin. She looked from Ritchie to the judge, sensing the play between the two. She was going to enjoy the confrontation. She almost felt like an observer, not a participant. She became drawn into the web that Ritchie was spinning between himself and the judge. She could feel the glare that Mashburn was casting down on her lawyer. She knew what Ritchie was doing. Playing the clown, the picador, dancing in front of the bull, drawing away his attention and his strength. And the ease with which he did, brought gladness to her heart. She knew he would win. At least the confrontation with the judge. He was much too sharp for him, that she could tell.

What she wasn't sure of winning was the minds of the jurors. She knew what delicate balances her life was held in. But Ritchie knew these people. He was talking to them, each and every member of the jury. Not down at them or over their heads. Dead in the eye. That's the way he approached them. And he was making her a real person. Making the jury aware that it would be her going to prison if they voted guilty. Sweet, innocent little ole Natalie. She smiled at the thought of her being considered for the sweet and innocent category. Ritchie pointed to her just as she smiled, and the jury all laughed as a whole.

Ritchie may not have been through, but he chose that moment to cease. He turned to the judge and informed him that his opening statement was over. He had the jury laughing. What more could he want?

Judge Mashburn looked at his watch and then over at the prosecutor. A slight nod of the DAs head and the judge slammed his gavel down. "Court is adjourned until eight tomorrow. We will begin with the state's case."

Ritchie and Natalie stood as Heartburn left the bench and disappeared into the hallway behind the courtroom. While Ritchie was stuffing papers into his brief case, Natalie turned and looked at the sparse crowd left in the huge courtroom. Jeff's mother and father were the first ones she saw. And then his brother and sister. She hadn't seen them since Jeff had been killed. She had been in jail at the time of the funeral. She had simply dismissed them from her mind, along with Jeff. Now they were here. All four glaring at her, accusing with their eyes.

The Dunn family had never liked Natalie. Partially because they had never known her. Jeff had married her so suddenly, they hadn't time to prepare for her. He had simply brought her home one day and told them they were getting married. Later Natalie had caught the tail end of a conversation as she came out of the bathroom and walked by the bedroom where Jeff's mother and sister were huddled. "...picked her up in a diner where she was a floozy little waitress."

Natalie never forgave Mrs. Dunn for that pre-judgment. The tone of those words came back to her as she looked at the Dunn family standing in the McCord County courthouse. She turned to Ritchie and said quietly, "Jeff's parents are in the audience. I don't want to walk out past them."

"You don't have to, Dear Lady," Ritchie said with a swirl. He took her arm and swiftly led her to the door through which Judge Mashburn had disappeared. A quick turn left and then another right and down a set of steep back stairs, and they were in the hallway below, standing next to the door leading out to the wheelchair ramp. Ritchie pushed the door open and they trotted up the ramp that led to the yard on the north side of the courthouse.

"How was that for a quick escape?" he said as he pointed her toward his office on the west side of the square. She smiled at him as he took her arm and pushed her across the double lane of traffic and up the steps to the sidewalk in front of his office. When they were inside, she collapsed in the big stuffed chair across from his desk. She let her head fall back. She allowed herself to relax for the first time in eight hours. The scenes from the day in court rolled through her mind. Good scenes, making her feel nice about her chances. She dozed as the cares melted away.

The scritch, scratch, scritch of Ritchie's pen on paper slowly seeped into her brain. Her eyelids fluttered and she became aware of where she was. It was growing dark and Ritchie had turned on his desk lamp. In a pool of light much like a miner's helmet light in a pitch black coal mine, his head bobbed and weaved over the paper as he furiously wrote. All she could see of him was the top of his head, his shoulders, and his hand. He reminded her of a schoolboy hunkered over a difficult assignment. She knew he was lost in thought so she closed her eyes and allowed the scratching noise of the writing instrument to calm her.

Her mind drifted to Dave Warren. Was she in love with him? The question came to her. And then the bigger question came. Had she ever been in love? Did she know how to love? What she did know was, she fought it. She felt herself feeling something for Dave Warren, and as soon as she recognized what was happening, she began fighting. But it hadn't worked. Something about him had captured her. She felt a hot flush of embarrassment as she thought of how easily she had gone to bed with him. But something more than physical had taken over. She could remember how she felt the first time. A powerful need to surrender, to submit. And then to take hold and over power, all at the same time.

But she didn't know how to pigeon hole the feeling and stick it in the love section. She felt her hands clinch, making fists. The frustration at not being able to sort through the jumble of her feelings and come up with the one that she could stretch out in front of her and run her hand over and say to herself, "This is the one. This is how I feel and this is how I am going to be."

A prayer sprang to her lips and she had the strange feeling that she had never before in her entire life, prayed, but somehow it was a natural and easy thing to do. Silently she spoke to the listener of the universe, knowing within her heart that she needed help, and that out there somewhere, wherever, there was One. Of all the trillions of miles she had travelled, passing through the millions of worlds that existed in time, both before and after, of all the disorder and confusion that seemed to leap out from every dark hole she passed, of all this multitude of deities and gods that man had let creep into his thinking, each one competing with the other for the soul's affection, there had to be a Oneness. Otherwise man was doomed.

Natalie suddenly realized that she had to find this Oneness. That was her task. If it involved Dave Warren, then so be it. She felt the shadow of the task coming over her, descending from the throne somewhere up above. Dank, musty breath assailed her as she realized that the gods were trying to kiss her.

"Hello, Sleeping Beauty," came from the mouth as she opened her eyes to look into the pale blue eyes of Dave Warren.

"Oh, Dave! You're back! She flung her arms around his neck, loving the warm glow the feeling gave her. The feeling of making someone happy. And there was no doubt that the reception Dave got made him happy. He pulled her from the chair and wrapped his arms around her, crushing her to him. Then he pushed her to arms length, holding to her hands as he let his eyes travel over her.

"You look wonderful! I don't know how to tell you how good you look. But I do know that I missed you. And I love you."

Natalie was overwhelmed. The pure and utter pleasure of knowing that someone loved her simply for herself, was unbelievable. And it was obvious that Dave Warren didn't care what or who she was, or had ever been. He loved her. And would always do so. That saddened her. A slow, sure, creeping sadness that moved her to tears and to his arms.

The tears came, not because she knew she would leave him, but because she simply didn't know whether her heart would rule and tell her to stay, or her mind would take over and tell her to move on in the continuous search for her god.

"Dave," she began. "I simply can't begin to tell you what you mean to me. And I don't mean to avoid telling you that I love you. I just can't get it all sorted out just yet."

"Okay lovebirds. I'm in this room, too. Let's talk about a trial and evidence from New York. You two can bill and coo later." Dave looked at Ritchie and grinned. He hugged Natalie and looked down into her eyes. "Can you believe this guy? Here I am trying to make love to you and all he wants to talk about is a trial."

"If this trial doesn't come out right, you two will be making love through prison bars. How romantic does that sound?"

Dave dropped his arms from around Natalie and walked over to Ritchie's desk, still holding her hand.

"Sorry, Ritchie. How did it go today? Any surprises?"

"No, other than the prosecutor kept objecting to my opening statement, and Heartburn kept sustaining. But I think I've got the jury on my side. At least a couple of them.

"What do you need from me?"

"The killer. Did you find out anything in New York?"

"I had just gotten started when you told me the trial was starting. But I did talk to the woman who lived across the hall from Natalie Hill and her mother. And the police were real helpful. A Detective Joncik is tracing the disposition of the Hill property. Hopefully by tomorrow we'll know who the real owner is, and can put a name to the man out there."

"What we've got to do is put our hands on this man, Dave. I've been thinking about him." Ritchie looked at Dave and Natalie standing before him. They resembled two runaways seeking to get married. He pointed to the chairs in front of his desk. "You two get over there and sit down. You're making me nervous."

When they were seated, their hands still linking them, he started talking again.

"Now, as I was saying about this man. I don't think that his presence or name should be even brought up, unless we can produce him."

Dave leaped to his feet and a loud "wait a minute!" came screeching out of his mouth. Ritchie held up his hand like a traffic cop and started shaking his head at Dave.

"Sit down! Sit down! Dave, my good man, I know what I'm doing. Just listen to me. Then I'll listen to you. Now, I've outlined everything the state has against Natalie. It's pretty thin. I think we can create all kinds of doubt in the juror's minds about the validity of their evidence. But if we start talking about a wild man living in the woods back there behind her house, a man only seen by you two, the jury is going to start doubting us. We'll lose credibility and then they'll start to think that maybe the state does have a case. No! We can't chance it."

Dave was tired and he wasn't thinking too clearly, but his mind began to see what Ritchie was talking about. In fact, he had to finger the cut along his belly to keep reminding himself that he had actually fought with the man. It slowly dawned on him that it would be hard to convince anyone that the story wasn't farfetched.

"Then I guess I wasted my time going to New York, didn't I?"

"Oh, no. Something might happen and we'll have to go with the man back there. So we'll need to put a name on him even if we can't catch him. That is, if the New York police can trace the property." Dave's eyes started to droop. He jerked his head up from his chest as he nodded. He grinned at Natalie. "Very little sleep in the last three days." Then he turned to Ritchie. "So, what do you want us to do?"

"Now that you've put it in the plural, I'm going to say something that you two probably won't like." He stood up behind his desk so he could look down on each of them. "I don't think that anyone knows that you two spent the night at my place the other night. But if the prosecution thinks you two are sleeping together, they'll crucify any testimony you give, Dave."

Dave's face turned red and he stared straight ahead, refusing to look aside at Natalie. He could feel her hand loosen its pressure on his. Ritchie continued.

"So, no more. I don't know what kind of arrangements we need to make for you, Dave, but just stay away from Natalie."

"What about you? Doesn't it look bad, her staying in your house?"

"Whoa! Whoa! She's not staying with me. I guess we didn't tell you. I took her to one of my girlfriends' house. I know how people talk. I don't want the prosecutor to link any of us together."

"Then why can't I stay with you, Ritchie?"

"Is there any way you can go back to Betty Lou until this is over?"

"Absolutely not!" Dave shouted. He stood up and advanced on the desk. "I don't see anything wrong with me staying with you. What can they say about that?"

"That's just it, Dave. We don't want to give them a chance to say anything. It would just be better if we were all three separated."

Natalie spoke for the first time during the discussion. "You could stay in my house. Nobody would know you were there. You won't be in the house much anyway. And if anyone finds out, I'll lie and say the thought of you in my house makes me sick."

"There you go," Ritchie laughed at Natalie's comment. "You're going to be looking for our wild man anyway, aren't you?"

"I'm beginning to think that will be a waste of time."

"Why?"

"Because I don't think there is any way to capture that man alive. There won't be but one way to bring him in, and that's dead. But then again, I might not have to kill him."

"Why's that?"

"He might kill me first."

Chapter 30

Dave would have died. He realized that now. It was bad enough just thinking about the trial. It would be torture to have to sit there and listen to what was being said about his Natalie. His mind transported his body to the audience and allowed him to see himself watching the prosecutor accuse Natalie. It didn't surprise him in any way when he saw himself get up out of his seat in the spectator's area and walk slowly down the aisle, through the swinging doors and step up behind the man pointing a finger at Natalie. He saw himself calmly reach up, put his hands around his neck and choke him to death.

The dawn was coming. It was as slow as Dave's walk down the aisle. Until right before daylight. Then it would burst forth with such swiftness that it would be upon him before he could move. The objects around him, trees, bushes, fence posts, would be just dark shapes in the blackness. Then suddenly they would become lifelike as the pre dawn arrived, giving each object a shape that in no way resembled it in daylight. Fence posts became sentries. Small trees became knots of people talking, the leaves fluttering in the faint breeze became hands gesturing. The truck he'd borrowed from a buddy suddenly became a four eyed monster, the sound being supplied by the larger monsters on the interstate.

Dave lay on the knoll above the interstate on the Garrett place and tried to control his breathing. He knew that the dawn could fool him if he let his imagination run wild. He dropped his head into the leaves and thought about Natalie getting up this morning and preparing for the first day of her trial. If she had been like him, she would have slept fitfully, even though the body was tired and worn out.

She would be nervous, anticipating the day's events in the courtroom. But he had spent most of the night lying in Natalie's bed at her deserted house, going over in his mind how he was going to track down the man with the spear.

A dry stick snapped and Dave jerked his head up. Dark shapes loomed around him and he swiveled his head in all directions, looking for something which might be attacking him. The clumps of bushes and the trunks of trees danced in the darkness, but came no closer as he fended them off with his eyes.

But the snapping twig was real. Maybe it was a deer? He hoped it was. He didn't want to fight the wild man in the dark again.

As he had expected, the light came before he was ready. It surprised him with its brilliance. Especially after the intense darkness that had preceded it. He felt naked as the gray sky opened up like a camera lens and exposed him to any and all who could see. He looked slowly around his position at the top of the hill, hoping he was as well hidden in daylight as he thought he was at night. He was certain that anyone would have to step on him to find him.

The sun glinting off the antlers of the buck caught his eye. The big one he had been looking for was right in front of him. A huge buck that would easily field dress at 250 pounds, stood down the slope about fifty yards away. He was under the big oak tree, eating acorns that the tree had dropped in layers around its base.

Dave's mind raced but only his eyes moved. He knew any movement would be seen by the deer, and by the man if he was near. He knew that he had to begin now and concentrate on every move he made. A false move could result in death. But the most important thing lay not here with him. On Ritchie's shoulders rode the fate of Natalie.

Suddenly he was there. Like an apparition rising from the mists of Hell, he appeared down the slope from the deer, walking toward the buck with his hand outstretched. The deer watched him, wary, but not afraid. Not running away.

The man's shirt and pants hung in tatters on his scrawny body. His black hair was matted and long, hanging down around his shoulders. The beard covered his face and upper chest, giving him the appearance of only having eyes and a nose. His lower face and mouth was completely covered with the matted black beard.

Dave watched, fascinated, as the man approached the deer. He had no weapon that Dave could see. He was not trying to kill the buck. He was trying to tame it! The thought came to Dave so quickly that it surprised him. Taming a deer? But that's exactly what the man was doing. And it was evident that he had been working on it for some time. The buck sniffed the air repeatedly as the wild man approached. But he stood there. However, his legs were braced, ready to run at the slightest sign of danger.

Something was in the man's hand, and the deer snaked out his long neck, laying the antlers back along his shoulders. The man put out his hand and the deer's tongue came out, flicking at what looked to Dave like grain. After two bites the man moved a step away and waited with his hand outstretched. The deer moved toward it and took another two bites of the grain. Again the man moved back.

"He's trying to toll him. Trying to lead him," Dave said to himself as it dawned on him what was happening. He watched as the man would move two steps back and the buck would move two forward. One of the man's hands would slowly reach in his pocket and get more grain to replenish the supply in the open palm.

And then they were gone. The brush and low trees swallowed them as they moved down the slope toward the highway. Dave waited a few moments and then rose and moved in a crouch slowly down the hill toward where the man and deer had disappeared. Entering the bushes, he saw the v-shaped tracks in a bare spot and knew he was on the right trail. It led down into a small bowl in the earth where a tree had blown down years ago, the roots lifting out of the ground and forming a depression that looked like a man dug pit.

Dave froze. Just beyond the hollow in the ground, the man and deer had stopped. The deer unwilling to go any farther. The slope leading to I-65 was just ahead, and it appeared to Dave that the deer didn't want to step out into the open spot beyond the trees.

Dave slowly sank to his knees and watched as the man backed out into the opening. The interstate highway was far below and Dave knew no one in the traffic would look up and see the man and deer. Still the deer was hesitant. But the lure of the grain was too great and he slowly stepped out and walked toward the man who stood about ten feet down the bare slope.

Crawling on his hands and knees, Dave moved to the edge of the brush and watched the two animals. It was hard not to think of the man as something feral.

The air horn boomed loudly when a trucker pulled the cord as a car changed lanes in front of him. The sudden sound, even though the buck had heard it before, scared him. He threw himself to the side, almost stumbling, then scrambled toward a small outcropping of trees to his left, his sharp hooves throwing dirt toward the disappointed man.

Dave watched the wild man slowly return the grain to his pocket, and then turn and walk down the slope toward the interstate highway.

As the man sprinted toward the dark opening of the tunnel that ran under the road, Dave left the shelter of the trees and ran, slipping and sliding down the bare slope. He could see that the man was going to cross under the interstate and head back to the Hill Place.

"I'm going to follow you, Spear Chucker. We'll see how good you are," Dave muttered to himself as he scrambled down the hill. He was winded when he got to the bottom. He approached the tunnel cautiously and peeped around the opening and then quickly jerked back. He could see the shadowy form of the man crouched at the other end.

"He's waiting for a break in the traffic so he can leave without being seen," Dave thought. Then it hit him. He had seen the man that evening when his headlights had caught him as he was leaving the Garrett Place a few weeks back.

When Dave looked again into the tunnel, the man was gone. Dave quickly entered the darkness and ran stooped over to the other end. He was just in time to see the man flit from the last cedar bush into the thicker bushes beyond the open field.

In a running, tip-toeing jog, Dave crossed the field and entered the woods at the same spot the man had. As he rounded a slight curve in the path the man had chosen, Dave saw him up ahead, moving steadily forward. He constantly scanned the area in front of him but he never once looked behind. Evidently he had never thought about anyone following him. He was just being cautious about running into someone in front of him.

So Dave followed. He kept the man just barely in sight. Even though the man wasn't looking backward, Dave didn't want to be exposed if the man took a sudden glance along his back trail.

The man moved steadily, knowing exactly where he was going. He took routes that Dave would have had difficulty spotting.

Then the ground began rising and Dave knew that they were climbing the steep ridge that loomed behind Natalie's house. But they were skirting the open areas where the thick thorns and honey locusts grew. They were following a faint trail through the woods, moving steadily toward the top of the rocky and wooded ridge.

At one point the path ran in a straight line up through a rock outcropping, and Dave hung back at the bottom, not wanting to be exposed on the path until the man had gone over the top. When he finally got to the top of the outcropping, the man was gone. Dave took a chance, hoping he had turned right, continuing on up toward the summit. He raced as quickly and as quietly as he could and when he emerged at the top, he saw what he thought was a shadow turn off the trail to the left and start down the slope.

As he ran along the path that snaked along the top of the ridge, Dave realized that this was the path he had seen from the air the day he had flown over the Hill Place.

"That means the house with the tin roof is just below. I'll bet that is where my man is heading," he grunted.

When he got to the big tree where he had seen the man turn, he stopped. Looking around the trunk, he saw the man far down the hill, heading toward the house. He spun and looked back up the slope for the first time and Dave flattened himself against the rough bark of the tree.

Had he been seen? He didn't think so. The man probably just realized that he should look back over his shoulder. But Dave's mind raced. He didn't dare follow down the hill. The man could be lying in wait to see if anyone was doing just that.

"I'll just out wait him," Dave said to himself. He slid down the trunk to the ground and flattened himself on the dark earth beneath the tree at the top of the ridge. Ever so slowly he eased his head around the trunk at the base and looked down the slope. There was a small buck bush whose leaves he kept his face behind. His eyes searched the slope for any sign of movement. There was none.

The tin on the roof of the house shone dully as the sun rose in the sky. And still Dave waited. Unmoving. The man was probably used to waiting and watching, so Dave wasn't going to make the mistake of moving and letting the man see him.

The morning wore on and Dave eased his arm up to his face so he could see his watch.

"Two hours! I've been lying here two hours!" It was almost ten o'clock. Dave's senses had been on alert for the past five hours and he was beginning to feel the effects. But he knew he couldn't drop his guard. Evidently Jeff Dunn had made a mistake against this man. And look what it had gotten him. A spear rammed through his guts.

The sun popped through an opening directly over head and Dave looked at his watch again. It was noon. Evidently the man had not seen him, Dave thought. But either way, Dave was not going to take a chance. He began backing on his stomach away from the tree. He backed across the trail and into the woods on the other side. He slid down the ridge, keeping the trail in sight so he would know where he was. When he got to the bottom, he stood up and brushed off his clothes. He felt safe now. He had checked his back trail and didn't think the man was following him.

He began a swift, silent lope back along the path he had followed to the top, and by the time he reached the open field beside the interstate, he was sweating heavily. The coolness of the tunnel refreshed him, and when he emerged on the other side, he turned right and headed to where he knew the truck was parked. By the old milk barn.

As he ran he thought about Natalie. If he couldn't catch the man in time to present him as evidence in her defense, then the prosecution could very well convince the jury that she had killed her husband. He could hear the snickers from the state's lawyers if he tried to tell them about this man he had just followed. The safe and secure, government controlled, air conditioned world that people lived in today didn't even have a word for people like this man. The word "hermit" was used only in jokes and stories. Fairy tales and such as that. To convince people that he existed a few miles from their manicured lawns, would be impossible. The jury would look on it as the desperate attempt of a man in love to save his guilty lover.

On the way back to town he thought about the awaited phone call from New York. From Joncik. He had been anticipating the call, hoping it would be the saving grace for Natalie. But now he doubted whether it would help. Not unless Joncik came down here and captured the man once he was identified.

As Dave nosed into a parking place in front of Ritchie's office, he saw the front door open and Natalie and Ritchie come out. The look on her face was one of shock when she saw Dave. Her eyes wandered over his body when he got out of the truck. He looked down at himself. The difference between them was suddenly never more apparent. She, crisp and cool in her thin dress. He, dirty and disheveled in his army surplus clothes, his face painted green and black to cover the stark whiteness.

Her eyes went to his left armpit. His hand went quickly there to cover the butt of the Colt in the shoulder holster. He had forgotten it. In the woods, it was almost a part of him.

"Did you find him?" she asked quickly.

"Yes, but I lost him. I followed him without him seeing me, but then when he got close to an old house back there in the woods, I had to drop back and he disappeared."

"Maybe he lives in the house. Did you check it out?" Ritchie asked.

"Not by myself. I would be afraid to go into this man's lair and face him on his own terms," Dave said. He searched the faces of Natalie and Ritchie, looking for any sign of hope after the morning session of the trial. When they didn't volunteer any information, he asked. "Well, how did it go this morning?"

"Not too good," Natalie said.

"Now, I wouldn't say that," Ritchie put in. "We made some good points."

"What did they present that was so damaging?" Dave asked insistently.

"The insurance policy recently taken out on Jeff, and then the letter to her friend, talking about coming into a lot of money," Ritchie said. "These were the two things that hurt us the most."

"I never did read that letter. Do you mind if I do that?" Dave lied, looking into Natalie's dark eyes. He wanted to let his eyes wander over the rest of her. She looked so lovely in the dress Ritchie had chosen for her. But he knew that he would be tempted to take her in his arms right here on the sidewalk. And that wouldn't look so good.

"There's a copy on my desk in the folder marked Natalie," Ritchie said. "You don't mind, do you Natalie?"

"No, I guess not."

There was a reluctance there. Dave touched her arm as she moved away from him, Ritchie at her side. Together they headed across the street toward the courthouse. Dave watched them go. Natalie, so brave in the face of unjust accusations. Yet so unwilling to help in her own defense. It was almost as if she wanted to be convicted. Ritchie had lectured her several times because she seemed to be hindering their efforts to free her. She had gotten mad at Ritchie because he had used the fact of her orphan birth and subsequent raising by foster parents, in his opening remarks.

"Natalie! I'm trying to get the jury to feel sorry for you so they will have trouble finding you guilty," Ritchie had told her that night when she objected to the orphan tag.

"I don't want these pitiful people's pity!" Natalie had yelled at him, standing in the middle of his office, the late evening sun casting shadows across her face, making her eyes appear dark and evil.

Dave had watched her as she paced the room. He had seen it then. Seen what she was seeking. Martyrdom. Could that be her one great fault? Was he correct in his judgment of her? He thought so. That had to be it. She wanted the fame of being unjustly convicted. There was no other answer for her actions. Dave knew then that he had to save her from her self. And he would never do it with the wild man behind her house, because he knew that he could never capture the man alive. Unless he spent days, maybe months, lying in wait.

Dave turned and walked into Ritchie's office. The letter. He had read it in the Sheriff's office, but now things were different. Now an eerie feeling came over him. Knowing Natalie the way he did, he knew he could interpret the form and style of the letter. He could tell whether it was real or not.

He spoke to Ritchie's secretary and told her he was going to look at the folder, with Ritchie's permission. It was so. He had been right. The letter was a genuine fake. A product of Natalie's mind. A perfect missile to be used by an enemy to show the evil intent of her heart. But it appeared to be so real that the prosecutor had no trouble believing that it was the perfect piece of evidence.

As he neared the end of the letter, Dave slowly came to an awareness. He knew what he had to do. The path before him lay as open and as straight as before. Now it just had a different goal. This morning it had been the wild man who stood at the termination point. Now it was someone else. Natalie Dunn. The real Natalie. The wild man was simply an obstacle to be skirted to get to her.

The letter he needed. He carefully slipped it inside his shirt and then stood up behind Ritchie's desk. He looked over at the courthouse. He desperately wanted to go over there, but he knew that the sight of Natalie sitting alone in front of the jury that was going to condemn her, would only confirm his suspicion. That she was building her own martyry. And he didn't want any part of it. He quickly left the office, knowing what he had to do. If the trial went as quickly as the judge had said, he would be up all night preparing for the defense tomorrow. But there was one person he had to see before he started. Had to ask for her help in the defense of Natalie. He knew what she would say before he asked. His old friend and confidant would help him with anything he asked. As long as it involved her one and only love. Psychoanalysis.

****

Lana Middleton should have been a college professor. After all, she had a BA in Psychology. Lana Middleton should have been a therapist in one of the hospitals in Nashville. After all she had a MA in Clinical Psychology. She should have been anything but what she was. The bookkeeper in her husband's plumbing and electrical business.

Middleton Plumbing and Heating was the largest plumbing and electrical contractor in Lewiston. Bob Middleton had built the business into what it was. Through his hard work and the help of his wife, Lana. But Lana wasn't a numbers person. Figures and statements and invoices weren't her thing. She was the accountant of the firm in name and body only. Her heart and soul was with people.

Lana did the books for the company while she talked. With people seeking help from marital problems, money problems and a whole host of sundry and assorted other personal problems. Dave sat down and talked with Lana every time he went by the Middleton business. And he stopped frequently, whether he needed any plumbing or electrical materials or not. Usually he had to wait in line.

Although she never said so, Dave suspected that she felt trapped. Not so much a big city person trapped in a small burg, but a large and overflowing mind surrounded by nothing with which to challenge it. Like a fortress never attacked, or a team never tested by stiff competition.

A challenge. That was the thing. Dave hoped that Lana would conclude that the challenge he was bringing her was as great as he thought it was.

Lana was in her glass enclosed office in the center of the large, open building that was the warehouse of Middleton Plumbing and Electrical. As Dave walked across the floor toward the office, it appeared to be an oasis in the midst of a sea of ignorance and indifference, he could see Lana hunched over her books, the telephone clamped between her shoulder and ear.

She would look up at him as he opened the door, would grab the phone with her left hand and point with her right hand to the chair beside the desk. She would continue talking to whoever was on the other end of the line. Giving them every thing they asked for in the way of advice, understanding, or just a listening ear. Lana liked to talk, but she knew when to listen. If she was in a listening mode, she would continue her book work while the person on the other end talked.

Lana rolled her big eyes at Dave and motioned him to the chair just like he knew she would. Dave knew why she did it. She didn't want anyone to leave just because she was talking to someone else.

Dave sat beside the desk and watched her talk and work. Her right hand darted to the calculator in front of her and a column of figures was added between two "I sees" and a "Uh,huh." He ticked off in his mind the things he was going to tell Lana about Natalie. He hadn't as of yet talked to her about this case, but he was positive she knew something about it. He just hoped she hadn't been listening to the wrong person.

The thudding of the phone into its receiver brought Dave back. He looked at Lana as she beamed her big toothy smile at him. Old Egghead Lana. That's what the boys in high school had called her. Because she was smart and studied and didn't chase boys like the rest of the girls. Dave remembered very little about her from school. He had been one of those guys who had cared very little about girls until his senior year. That's when he had run into Betty Lou. They had fallen in love, or at least they thought they had. Two months after graduation, they married. That was one of the reasons Dave had not been by to see Lana in awhile. Betty Lou. He knew Lana would berate him for leaving her.

"What's this I hear about you running out on your wife, boy?"

"I don't know. What have you heard?"

"That you fell for this Dunn woman who is on trial for killing her husband. That's what Betty Lou is telling at work."

"I wouldn't use the term, "fell for," Dave said. "I just believe she is innocent and I am not going to stand by and see her to go to jail for something she didn't do."

"Everybody says she killed him for the insurance money, and so she could run off with you," Lana said, crossing her legs and leaning forward across the corner of the desk, her eyes boring into Dave's.

Dave knew better than to lie to Lana. But he also knew that he couldn't tell her the truth, if it was unbelievable. But he dare not batten his hatches and draw back within a shell. That would be worse than baring his soul. He would tell her most of the truth, leaving out the part about his being so much in love with Natalie that it was threatening to control his life.

"At the time her husband was killed, she couldn't stand the sight of me, so I know that part is a lie. As for the insurance money, she doesn't need it. She is going to be wealthy without it."

Lana perked up at the last part. She pushed her large round glasses up on her nose and scooted forward in her chair. She didn't have to say anything. Dave knew she was waiting for him to explain that last part. But he knew that was the part that was going to take the rest of the day and all of the night. Maybe part of tomorrow. But Ritchie could stall until they were ready. What he needed from Lana was time. Now that he had her attention.

"I need your help on this in the worst way, Lana. But I've got a feeling it's going to take all night. The judge is not going to let this trial go past tomorrow, so tonight is all we have."

"What are you talking about, Dave? I'll help, but you've got to tell me what you want."

"I can't tell you in five minutes. What I'm asking for is the rest of your afternoon, all of tonight and tomorrow. It'll take that long for you to look at what I've got to show you. Then you'll know that Natalie Dunn is innocent like I do. But I can't get up there and tell the jury that. Only somebody like you can."

"Why? Because I'm not in love with her, like you are?"

Dave ducked his head at this. But he knew that he was going to have to put up with things like this from Lana. She didn't pull any punches. But he had his answer ready.

"No! It's because when they see how passionately you believe she is innocent, they won't question your motive, like they would mine."

****

Bob Middleton was used to Lana's involvement in other people's lives. Usually the person was present whose life she was delving into. Not tonight. This person was being pulled apart and put back together on the living room floor, and she was not even here. Every time he went by the door to the living room, he could hear Lana and Dave discussing Natalie. But there was no Natalie there. Only a mountain of paper. Little stacks of it here and there. And Lana's constant reading and vocal outbursts when she got to something good.

"Listen to this, Dave!" Lana cried. She read a passage to Dave, who was sprawled out on the floor, looking up at the ceiling. He grinned. Lana was hooked. On Natalie. Just like he was. "This is fabulous!" she continued. "This woman is something else."

Dave rolled over onto his side and watched Lana read. She was sitting in the middle of the floor with her legs crossed, totally absorbed in the being of Natalie Dunn, which was spread out in little stacks around her. The only problem Dave could see was Natalie. She would be furious when she discovered that he had invaded her private lair and had brought her innermost thoughts and musings out into the harsh daylight where they could be snapped up and picked at the way stray dogs fought over picnic scraps.

But by two a.m, Lana was through. Exhausted but finished. She raised her head from the slump it was in and looked at Dave. He had nodded off. He was lying on his back, his head turned to the side, his mouth slacked open. The way men slept. She knew after reading what she had just been through that he was in love with the woman called Natalie. And not just an infatuation, but a real, soul twisting, fire in the belly kind of love that could see its way through whatever kind of adversity life threw its way.

She looked at the closed eyes and started to speak, but the lids raised quickly, revealing the cold, blue stare that told her the fire was only smoldering.

"Are you ready, Dave?"

"Hell, yes!" He said, rolling over and coming up on his knees.

"Well then, get you a pad and pencil because I'm ready to start. The first thing I need to know is what the evidence against our fair maiden is. Then we're going to start taking it apart bit by bit." She paused and looked at her watch. "It's two o'clock in the morning. By two o'clock this afternoon we might be ready. Do you think the judge will allow us to come in marching and chanting?"

"Chanting? What?"

"Free Natalie Dunn! Free Natalie Dunn!"

Chapter 31

"Your Honor, I would like to call Natalie Dunn to the stand." Ritchie turned and smiled at Natalie as she rose from her seat beside him and walked toward the witness chair. Out of the corner of his other eye, he saw the prosecutor greedily "washing" his hands.

Natalie looked so fresh, clean and pure. She had on a light beige chiffon dress with low heels. The sleeves covered her shoulders and tied with lace halfway down to her elbows. Ritchie had purposely dressed Natalie. Exactly like he would have dressed his teenage daughter to go on her first date. He wanted her to look discrete and demure. Not alluring and appealing.

But the hardest part had been the decision to put her on the stand. At first he had said that she would not be allowed to testify. But after the prosecution had thrown haymaker after haymaker at Natalie yesterday, Ritchie had decided to put her on.

Of course, the decision had not come lightly. It hadn't come until early this morning. After most of the night had been spent rehearsing. When Ritchie was convinced that Natalie could respond calmly and without anger to any question the prosecutor could throw at her, he decided that it would be in her best interest to go on the stand. That, coupled with the assessment he had made of the jury.

Ritchie had watched the jurors as the prosecution had fired its broadsides at her. The little, short, chubby prosecutor had walked around the courtroom waving the letter she had written to her friend Joan, telling her that she would be free of her commitments and would have plenty of money to do as she pleased. Then he had picked up the stick and waved it around as the medical examiner pointed to it as the probable death instrument.

That's when Ritchie had really made the decision to put Natalie on the stand. He had stolen a glance at the jury box. Several jurors were looking at Natalie, seemingly trying to decide whether this sweet, innocent looking woman could have done what they said of her.

As Ritchie approached Natalie when she sat down in the chair after taking the oath, he thought that now they would get their chance. What she would say, or better yet, how she would say it, could make or break them. It didn't look like Dave was going to come up with the wild man. In fact, he hadn't heard from him since noon of yesterday. Maybe he was lying dead out there in the woods behind Natalie's house.

"Mrs. Dunn, or do you prefer Natalie?"

"I prefer Natalie."

"Fine. Now, Natalie. Do you remember what you did on October 14 of this year?"

"Yes, that was the day after Jeff came back from New Orleans for the last time. That was the day I left him." She said the words almost perfectly. Ritchie could have applauded. Not too much triumph. Just a touch of sorrow.

"And what made you decide to leave your husband, Natalie?"

"I discovered that he had been visiting a house of prostitution in New Orleans." Again, said with just a note of finality. Maybe even a touch of sadness for Jeff.

"How did you discover this, Natalie?"

"I found several match books in his pockets and in the glove box of his car from one of these places."

Ritchie walked back to the defense table and picked up a matchbook and went over and handed it to Natalie. "Is this one of the ones you found?"

"Yes, it is."

"Would you read what it says."

"Cats Place. Girls, Girls, Girls. Any sizes. Any shapes. All to please you."

"Did you confront Jeff with this, Natalie?"

"Yes, I did."

"And what did he say?"

"He just laughed and said that girls like that didn't mean anything to a man. They were just something to pass the time. He said it didn't meant he didn't love me."

"And what did you say to that?"

"I said I was leaving him. That I wouldn't live with a man who was unfaithful."

"Did you ever cheat on Jeff, Natalie?"

"No, Sir!" Just the right touch of defiance. If Ritchie didn't know better, he would swear that Natalie had been an actress.

Ritchie walked over to the prosecutor's table and picked up the stick that had been adjudged to be the death weapon. He nodded to the little man. "If you please, Sir." He walked back to Natalie and attempted to hand her the stick. She kept her hands in her lap and drew her head and shoulders away from Ritchie and the stick.

"Natalie, would you take this stick?"

"No, Sir! I would not!"

"You do recognize this, then?"

"I do. Jeff used it to hang deer on that he had killed."

"And where did he keep it?"

"Under my kitchen sink."

"Did you like it there?"

"No, Sir."

"Why didn't you move it?"

"I couldn't touch the thing. I told Jeff to get it out of the house, but he told me to put it where I wanted. So I left it there. I couldn't stand the thought of touching it."

Ritchie looked at her and then spun and walked to his table. He retrieved a framed photograph and walked back and handed it to Natalie.

"Do you recognize this, Natalie?"

"I should. I took it. It's a picture of Jeff's first deer."

"And this stick that is run through the deer's legs, by which it is hanging from the tree limb. Is this the stick? The one Deputy King took from under your sink?"

"It is."

"And you have never touched it or laid hands on it?"

"Never! I told Jeff it could rot under there before I would move it."

Ritchie reached up and handed the picture to Judge Mashburn, who in turn handed it to the bailiff. A commotion in the back of the courtroom arrested his attention, and when he looked, he saw Dave and Lana coming down the sloping aisle toward the front of the courtroom. Dave had two large boxes in his arms. He was grinning from ear to ear. He and Lana sat down on the front row beside George Emmons and smiled at Ritchie, each of them looking like the cat that swallowed the canary.

Ritchie turned back to Natalie before he lost his train of thought. He couldn't imagine what they had for him.

"Now, Natalie. This Saturday that you were preparing to leave your husband. What was he doing?"

"He was getting ready to go hiking to the top of the ridge that is on the property behind our house."

"What did you say to him?"

"I told him I wouldn't be home when he got back."

"And what did he say to that?"

"He cursed me and made an ugly finger sign at me when I backed out of the drive."

"And that's the last time you saw him?"

"Yes, Sir. Until Dave Warren came and got me and took me to the hospital to identify his body."

"Natalie." Here Ritchie paused. He and Natalie had discussed the next question and had decided to ask it anyway. They both figured that the prosecutor would ask it. "Did you love your husband?"

"I did when I married him. But after he was unfaithful to me, I found I no longer could have any affection for him."

Ritchie looked at Natalie. Naturally, his questions had been carefully chosen. There had been nothing there to upset her. But it would be different with the prosecutor. He would jump on her with both feet. Ritchie had tried to prepare her for it by asking her tough questions last night. He hoped she wouldn't rattle when the little fat man started getting to her. He looked at his watch. It was eleven thirty. It would be nice if he could keep the prosecutor away from her until afternoon. Out of the corner of his eye he caught Dave waving at him. When Ritchie turned toward him, he saw him pointing first at the boxes in his lap, and then at Lana. He spun to the judge.

"Your Honor, it is very close to noon. Do you suppose I could ask for a short recess which might stretch on into an early lunch? If it pleases the court?"

Judge Mashburn looked at Ritchie. He wondered what kind of bull this con man was up to. He hated to grant any request that Ritchie applied for. But it was close to lunch time, and he had asked nicely. And the prosecutor had told him he could take the defendant apart in thirty minutes, but maybe he needed some time to get ready.

"Court adjourned until one o'clock!" he said with authority, as if he had thought of it all by himself.

Ritchie stepped in front of Natalie as she came off the stand and started toward Dave. He looked at her and moved with her as she tried to get around him.

"Remember. You don't like him. So no show of affection." Natalie looked at him, irritation showing in her face. She started to say something but Ritchie cut her off. "The jury is looking at you." He smiled. She smiled back and put her hand on his arm. "Let's go see what Dave has for us."

Dave and Lana were crowding through the swinging gates that separated the spectator area from the floor of the court. Lana grabbed Natalie by the arm and pulled her into an embrace. Like she was a long lost sister. Natalie was confused by the show of emotion and let her arms drop to her sides.

"Girl! I've been wanting to meet you since I heard about your trouble. I'm Lana Middleton. Dave, you didn't tell me she was beautiful."

Ritchie grabbed Natalie's arm. "Okay, people! Let's get out of here and over to my office. I'll have the Chinese restaurant next door bring us something to eat. Out! Git!" He steered Natalie toward the back door they had escaped through the day before. He didn't want any loose talk that the jury might overhear. They were still in their seats. The foreman was getting them ready to go to lunch.

They fled across the lawn of the courthouse, Ritchie and Natalie in the lead, he with his hand grasping her elbow. Like refugees fleeing across no man's land, they ran. Heads swiveling as they crossed the two lanes of traffic, stringing out in a ragged line as they ran up the steps to Ritchie's office.

Ritchie called next door and ordered four boxes of "something good." He never did know how to order Chinese food. As he hung up the phone, he looked at Dave and Lana. They had the brightest looks on their faces. Almost as if they had been drinking. Their faces glowed.

"What do you two have? You act like you're on dope."

Natalie had dropped into the chair beside Ritchie's desk. Her eyes had been resting on the boxes in Dave's lap, idly wondering what was in them. Suddenly she knew. She recognized the boxes. They had come from her house. From her room, from her very soul.

She grabbed the arms of the chair and bolted upright. Her eyes blazed as she lunged across the room toward Dave. Coming to his feet, Dave braced himself, awaiting the charging Natalie.

"What have you got in those boxes?" she yelled, advancing on him as he turned his shoulder to her, the boxes shielded by his body. He hunched his back, further protecting the precious cargo he carried. He felt her hands clawing at him in attempt to get the boxes.

"Dave! I want those boxes!" Natalie was screaming now. Her fists began pounding on his broad back. Ritchie came around the desk and grabbed Natalie from behind as she flailed at Dave.

"What's going on here?" he yelled, trying to make his voice heard over the loud noise coming from Natalie.

"You're not going to use that, Dave!" Natalie screamed as Ritchie pulled her away. Dave turned toward her when Ritchie turned her loose and she made another lunge at him, grabbing at the boxes in his arms.

"Would somebody explain to me what is happening here?" Ritchie yelled above the melee. "I'm the lawyer here and I need to know what is going on! Now, everybody settle down!"

He literally slung Natalie around toward her chair and positioned himself between her and Dave. He crouched with his back toward Dave and faced Natalie. He pointed his finger at her. "Now! You! Settle down. If the jury saw something like this, they would convict you in a heartbeat."

"He's stolen something out of my house and he thinks he's going to use it in court." Natalie's breath rattled in and out of her lungs as she struggled for air. "Well, it's not going to happen! I won't allow it. Now, give it back." She stepped toward Dave and Ritchie again. Ritchie put his hands up, traffic cop style.

"Whoa! Just wait a minute. Set down, Natalie. I don't know what's going on here, but I don't have time to spend the next hour keeping you two separated. Now let's talk about what's going on." He turned to Dave and pointed to the chair. He looked at Lana, who had remained seated through the whole shouting match. She seemed under control. He turned back to Dave, who had obediently taken a seat.

"Okay. You. Begin." He spun to Natalie. "And don't you butt in until he's through." He turned back to Dave. "Now, what is this all about?"

"It has to do with the letter the prosecution is saying Natalie wrote to a friend telling about how her money troubles would soon be over," Dave began. "Yesterday when I read the letter in your folder, I knew I had seen another one just like it."

"You're a snoop!" Natalie yelled across the room.

"Natalie! It's the only way. I had to do it. I can't let you go to jail for something you didn't do."

"I'm not letting every sonofa..."

"Hey! Hey! Hey! Enough! Now, I'm tired of this yelling you two are doing. You act like you're married. At least that's the way I remember marriage," Ritchie said. "Let him finish, Natalie. Quit interrupting."

Dave continued. "So I went to Lana to ask for her help and..."

"Let me interrupt here," Ritchie said. "What does Lana have to do with this?"

"Lana has a masters degree in psychiatry."

"Clinical Psychology, Dave," Lana said quietly.

"Okay, whatever. And she has a counseling license from the state. So she would be an expert witness. And she does book reviews for the Nashville Tennessean, so she is well read. In other words, Lana here is pretty smart."

"I get your drift," Ritchie said, pointing to his watch. "Get on with it."

"Okay! Okay!" Dave said, getting up and placing both boxes on the desk in front of Ritchie. "Now, we were talking about letters. Read these two and then tell me if we don't have something." Two loose sheets lay on the top box.

Natalie let her spine slump, and she slid down in the chair. Her neck bent and her head dropped onto her chest. Dave's words started a buzzing in her ears that became so intense, she had to swallow to equalize the pressure.

A steamy sort of haze descended over her and she had the strangest feeling that her eyes would not focus further than two feet in front of her. It was as if her eyeballs themselves where extendable, and two feet was the limit of their range. Then like periscopes rising above the surface of the ocean, they turned and focused back toward Natalie. She saw nothing.

Natalie felt empty. After years of struggle to build something inside, something strong and permanent on top of the hollow and wasted foundation she was born upon, she felt it all melting away. Sliding beneath the green, slimy surface without even a ripple. Nothing to even mark her passing.

She tried to look at Dave who was leaning over Ritchie's desk from the front, his arms placed beside the boxes. The haze kept her from focusing on him. He remained fuzzy. His words still a buzz.

Then Lana What'shername was up, talking excitedly, pointing into the pure and undefiled heart of Natalie that Dave had stolen from her house, and then had carried it to town and flung it down on a cheap desk for everyone to gawk at.

Everything has a price. Natalie slowly discovered this fact as her glazed eyes forced her mind to search inward, probing into its limitless expanses for the ultimate answer. Priceless treasures? No such thing! Wouldn't sell it for any amount of money? Only a fool makes such statements.

Natalie watched the dollar signs roll in front of her eyes, intermingled with lemons, cherries, and grapes. Slot machine eyes, simply waiting for the right amount to show. Then she could determine what price for her soul. Like an auctioneer taking bids, she waited for the price to become high enough so she could point to the high bidder and say, "Sold!"

The magic number rang in her ears and she looked to see who had won the bid. Who had bid the high dollar for the soul of Natalie Dunn. It was she, herself, and the price was her life.

She rose to her feet. Somebody was talking to her. The words coming through the haze like a mirage dimly seen in the heat of the desert. In and out, the volume rising and falling as the words were sucked this way and that on the heat thermals rising from the baking sand.

"Do you understand what we are going to do, Natalie?" It was Ritchie talking. But she looked at Dave. Did he know what he had sacrificed for her life? Did he realize that he could not win all? That he could only win a part, and the part that he lost, the part he gave up as a sacrifice, was the greater? That simply capturing her body did not give him access to her soul?

What thinketh Abraham when his hand was stayed from killing his son Isaac? That he was only saving the life of the boy? No! The boy was only flesh. Flesh that would rot and decay. Something that the soul inside of Abraham would never do. Because, through the soul of his son, would he pass on all life. The son could die and he could get another. But when the inside of a person died, it could never be replaced.

Natalie then found her priceless treasure. The only question, could she keep herself from selling it?

"Let's go, Natalie." It was Ritchie talking to her. Had he been talking to her before? Had she answered him and been unaware of what she said?

"Are you okay? Do you understand what we are going to do?"

"I'm not going to testify anymore." It was flatly said. No emotion. Just a plain vanilla statement.

"You will have to, Natalie. Once I put you on the stand, the prosecution can question you all it wants."

"Then I will answer his questions, but I will not answer anymore questions from you."

She was aware of Dave turning toward her as she walked beside Ritchie across the street toward the courthouse. But he was out of her two foot range, so she never saw the look of consternation on his face. She realized he would never see inside her, ever again. Not because he couldn't. In spite of all his lack of education and polish, Dave Warren was more capable of understanding and warmth than any person she knew. So, no. Not because he couldn't, but because she would never again let him. He had searched too deep. Peeled away too many layers, exposed too much of her soul. The very thing she wanted him to do, but when it was done, she hated him for it. Hated him for making her love him. Making her look at herself and see the price she had put on her life. But most of all for bringing this Lana What'shername into her life and trying to make of her a friend. The search was not yet over, but Natalie knew that it involved no friends. No one as close as Dave had become. She longed to reach out and touch him. To feel the smoothness of his skin, the bulkiness of his body. To wrap her arms around him.

As they walked into the courtroom through the door behind the judge's bench, she gritted her teeth to keep the feeling down. She could feel Dave's nearness behind her. Her face flushed as she realized that she wanted him. Just thinking about him made her hate herself. She had almost released herself upon him. Had in fact, given completely that one time. But had caught herself before she went over the edge. She must never let that happen again.

The haziness crept closer as Ritchie and the prosecutor popped up and down objecting and arguing over her soul and Dave's finding of it. Over her not continuing and the relevancy of it all. She felt her eyes pull her whole body along with them as they left her Isaac at the altar and swept through the curtain of mist into the world of life for life and eye for eye. Never again would her eye be dimmed or her life be encased by another. From this day forward, no one could ever accuse her of killing another. There would never be another human close to her, close enough for her to touch or be touched by.

"...call Dave Warren to the stand," was all Natalie heard and she idly watched Dave move to the seat where she had sat all morning. Detaching herself from the anger she felt at his betrayal and his unauthorized snooping, she slumped in her seat behind the table. It was her favorite position when she was attempting to keep her emotions under control. She knew that if she sat up straight and got into the flow of the moment, she would likely lose her temper and come up out of her chair and yell at Dave to shut his mouth.

Dave's voice billowed and flowed in and out of her head, sounding hollow and strange as he told of finding the secret compartment in her desk, and the treasure it held. One complete, the other partial. The completed one, accepted, the partial one, given much praise and the author urged to continue until it was completed.

"...being the letter of acceptance from the publishing house of Fulmer and Son. And here I have a copy of a contract from a literary agency in New York, which is an agreement to represent Natalie Dunn and market her literary works."

Natalie looked at the letters being waved around. The letters she treasured as much or more than the mounds of paper they alluded to. The letters were acceptance, approval, praise. Glory and honor. Directed at her and her alone. And not a damn person could say they helped. The book, the novel she had written was the ultimate tribute to her strength of character. It represented over a year of gut wrenching labor. Labor that had taken more out of her than childbirth ever could. Then when it was down and done, ink on fiber, she felt part of her go with it. Because what no one would ever know was, just how much of it was her and how much was created. It was then she realized that no one who ever wrote could do so from pure imagination. There had to be something real in the words. The secret was to never let the reader know which was which.

"...second one is the one we are concerned with. Here I have a letter from the same publisher, telling Miss Dunn that the outline and sample chapters from her second book are very impressive. The editor says that the concept and plot are unique, and an advance of ten thousand dollars is offered for the book."

Dave was handed the second letter and asked if it too was found in the file in the secret compartment. When he answered yes, she knew that what was coming next was the real reason for this whole thing. She listened, but she didn't really want to hear. Lana Who took the stand as Dave stepped down. Natalie listened as Ritchie took her through her qualifications. Heard her tell why she should be allowed to testify in open court as to the inner workings, as she saw them, of Natalie Dunn's mind.

"...mind if I call you Lana, do you?" Ritchie was saying.

"I would prefer it."

"Now, Lana. You have read both of these books and the accompanying letters?"

"Yes."

"What is your impression of the writer of these works, especially the novel?"

"Very creative. Very sensitive. A person who is immensely talented and sure of herself."

"Now, Lana, let's go to the second book. The incomplete one. You have read it?"

"Yes, I have."

"And what is it about?"

"It is the story of a person who gives advice to people through a column in a big city newspaper. Kind of an Ann Landers type person. The book delves into the lives of the people who write to this person for advice. It is written in the form of letters back and forth between the columnist and the people who confide in her."

"Now, Lana, have you read this letter that the prosecution has introduced into evidence as being written from Natalie Dunn to a friend of hers?"

"Yes, I have."

"In your opinion, what is this letter?"

"It is one of the letters in the book being written by one of the characters to the columnist. It is addressed, Dear Joan. The name of the columnist in the uncompleted book of Natalie Dunn, is Joan Daley. The column is called Joan's Daily Advice."

"So, this letter that is supposed to be written by Natalie Dunn, is actually a letter from an advice seeker to Joan Daley. It is just a part of the story in the book?"

"That's right. If you read the letter written previous to the last advice given by Joan, you will see that it ties in perfectly."

"Lana, how long have you known Natalie Dunn?"

"I just met her this morning, but after reading her two books, I feel that I've known her for years."

"In what way?"

"I've found in my counseling and dealing with people through the years, that there are two kinds. Those who can verbalize their troubles and dreams, and those who can't. But many of the ones who can't verbalize, can write. These are the special ones. Grand dreams and ideas spoken come often from shallow and insecure people. The ones pondered over and then written down, most often come from a secure and self-satisfied person. A writer is less prone to violence than the orator. Oratory can be full of bluster and threats. Writing must be calmer. Consider the difference between Hitler and Gandhi."

"Your Honor, I must object to this line of testimony. What is the purpose of it all?"

Ritchie was wondering when the prosecutor was going to object. But Lana was so fetching and convincing that Ritchie was sure he didn't want to appear to be badgering her.

"Your Honor, I am merely trying to show that this person is incapable of murder, and that the main piece of evidence that the prosecution has, is a part of a novel being written in the home of the accused."

"Overruled."

"Thank you, Your Honor. So, Lana. In your opinion, if Natalie Dunn had a problem, how would she solve it?"

"By writing about it. Putting it down on paper and then watching it go away."

"And how much problem would an unfaithful husband be?"

"No problem at all. He would simply be more material for her book. And with the money rolling in from her books, she wouldn't have any financial problems."

"Objection!"

"Sustained! Strike that last statement."

"Thank you, Lana. That will be all." Ritchie nodded toward the fat little prosecutor, who seemed bewildered by the swift turn of events. He rose from his seat and looked at Ritchie, who was back at his table preparing to be seated. He looked back at Lana and decided that he didn't want the jury to hear any more praise from her about the defendant.

"No questions for Miss Middleton, Your Honor. But I would like to ask ex-deputy Warren a few." He stressed the "ex."

The bailiff stepped forward and summoned Dave to the stand, and he walked slowly toward the witness chair. Dave was in a daze as the judge reminded him he was still under oath. He hadn't really thought about this. Hadn't prepared himself for what he would say when he was asked questions about he and Natalie's relationship.

A faint smile appeared on the fleshy face of the prosecutor as he approached Dave. "Now, Mr. Warren. You were once a sheriff's deputy. Is that right?"

"That's right. The Sheriff didn't like it when I said I thought Natalie Dunn was inno..."

"Your Honor," the fat face said loudly, cutting off Dave's words from the jury. "I must insist that the witness answer only the questions."

"Just answer the questions, Mr. Warren."

"Now then, ex-deputy Warren." A smirk came over the prosecutor's face and Dave looked at him with a bewildered look. He couldn't imagine why the fat man was asking questions that would only be damaging to his case. And then he knew why. Out of the corner of his eye he saw the Sheriff trying to signal the prosecutor. But the man didn't see the frantic signals and continued his questions. Questions that he would never be asking if the Sheriff hadn't lied to him.

"Isn't it true that the Sheriff fired you because you refused to arrest Natalie Dunn?"

"No, Sir! He fired me when I threatened to tell that Deputy King had beaten Natalie Dunn when her hands were handcuffed behind her back."

"That's a damn lie!" the Sheriff roared from his seat at the side of the jury box.

Mashburn slammed his gavel. "Quiet! That's enough! Warren, I'm instructing you to just answer the questions. Your off the wall comments are putting you in danger of contempt."

Dave followed the prosecutor's eyes to the Sheriff who was making the "cut" sign across his throat. Dave grinned at the fat man as his eyes came back to him. He knew the man had committed the lawyer's unpardonable sin. He had asked a question he didn't know the answer to. Except, in this case, he thought he knew the answer. He had just been given the wrong information. Dave tried to wipe the grin off his face, but he found that he was enjoying the discomfort of the prosecutor too much. He lowered his voice so that the jury couldn't hear.

"If you want, I'll point out a witness to the whole affair, and he can back up my story."

The prosecutor glared at Dave, and then suddenly changed his whole line of questioning.

"Mr. Warren, is it not true that you are madly in love with Natalie Dunn?"

"Yes, Sir. And I'm glad you used the term "madly." Because that is the word to describe it. I just hated to use it."

"Why is that?" the prosecutor said, stumbling right into Dave's trap. Dave now had him answering him.

"From the first, I believed she was innocent. The evidence just didn't support her doing anything like she was accused of. But I didn't fall in love with her until I read the two books she had written. The ones I found in her desk in the house. Then I became a fan of hers. It was like I had discovered her. I've never read many books, but all of a sudden, here was a book written by somebody I knew. And it was good. It was..."

"Mr. Warren, that's enough."

"I'm not through answering your question. You asked why and I'm telling you why. I fell in love with Natalie Dunn the way people fall in love with Elvis Presley. Like people fall in love with sports stars or movie stars. Here was a famous author, and I knew her." Dave paused. "Did I answer your question?"

"Mr. Warren, have you had sex with Natalie Dunn?"

"Heavens no! I'm just an adoring fan of hers. Not her lover." Dave knew he had lied perfectly. Cleanly, wholesomely, and with just the right hint of indignation. He had never dreamed that he would be able to fool the prosecutor that easily. He walked in a daze back to his seat beside George and Lana when he heard the fat man say, "no more questions."

Through the whole time he was on the stand, he had not once looked at Natalie. Now he looked at her from behind as she sat beside Ritchie, who was standing and telling the judge that the defense was through. Resting. Natalie looked so calm and relaxed that she appeared to be sleeping with her eyes open. Dave continued looking at her. He wanted her to turn to him. Give him a sign that she had heard and appreciated what he had done for her. Lied under oath to protect her. To save her from the guilt the jury might infer from knowing they had been lovers.

Natalie didn't look at Dave. She didn't look at anyone but herself. She had heard Dave on the stand. Heard him deny loving her. Maybe it was true. As far as she could tell, it had never happened. Her body seemed to her as unspoiled as the day she was born. She stretched her long legs under the table, feeling the tenseness leave her. As the mental strain drained away and left her relaxed, she felt a physical need arise. She thought of Dave's smooth body against hers. Then she remembered his denial on the stand. How different would have been her answer. She would have told how wonderful had been the experience and then would have dared anyone to imply that she and Dave had conspired to kill her husband.

She heard the incredulity in the judge's voice when he asked the prosecutor if he was not going to question Natalie Dunn since she had been put on the stand by the defense. When the fat man said he had no questions for her, the judge turned to Ritchie and asked him why he couldn't begin his closing argument immediately. The prosecutor had earlier told the judge he would have no problem launching immediately into his summation, since it was an open and shut case.

Ritchie made his decision after looking at Heartburn for a good ten seconds. Strike while the iron is hot. He felt that he had the jury on his side. He would go with them and with whatever they were feeling at the moment. He didn't want them to sleep on it.

"I'm ready, Your Honor."

The prosecutor had an open and shut case. He opened his mouth and let the bluster out. Natalie shut her ears and didn't even listen. Ritchie made a few notes, but mainly watched the jury. He wanted to see how they were reacting to the little fat man parading in front of them. In his heart, he knew they weren't buying in.

When it came Ritchie's time to give the jury his summation, he approached them and when he was in front of them, he bowed.

Natalie almost laughed. It was the same bow he had given her when he had first met her in the corridor outside her jail cell.

Ritchie found his calling that day. As he talked in front of the spellbound jury, he realized that he should have been an actor. Not a movie star, but a real actor. On Broadway. So he could respond to any twitch of the head, as one juror did. He spun and directed his next remark right at her. So he could pause when something he said elicited laughter as it did from the spectators. So he could hitch up his pants and stride forward, a prop, in this case the stick, in his hand. So he could bend forward, outside the footlights, in this case the rail in front of the jury box, and speak directly to the audience.

And the jury listened. When he showed them how preposterous, he actually used the word, it was to believe a woman could ram the stick through someone and then carry the body several miles and dump it in a trash can, they, as a group, nodded.

"This letter, ladies and gentlemen? The one written, the prosecution says, to a friend?" Here he paused again, looking at each one. Then he picked up the box off the table. He raised it over his head. "Read the book! This box is full of letters just like it. All addressed to Joan. You'll see. It fits right in."

Then he went straight to the women. He was better with them, anyway. "And what would you do, ladies, if you discovered your husband was frequenting, shall we say, cat houses? Kill him? Again, preposterous! Maybe if you came home and found him in bed with your best friend, but that was not the case with Natalie Dunn. So what do you do?" One woman nodded and Ritchie spoke to her. "That's right! You pack up and leave. And that's exactly what Natalie did. And the prosecution wants you to believe that's an act that shows guilt?"

Ritchie turned and found Natalie looking directly at him. Something she had not done in a while. Her eyes said she had had enough. Maybe the jury had, also. He turned back to them.

"Kind sirs and ladies. I have spoken enough. You know what you have to do." He bowed again and Natalie wanted to gag. "I thank you."

Heartburn spent five minutes explaining to the jury what they must find and how they must use the evidence to find it. When they had filed out and into the room behind the bench to begin deliberation, Ritchie was still in deep thought, wondering if he had done enough.

Lana's droll voice brought him out of it. "Let's go, Hamlet. Me thinks this fair lady needs some rest from all the BS you've been slinging."

Natalie laughed. A clear, ringing, for all the world innocent as a school girl, laugh. It floated through the courtroom and every eye turned toward her. The people shuffling up the aisle toward the rear doors, stopped. The prosecutor gathering up his papers, paused. Judge Mashburn, who was just before disappearing through the door to his chambers, halted, the doors pushed half open. Dave froze. His eyes on the woman he loved. To everyone but him, the laugh was the jubilant sound of innocence released.

But Dave saw it. In the head thrown back, revealing the sharp incisors. In the eyes that darted to the prosecutors and gloried in his coming defeat. In the strong hands that went around Lana's waist as the two hugged, this time Natalie accepting the show of affection.

And then he knew. Natalie hadn't killed Jeff, but he knew she could have. And could have laughed as she wiped the blood off the stick. And could have lied about it as perfectly as he lied about their love.

Dave was now a follower. Across the street and up the steps to Ritchie's office. Lana with Natalie and Ritchie. Dave alone. Ritchie's secretary, Pat, gave him a note. It was now meaningless. It simply said, "Call Det. Joncik. He said you'd know. It's important."

It was growing dark and Dave idly watched Pat pick up her purse and get ready to leave. She looked at her watch and indicated the phone on her desk. "I'm leaving in a few minutes. As soon as the jabbering in there stops long enough for me to ask him if he needs anything."

Dave stepped to the door and looked out across the square. Leaves were starting to blow off trees. Normally, this time of year brought his blood to a fever pitch with the thought of deer hunting. Now he wasn't feeling anything. He thought about the big buck on the Garrett Place. But the image of the wild man trying to get the deer to follow him, was fresh on his mind. Dave still hadn't figured out what the man was trying to do. Maybe he had no way to kill the deer and was trying to lure him into a trap. Then he thought of the spears. No! He could kill a deer if he wanted. Simply wait up in a tree for one to walk under.

He looked at his watch. Would the jury recess or would they deliberate on into the night? This kind of waiting, unlike waiting on a deer, was nerve rattling.

"Excuse please! I'm leaving. You people can wait all night. I'm going home." Dave watched Pat hurry down the steps and out to her car, and thought about killing. Not her, but just killing in general. He wondered how killing a person would feel. He had killed deer, but a dead deer had never given him a hint at how it would feel to kill a person. It suddenly fascinated him.

Natalie, a killer. He thought of her on the doorstep with her head buried in the dead body of her dog. Crying over the dog. And then he heard the laugh. The laugh he imagined she would throw out over the body of a person she had just killed. Like the victory yell of the savage over the body of an enemy. Pure, wild, coarse and naked. The hands dripping blood as they are raised to the sky in salute to the gods of death.

Dave turned and went to the phone on the desk. The door to Ritchie's office was closed and the sounds coming inside were foreign. No weeping. Laughter and victory.

"Detective Joncik, please ma'am." Dave knew that would get a response. He laughed. "Please ma'am to a Yankee?" he said out loud.

"You must be calling from the South. The operator is going crazy," Joncik said as he came on the line.

"I figured that would get a response," Dave laughed.

"It did. How's the trial going?"

"It's over. The jury is deliberating now."

"Then I'm too late, aren't I?"

"It's not going to matter. The jury will find the woman not guilty. Then I can go after this guy." Dave's voice was low.

"You're sure of the jury?"

"Positive."

"Hope you're right. The reason it took so long was, this guy really covered his tracks. But I'll tell you what I found." Detective Joncik paused as if he could see Dave scrambling for a pen and paper.

"Okay, I'm ready."

"His name is Benjamin H. Jamison. He's a lawyer. His old law firm handled the estate of Minnie Hill. That's what threw me. It all looked so innocent. The phony paperwork says the property in Tennessee was sold at auction and the money went to charity. No problem." Dave listened. He loved the way Northerners said problem. "Praeblem." Joncik continued.

"I didn't even suspect this law firm. Everything looked up front. Then I just ran a check on them. One of the documents looked funny, so I said what the heck. And guess what?"

"You found a lawyer with a record?" Dave guessed.

"Right! This Jamison. Arrested for fraud. Put on probation by the New York Bar Association. Plea bargained out of it. Reinstated a year later. Then guess where he went to work?"

"I have no idea," Dave said. He could tell Joncik was having fun and he didn't want to spoil it. He just enjoyed listening to the man.

"A Wall Street brokerage firm."

"The same one Natalie Hill worked for?"

"Hey, hey. Who said hillbillies were dumb?" Joncik rumbled his throaty, cigar smoke infested laugh.

"So he knew her and probably knew about her mother and the property here in Tennessee, and started making plans to steal the property when he worked at the law firm," Dave blurted.

"Right! But now it really gets interesting. Remember you told me Mrs. Schuburt told you Natalie Hill's boyfriend was killed the same night. I had Neuman do some digging and he discovered that the man we never identified was named Morgan Vandiver and he was Natalie Hill's boyfriend. He was a lawyer and guess who one of his law partners was?"

"Our friend Benjamin H. Jamison?"

"Bingo!" Joncik rumbled.

"Mrs. Schuburt mentioned to me she had a boyfriend."

"She never did to me, and I didn't discover him until I got to checking. Nobody came forward with this until now. Maybe it was because he was a drug dealer. We knew that at the time and just assumed it was a drug killing and forgot about it. But now it appears that she was killed the same night as her boyfriend was. And guess where his body was found?"

"In Natalie's apartment?"

"No, wrong there. In a trash can."

"Just like Jeff Dunn."

"I remembered you telling me that. But there's more. The father of this Vandiver who was killed, is in a mental hospital now. That same night his son was killed, somebody punched out his eyes and ears."

"Damn!" Dave swore softly. "What was going on? What was the reasoning behind this?"

"Drugs. Revenge. Who knows? My nose tells me that the son killed Natalie Hill, ran her down in the street. And then this Jamison killed him and mutilated the father. Jealousy, maybe."

"And what happened to Jamison?"

"Disappeared. No trace of him. I found a copy of the deed with Minnie Hill's signature on it. It has been recorded in this Jamison's name. He either coerced her to sign it, or it's a forgery."

Dave went silent. The whole thing had taken on a dark and sinister twist. The man on the Hill Place had not only killed to keep people off. He had killed to get the property to begin with. And he was a mutilator. Men's eyes. Dog's guts. It apparently didn't matter.

"You still there?" Joncik rumbled.

"Just thinking. Is this Jamison wanted by New York? Is he a suspect in any of this?"

"No, the case has been closed. But it could be reopened if I could persuade my boss that this Jamison is still alive. But I don't know about convincing him that he's been living in the hills of Tennessee for the last ten years."

"But he's never been charged in this case. Right?"

"Right. But if you capture him, let me know. We would want to talk to him."

"What about the man who had his eyes punched out? Have you talked to him?"

"I talked to him, but it was a one way street. He hasn't spoken in ten years. Evidently his mind snapped when his son was killed and he was mutilated."

Dave started to tell Joncik about following the man to his lair, but hesitated. Jamison looked harmless enough, but Dave knew that cornered, he would fight like a wounded tiger.

"I'll let you know if I can get within ten feet of him. He's evidently like a ghost if he can stay hidden this long."

"Just be careful. From all appearances, the man is dangerous," Joncik said. "But of course you know that, Scarbelly."

Dave laughed. Joncik remembered the long gash on his belly. "I will. Thanks for all your help. Call me anytime if you need anything down here. I'll call you if something comes up."

Dave heard the phone click. Dead. Connected, now gone. He was alone and free to go after Jamison. He now had a name to call him. He wondered if Natalie would be interested in knowing the name of the man who had killed her husband. He got up and opened the door to Ritchie's office.

"I just talked to Detective Joncik in New York. He found out the name of the man on the Hill Place. Or at least, who we think it is. His name is Benjamin Jamison." Dave looked at Ritchie and smiled. "And guess what he used to be before he went crazy. A lawyer."

"Sounds like he went from crazy to smart if he got out of this racket," Ritchie shot back.

Nobody looked at Natalie. If they had, they would have seen the color drain from her face.

Lana was up and looking out the window. She could see the light in the jury room on the second floor of the courthouse.

"I feel like the people in Saint Peter's Square watching the chimney of the Vatican to see what color smoke is coming out," she said. "I wonder how long the jury will take?"

"I've got this horrible feeling that the verdict is going to be guilty." Natalie spoke, her voice weak and low.

"Natalie, don't say that!" Lana yelled, whirling away from the window.

"And Deputy King is going to come leaping across the courtroom and throw me down and handcuff me again."

Lana was across the room, standing in front of Natalie, grabbing her hands and holding them together in front of her. Being the eternal optimist that she was. "Listen to me, Natalie. It's not going to happen that way. I have the fullest faith in that jury. They will see what we all in this room see. That you're innocent.

"And what if you're wrong?" Natalie asked.

"I'm not wrong! You've got to have faith."

Ritchie suddenly got up and came out from behind his desk. "I should have waited until tomorrow and given a better closing argument. I shouldn't have let the judge rush me. Damn! Why didn't I resist?" He slammed his fist into his palm.

Dave knew what he had to do. He felt like an alien in another world. Like he was standing alone on the windless surface of the moon, watching the antics of earth people a quarter of a million miles away. Dancing and kneeling and praying to whatever god they happened to fancy at any particular moment. And then wondering why each god let them down at a crucial moment in their lives. Then switching to the next god, hoping that it would be better than the last. He remembered a conversation that some of the guys had about which beer gave the least hangover. Kind of like which god would let you down the least.

"I have to go. I'll be at Natalie's house if you need me. I've got some hunting to catch up on," he said.

"What about the verdict? You not going to stay to hear if they decide tonight?" Lana asked.

"I know what the verdict is. I don't have to hear it from them."

"Dave!" Ritchie yelled.

But he was gone. Like he had never been in the room. Lana and Ritchie looked at Natalie. She arose and walked to the window and watched Dave get in the borrowed car and back out into the street. The car bucked once and then moved smoothly away. Taking Dave away from her. He had not spoken to her since yesterday. Did he know? How could he? Maybe he had read her mind? Maybe it had come through when she thought she was only thinking? Words instead of thoughts. She couldn't remember.

Natalie turned to the empty room. Just like her life. Full of people, but empty. She walked over to the chair and sat down. "I'll find him tomorrow. I'll tell him. I don't want to bother him tonight."

But in her mind, she knew she would.

Chapter 32

Dave knew she would come. When he heard the broken back door push open, he put his hand under the pillow and touched the Colt. But he knew he wouldn't need it when he heard the couch being pushed back in place in front of the door. The rustle, faintly heard, of feet bare, of cloth being dropped to floor. Then whisper-like sound of hand on wall in darkened hallway. Feeling the way, no light needed. To the familiar bed where the white sheets shone in the dim light from stars and quarter moon.

Gasping, ever so slightly, her hand ahead, probing, feeling the smooth skin that awaited her. The surprise that he knew of her coming and expected it, quickly gone as the two smooth skins began their slow dance to a new god. One which demanded silence with only the moist sounds of secret sin as sacrifice.

And time. Time must stand still. But that comes with silence. The joy, the ecstasy, the pure enchanting mistress of desire that floated over the bed, demanded that silence be enforced. For only then could two become as one. Joined in silence save for the sacrificial sounds. The low moaning of wind as it passed over cords and mucous membranes.

Then the rising and falling as the peak was reached time and again. The heaving breath that was forced from the lungs by the thin atmosphere at the summit.

"Ooh," the wind sighed as it came gently from the lungs inside the smooth skin. The god quickly pressed finger to lips, sealing them to any sound but this.

Natalie rose over Dave, conquering him even as he slipped deeper and deeper into her silent smoothness. Her mind reeled with the sweet waving finger tips of passion playing in front of her dark eyes. But the silence. Fingers could speak. Tongues could caress, enforcing the silence. Keeping the words from coming. The awful words that hurt, making the tongue bitter and evil.

Again the lungs inside the smooth skin tried to force wind over the cords, seeking for words to speak with the tongue. Longing to break the silence and speak some meaningless words, forcing aside the sweet sounds of moist skin touching, replaced by harsh sounds of wind raging across jagged teeth.

But Natalie felt his chest rise in the darkness and summoned the god who, with light petals that only spoke with silence, touched his lips, sealing them forever shut to sounds from the tongue. Teaching the language of silence.

The joy of reaching the summit inside the void of the new language, came slowly to Dave. Frenzied movements, opposite but matching, rushing toward one another, then falling away, the softness of the collision causing his eardrums to split open with the deafening silence. His fingertips began speaking to Natalie, and as they crossed the peak he pulled her to him, praying to another god that the sweet moistness that began to slowly spread over their smooth skin would, when dried, bond them together into one floating, touching traveller;

climber of mountain tops where words were written in stone, not chattered with mindless unfeeling.

But the falling, rather the floating down the other side after the sweet silent ascent, with the lessons learned, the lips sealed, brought Dave to a new awareness. With eyes closed, he saw the green, lush valley below come drifting up to meet the falling bodies. The waving tips of soft grass and the swaying branches of gentle old trees shushed the words the ancient language tried to force from him.

He remembered the simple lessons. Speak with finger tip. Caress with tongue. Let soft, smooth skin touch to create the backdrop of sound, if that is what is needed to enhance the silence. But never speak.

Sleep is speaking. It says, "I am contented." Dave and Natalie spoke these new words and floated in and out of the new world. Arising at least once, maybe twice, to climb again the mountain where the new god lived. Then cresting the top, barrel rolling like swimmers locked to one another, jack knifing into the heavy moist air over the valley and again coming to rest in the soft grass.

****

The sun was silent. But it spoke. It said, "Awake." The wind blew, even though the soft skin had dried of its moist sweetness. It made no sound, but its voice was heard whispering through the waving tips of grass and the fluttering tree leaves.

The movements of the two on the white sheets, spoke. But it was a language last spoken centuries ago. In halting, trembling attempts at remembering. Afraid of saying the wrong thing. But unashamed of the daylight penetrating the valley. One arose and pulled at the other for one last climb. A methodical, eyes wide open, searching the other for any sign of fear, climb. One in which every foothold is looked at. To be remembered for the next time. When they arched over the jagged peaks for the last time, panic set in. They knew and looked back for that last glimpse. But it was gone and the fall into the soft valley came much too quickly.

Tears for one. Dave. Natalie's soft, silent hands brushing them away. She knew that he knew. Just like he knew she would come. Just like she was surprised at his awaiting her, she would be surprised at her leaving. But she knew he would not be. He had learned the language too well. She had taught him. With her own selfish words flung at him, stinging and biting, unable at times to use the language she had perfected.

Dave's eyes spoke to her and his fingertips traced hungry words down her belly. But there was only one more mountain to climb. And harsh words awaited in the valley, not smooth, moist skin.

****

Natalie knew where Dave was going, and she knew that she must follow. Somewhere between the house and the top of the ridge she would tell him about the call from the courthouse and the announcement that the jury had reached a verdict. But the silence had imposed that only her racing heart could speak. And it spoke fear. On the walk to the courtroom, the silent fear threatened to betray her and she could hear words of guilt come forth from the tongues of the jury.

But as her heart reached its bursting point, at the exact moment she soared over the peak in the old world of shouting and slinging accusations, she heard the foreman of the jury speak. One of the few men who could impose silence on her. A silence she did not want. His words were, "Not Guilty."

Had she really believed they would come? Like Dave did? He seemed to know. She could tell by the sudden jarring stop that never came. So indeed, she had known all along. Just like Dave had known she would come. It was his testimony to her innocence. And she had repaid him with a new tongue. An unwritten, unspoken manner of speech that would forever exist between them.

Jeff would have screamed, "Where in the hell do you think you are going?" Dave's eyes simply looked at her as she pulled the long socks up over her pant legs, sealing out the briars and thorns. His fingertips sought the gun under his armpit. Silently working the slide, the smooth metal making the same sounds as their skin touching in the night. Then into the smooth leather. Nestled like he in her.

She watched him move. Loving him. Loving the way he took up the language of silence. He touched her on the arm with the same fingertips that had probed her soft skin during the lessons she had given him. Then his hands came to her face and he gently pulled her to him, not like in the night. He kissed her goodbye one last time and then together, they began their ascent of this one last mountain.

Chapter 33

Two hours later they reached the top of the ridge as they had begun. Silently. Natalie followed Dave as they crawled the last hundred yards to the top. As they lay side by side in the leaves, he had asked the question with his eyes and she had whispered in the old language, the words of the man telling her she was free. Then she whispered how the little fat man had stood and told about dropping kidnapping charges because the little girl told an unbelievable story about a silent wild man. Not Natalie.

But they hadn't believed it. They had simply known that the little girl couldn't be counted on for any consistency in her story. And they were a little afraid of the beating King had given Natalie. Ritchie had threatened to subpoena the newspaper editor and the pictures George had taken. So the charges were dropped. And silence again reigned in Natalie's life.

Natalie lay beside Dave as they studied the downward slope in front of them. The tin roof of the house below shone dully in the morning light. The leaves that had fallen would make moving silently difficult. Unless there was no one to hear. If the house was empty.

Dave took a small pair of binoculars from one of the cargo pockets of his army pants. He scanned the house and the area around it.

Natalie studied Dave. She had forgiven him his sin of soul stealing. And later even felt proud when he recited from her book on the witness stand. And then Lana had praised the work as art and her as a great talent. After all, she thought to herself, why write it if not for someone to read it?

So she looked at Dave in a different light. Especially after last night. A wonderful night of silence. She had led him. And he had been a willing follower, not a driving dominator. She had seen his lungs bursting with air, struggling to talk, but he had allowed her to gently push fingertips to lips, shutting off the sounds. He had been willing to learn the silence, and now when he looked at her, he spoke with his eyes. Or touched with his fingertips. Using the new language he had learned from her in the night, during the numerous climbs up the mountain.

She watched him lower the glasses and turn to her, his eyes telling her they were going down the slope toward the house. She answered, her hand touching him gently on the side as he slid over the crest and began inching on his belly toward the rear of the silent house. Her face remained inches from the bottoms of his cleated boots as she crawled in the path he left in the leaves. She saw over his shoulder that he was headed for a mound behind the house. One covered with large rocks and fallen branches.

They were close to the mound now, unable to see the back of the house because of the rise of the rock and dirt. Suddenly, she felt Dave's legs stiffen. She almost bumped his feet with her face. Then his feet began moving backward into her. She scrambled back and to the side, letting him come to her. When his head was even with hers, he stopped. He pushed his face to her ear and whispered hoarsely, "It's him. The smell. In the rock pile. I smelled him."

Natalie watched as his eyes darted back to the pile of rocks and dirt. His hand crept inside the jacket to rest on the butt of the gun she had seen there. She pushed her face to his ear and whispered, "What are you going to do?"

"I'm going around that rock pile. He must be on the other side." His lips excited her as his quick breath rushed in and around her ear. She grabbed his head and turned his ear to her mouth. This was no time for silent signals being misunderstood. "I'll be right behind you."

He started forward again. When his hand came out from under his shoulder, the gun came with it. Its muzzle led the way, like the dark eye of Satan, searching the shores of the burning lake, looking for feeble victims who had managed to crawl out of the molten waters.

When they reached the side of the mound facing the house and had not seen the man whose scent they were following, Natalie panicked. She quickly quelled the feeling and spun onto her back, searching behind them, afraid the man was coming up on their rear. Nothing. Dave felt her sudden movement and spun also, the gun coming to bear on the empty space above Natalie's drawn up knees.

He sniffed. No sign of the odor. He came to his knees and looked quickly around. The man was not in sight. He beckoned to Natalie who was up on her knees by now. He started back to where they had begun on the upper side of the mound. He sniffed again. The smell was back. Dave raised his eyes and looked into the pile of rock and branches and dirt. He came to his feet and in a crouch, started into the pile.

Near the top of the pile, hidden by a dead cedar bush that still retained most of its thick branches, he saw the dark hole that seemed to lead downward into the pile. He fell to his knees and picked up the bush and laid it aside. The fetid smell rushing out at him almost made him puke. His head jerked back and Natalie put out her hands to keep him from hitting her. He spun toward her, stopping before the gun barrel swept her body.

The silence between the two since the whispering start was satisfying to Natalie. She had no problem understanding Dave's move. He had thought she was the wild man. She saw his eyes dart over her shoulder and then to the woods behind her. She knew he was grasping every opportunity to look for the man. She also knew she was not going to be separated from Dave. Whatever happened, was going to happen to both of them.

Dave turned back to the hole and ran his left hand down inside the cargo pocket on his thigh. He came out with a small, black flashlight. He then turned and looked into her eyes for one brief moment, then flicked the light on and began belly crawling off into the hole.

It didn't go straight down. It went at an angle. Toward the back of the house on a gentle slope. Natalie could barely see past Dave's head to where his light made a path in the dark. She could feel the top of the tunnel over her head, but her main concern was keeping Dave's feet in her face. The bottom of his boot scraped her face occasionally, but that was a small price to pay for the comfort of knowing that he was there for her to grab in case she needed him.

She bumped the Vibram cleats with her nose when he stopped. She looked over Dave's shoulder. The area he had stopped in was larger than the tunnel they had crawled down. She inched her body up beside him and watched as he played the beam of light over a set of concrete steps that led downward to a door. She looked upward as he brought the light to the roof of the tunnel. A heavy piece of sheet metal overhead, supported by several concrete blocks, made a sort of awning over the steps. A small space to crawl through led down the steps to the door below.

Dave turned and looked back the way they had come. Flashing the light back up the tunnel. It was empty. When he turned back to the steps, Natalie was already crawling down them. He quickly followed her and touched her on the shoulder when they got to the bottom. He pointed to the low roof over their heads which would allow them to stoop in front of the door.

Natalie put her hand to her face and pinched her nostrils. The smell was worse down here and it was so bad it almost made her sick. Dave just sniffed. He had to be sure he knew where the man was, but the smell was so bad, the man could be anywhere. But it was his smell, and this was his lair. And the cellar door in front of them, with its old white porcelain knob, was the portal to his life. If he was like the only other hermit Dave knew, Old Stinking Joe, he would regard the hole he lived in as a castle. He would defend it.

But Dave was tired. This whole stinking mess was getting to him. It was the thing between him and Natalie. And until it was gone, done away with, he could not rest. Could not enjoy the silence of her.

The door would swing inward. He pointed to the knob with the flashlight and moved to the side of the door with the hinges. Natalie put her hand on the knob and turned it. The old door swung open without the slightest sound. It stopped about halfway through its arc and Dave could see into the old storm cellar. He flashed his light into every crevice and cranny he could see. Up the walls to the overhead. No sign of the man. Natalie remained standing beside the frame, following the beam with her eyes.

Behind the door! They couldn't see behind the door! Dave pushed the door against the wall with the flashlight. It bumped the wall.

A dark spot on the floor below the hinges told him that someone regularly oiled them so they would not squeak.

The rest of the room showed empty under the sweep of the light, and before Dave could move, Natalie stepped into the room. Dave came quickly behind her and grabbed the door and pushed it back to its closed position.

Natalie was standing in the middle of the room, looking around. Dave walked to her side and stood with her as she pinched her nose and gazed at the underground room. The filthy cot in the far corner was obviously the source of the smell. That and the old chair in the middle of the room.

The beam of light led Natalie's eyes around the room. Sweeping across the shelf to the left of the door where canned goods used to be stored, but now holding bits of clothing and scraps of cloth. There was a box on one of the shelves and Natalie walked over to it as Dave held the light. Some apples, part of a loaf of bread, cans of something with the labels torn off. The man's larder. Slim pickings.

Then as the light moved downward, Natalie saw the briefcase. She stooped and picked it up as Dave knelt beside her. She felt his nearness, knew that the smooth skin under the camo clothing awaited her. Knew that the contents of the case would shortly be exposed to the glare of the flashlight.

She gently placed the case on the shelf beside the box of food. The small brass plate between the hinges of the handle read "BHJ." The silence still prevailed. The two pairs of eyes met for an instant. In the dim wash from the light focused on the briefcase, Dave saw something in Natalie's eyes that he had never seen. Fear, love, desire, defiance. He had seen all that. But now this. Was it hate, or simply determination? He couldn't tell.

The clasps clicked. The case creaked when the lid started coming up. It hadn't been opened in a while. A blue backed document that Dave recognized as a deed was the first thing he saw. He reached in and opened it with one hand as Natalie helped him spread out the creases with her free hand. It was a trust deed with Minnie Hill giving the described property to Benjamin H. Jamison.

Natalie sucked in her breath, breaking the silence. Dave looked at her but couldn't tell which emotion she was dealing with. He flipped the pages to the last one and there saw the elderly, squiggly scrawl of Minnie Hill, or a very good forgery. Under it the bold signature of Benjamin H. Jamison.

"The sonofa...!" For an instant it was unclear which one of them had uttered the oath. Which one had cursed the man who had stolen Minnie Hill's property. Then Dave knew. It was Natalie. He had started to say it, but then she had blown the words by him. Maybe even sucking them from his throat. He knew that was the case when he tried to swallow and his throat was too dry to even do that. He looked at her but she was picking up something under the deed. A map.

Dave held the light with one hand and spread the map with the other. It was a property map of the Hill Place. Someone had drawn a red line around the entire boundary. Until part of it had been crossed out. Down at the bottom of the map the red had been blacked out and then re-drawn, causing an indention into the belly of the Hill Place. Dave recognized it as the property that Natalie Dunn's house sat on. Something was written in the space that suddenly had intruded onto the acres of Benjamin Jamison. Dave twisted the map sideways so he could read it.

"Natalie! Risen from the dead!" The words were printed in neat block letters. Not a hasty scratching, but a deliberate printing.

Natalie quickly flipped the map, closing the folds back to where they had been. She brought her other hand up to grab the lid of the case and close it. Dave wedged his elbow into the opening, stopping the closure. He looked at her but her face had gone blank. She wouldn't look at him. Her eyes were focused on the inside of the briefcase.

Dave reached for the newspaper clippings that were under the map. They were old. He saw by the date on the top one that they were from eleven years ago. When he spread the top clipping open, he saw that it was the business section of a New York newspaper. The headline stated that "Successful Broker Operated in Man's World". Natalie Hill's name leaped out at him. The article was about her. He wondered if the little county historian would be interested in seeing it. He didn't think the little man had shown him this one. But then maybe he had. It looked familiar. Maybe it had been in the folder that Joncik handed him. No! But as he scanned the article, he got the distinct impression that he had seen it before.

Dave's brow became so furrowed and his mind raced so, trying to remember where he had seen the story of Natalie Hill, that he almost failed to hear a scratching noise outside the wall. He might not have heard it if Natalie hadn't touched him on the arm and pointed with her slim finger.

Instantly he closed the case and grabbed Natalie by her arm and steered her toward the easy chair. He put his arm around her shoulders and pulled her down to squat behind it. He flipped the flashlight to his left hand and turned it off. His right hand went easily to the left armpit and returned with the .45 Colt pistol.

A scuffing, sliding noise. He heard it but didn't know what it was. Then a scraping of something outside the wall, followed by a draft of cooler air and then by the smell even stronger. Dave's heart raced as he heard breathing and whisper of clothing as someone, the wild man, came into the room. But from where? He wasn't coming through the door they entered. And Dave hadn't seen any other door. But, he was in here. He felt Natalie tense beside him and wondered if the man could sense them the way they could feel him. He was even more attuned to his senses than they.

The darkness was total and Dave felt his eyes literally pop forward out of his head as he attempted to penetrate the black and find the man inside the room with them. His ears became his eyes as they followed the sounds the man made as he moved along the wall away from them. He felt his hand holding the Colt track the sounds as his ears fine tuned in on them.

A rattle? Like beads in a box? What was it? Seed in a sack? Then scratching! Again he tried to identify it. Like a fingernail on sandpaper. What was it? Then a smell, familiar but so unexpected that he couldn't identify it at first. Until the light flared in his eyes. A match! A large kitchen match putting off fumes of sulphur. Flaring brightly and throwing the whole room into relief.

The man stood there, his back to them. All shaggy and tattered. The light outlining him as he lit a candle on the shelf beside the briefcase. It took a second for it to register, then he stared at the case on the shelf where he had not left it, and then whirled about, blinded by the match that had flared in his eyes. Then by the light as Dave pressed the button and threw the flashlight beam directly into his eyes.

Like a rabbit frozen in the headlights of an oncoming car, awaiting the rushing death that bore down on him, the man stood. Unmoving.

Dave's heart raced. He had never killed anyone. He had awakened every single morning of his life the last fifteen years and realized that it might happen today. But until now, he had never been so close to popping a cap on anyone.

His eyes locked on the knife handle at the man's belt, but as yet the hand had not moved toward it. He silently prayed to the god of peace that the man would not do anything to make him kill him. He honestly didn't know if he could do it. He might freeze, just like the man in front him was frozen.

"Ben. Benjamin Jamison. We want to help you. Do you understand? Natalie and I want to help you. We are not going to hurt you." Dave felt himself saying these words slowly and distinctly. If he had been writing a script, he would not have used such language. He felt himself standing afar, away from himself, listening to his own speech. It sounded so stilted. So childish. He could have been a teacher talking to a three year old.

The man's hands moved. Dave pressed his thumb to the top of the safety on the Colt, ready in an instant to push it downward and then press the trigger. If he could.

But the man's hands continued upward, into the air around his head. As if questioning the actions of Dave. Asking why are you doing this to me? Then Dave realized that Ben's actions were those of the street punk who had been arrested several times. He was assuming the position, what he could remember of it.

Dave took two cautious steps toward the man. He felt Natalie beside him, moving with him. The man could see her in the side wash of the light, and his eyes went to her, his hands stayed up somewhere beside the shaggy head.

"I once had a knife like that. It is a nice one. Can I see it?" The sing-song voice would have made Dave gag if he had been listening to anyone else use it. But it seemed to disarm Ben. His eyes locked on Natalie as they moved closer to him, and then his right hand moved slowly toward the handle of the knife.

Dave felt himself push the safety downward to the off position. The gun was now unlocked. Slight pressure on the trigger would send the 230 grain Hydra-Shok bullet into the man's chest. But the hand, gently and almost absentmindedly, pulled the knife from the sheath and handed it toward Dave behind the light. The wild eyes stayed on Natalie.

Easing the safety back up, Dave reached for the knife with the hand holding the flashlight. When he had the handle clamped between his fingers and the barrel of the light, he backed up a step. The man didn't notice. He was enthralled with Natalie. He probably hadn't been this close to a woman in ten years.

Dave's mind was now confused. What was he going to do now? When he first came into the den of the wild man, he fully expected to kill the man. At least he was convinced that he would have to. He was sure the man would fight to the death to defend his home. But all that had suddenly changed. Here was the man standing in front of the two of them, as meek as a lamb. Of course, all that could change with the wrong word or action.

He must continue talking to the man. "Why don't you sit down, Ben. We can talk better that way. Natalie, why don't you go over to that shelf and light some more of those candles so I can turn off this flashlight?"

Natalie moved around Ben to the shelf behind him. He turned to watch her, leaving his back exposed to Dave. Dave thought of getting his handcuffs and attempting to subdue him, but then decided against it. The man would probably go crazy. Instead he reached back and put the knife on a small table made of crates that stood behind the easy chair.

Then he watched as Natalie lit two more candles. Her face seemed to glow as she stuck one of the matches into the flame of the burning candle. When the match flared, she stepped back, then reached forward and put the burning match to the other two candles. When they were burning brightly, she turned to face the two men.

Dave felt his heart leave his body as he knew without a doubt that he loved her beyond all reason. She was forever pressed to him. Imprinted on him so that no matter how far she soared from the nest, she would always be the only one he would go to when the flock returned.

"Sit down, Ben. Please, we just want to talk." Again the soft, gently pleading voice. Dave couldn't believe himself. Two months ago he would have been slamming the man up against the wall, screaming at him that he was going to blow his brains out. Now, here he was treating a murderer like a little lamb.

Ben sat down, his chin coming up so he could keep his eyes on Natalie. Dave watched the way he eased himself into the chair and realized that the man was under a spell. At least partially. He slipped the Colt back into the shoulder holster. He didn't think he would need it now. He watched Natalie step backward to the wall, press her back against it, then slide down to a squat, her arms resting on her knees.

Dave moved around behind Ben. He didn't want to cross the vision lines that ran between the man and Natalie. He stepped over to the shelf where the briefcase lay. He knew he must be careful. He didn't want to accuse the man or say anything that would send him out of control. But he did want to find out about Natalie Hill and the events surrounding her death.

He opened the case and pulled the newspaper clippings from the top where he had left them. He turned, holding the papers up to the flickering light from the candles. The man in the chair never saw him. His eyes were still locked on Natalie. Dave wondered if the man remembered coming at him with the spear outside Natalie's house.

Dave opened his mouth to speak, but Natalie spoke first.

"Hello, Ben. You act like you don't remember me. Did you think I was dead?"

Her voice was from somewhere else. A change had been wrought. Dave had been looking at Ben as Natalie began to speak. Ben remained the same. His head slightly tilted to one side as he watched and listened to the Natalie he remembered. But the voice was not one that Dave remembered as coming from the Natalie he knew before the silence. The papers in his hand fluttered to the floor and he felt himself going limp as the new voice settled over him.

Suddenly he knew the voice was not new. He had heard it before. Just as he had read the article about Natalie Hill before. The night in her house. The night Ben had almost run him through. The book! The first book. Not the partially completed one that was used in the trial. But the first one. A story about a woman in New York who rose to the top of a brokerage firm.

But the story was not new. Just like the voice was not new. It was the story and voice of Natalie Hill. When the voice began again, it was the same voice he had heard in the words of the book written by Natalie Dunn.

"You killed Vandiver because you thought I was dead, didn't you, Ben?" Natalie pushed with her back against the wall and slid up to a standing position. She stood there, her head highlighted by the candle on the shelf behind her. Her eyes became deep pools of darkness.

Tiny pinpricks of light, blinking from far beneath the surface, shone in each. She took a step toward Ben and he slunk backward into the chair, pushing himself deeper into the saggy material with his hands on the arms.

Dave watched her. Like a moth transformed into the only thing it truly can become and be free, Natalie sprang to life before his eyes. Not only did her voice change, as Dave stood there transfixed, but her presence became new, at least to Dave. To Ben it must have been the same one he remembered. A commanding presence of a woman that demanded respect, then subjugation, as the awe and adoration gave way to pure love.

Ben was hers. Dave slowly moved his eyes to Ben and saw that the man was incapable of movement. The images of Natalie were driving with such power through the lenses of his eyes, exerting tremendous pressure on his brain, that his head was pushed back into the headrest of the chair with the force of several g's. The man's mouth and jaw went slack as his facial muscles collapsed under the terrible force.

"You killed Vandiver and then tortured his father until he lost his mind. Didn't you, Ben? You couldn't stand it because I loved Vandiver, could you? But why did you kill him after you thought I was dead? Did you think he had killed me?"

"Yes." The word was whispered. Barely audible to Dave above his own breathing and the words of Natalie dying in the room. It was a rasping, choking word. One which barely escaped the throat of one who talked very little, if at all.

Again words came from the unused throat. "He...I saw...You..." The man's left arm came up and his right hand came over to it, the forefinger and middle finger crooking and the thumb making a pushing, plunging motion toward the crook of the left arm. There was no mistaking what he was demonstrating. A needle going into an arm.

"That was over. The only way I could escape it was to die. Vandiver was going away with me. He was going to escape also. But then you killed him and ruined it all."

Dave listened to the voice of the dead Natalie Hill. The woman who died on the streets of New York and then was suddenly resurrected in this underground tomb in Tennessee. He fought his ears to keep them from rejecting the new voice. It was so different. He didn't want to get used to it. He loved the old one. But he could tell that the lamb, the one cowering on the altar before his high priestess, was mesmerized by the one he remembered as old.

Dave understood now why she didn't want to talk when they were climbing the mountain last night. She was afraid she would forget, under the sensuous pressure of the high altitude, and speak in the wrong tongue. Dave wondered if he would ever again be able to speak to her. Unless it was in halting, simple, one syllable words like those of Ben.

"How did you find out about this farm, Ben? You must have stolen the file from Vandiver's office. You're sneaky, Ben. Stealing from your own law partner." She moved closer to him and he sunk deeper into the chair and into his fear. "How did you get my aunt to sigh the deed, Ben?" She was in his face now. He cowered before her words and presence. "You probably just put her hand on the line and made her wright. What did you tell her? That she was signing the place to me?"

A single drop of sweat released from the hair line of Dave's head and ran down the middle of his back. He shivered, his shoulders twisting suddenly in an uncontrolled movement. He realized that he was a slave to Natalie, to her being and will. The only thing to override it was the automatic jerks and flinches of his body reacting to natural stimuli. Much like he rose and fell with her as they peaked and valleyed in the throes of passion last night.

Her feet shuffling on the concrete floor he heard. Natalie moved around behind Ben. His head swiveled to the side and upward, following her in her priestly duties. She grabbed the wings of the chair beside Ben's head and pulled backward. "Look at me, Ben!" she demanded in the new intimidating voice.

Ben arched his body, his chest rising from the chair, his head going back to look up into the face of Natalie. His arms were braced straight and rigid on the arms of the recliner.

Natalie's face took on a new glow as she moved to the rear of Ben, the light of candles now in front of her. Droplets of sweat glistened on her smooth skin like tiny pearls brought by her many adoring subjects. The flickering flames of the candles danced in her eyes like fireflies, as the sacrificial body was about to be offered to the pagan god by the naked priestess.

Dave saw Natalie lean suddenly backward, her arms swooping down as if preparing for a high dive from a cliff. As she came back up and the light again twinkled in her dark eyes, her arms came up over her head. The flickering flame of the candles bowed and swayed with the movement of the air currents that her body stirred up.

The pinpricks of light went out in her eyes as the pupils shut down and her face looked upward. Dave followed her line of sight and saw the millions of fireflies swarm toward the object in her hand. The shining scepter of the holy one descending toward the adoring subject. His chest arching upward to receive the blessing. His eyes looking toward her face for one last favoring glance.

"AAAhhagggahh!" Natalie screamed as she plunged the knife into Ben's chest. The force of the blow drove his body back into the chair. Then he arched upward again, the pierced heart striving to keep beating for the one he loved. But the scream came again as the knife was withdrawn and blood flashed heavenward as the fireflies were drawn to the tiny droplets flying through the air. Again the scepter came down, and with a thud the blade sank into the still beating heart. And the head of the priestess bowed in sorrow as the twitching body beneath her hand, still on the handle of the knife, slowly sank into death and sleep.

Then the judgment. Her defiant head came up to look into the eye of the accuser. Her mouth came open to scream the curse into the courtroom that what was done was done in the name of justice. And with a bloody hand to point to the jurors and demand a "not guilty." But the face of the accuser was the one of the silent speech. The one she had taught so well to speak with the words of touch and feel. And with his eyes. They now spoke. She knew his words would betray, hence the speaking eyes. His love could not stand the words that might come by accident from the mouth.

Dave turned and walked to the door through which they had entered the burial chamber. He opened it and stood waiting for Natalie. The scream that had risen in his throat when he saw the knife in Natalie's hand, had died when her own hoarse, throaty roar had preceded the fatal plunge of Ben's own knife into his chest.

He had wanted to stop her, do anything to keep her from committing murder right in front of his eyes, but he had been unable to function, unable to do anything but watch. It wasn't real anyway. Nothing seemed real anymore. The scene of the knife flashing high, then descending in a shiny, twinkling arc toward Ben's uplifted chest, now seemed like an old yellowed movie he had watched as a kid. The actors were bad. The music was added as an after thought. The candles were put in for dramatic effect, and to make the light so low that the audience couldn't see the cheap props and the lack of makeup.

But the worst part was, when it was over nobody seemed to know that the show had ended. They all stood around and looked at each other, wondering if there was more, or if this was what they had paid their money for.

The lovely murderess stood like a statue behind the victim in the chair. She was looking behind the camera toward the director, who had dozed off. She seemed to be asking if the cameras were still rolling.

A slight breeze filtered down the tunnel and swept through the open door by which Dave stood. It rustled the papers on the floor that had been dropped ages ago when Natalie Hill had emerged from the embryo of the Dunn woman. Dave stepped quickly over to them and stooped to pick them up. His eyes darted to the man in the chair, expecting to see him come leaping from the chair onto his back.

Natalie moved. Dave jumped upright, his senses and alertness back. He was starting to come out of the stupor that had settled over him when the sacrificial ceremony had begun. The ritual he had watched Natalie perform with exactness and precision as if she had practiced it a thousand times. It was now playing back in his mind, and it seemed as if he had watched it again and again. He felt like the child at the movie watching his hero about to be attacked from behind. He was yelling "watch out!" knowing all along that he couldn't hear. But still knowing that each time he watched it, he would yell out his warning. Of course with Natalie, the shouts had to be silent.

Dave backed up toward the briefcase on the shelf. Natalie followed him, walking in front of the dead Ben, his sightless eyes focused on the ceiling. If she saw him she seemed not to notice. Dave flipped the clippings into the case and snapped the lid shut, and grabbed the handle. Natalie stood and watched. If she was affected by the killing of Ben, she didn't show it.

He took her arm and pointed her toward the door. She moved toward it, she the servant now, he the master. Dave followed her and watched her drop to her knees and begin crawling up the steps toward the sloping tunnel that led to the daylight. He turned and took one last look at the room. The candles guttered, then flared in the draft from the tunnel. The shadows danced over the face of the man in the chair, making him seem to move as the eerie light played back and forth across the room.

Dave took a step back into the room. He needed to blow out the candles. The wind jerked the flame and something seemed to move in the dead, sightless eyes. Dave screamed at last. The desperate, agonizing cry came from his lips, a banshee wail, flinging itself around the walls of the tiny soundproof chamber, flogging his hearing with the sound. The pitiful tears coming as the cry died in his throat. Died. Like the soul he once thought he possessed. Dead like the man in the chair. Every right thing he had learned and knew to do, he was leaving in this awful room. He knew in his heart he was now a murderer. Unable to kill, that he now knew. But still one who could do murder.

His desperate feeling, on coming into the room earlier, that he might not be able to kill the wild man, had been right. He couldn't have done it. He felt as one with the man. He felt the knife from Natalie enter his chest and knew that he too, just like the man in the chair, would have risen upward, offering his breast to the blade. But the awful feeling came when he realized that he would have murdered the man for Natalie. Would have sacrificed his soul for one more trip up the mountain. In fact, he may have done just that. Like Ben who had killed for her, he had stood and watched as Natalie killed for him.

Dave stepped quickly toward the door. He no longer wanted to blow out the candles. The man needed as much light as he could get where he was going. The door slowly shut as Dave pulled the knob. The haunting, flickering scene of the light flittering across the body of Ben as he lay in state upon the altar where he had died, was now Dave's own special memorial to Natalie. Insane, crazy, whatever he wanted to call it, Dave now knew that he was tottering on the brink.

He took one last look into the room and then forever shut it out. He knew that if anyone, even he in his dreams, ever opened the door again, he would go completely and absolutely out of his mind.

****

Natalie was at the top of the ridge by the time he got to the end of the tunnel. He saw her turn right and head down the trail toward the bottom and her house. He quickly pushed the brush over the hole and picked up the briefcase and started up the trail after her. He knew that he must come back and completely destroy and cover up the entrance to the room under the ground. But it would be a detached activity. Simply a groundskeeping function. Just something to keep the inmates busy.

Dave moved after Natalie as fast as he could. He had to slow down when the tears started coming again, clouding his vision and making it difficult to see the rocks and sticks that littered the trail. She stayed ahead of him, moving quickly through the crisp fall air.

He wanted to catch her, but in his mind he knew that the mountain they were leaving was the last one they would ever climb. So he slowed down. He wanted to prolong the descent. To make the landing as soft as possible. Maybe she would land hard and the jolt would awaken the Natalie that he had caught fleeting glimpses of as she climbed ahead of him through the mist that enshrouded the crest of their passion.

But by the time he got to the house he knew that if she had landed hard, it had been on her feet and she had been running. Her car was backed up to the rear door and she was moving quickly from somewhere inside to the shattered opening and throwing things into the open trunk.

Dave stood by the open lid and watched as an armful of shoes, clothes and toilet articles came flying out the door. He stepped inside as she headed back down the hall toward the spare bedroom. She came out with her typewriter and deposited it on a bed of clothes in the back of the car. Two more trips brought out boxes and books. Then she was done. An agonizing period of silence descended upon the two as they stood in the room, looking at each other. Of all the stupid questions he could have asked, Dave picked the stupidest one.

"Are you leaving, Natalie?"

"You dumb sonofa…! What does it look like I'm doing?"

"Why?"

"Why, what?"

"Why are you leaving me, Natalie? It's over now. We can start from the beginning. Just us together."

"You're completely arrogant, Dave Warren! You think you own me just because we went to bed?"

"Natalie! Please! What's happened is over. I don't care whether you're Natalie Hill or Natalie Dunn. I just know that you're my Natalie and that I love you." He looked at her. Remembering the days when he had first loved her. The very day she had called him arrogant and slapped his face. Then to the nights of silence. That's when she became a different Natalie. But he loved both of them. Even the one that stood before him now, he loved. The smart mouthed, haughty, hateful one. The one he wanted to know more about, even if it hurt him beyond all hope of recovery. And too, if she would talk, she would stay longer. Maybe so long that she would never leave.

"I want to know, Natalie," he said. His voice grew soft, almost a whisper. Silence he needed. "I want to know about you. Who's Vandiver? How did you know Ben? Please, tell me."

She stood by the door, the open car trunk over her shoulder, and looked at Dave. The life behind her was so sordid and full of sorrow and grief that it would take her several more books to write it all down. How could she tell Dave about it in the ten minutes she had before she knew she would have to go? Maybe he deserved to know. After all, he had invested a wife, a career, and probably his sanity in her.

"Vandiver was the man I loved. He was a drug addict and got me hooked. His father was a dealer. I know it sounds crazy. Me a successful broker. I had the world on a string. But suddenly, one day, I was addicted. I woke up one morning and decided to do something about it. Vandiver came up with the idea of both of us dying and then starting over. We cashed out our assets, a couple of million for both of us, and with his connections, he was going to arrange for both of us to "die" in accidents. But something went wrong. I "died" in my accident, but Ben must have found out and thought that Vandiver had really killed me, so he killed Vandiver and took our money."

Natalie's breast heaved as she recalled the things she had tried to forget, but now came rushing back from the past.

"Who was Ben?" Dave asked.

"He and Vandiver were lawyers in the firm that handled my mother's affairs when she died. He wanted to go out with me, but I wouldn't go. He followed me around. I guess I became an obsession with him. We caught him looking in windows at us. Hiding in the hall. The night we both "died", I was waiting for Vandiver to come and get me, but Ben shows up with a vase of flowers."

"I thought he thought you were dead."

"Vandiver must have told him before he died that I wasn't really dead. Maybe Ben tortured him like he did Vandiver's father. Ben wanted us to go away together. He told me he now had all the money and papers that Vandiver had, and that I would have to go with him. I ran. He chased me all the way out into the street where we ran into two cops with a dog. They must have been on a drug bust or something. Anyway, the last sight of Ben I had was the dog chasing him across the street."

"And what did you do?"

"I got in my car, which was already packed, and left. I never went back. I spent the next several years up and down the east coast, working at whatever I could find. As long as it didn't require a background check. I worked at a casino in Atlantic City. I sold popsicles on the beach in Daytona. I was working in a diner in Charlotte, North Carolina when I met Jeff. I told him I was just a kid who had flunked out of college and he fell in love with me, I guess. Anyway, I married him and moved here with him when he dropped out of school."

"Why here?"

"His parents were from Franklin, just up the road. This property was for sale. We saw the sign from the interstate. When we looked at it, I knew where I was. I was five years old when my mother took me to New York, but something told me I was close to home when I saw this place."

"So everything on the deposition was a lie. You were no orphan adopted by a Smith family. "

"I had to make up my identity after I left New York where I was supposed to be dead. I couldn't tell you who I really was."

"And you had no idea that Ben was here right behind you?"

"No! I swear to you, Dave. I didn't know he was here. After Jeff was killed, I started to suspect it. My mother and Aunt Minnie both insisted the place be sold. And they didn't want me to have the money because I disappointed them by not wanting to be an actress. But Ben saw his chance and must have gotten Aunt Minnie to sign the farm over to him. She didn't know what she was signing."

Dave saw his chance. His hope to keep Natalie here. The land. Surely she would feel something for the place where she had been born. "Natalie! It's yours now. We can get Ritchie to change it. You don't have to go anywhere."

"And you could come and stay with me, couldn't you?" Natalie deadpanned.

Dave looked at her and wondered how they had been so close to each other, and now seemed so far apart. He remembered her accusing him once before of wanting to come and live with her. Then she had accepted him in love and now was willing to leave all that behind. Had given him more in one night than he had gotten from Betty Lou in the last fifteen years. Now she was standing ten feet and three seconds away from leaving him forever.

"What about this house? What will happen to it?" Dave asked.

"I had Ritchie put it in both of our names. You'll have a place to stay as long as you pay the taxes. That's the least I can do, after you left your wife and home for me." Natalie paused and looked at Dave. He was so helpless at times. Other times so strong. If she ever…No! She couldn't think of it. She had to leave. That's all there was to it. She couldn't stay. Trapped in this house with all the duties that would come with being a wife again. The years between Vandiver and Jeff were the most blissful days of her life. Hard and lonely, but that was what she wanted. No more love, or what she thought passed for it. Just her and her search for what she wanted to leave behind in this world when her days were done. And that wasn't husband or kids or land. It was the written legacy that only she could provide. And it wasn't going to be done in a corner of the kitchen with supper boiling. Or between naps of babies. Or early in the morning after hubby goes to work and before the kids start making a racket.

"Dave. You know enough about me to know that I'm not what you want. Don't try to follow me and don't try to find me. If you'll promise me that, I'll call you. Or even write you. But don't try to get me to come back. I won't come."

"Do you know where you are going, Natalie?"

"Yes, but there's only room there for one. There's only space in my life for me, Dave. I know that sounds selfish, but that's the way I am. That's why I didn't cry for Jeff."

"Then why did you let me love you, Natalie? If you knew that it could never be."

A tear formed in the corner of one of her eyes. Just one. A lonely, solitary tear. And it was for Dave. That was one more than she had shed for Jeff. Her voice dropped to a whisper and Dave saw the pain in her eyes and felt the tremendous effort it took for her to speak the next words.

"Because I love you, Dave. I don't want to hurt you or give you false hope, but I truly love you. Because you're so honest and open and the most unselfish person I've ever known. I didn't want to, but you made me love you. Just being your simple, unpretentious self. That's why I tried. I really tried. But now I have to go. And it's not you. It's me. You see that, don't you? Oh, Dave! Please forgive me."

She moved into his arms as the tears started down his face. She felt the wetness in her hair as she buried her head in his chest. She felt his arms go around her, the hands touching her as if they wanted to imprint her memory on them forever. She pulled away before they could start speaking the language she had taught him.

"I have to go," she said. The finality of the words struck total fear into the heart of Dave. He brought his hands up to capture the face and head of Natalie. Through his tears he saw her face slowly come into focus in front of his eyes as he held her head in his hands. He had her so close. Why couldn't he keep her? She was reasonable. He would appeal to her reason.

"Natalie, you love me. You said you did. I know you do. You can't leave somebody you love!"

"Dave! I have to go. Now let me go!" Her voice had changed. Gone back to the old Natalie.

"But you love me!" he pled.

"That's why I have to leave."

"Why?" he screamed, losing his reason now as he watched her walk out the door and slam the lid to the trunk. He followed her as she got in the car.

"Natalie! Why?"

"Because every person I have ever loved has either died or gone crazy."

Her brown, slender arm snaked out and pulled the car door shut. The hard, sharp slapping sound sent tremors through Dave's soul. Like the trap door slamming on the deep, dark oubliette that was to become his life. He stood in the back yard and watched the car carrying Natalie away. Transporting her into her solitary world where she could be one with herself. But leaving him in agony, and alone.

He looked out over the Hill Place. Where it had all begun. Where Natalie's search had started and his had ended. He had found his Natalie, but she had found the beginning of the trail of her life. A narrow, one lane foot trail. He could see now that it was leading to her Shangri-La, but just like every dream worth dreaming, the tiny portal in the wall of the massive fortress was only small enough for one person to slip through. And through it, just before his eyes clouded with tears, he saw her steal. With a tiny, maybe careless backward glance over her shoulder, her face forever framed in the fading light of his memory, she looked at him one last time. There were no tears in her eyes. Instead they shone with the brilliance of a new day. A bright sun that would come streaming into the valley where she would spend her days. That same sun would awaken Dave to a day of bitter memories.

He turned and looked at the shattered back door of the house. How wonderful it looked. At least it matched his life. Un-shattered would have been so out of place. His hand slowly lifted to the walnut grips of the Colt under his arm. It would be so easy. One life gone. Natalie's. Then his. Gone. Just like that. No one to care. No one to grieve. Then he would be forever alone. How lonely it must be for someone who crawls into the pit that way and pulls the dirt in on top of themselves.

Dave's hand shivered. His whole body shook. He couldn't believe that he had even thought about it. But he had. For one awful second he had wanted to end those dreams of the climb with Natalie. Because she would no longer be with him. And he would have to climb alone.

The sky parted over his head and he saw again the wall of the hidden paradise where Natalie had disappeared. The door in the side was hidden. Maybe there was one there for him. Not into the same part of the citadel where she was, but somewhere inside the massive walls there had to be another chamber. Another room just for him, or somebody like him, who only wanted to be alone. After all, isn't that how this started? Betty Lou had never been with him on his serious jaunts up his own secret mountains. The times he had spent hours in a deer stand, not even looking for a deer. In fact, hoping one wouldn't come by to spoil the careless, pleasant wanderings of his mind.

Dave suddenly smiled. Then his arms slowly encircled his own middle, hugging Natalie for one last time. Thanking her for loving him, showing him the way that all solitary travelers must go. It was that one last look before she disappeared that had done it. She wasn't beckoning him to follow her. She was just showing him that there was still room inside. But, all the rooms were singles.

He felt eyes on him. He froze. Could the man have gotten out of the room and crawled this far. Had he not been dead? Dave was facing the house. The presence behind him, that he could feel as certain as he had felt the spear point against his belly, was overpowering. He wanted to whirl, his hand going to the .45 under his arm. Then to throw himself aside to the protection of the picnic table. Anything to escape the eyes he felt boring into his back.

Instead he slowly turned. One foot shuffling, the other pivoting. The buck, the big buck that Ben had been trying to get to come to this side of the interstate, was standing at the edge of the yard looking at Dave. His ears were flared, his nose was in the air sniffing, his sightless eyes closed forever to the light of day.

Something had blinded him. Had the wild man somehow put out his eyes hoping that would make it easier to get him over here? Dave moved. The deer's head didn't. Dave brought his hands up and waved. The deer never saw the movement. Dave moved toward the buck. He shifted his nose trying to catch the scent. Like Natalie. Looking but not seeing. Dave opened his mouth to speak, but knew that the words would not come. He had almost forgotten. He had learned a new language. He would speak it with the deer. And over the years he would silently tell the deer about Natalie.

And about how much he had loved her.

END

Epilogue

"We would like to welcome to our show this morning a very special visitor. This lady has written a book that the critics are calling a new voice. One has even called her the new Ayn Rand. Her writing is that conscious of the new world around us and the new language we speak. Ladies and gentlemen, CNN would like to welcome Natalie Warren to the Literary Showcase." Dave's eyes took a few moments to adjust. His ears took even longer. But his brain took forever. There was no Natalie Warren. How could she exist? How could she be, when she had disappeared forever?

It had been a year. She had been gone a whole year. Now she was back. He couldn't move. He was on the couch in her house in front of the television. It was where he spent every morning after he got in from his midnight to seven job of keeping Jerry's Market open down at the interstate.

In time and space he floated. Somewhere between both. And there Natalie drifted in front of him. In and out. Telling him nothing. Leaving him helpless.

"Oh, please ask her where she's from?" he pled to the screen. Instead, silly, pointless questions about her book. Some asinine remark about how her mind must work to be able to create the worlds that were displayed in her writing.

He knew how her mind worked. He watched in agony as she talked about the pleasure of creating. His only pleasure was in agonizing moments of remembering. She mentioned a lonely childhood as contributing to her wanting to be a writer. She never said one word about the man who had spent his whole life searching for her. Then upon his finding her, she had touched his lips, sealing them forever to speak only the silent new words she had taught him.

"Your books have so much of life and death in them," the interviewer said. "You must be an expert on the subject."

"I once contemplated suicide," Natalie said. "In fact, I had the gun in my hand. But then I buried it behind the house. My symbolic gesture of burying my troubles and starting over."

Then toward the end of the interview, after Dave had wrenched his guts out of his belly with his bare hands, she broke the silence. Went back on her word. And as sure as the spear that had pierced the body of Jeff, she sent the next words straight into the heart of Dave.

"I would like to thank my husband, Dave Warren, for being so patient and loving with me through all this. Without him, it would have been impossible."

The scene changed on the screen and Dave's mind raced back over the interview. If he had been prepared, he could have taped it and watched it over and over for the rest of his life.

Suddenly the word popped out at him. "Buried!"

"From the air!" he said loudly. "I saw her burying something in the back yard by the tank."

Dave leaped up and raced for the door. The wet grass of the back yard soaked his sock feet but he hardly noticed. He fell to his knees in the area where, from the air, he had seen Natalie burying something. Finally he found a small depression in the ground and began digging frantically with his bare hands.

It wasn't deep. Only inches. When his fingers scraped the cold metal, his heart felt an icy chill.

Slowly, ever so slowly he brushed the dirt away from the small black box and opened the lid to reveal the .38 revolver that Natalie had once held to her head. Her lovely hands had once been on this very gun. This close, oh, he was so very close to her.

Dave's hand carefully closed over the small wooden grips. Maybe now was the time. If only his hand would stop shaking long enough for him to steady the gun. Natalie's face drifted in and out of focus as he looked down the barrel. If she really loved him, she wouldn't mind him joining her this way. But no, if she truly loved him, she would come to him again as she did after the trial. And he must be here to go with her for one more trip up the mountain.

FINAL

CPSIA information can be obtained at www.ICGtesting.com
Printed in the USA
LVOW10s1300170416

484006LV00002B/4/P

9 781622 172412